in(alculable

J Palazzo

Cover design by Scott Barrow

www.scottbarrowart.com

Editing by Inky Pen Editorial Services

www.inkypenediting.com

ISBN : 979-8-9919541-0-5

in(alculable

1

(silver)

The colors were a curse. As a child, she'd seen them in numbers and symbols. Didn't matter if they were printed in black and white. Five was red. Six, royal blue. Seven was gold. The longer she focused, the more alive they became.

It had started as a game and turned into an obsession. She'd stare until the colors lifted from the numbers. In time, the colors shifted and spun. With practice, more focus, soon she could alter their shapes. She'd get lost playing in them.

They infected her experiences. Dull yellow and purple spots had shaded how she'd felt about standing in front of the class for show-and-tell. Electric blue while soaring high on the swing set. Cold gray and olive walls had closed in when monsters had jumped out in scary movies. As she'd gotten older, it had made driving somewhat dangerous. At sixteen, her license had been revoked after four months for running stop signs.

Other people with synesthesia were famous artists and musicians. Syd Barrett. Kristin Hersh. Billy Joel. Billie Eilish. Her synesthete idols were physicist Richard Feynman and inventor Nikola Tesla. They were legends. Beloved icons with cult followings.

Nobody likes you.

Years ago, Gideon had taught her to count cards. They'd road tripped to Vegas, talking about how they'd spend their winnings. New car. New shoes. Leather jacket she'd had her eye on. But the second they'd turned onto the Strip, corroded rust and mauve had filled her vision. She'd broken into tears. He'd pulled into a gas station. Talked her down.

They'd grabbed lunch at Magnolia's Veranda inside the Four Queens. After a couple Bloody Marys, she'd worked up the courage to walk into the Golden Nugget. She'd played six hands of blackjack before the blue-gray clouds and orange squiggles had become too much. The pit boss, security—they'd been watching her. She could feel it. After gas and lunch, her short gambling career had netted them one hundred and forty bucks.

You suck.

Now she was screwing up invoices. Well, the invoices themselves weren't wrong—

"Eve."

The colors faded as her eyes lifted to her supervisor, Greg, a chunky guy with thinning hair.

"You forgot to put the requisition numbers on the purchase orders again."

And an insufferable tool.

"And if we don't have the requisition number on the purchase order, we don't get paid and then we have to resubmit our invoices and it takes another two weeks before we get reimbursed, which affects revenue."

Go ahead. Tell him about the lime-green stripes and bubble gum-pink splotches.

Aside from being unappetizing, it threw off the whole composition of the form.

"Well?" he asked.

Her lips bobbled for words like a goldfish.

"Everybody." Greg turned to the row of cubicles. "Don't be like Eve. You need to make sure you're putting requisition numbers on purchase orders—otherwise we have to resubmit our invoices and that affects revenue."

He handed her a stack of papers. "You need to re-do these. And update the system."

Eve sighed.

She'd been in the accounting department at Pierce Technologies for seven years. Not her ideal job, but they promoted themselves as a green company. Industrial mining without the industry, no harmful byproducts. And they were expanding their research division. Always looking for the best and brightest.

And that's not you.

Seven years. Five with Greg as her supervisor. And he hadn't learned her birthday. No one had. She checked her phone. No messages.

Not even from her mom.

You know why.

Her sternum clenched. Crimson and magenta flashed in her periphery. Laurel green grayed into desert sands. A dingy purple pit opened up.

She took a deep breath and wrung her fingers.

They all hate you.

No—she'd stood up for herself. And it had felt good. At the time.

Not so great now, is it?

"Stop," she whispered. "Stop it."

She stood, peering into the next cubicle where a young woman in a pink sweater texted on her phone.

"Hammock-zen-see—mmph." Eve winced, then cleared her throat, not much louder. "What's everybody doing for lunch?"

Mackenzie glanced at the pale little woman in all black. "We already ordered."

"I—I asked you like a half hour ago."

Mackenzie's phoned pinged. She giggled and resumed texting.

"Whatever." Eve sank back into her cubicle.

She slumped in her chair, pushing aside the purchase orders. She scowled at the monitor, the numbers flickering with color. Her eyes drew to her phone.

Nobody likes you. It's always been that way.

She snatched the strap of her beaten-up black shoulder bag and walked out.

* * *

Eve wasn't interested in the lunch options around the corporate park. Get in, get out, get the day over with. The notion she should treat herself suffocated under the pesky fact the rent check hadn't cleared. She'd told herself it was worth it—spend the extra four hundred for a little less space in a better neighborhood. But they raised the rent. Every year. All over California. Finding a cheaper place was like proving the Riemann hypothesis.

She picked through the convenience store's refrigerator case inspecting prepackaged sandwiches, checking the dates, and sniffing a soggy cucumber and roasted red pepper hoagie—the only vegetarian option—before settling on a roast turkey and cheddar.

Way to save the planet.

She slouched in line for the register, again troubled by her phone's silence.

They all hated her. But today?

Preoccupied with her nonexistent social life, a college student with a man-bun cut in front of her.

Eve stepped forward. “Hey, I was—”

He didn’t acknowledge her, and neither did the cashier. So much for that next-in-line thing.

With a pass of his phone over a scanner and a wave to the cashier, Man-Bun College Kid was on his way.

Eve dropped the sandwich onto the counter. The cashier focused on the screen.

Tell her off. She already doesn’t like you. Who cares?

“That’ll be seven sixty-five.”

Eve went to swipe her card, then yanked it back. Silver, blue green, purple. That was what would be left in her account until payday.

She dug into her purse, berated by the customers’ annoyed sighs and grumbles behind her.

Loser.

Eve lowered her eyes, handing over wrinkled bills.

* * *

She crossed the street, back to the corporate park. Office workers intermingled along a winding path through a thick, verdant lawn. A travesty. The water required to maintain the grounds boiled her brain. The one redemption—and probably just for cost reasons—were the native trees dotting the path. Black oak. Cottonwood. Ponderosa pine. But no one cared, they were all too absorbed by their phones. Which only made Eve think about hers.

She sat on a bench, unwrapped her sandwich and played a game—find two or more people not on their phones. She scanned the campus, relieved to find others eating alone, then surprised at a small cluster of older men chatting on the lawn. Polo shirts and khakis. Except for a guy in a brown suit. He was stout and on the shorter side. She gambled with herself. Which of them would get a text message first? Or want to show the group something on his device?

No such moment arose.

The stout man glanced in her direction.

Her eyes darted away and she resumed her scan.

A young couple in an intimate conversation under a shady tree. Her arms draped over his neck, his hands on her hips. They kissed.

“It won’t last.” Eve muttered. “Dumbasses.”

She took another bite, mustard and mayonnaise splattering onto her pant leg.

“Dammit.”

She brushed it off, then rubbed out the stain on the fabric. A glint on the asphalt path caught her eye. Tiny, shiny, metal and glass. An earring? Or a charm from a bracelet? No. Too small. She reached down, pinching it between her thumb and forefinger. Eyeglasses. Round frames. Gold. Less than half an inch. Eve squinted, scrutinizing their detail.

Her phone chimed.

She pocketed the glasses in her cardigan, then bundled up her half-eaten sandwich and shoved it into her purse. She hopped off the bench and hurried back to the building while closing the calendar reminder on her phone:

DR.PIERCE 1:15 (silver, blue, silver, red)

Eve rode the elevator to the executive floor, captive audience to the corporate promo on the screen overhead. It opened on a polished office. Their twenty-eight year old founder and CEO, Dr. Simon Pierce, stepped into frame in a tailored lapis lazuli suit and tie, his ruddy hair coiffed to perfection. He sat on the edge of a marble-topped executive desk, facing the camera with an engaging smile.

"I remember when I built my first high-powered laser cannon in my step-dad's garage. The police told me I was lucky I was a minor. I told them they were lucky I didn't blow a hole in them the size of a cantaloupe."

He turned to another camera. "A lot's changed since then, and today there's nothing on Earth I can't penetrate."

Cut to a mountainside mining operation. A Pierce Technologies-brand laser cannon blasted into solid rock, triggering an avalanche. The hardhats fled in terror, the wall of stone collapsing. The clip cut, rejoining Simon on a brisk walk through Pierce Technologies's laboratories, dozens of scientists tinkering in the background.

"But Pierce Technologies isn't just the global leader in advanced mining operations worldwide. It's also a trusted source of innovation and design, providing highly skilled scientists and researchers for lucrative government contracts."

The scene wiped, Simon still at the same brisk pace outside the building. "So whether you're looking to build the future or burrow out of it, Pierce Technologies can help make that vision a reality."

He stopped in front of teams of miners, engineers and scientists, pivoting to yet another camera. "Pierce Technologies. Can you dig it?"

He pointed to the same camera. "Because we can."

Eve scowled as the promo ended. He was just so fake. Always smiling all the time. Nobody was that happy. No one. And his immobile hair and blemish-free skin—like plastic. Probably built like a Ken doll, too.

Ding.

The elevator doors opened.

***

Simon exited the men's room, straightening his platinum suit jacket and checking his smart watch—1:15 pm.

"Train's running on time, I see, Dr. Pierce," a passing executive commented.

"Key to long life is a regular colon, my friend." Simon snapped his fingers, punctuating with a point in the man's direction.

Simon turned the corner as Eve stepped off the elevator, coaching herself.

"All right," she whispered. "You already know what you're going to say. Just—breathe. And—eye contact."

Her research proposal. Simon backpedaled. He hurried to the glass doors of the executive offices. An elegant woman in a flowery pant suit was also looking for him.

She smiled. "Simon."

He grinned, gliding toward her. "Deepa."

"Have you seen Dr. Freitas?"

"Can't say I have," he answered, his next words a rushed hush. "Could you do me a favor and talk to me really quick? I want her to feel guilty when she interrupts."

"What?" Uncharacteristic wrinkles formed in Deepa's brow.

"It can be anything," Simon said in a low tone. "Your weekend—anything."

***

Eve rounded the corner and took a deep breath, unnerved by the tall, well-dressed people.

She approached like a child waiting for the adults to finish.

"Uh, all right," Deepa was saying to Simon. "Well, my partner and I are really into canoeing, so, we're building a dugout from a tree log, where you hollow out the insides with small coal fires."

"Oh. Well, that's actually pretty interesting."

"D-Dobter Rears?" Eve sputtered. "Peerbs." She winced in frustration.

Nice.

He smiled. "Eve Kincaid. Great to see you. How've you been?"

"Uh—well—that's kind of why I wanted to talk to you. When I started here I was told you were always looking for talented people and that I could move into research—"

"Well, talent is subjective, and we do prefer our lab assistants to be working on their doctorate."

"Well, technically, I—I still am."

A smile crept across Deepa's face.

She thinks you're stupid.

"And this... " Eve stood straighter. "This is the fourth time I've applied, so—"

"In all fairness," he said. "I know my name's on everything here, but I don't make all the hiring decisions. You'd have to take it up with Human Resources."

Lying, dickless plastic prick.

Her eyes buckled, searching for the floor. "I...I'm—I'm sorry. Thank you. I'm sorry."

Head down, she scurried toward the elevator.

Simon turned to Deepa. "So, did you chop the tree down yourself, or—?"

* * *

Eve hunched over the keyboard. Her bony fingers dug into her chaotic mop of hair. Her gray eyes stared at the monitor, only registering unrealized dreams as the numbers and symbols illuminated with color. 4,795 shifted into bands of pink, gold, brown, and red. 3,457 was blue green, magenta, red orange, and amber. They drifted apart, losing their shapes, recombining and weaving into complex mutations. Cerulean integrals. Burnt orange sigmas. Coral phi. Neon-green psi. Little garnet partial derivatives interspersed with plum xs stretching into endless space.

"Did you really think I'd forget?"

Her head snapped aside. The colors dissolved to reveal Greg.

They'd gotten her a cake?

"These all need requisition numbers." He stuck out a stack of papers. "Before you leave for the day."

Eve snatched them from his hand.

"There's more on the printer." He walked off.

She huffed and stood.

You couldn't handle all that attention anyway. Peerbs.

She walked to the copier and picked up the warm pages, cursing the sacrifice of trees. Maybe there was an acceptance letter hidden among them. She'd been selected for the research position, and Simon couldn't tell her himself because it had to go through formal channels. Greg was upset to see her go.

Yeah, that sounds logical.

She thumbed through them. All purchase orders. She had hoped her photonic microprocessor design for a quantum computer would dazzle the R&D department.

It was conceptual. And you're not an engineer.

"Hey, did you want to come out with us tonight?"

Taken off-guard, Eve didn't have a ready answer.

But when she met Mackenzie's eyes, she realized the words had been directed at Ashley, the new girl, who was returning to her cubicle.

"Oh." Mackenzie frowned. "Not you."

Eve slunk back to her desk.

"Let me get your number so we can avoid that confusion again."

Eve dropped into her chair, and slapped purchase orders atop the others. She searched the database for the original she'd sent without the requisition number, canceling its status, creating a new order and entering the information all over again. Head braced against her fingers, she slouched forward, her right hand switching between the keyboard and mouse as she jumped through windows and prompts, the same ones over and over. The familiar patterns blended in blurs of colors.

She sighed.

She'd wanted to unlock mysteries of the universe with Gideon. Uncover invisible realms. Discover their deeper meaning. Share them with the world.

There's nothing. This is all you're good for.

Her coworkers left, saying goodbye to each other. The cleaning crew changed out trash bags. A vacuum roared down the hall.

Eve flipped over the last purchase order and grabbed her phone. If anything was going to happen, she would have to make it happen.

Oh, yeah, let's see how this turns out...

She texted Georgie.

Hey! Want to grab a drink? My treat!

Send.

You sound desperate.

She logged out and stood, slinging over her shoulder bag. Her phone chimed. She dug into her purse to check the reply.

Hey girl! Thanks but can't. Helping the kids with a school project. Maybe some time next week?

There's no next week. She's dodging you. Again.

She scrolled through previous replies from Georgie, all rescheduling for another time which never materialized.

There might be a bottle of wine in the fridge. Too much trouble to stop on the way home. And no money. But she didn't really want to drink. She just wanted to pull the covers over her head and sleep forever.

After six, security maintained a skeleton crew. One guard manned the lobby check-point by the elevators.

"Have a good one." He smiled, holding the door open.

"Good night," she croaked.

Her steps echoed in the lobby.

Georgie had blown her off. Again. Everyone had blown her off. But she'd at least thought Georgie would come through.

Eve shoved open the door. "Oh, sorry I can't hang out with you, I'm too busy with my awesome career and my perfect life in my big, expensive house with my adorable kids even though I married Jeremy, of all peop—"

A loud, cracking pop. The entire corporate park lost power. She stopped cold, hovering in the darkness, ears delving the dead air.

With a thrum, Pierce Technologies lit up, startling her.

The other buildings remained blacked out. She used the back light to scan her surroundings. Bars of yellow cluttered her vision. Trees and an empty path. Blackouts weren't uncommon, but she could see lights on across the street. She dug into her bag, pulling out her mace, and secured the strap on her wrist, keeping her thumb on the button.

Deep breath.

Eve edged around the corner, hesitating, wary of a lone black van parked alongside the building.

Had it been there earlier?

Maybe somebody had cut the power. Maybe whoever had cut the power was in the van. Or one of them had cut the power and another one was waiting in the van. Either way, the second she got close, she'd be jumped, taken hostage, raped, murdered, and left somewhere in the desert in a shallow, unmarked grave.

Of course, that was just one possible outcome. More horrific scenarios ran through her mind as she crept toward the rear parking lot because—well, she needed to get home and forget today had happened. She didn't have clearance to go back inside after hours. The north end of the building was lit even less. Besides, most likely she'd be stabbed for her purse and left to bleed to death. Joke would be on her attacker. He'd find dried-out makeup, four tampons, a half-eaten sandwich, and two dollars and thirty-five cents in change.

Footsteps behind her. Yellow and charcoal.

In the van's reflection, a figure darted up fast. Her molars ground. She held her breath.

Eve whipped around, soaking his eyes, spraying up his nose, even getting a little in his mouth. But he'd aimed something at her—a flicker—and missed.

He'd tried to taze her?

Under normal circumstances, she would've run and been relieved to get away. But not after today. Every indignity replayed. And now this. That was all she was good for. Somebody's disposable target. Charcoal and crimson. She growled, plunging a fist into his head. The gratifying collision of her knuckles stoked her rage.

He dug his fingers into his eyes, still trying to aim the taser as she swatted a fist into his head.

The mace swung from the strap on her wrist.

"N-N-N-No!" She gnashed her teeth. "No! No!"

She grabbed his jacket, tugging him closer, and drubbed his face. Her left hand grappled for the taser while the right pummeled his head.

He tried pushing her back, but she seized his wrist.

Her knuckle jabbed his eye. She jammed a knee into his groin. Another knee thrust, and she struck his gut.

His grip loosened. With a stomp of her heel into his pelvis, she pried the taser free, and they stumbled apart. Her thumb landed on the button—a flash.

And he was gone.

Bewildered, she backed away. The spots in her eyes faded. Movement. On the ground.

A little man, no more than three inches tall, cursing, and twisting about in agony. He staggered, bent over, rubbing his face. It wasn't possible. She checked over her shoulder...the van was gone—no, it'd been shrunk, too.

She turned around, awestruck by the matchbox-sized vehicle in the building's dim glow. It wasn't possible. She couldn't remember if she'd inhaled or exhaled last, just that there was no air in her lungs and she seemed to have forgotten how to do either.

She stared at the device in her hand. Clearly not a taser.

Who was he?

"And why—"

Brown-suit guy. The men on the lawn. When she'd found the tiny glasses. He must've seen her find them. And he'd known they were there because he'd shrunk whoever had worn them.

She gasped and backpedaled. A lump squeezed under her heel with a crunch.

Her jaw dropped.

She lifted her heel, dreading the mess. Yellow bars faded in her vision, revealing a shimmering wet stain on the pavement.

She gagged, bolting toward the parking lot. Eve slowed, her breaths labored as she turned around. She couldn't just run away, but she couldn't go to the police.

"What am I supposed to say? He would've shrunk me if I hadn't fought back? Stepping on him was an accident?"

No one will believe you.

Then there was the device itself. She checked it under the pale lamplight. A dial and an antenna—which she figured was the firing end. One marking in the center stood out: *oo*. Infinite black. And with any luck, neutral.

She rolled it into position with her thumbnail. She approached the crushed body, pulling out the plastic convenience-store bag from her purse. The uneaten half sandwich fell out inside.

She scraped up the mushy wad, suppressing her gag reflex. "Oh god oh god oh god oh god oh god."

And tied the plastic bag closed.

She lurched across the pavement, snatching up the van, and raced to her car.

2

(yellow)

Eve burst through her apartment door, short of breath, and locked it behind her. She grabbed her chest. Her eyes drew to the bloody plastic bag. Her gasps intensified into dry heaves. She dropped it, rushing to the kitchen as the whirl in her gut crested.

She made it to the sink just in time.

Afterwards, she wiped her mouth and rinsed her hands. Then she flipped on the garbage disposal for good measure. She braced her forearms on the counter's edge, thinking she might have another go. Drained, she twisted around and slid down the cabinet.

She rummaged into her shoulder bag and plucked out the tiny van. She examined it between her thumb and middle finger. It made no sense. She reached up, tossing it onto the counter, and dug around for the device.

The crude remote had a short antenna and tiny screws on the cover panel. The most complicated element was the dial button—a black disc around a smaller white disc, and a pale gray push-button in the center. The black disc was aligned in the neutral position, marked by gradients using circles increasing or decreasing in size. The white disc had a different set of markings spaced farther apart in numeric decimals from 1.4 (silver, pink) to 8.0 (purple, black).

She used her thumbnail to adjust the white disc, careful not to put pressure on the push button, finding the parts firm. The larger dial had more give than the white one, which clicked into each position. She rolled the main dial a few degrees down and aimed at a wooden kitchen chair. A thin beam shot from the antenna, striking the nearest leg. The chair drew in on itself, lower and narrower, until it was six inches high.

She sat up. "But where does the mass go?"

A quarter turn of the white dial. The main dial a few degrees up. Another bolt, a wider beam.

The other chair pushed outward, rising and widening. It shoved the little breakfast table aside before it stopped at the ceiling. The rush of its expansion sent napkins flying. She followed a napkin with the antenna as it floated down. She hit the button.

The napkin enlarged, filling the space around it. Too heavy, it dropped onto the spindle of the giant chair. Eve sprang to her feet, placing the device on the counter. She ran her fingers along edge of the giant napkin. Less like paper, more like canvas. Amazed at its heft and starchiness, she gripped it with both hands and pulled. With all her might, she couldn't start the slightest tear.

"What? No."

Matter didn't increase in size and dimension, mass and density—and sure as hell not without adhering to the laws of physics. She cocked her head to the side, eyebrow raised like a quizzical bird. It demanded experimentation.

She adjusted the dial to *oo* (infinite black) and pointed at the giant chair and napkin. Their compression to normal size was quicker. They weren't being drawn but yanked. She aimed at the tiny chair. It was thrust outward into its original dimensions.

Eve scoured the cupboard for a suitable test subject. She settled on a single dry linguine noodle. Then she scanned at her messy apartment. Collections of rocks and pine cones, seed pods, dried leaves, and bird feathers were strewn at random on dark hardwood furniture, shelves, and counter space. Books, notebooks, papers, and mail were piled in the same manner. Most books were marked with a pen or dried leaf to save a page. Science-related artwork lined the walls. A Fibonacci spiral overlaying a curled cat. A large portrait of planet Earth hung above the television.

After dragging the coffee table aside, she pushed some book piles to the walls. Then she arranged the kitchen chairs back to back in the clearing. She balanced the linguine along the top rails and adjusted the device's dial.

The noodle expanded to fill the length of the room, knocking over a lamp before tumbling to the floor.

"That—that's not right."

The noodle's center should have snapped in half under its own weight. She jabbed it with her heel. Pain shot through her leg and she stumbled back. She jumped onto it with both feet, determined to break it with repeated stomps.

Mere cracks formed.

Her brow pinched with puzzled disdain. "So...it's magic."

To reduce matter, atoms would have to be removed or forced out, but that didn't appear to be happening. The little man hadn't splattered until she'd stepped on him. Orange and chartreuse. Nausea bubbled inside.

Not the first time you'd be responsible—

"No, no, no." She shook her head and exhaled. "Focus, focus."

Eve returned the noodle to normal. She placed the device on the counter and moved the chairs back into the kitchen. Her heart lunged ahead of each step into the living room.

"Maybe I should just find a box for this thing..."

But the device represented a radical challenge to long accepted principles. What was happening to the mass and energy? How was it possible? She had an idea—her own ideas—but maybe this guy had discovered something else.

She had to know. She couldn't not know. Not knowing was painful.

Another study of a dial. From what she could tell, the device was safe to use on living organisms. No way she'd reduce herself. Her ground floor apartment had a persistent bug problem. She shuddered thinking about the overpowering strength of ants, the lethality of a spider's venom, or a roach the size of an Escalade.

Her thumbnail adjusted the dial. She bit the side of her lip and turned the device to herself.

A jolt raced through her. It didn't hurt. Kind of a rush. She shifted up, spreading out. Her body enlarged to over six feet, her clothes and the device with her. Why was it affected? A field?

She felt more substantial. Heavier. Everything was brighter, louder, clearer. Her vision, her hearing, her sense of self—all magnified.

If this was six-foot-something, what would more feel like?

The reality of physics rattled her. She could grow too heavy to move, her muscles unable to lift her larger mass. Or they'd become so heavy, her bones would break. Or her heart could give out, unable to pump hard enough. But, what about the miniaturized man? How had his lungs been processing oxygen? How had any of his biological systems been functioning?

"Well, any sufficiently advanced technology, looks like magic."

The crude machine didn't conjure notions of advanced technology. The housing resembled a gaming controller from the eighties, Intellivision or Coleco, but thinner. He'd melted plastic to seal up the keypad. The dials reminded her of old rotary knobs, cut and flattened to streamline. On second thought, he'd put a lot of time into it.

She hesitated, thumb over the button.

Of course, there could be limits she wasn't aware of. What if the miniaturized man had been running out of oxygen and would have died within minutes?

What if that had been his plan for her? Then it had been self-defense. Maybe what she'd done had been quicker, painless.

Oh, please. You know that's not true.

Laurel green and blue gray. No, not now. She squeezed her eyes shut, gritting her teeth. She focused on the black behind her eyelids and inhaled. She swallowed hard and exhaled, opening her eyes.

Worst-case scenario—all of the bones in her body would shatter and she'd die of heart failure. The authorities would find her huge rotting corpse the next day, the device crushed under her enormous weight, lost forever.

But then, she considered the napkin. And the linguine. They shouldn't have grown denser and stronger. The noodle's center should have become its weakest point, the same way she was sure her bones would snap. Except now, she wasn't sure.

Each horrible fate played out in her mind. And after. Who would show up at her funeral?

No one. Nobody loves you.

This was all she had. Someone else's breakthrough. She could hide it and his death. Or turn herself in along with device. Or risk everything, and advance the canon of human understanding. Be something great.

Deep breath. She closed her eyes. And hit the button.

A tingling wave pushed the edges of her form. She rose and spread out, the device with her. Soon she was forced to crouch below the ceiling. Her butt knocked something over, her right hip pressing against the bookshelf. She stopped at over twenty feet, crammed inside her apartment, her elbows on her knees.

Her heart raced, but didn't pound. Not breathing hard, but—she wasn't breathing. A breath. No strain on her lungs. Her heart wasn't straining to pump. People over eight feet in height struggled with cardiac and pulmonary problems, yet here she was three times their size and aside from the adrenaline coursing through her veins—which probably should have given her a massive heart attack, she was fine. With little room to maneuver, she managed a slight twist of her torso and a careful swing of her left elbow, gauging the weight of her more considerable form. Not laborious or exhausting to move.

She focused on the Earth portrait above the television a few feet from her face, envisioning a gigantic version of herself stepping across the North American continent. The portrait-self turned a gaze upward to meet her own eyes. An eyebrow rose and a smile cracked across her face. She watched her gigantic portrait-self wade into the Pacific, gathering up the Great Garbage Patch with a massive mesh net, seawater draining out. Portrait-Eve used the device to shrink it. Pollution eradicated!

Her gigantic self waded into the Arctic, using the device to enlarge icebergs. Global warming halted!

Gigantic Eve next stood along the San Rafael Mountains, dumping sand onto raging wildfires to snuff them out. Devastation, limited!

Portrait Eve dusted off her hands, satisfied. Then, the scream of fighter jets distracted her. Missiles screeched through the air, bombarding her. A nuclear warhead. Mushroom cloud.

Daydream over.

Eve shook off the fantasies. She glanced at the ceiling and stifled a laugh. Her attention returned to the device and she dialed to neutral. With a press of the button, she dropped down and inward, yanking the ceiling fan tangled in her hair.

"Ah, shit!"

The fan landed with a crash. Dry wall rained on her as she returned to five foot four.

She brushed off the dust. "How did you do this? How...?"

Her eyes drifted to the bloody plastic bag. Decomposition would be in the early stages—would she be enlarging bacteria if she made the body normal sized? Would they be too large to affect her? Or would their enzymes devour her flesh? Or would the membranes of their single cell bodies be unable to survive the macroscopic world? And what about parasites?

"I have to know."

In an hour's time, she'd stitched together a make-shift hazmat suit of garbage bags, duct tape, cleaning gloves, scuba goggles, and a respirator mask. She cocooned the kitchen table, kitchen floor, and breakfast bar with garbage bags and plastic wrap. Then she dug a microscope out of the closet, the same one she'd had since she'd been ten. She tore off the edge of the bloodied sandwich bag and slid it under the lens. At four hundred times magnification the blood cells were tiny dots dwarfed by huge sand grains.

Eve placed the microscope on the kitchen counter. Head turned aside, she unwrapped the sandwich bag, exposing the hideous mass inside. She picked up the device, eyes cracked just enough to aim, and hit the dial button.

Instant full-sized smashed corpse. Without the benefit of clothing mashed into it, it would have been impossible to tell which end was what.

She choked in disgusted shudders. "Oh god, oh god, oh god."

Teeth clenched and eyes closed, she squeezed her hand into the pants pocket, glued shut with pressed flesh, and pried out a wallet. She dropped it into the sink with a thunk.

On her second pass, she reached across the body, gagging as her fingers dug into the wet fabric and dislodged a set of gore-soaked keys with a key card stuck to them. Those, too, clanked into the sink. She snapped off the gloves, letting them fall into a nearby trash can, then pulled on a fresh pair and grabbed the device.

The body reduced to inches.

Hot water filled the basin with a healthy douse of bleach and a long squirt of green dish soap. She pulled edges of the tape from the table, wall, and floor, and folded the plastic into a bundle. With the device, all of it reduced to a little ball she held between her fingers. She could reduce plastic and toxic waste to zero. Then she considered the mangled body. Someone was probably looking for him.

Are you kidding? He invented a shrink ray. Probably in his basement. Nobody's looking for this guy.

She sighed. His family couldn't see him like this. He needed a proper burial. And they'd need closure.

"*Fuck.*"

Faucet off, she reached into the foam. First was the key card, floating on the surface. Pierce Technologies. She held her breath. He'd worked in the same building? She reached back in, grasping the wallet. Shaking off the suds, she struggled to push the driver's license from the slot with gloved fingers.

Dr. John W. Talbot.

And he lived at 1502 (silver red black yellow) North Hazelton.

* * *

She and Gideon used to watch heist movies with an intellectual passion. They'd hit Pause early on, trying to guess the plan. At key points they'd pause again, troubleshooting what would go wrong, or what the double-cross would be. Afterward they'd poke holes in the plot. Brainstorming the perfect caper had become a pastime. At a diner or coffee shop, mid-conversation one of them would drop in details. She'd hazard the security precautions with clinical apathy. He'd solve for the variables. A hypothetical Bonnie and Clyde.

She wished he was still around.

Eve scouted the quiet hillside neighborhood. She rolled past Talbot's a couple of times, then parked at the end of the block. His house was a Dutch colonial style with a row of Italian cypress trees and a maple in the yard. No car in the driveway. Only a light or two on inside. She checked over her shoulder as she hiked up the lawn, slipping on a pair of nitrile gloves.

"It's not breaking and entering," she whispered. "I have the keys, so, it's just entering, right? Right."

She tried one. And then another. And another—which almost got stuck in the lock. On the fourth attempt, the knob loosened. She coaxed the door open, expecting an alarm, but...nothing.

She slipped in, easing the door shut.

Stillness.

Eve pocketed the keys, hovering in the wainscoted foyer. She peered down the hall to the glow coming from the living room, and another light. Maybe the kitchen? She just needed his computer, anything that would tell her who he'd been and how the device worked. Take whatever she could, leave no fingerprints, and run.

After stalking the hall, she reached a door and tested the knob. It opened. Darkness inside. She hit the light, revealing a staircase to another door below with a keypad alongside it.

Called it. Basement.

She descended with delicate steps.

"John?" A woman's voice asked. "Is that you?"

Eve spun around. Hot yellow and slate rippled her vision.

A tawny-haired woman in a bathrobe stood at the top of the stairs, pointing a small revolver at her.

"Who are you?" she demanded.

Eve put her hands up. "I—I work with your husband! Th-There's been an accident."

"An accident?"

"Look, I-I-I have proof." She lowered a hand.

"Don't move!"

"Please don't shoot me!"

"Then stop moving!"

"Don't shoot!" Eve reached into her cardigan.

"Stop. Moving."

"I-I don't know how else to explain it!" Eve whipped out the device and hit the button.

A flash and a deafening snap. The tiny bullet plinked against the wall alongside Eve's head.

Ears ringing, Eve raced up the stairs as the two-inch Mrs. Talbot ran.

"N-N-N-No!" Eve pleaded. "Wait! Come back! I just didn't want to get shot!"

She clambered up, catching a glimpse of Mrs. Talbot darting into the living room.

Eve slowed. This wasn't going according to plan.

There was a plan?

Time to come clean. Return her normal, explain what happened.

A careful step onto the carpet. Mrs. Talbot was near the coffee table, winded, shifting back and forth as she gazed up at Eve.

Fearing she might run, Eve hesitated, trying to gauge the woman's next move. Neither was prepared when a large tabby cat pounced from the floral-patterned sofa and snatched up the tiny woman.

"Oh god!" Eve cried.

She lunged for the animal. Mrs. Talbot's screams bounced in and out as the tabby scampered around the living room and back again.

"No, no!" Eve darted back and forth in a haphazard chase. "Wait! Wait! Wait!"

It slipped past her, running down the hall and disappearing into a pet door. Eve thrust open the human door.

Twelve more cats. Three of them ripping Mrs. Talbot to pieces in a vicious tug of war.

Eve slammed the door and clasped a hand over her mouth. Yellow spots and chartreuse ripples. She bolted through the hall and then slowed.

"Oh my god." She gasped, resisting tears. "Shit, shit—*fuck*. Okay, okay—no more shrinking people."

Laurel green saturated her vision. It had been an accident. She hadn't meant to—

Nobody cares about you—why should you care about them?

She didn't mean it. She squeezed her eyes shut. With a long slow breath, her eyes opened.

All this couldn't be for nothing. Not now.

Eve searched the pantry shelves and grabbed an open can of cocoa powder.

Once at the bottom of the basement stairs, she shook a bit onto the lid and then blew it onto the keypad. The powder back shot into her face. With a cough and sputter, she managed to dust the numbers, revealing the combination and streaks hinting at their order. 4, 3, 7, 8 (pink, blue-green, gold, purple).

She pushed open the door, smudging cocoa across her face as she wiped her nose. The lights came up. There was a server wired to a desktop computer on a small wooden desk. A long counter ran against the wall to her right with a row of lab equipment. Three odd machines. One she recognized as a spectrometer. It had been equipped with different parts and additional displays.

Shelves of miniature vehicles lined the entire back wall. Dozens and dozens of cars and trucks, some with the license plates removed, along with jon boats and skiffs. Too detailed for scale models. And no bottles of hobbyist paint or glue.

The work bench to the left was dedicated to soldering. Three cube organizers nested dozens of little bins. Alongside it, another shelf full of binders. Two white boards of formulas and computations. The floor and walls were all concrete.

She scanned the whiteboard calculations. Complex, but not indiscernible. Familiar starting points. Green and purple. Energy and mass. Yellow-orange, gray and silver streaks blending to sky blue, olive swirling into pink, violet and cerulean. Unfinished. He was trying to violate the Pauli exclusion principle—that no two fermions could occupy the same state.

The white board on the right had more question marks. Rays of deep fuchsia, white, mint green, and electric indigo. A different approach, trying to use Minkowski space in quantum states. Intriguing. Too bad she'd left her phone at her apartment, afraid it would incriminate her.

She wiggled the computer mouse. A secure login prompt.

She took a guess.

Password1 (silver).

Error message: Two More Attempts—Failure & System Wipe.

She abandoned the computer and pulled down a binder. Schematics and diagrams. This was it. Hand-drawn hard copies of the device design. He'd built it. But then, what did it have to do with Pierce Technologies? She shelved it, reaching for another. Strange colors lifted from the pages as she skimmed the notes, unable to recognize the words.

Was she having a stroke?

No.

Russian Cyrillic.

"Aw—really?" She snapped the binder shut, then shoved it onto the shelf like it was cursed.

It all made sense. The gold glasses. Why he'd waited for her. Someone else had found out before she did. Another scientist, maybe? Talbot had stolen something—probably from one of the government projects—and repurposed it. That was why there was no alarm system in the house. The Talbots couldn't risk the police showing up.

Yellow, chartreuse, soggy purple.

"Oh my god." Eve backed away. "What was I thinking? You weren't! Because you're an idiot! I can't do this. I can't do this. What am I going to do? They're going to kill me."

The wheel of her mind spun, weaving her demise. No sympathetic ear from Russian intelligence. Nor would they believe it had been an accident. It would be torture and death unless she fled. And they would stop at nothing.

She could make an anonymous call to the FBI, but how anonymous would it be? They'd want to know how someone had discovered a Russian agent living in suburbia. If they weren't already monitoring him. Trace the call. Analyze her voice. Prosecute her for possession of stolen government property and double homicide. They'd confiscate the device. She'd never know how it worked.

Her belly wobbled with dread until a legion of shadowy assassins trampled her longing and regret. No one would take pity on her. They'd find her no matter where she hid and—

"Wait. Nobody knows I'm here."

She raised the device. No one knew she had it. No bodies, no murder weapon. The Talbots had vanished. And nobody knew where. Maybe they'd gone rogue. Maybe—

"Maybe he decided to keep it for himself."

And the two of them had taken all the research and fled.

Her scrutiny shifted to the server. If they'd been spies, maybe he hadn't been backing up data. Maybe they'd had a private email server to communicate with headquarters and avoid detection by domestic intelligence agencies.

She typed gibberish into the prompt and hit Enter.

Error message.

More gibberish. Enter.

System Overwrite—35 (blue-green red) *Passes.*

She rushed to the white boards, seized a cloth, and wiped them out of existence. She unplugged the lab equipment. Then she slid down the row, shrinking each machine, and plucked them up, shoving them into her pocket. With a blast, she reduced the binders and scooped up the lot of them.

Eve darted around for a container, grabbing a waste basket by the workbench. Her hand swiped across the lowest shelf, dumping in the vehicles until she'd filled the basket. She rushed to the desk for another container, then balked.

What if severing the connection to the server alerted Russian intelligence? What if the Talbots had handlers? What if they were coming to check on them right now?

Her throat closed, halting mid-breath. She backed away, ears probing the stillness. They could already be here. She faced the wall of miniatures. Cover what tracks she could or clear the shelves. Not worth the risk. She set down the waste basket and shrank it to a thimble, then pinched it between her fingers. She bounded up the stairs, chased by specters of her own creation.

* * *

The order of burnt coffee wafted from the kitchen. Eve remained hunched over her laptop. She'd found an online Russian keyboard which would translate to English. But the painstaking process of transcribing from the binder to the laptop to a yellow legal pad had taken hours for just a few pages.

Talbot had been trying to create a philosopher's stone, hoping to transmute lead into gold. In modern times, such a thing had been achieved with a particle accelerator, the amount of gold it produced only detectable by way of mass spectrometer. Somehow, in his effort to change the atomic number of aluminum, Talbot had altered size and dimension.

He'd called the device a *modifikator*, or modifier. And he'd kept referring to a fragment. At first, she'd interpreted this as quantum chemistry and the reason for his unorthodox, incomplete formulas. But as she translated more pages, it became clear the fragment was the experiment and the cause of the alterations. Her face scrunched. She flipped through the transcription, reading it in new context.

She dug out a small precision screwdriver set and removed the *modifikator*'s cover. Inside, a web of circuitry encompassed a black crystal shard. Though glassy, it didn't reflect light well. She tilted it back and forth. Instead of a reflection, a purple holographic honeycomb illuminated inside. A faint, deep hum filled her ears. She searched for its source, but in doing so, it vanished.

She tilted the *modifikator* to reproduce the holographic effect. It flickered, brighter this time. Talbot's unfinished calculations flashed through her mind. So did others. Ones she'd conceived of years ago.

Eve rushed to the bookshelf, pushing aside a magnolia seed pod, and pulled out a leather notebook. She flipped to a page marked by a photo booth picture of her making faces with a wily, bearded grad student. Gideon. Blue gray and pale green. She winced, heart dropping into the pit of her stomach, and turned it over. Her fingers ran over notes in Gideon's handwriting:

An extension of the holographic principle (maybe?)

Followed by a smattering of handwritten equations.

Her handwriting.

She returned to the couch, juggling the notebook, binder and legal pad between her knees and lap, melding her scribbles and Talbot's notes. She sketched out a new formula, a messy projection of unraveled quantum dimensions. A projection, from what she could tell, of mismatched information. Jagged dusky peaks and cherry blossoms. She could still see the drab sepia jacket Professor Beckett had worn during her doctorate proposal presentation.

"The notion that quarks engage in color change," she'd said with halting rigidity, "has been around for decades. I propose the language of elementary particles isn't spin or charge or mass, but tiny bits of information using an infinite palette of colors with infinite combinations. Blips."

Beckett had frowned, jotting notes as Eve had changed to the next slide.

"These bundles of color." She'd gestured to the screen. "Each trigger a mirror-image response called a *pilb*, confirming a blip was received and understood, and reflecting back its own information. This constant feedback creates what we experience as reality through a process I call blip-*pilb* projection. Furthermore, I hypothesize these channels of communication can be disrupted, distorting reality. My research seeks to prove information is the fundamental element of the universe."

Childish and ill-conceived.

Beckett's words.

She was sure he'd been the reason they hadn't let her back into the program.

Maybe he was right.

As much as she'd tried to push the memories to the back of her mind, they'd repeated in routine rumination. An insidious cycle. Though she had shelved the notebooks, she'd never stopped ruminating over her theory. Her eyes wandered to the fragment, captivated by its illumination. The strange hum returned to her ears as a never-ending equation of shifting colors spiraled out of the shard.

* * *

After an hour's nap, Eve changed clothes and brewed a fresh pot for the morning. The engine's whir masked the rattle of the Toyota as she sped down the freeway. She glanced in the rear-view mirror, ignoring the bags under her bloodshot eyes.

"It was an accident. I'm just going to give it back, tell them what happened, and explain my—my theory..."

Distracted by her view of the off-ramp, she gaped at the corporate campus. Pierce Technologies was surrounded by military vehicles and black sedans. Two utility trucks from the power company were parked on the north lawn. Dozens of FBI agents and military personnel were already stopping employees as they approached the building.

Her eyes widened. Yellow spots and white bands. The severity of the situation set in.

She'd be running from the Russians for the rest of her life under federal witness protection as Wendy Foster, living in Topeka, Kansas. The suburbs. Her brawny husband, Tom, was actually her FBI assigned bodyguard. Not ideal, but not terrible. He was kind, patient, well-read, handy, and funny. Faux-married life suited her. They worked well together. But her hopes for romance were dashed apart when he confessed he was gay and had begun a love affair with a neighbor down the street.

"Goddammit, Tom." She griped under her breath, clenching a fist in vain frustration at what might have been.

Her mind spun out further, at the mercy of its most vicious criticisms. Why would the government believe her? Why would anyone?

Nobody likes you. Everything about you is wrong.

Two spies died by accident? A tribunal of suits formed in her mind. Federal agents with sunglasses joined the expressionless professors from the university's interview panel and her current colleagues. Deepa's snickering. Simon's veiled mocking. Greg. They were never going to let her into their little club.

You're not smart enough. Not good enough.

She wasn't anything. Her insides crumbled with nausea. It was sixth grade all over again. She was the little weird girl nobody wanted to talk to. Altering reality at the most fundamental level and defying classical physics? Impossible! She'd have to be stupid or insane to suggest such a thing. But they'd know she was right, having been working with the fragment themselves. It would be easier to call her crazy, confiscate the *modifikator*—and her theories—and institutionalize her.

That's exactly what they'll do! Discredit and incarcerate you!

She gripped the wheel, lungs empty, eyes watching events unfold instead of the road. No trial, no appeal. Simon's smug face as they led her away. Orderlies wheeling her medicated body into the hospital's courtyard, settling her in front of the fountain.

She likes to watch the birds, they'd say.

But really, she was so doped up on sedatives she couldn't tell them the sound of the water made her have to pee.

Oh, it won't end there. You've got classified material. They're going to erase you.

She couldn't let that happen. She wouldn't. She'd been right last night. No one knew she'd been there. And they wouldn't. Not as long as she covered her tracks. Not as long as she had the *modifikator*. All she had to do was disappear.

She jammed her foot on the accelerator and sped past the exit.

If professionals needed tons of funding, Eve figured she'd need more as it would take her twice as long to understand the fragment and its properties. Maybe three times longer. Ten times longer. No—then she'd be dead of old age.

But, still.

Up ahead, a bank truck pulled off an exit ramp. She tore across the freeway to follow it. The armored car slowed into a sprawling suburban shopping center. It stopped behind the building, near a dumpster in a cement enclosure. Eve parked in a neighboring plaza and dashed across the lot.

"All right, I just need some start-up cash." She backed up against a tree in a dividing median. "Leave the country, get a new identity, then build a lab..."

Eve poked her head around. Several large trees surrounded the dumpster. She gauged the position and angle of the building's cameras. The foliage might be enough to block their view.

She ducked behind the tree. "And it's for a good cause. All the good I'm going to do totally outweighs this. And, I mean, I'm going to pay it back. It's a victimless crime. It's not even a crime—it's an anonymous loan."

She peered around the tree.

A muscular man in uniform headed to the building. The door closed behind him. She sucked in and blew out air a few times in an overzealous breathing exercise until she felt lightheaded. She flipped the hoodie over her head and pulled the drawstring.

She raced to the truck, then took the *modifikator* from her sweater and hit the button. The armored car shrank to two inches. She lunged forward in a single step and snatched it. She turned on her heel and took off running.

* * *

Most of her past stolen loot consisted of office supplies and pens. Years ago, she'd needed toilet paper so she'd grabbed a roll from a restaurant bathroom because they'd left them there in a stack and she'd figured it might have been an indication about the food. It had been, but she'd still felt guilty. Then there were the glasses from bars she'd shoved in her shoulder bag. And coffee mugs. Pretty much her entire cupboard of drinkware had been stolen. Although, the places she'd gotten them from had taken her hard-earned money with overpriced beverages and below-average service.

She placed the matchbox-sized vehicle on the kitchen counter, winded from the rush but relieved, and a little proud of herself. Her exuberance faded as the driver's-side door opened and a paunchy, uniformed man climbed out. The rear doors opened. Another man jumped out—younger, darker, much fitter.

She staggered back, reaching for a chair for support.

The half-inch tall men waved their arms, their voices inaudible.

So much for not shrinking anybody else...

Eve's fingertips dug into her temples. "Ohhhh no—no, no, no."

She pulled out the *modifikator*, circling her finger. "All right. Get near the truck. I'm going to enlarge you."

They moved in close, eager to be returned to normal. But when she hit the button, the narrow beam shot past them. The paper towel holder behind them enlarged. The top shot into the cabinet above, shattering glasses inside.

"Ah, shit!" She fumbled with dial. "Forgot to widen the beam—hang on."

She took aim and hit the button. The men rose to two and a half inches, the vehicle to the length of a smartphone.

"I could've sworn I saw someone go inside," she said, adjusting the dial.

"There's three of us in each truck," the driver answered. His voice was squeaky but not as faint as she'd expected. Though he did seem to be shouting up at her.

"Since when?" she asked.

"It ain't 1996 anymore, lady," said the driver. "Three guards, every drop."

You are so stupid. And fucked. Stupid and fucked.

"No, no, no, I—I can figure this out..." She hit the button, returning the paper towel holder to normal.

She couldn't do the same for the two men on her counter.

Poor innocent bastards. They have no idea how much danger they're in being anywhere near you.

They knew she'd stolen the truck. They could identify her. And they'd seen the *modifikator* in action. If she let them go, they'd tell the police. The police would report the robbery to the FBI, the tip would get forwarded to Counterintelligence. They'd lockdown the border, and she'd never get into Mexico. Not to mention the Russians could still be tracking her down. Her escape window was closing.

"All right, guys," she said. "There's no easy way to say this. Problem is—you know what I look like and I just stole all this money, so I can't let you go."

The men glanced at each other, unnerved.

"I know—but it's temporary, all right? I just need to figure some things out."

"So, what are you, like a scientist or something?" the younger man asked.

"Well, no, not—not technically."

They glanced at one another again.

She sighed. "This didn't turn out the way I thought it would, obviously. Because I should have figured there would be two other guards, I mean—*Heat!* The movie *Heat*! How did I forget that?! Probably because I should've slept for more than an hour last night... God! Why does this always happen to me?"

She tore her fingers through her tousled hair, blowing out a sigh. "Whatever. Point is, you're coming with me."

"With you?"

She wrung her hands. "Yeah."

"Where?"

Her focus receded inward, carrying her off with the new probabilities of her compounded threats. The Russians. The US government. The military. Pierce Technologies. The armored car company. The police. She needed to get to Mexico with the money, return these guys to normal, and ditch them. Leave Mexico and get to a place without an extradition treaty. Possibly the Maldives or Marshall Islands. But sea-level rise was making those places unlivable. Though she had always want to visit Madagascar...

Eve snapped back to the present as the driver glanced at his partner again. His partner shrugged.

"Uh, there something wrong?" the driver asked.

She squatted. "Everything. Nothing ever works out for me."

She swung open the cupboard below, rummaging through the pots and pans. "Gideon, school, friends, my stupid job! Yesterday was my birthday, and nobody remembered! My mom didn't even call! How messed up is that? Now I have this thing that can change the world and I think I can figure out how it works, and I can't tell anyone!"

The men glanced at each other, backing toward the armored car.

"Look, I know it's a lot to take in." Eve pulled out a Dutch oven and slid it onto the stove top. "And you guys don't understand, but it's really dangerous at your size, and I promise I'm going to do everything I can to make sure you're safe, so for right now you're going in the pot."

3

(blue green)

Simon straightened his jade suit jacket and logged into the videoconference. He'd neglected to put the meeting with billionaire Randal Chang into his calendar, though it had been arranged a week ago. Probably for the best. The Hong Kong mogul's business was under suspicion of being directed by the Chinese government. But Chang maintained his operations were legitimate. He claimed his success was due to the power of free market capitalism, and his vast wealth was evidence. Besides, after months of investigations, the FBI and SEC hadn't produced anything linking his company with Beijing.

Chang smiled, still in a pin-stripe suit and tie although it was midnight in his part of the world.

"Dr. Pierce," he said. "So glad you agreed to talk, in spite of all of the nasty rumors about me."

"Goes with the territory of being rich and powerful." Simon smirked. "Figured you'd be used to it by now."

"True." He nodded. "But it does put a damper on business. Hence the reason for our meeting."

Simon leaned in.

Chang spread his hands. "Due to hasty decisions by the EU, we have more operating space, if you will, in a couple factories. And I believe there would be significant savings in your production costs if you were to move them overseas."

"Well, the increased cost in transit—"

"We would offset that." He clasped his hands, fingers interlocking.

"And who knows? Maybe this could be the first of many more mutually beneficial arrangements between us."

Simon wagged his finger. "Funny you say that—"

A couple beeps from the desk phone. His secretary, Sasha.

"There is—"

More beeps.

"Just a moment."

He hit the button.

"General McCrae is here to see you," Sasha said with concern.

"Tell him I'm—"

"No—he's here to see you right now."

Simon hung up the intercom with a casual return to Chang. "I'll have to get back to you."

Chang raised an eyebrow. "Is there a prob—"

Simon logged out of the videoconference and snapped the laptop shut. Before he could stand, a husky uniformed man with a trimmed mustache barged in, followed by the more subtle glide of a statuesque blonde woman in a black pantsuit carrying a portfolio. A large man in a navy suit and tie took a sentry post at the door.

"General McCrae, and...friends." Simon grinned, reaching out for a handshake.

The woman slipped in, shaking hands. "Special Agent Kelly Callahan, FBI."

"And she's not your friend," McCrae said with a stern drawl.

Simon continued to smile and nod. Of course she was. Everyone was his friend.

"One of the fragments is missing," said Callahan.

The edges of Simon's smile sank but didn't capsize. "Well, that's—shouldn't it be on base?"

"Should be." The creases in the General's face tightened. "Somebody swapped it out with a piece of obsidian."

Simon brightened. "Well, one of your people must've—"

"One of your people," said McCrae. "Talbot was the last person who had access to it."

"That's not possible. I just saw him yesterday."

"Well, he didn't report to base this morning."

"We've sent a team to his home," said Callahan. "And we're going to need access to his office and any computers or devices he may have used."

"Absolutely." Simon nodded.

She gazed at him, expressionless, and opened the folder. "We've requested a list of anyone who's not present and accounted for." She skimmed the first page. "Oh, and there's blood outside your building.

We're looking into that, too."

"Wait—what?" asked Simon. "How much blood? Like a pint? Quart?"

"What can you tell me about Dr. Frederico Freitas?"

She held up a company ID photo of a middle-aged, olive-skinned man wearing a pair of gold, round-framed glasses.

"I know this one." Simon snapped his fingers, pointing. "Engineer in Research and Development. Dr. Bhandari was asking about him yesterday."

"Then we'd like to speak with Dr. Bhandari as well." She pulled out her phone, dialing.

"Of course," he said through a smile. "Anything you need."

Phone to her ear, Callahan flipped to the next page. An unflattering ID photo of a sullen woman with chaotic hair. "What about Eve Kincaid?"

"Oh, easy one." Simon flipped a dismissive hand. "She's in Accounting. Nothing to worry about."

"I don't care," said McCrae. "Somebody's gone AWOL with an extremely hazardous material. If she ain't here, I want to know why."

* * *

Eve filled a worn suitcase with clothes, shrunken possessions, and the items she'd looted from Talbot's. She took a small framed photo off the dresser. Hershey Park. Eve had been a geeky teenager, reluctant to smile alongside her sunny younger sister, Charlotte, whose arms draped around their kid twin brothers, Sawyer and Luke, each missing a front tooth. She wished she could go back in time, change the past. She stacked it with other frames, wrapping them in a T-shirt and shrank them. The bundle she placed into a ring box and then into the suitcase. She'd have to leave her collections of feathers, leaves, and rocks behind. No time to shrink everything.

Her closet excavation led to the discovery of a plastic bin full of Halloween costumes. A mess of wigs, two of which were unnatural colors of blue and pink. But the wavy blonde one was workable. Her eyebrows would be a dead giveaway, but it could pass for a dye-job.

She checked her disguise in the mirror. Black leggings, black skirt, black hooded sweater. Too much black. Too much like the way she already dressed. No more sweaters or hoodies. She had to channel Jamie Lee Curtis in *A Fish Called Wanda*—adapt a new persona to whatever situation unfolded.

She delved further, finding a herringbone skirt and a white button-down top. She yanked a stylish tweed blazer off a hanger. Buried among a pile of shoes was a lone whiskey-colored ankle boot. She tossed through the graveyard of footwear and unearthed its partner. Then she reconstituted her dried-out makeup with warm water and eye wash. A touch of mascara, wisps of eyeliner, and a streak of lipstick.

Sliding on a pair of sunglasses, she could pass for a sophisticated urbanite in a rush to get across town for an important meeting. With a press of the button, she enlarged herself to five foot ten to complete the look. Cyan and cerise. The jolt of sensory amplification and brief euphoria coursed through her. She felt like she could do anything.

Then she remembered everything she still had to do.

She zipped up the suitcase, adjusted the dial, and zapped it, sticking it into her coat pocket. She set the *modifikator* to neutral and rushed out of the bedroom, neglecting her phone in the billows of the comforter. A second later, she turned on her heel, darting back in to grab a handful of pebbles and acorns along with a Steller's jay feather off the dresser and shoving them into her other pocket before rushing out again.

Eve scooted into the kitchen, catching the chiseled physique of the younger man standing on the handle in an undershirt, his foot braced against the rim of the pot and using his uniform as a rope to help his heftier partner scale the side.

They froze as she entered.

Eve pulled off the sunglasses. "Aw, come on—you guys are trying to escape?"

"Oh, no, no, uh," the hefty man said. "We were just, uh—"

"We just wanted to check out your place," said his partner. "See if you had anything to eat."

"We've got to get out of here." She snatched her shoulder bag.

"Why?" The heavier man slid back into the pot.

"Yeah," said his partner. "I mean, maybe if you told us what's going on...?"

"Look, it's—If I tell you, I can't let you go. It'll ruin your lives, okay? They're going to find you and your families and do anything it takes to get to me."

"Who is?"

"The government. Our government. And the Russian government. And the company I work for. Or used to work for. I'm pretty sure I can't go back. It's why I stole the money."

The two men checked each other.

"We should tell her." The younger man shrugged. "I mean, if she didn't know there's supposed to be three of us in a truck, you know?"

His partner nodded. "Oh—yeah, yeah."

"What?" Eve darted closer. "What?"

He sighed. "You can't spend it."

"Wh-Why not?"

The paunchy man shrugged. "It's all logged. Stores don't keep track of it, but we do, because we got to report to the banks. So, they'll flag the serial numbers and figure out where you are."

He's bluffing.

"That's impossible," she said. "Every serial number on every bill...?"

"Well, it's all pre-scanned, you see." He turned to his partner.

"Yeah." The younger man nodded. "All we do is run the RFID chips on the bags."

Her fingers clenched into fists as salvation slipped away. "Shit! Fuck! Dammit!" She exhaled, pulling fingers through her hair. "Of course. Of course. Great. All right—I really appreciate you guys telling me that."

"Yeah," said the younger man. "So best thing you can do is let us go with the money, and, you're off the hook."

Her desire to believe him was outweighed by her nagging paranoia that they'd run to the authorities within an hour of being returned to normal.

"Yeah." She bit the side of her lip. "Except you've seen too much. You've seen me."

"For, like, two seconds." He shrugged. "Weren't you always blonde? I don't know."

"Yeah, and I'm old, so I don't remember nothing from five minutes ago."

"Look, I know this is probably a weird and uncomfortable situation, but you know what else will be uncomfortable? The Russians interrogating you while they torture your family. Or, the FBI handing you off to the CIA so they can take you to a black site and do god-knows-what to your balls. And that's just what happens to you guys. I'll be damned if I end up in Topeka living out the rest of my days as somebody's beard!"

She stuck the armored car into the pot. "Now get in the truck."

* * *

Eve locked the front door and sidled to her car, adjusting her sunglasses. Mid-morning. Kids were at school, parents at work, retirees watching syndicated courtroom reality TV shows. The best cover she could hope for. Her thumb rolled the dial down farther than ever before. She turned aside, pointing the firing end. A faint flash in the daylight. Her Toyota contracted. It shrank smaller than a soda can and smaller still, disappearing into nothing.

She dialed back to neutral, dreading an accidental misfire on herself. Then she hurried off, cradling her shoulder bag steady so not to jostle her passengers. She'd told them to buckle up, but fretted over giving them whiplash—or worse, setting the truck down and finding them motionless.

She passed the dumpsters to the second gate on a side street, stuck a third of the way open, as usual. She slipped out and walked up block to a bus stop.

Eve fed cash and coins into the farebox. She sat, grasping the shoulder bag in her lap to hold the truck upright. The bus pulled away as a black sedan rolled up to the apartment complex. She turned away from the bus window so whoever was in the car couldn't see her.

She had to let these guys go. They had lives and families. Just because she'd ruined hers didn't mean they should suffer.

But that's what you do.

Maybe that was all she was good for.

It is. Without the modifikator, you have nothing. You have no one.

She winced, tormented by memories of last Thanksgiving.

She'd flown to the East Coast under the impression it would be her parents, aunt and uncle, a few of her parents' friends. But then, to everyone's surprise, Luke and his wife, Gemma, had shown up with the new baby. Twenty minutes later, Sawyer had arrived, unannounced. He'd flown in from New York, making sure not to be on-call for any surgeries. And a moment before anyone could mention them, Charlotte and her husband, Samir, had knocked on the door. Twenty-seven hour flight, three stops.

They'd regaled everyone with tales of East Africa and their research helping children sick with a horrible genetic disease. Everyone had wanted to know about Sawyer's great work at Sinai Medical. Luke's promotion. Gemma's new business. And, of course, the baby. Whatever his name was.

Eve had faded into the background, glass in hand, sipping drink after drink. When her aunt had finally asked how she was doing, Eve nodded, words clogged between her tongue and nasal cavity, managing a single syllable.

Good.

For this she'd received a polite smile. Might as well have been a punch in the nose.

Her aunt had returned to her more entertaining siblings. They were more accomplished. Successful. Well-traveled. Well-off. Taller. Younger. And she was...the oldest. A seed that had never sprouted, languishing in a cubicle farm.

The way her aunt had dismissed her had replayed in her mind—

smarting, striking fresh, and smarting again. Charlotte's laugh had seemed to be at her expense. Sawyer had seemed to be deriding her. Luke had been ignoring her. Her parents too ashamed look at her. No one had spoken to her. Their eyes were filled with judgment, contempt, ridicule. Caught in a loop, each repetition had compounded her agony. Crimson and magenta waves had radiated her periphery as they'd sat down to eat.

Someone had asked Charlotte a question. She'd, of course, answered in the most delightful fashion.

Eve hadn't heard any of it. "What's it like to be so goddamn perfect all the time?"

"Eve!" her mother had scolded.

"Oh god forbid I question your precious babies."

Despite slurring a little, what had followed had been a barrage of profanity and cutting observations about her siblings fueled by wine and liquor. Their faux modesty. Their destination vacations. The fact that they'd coordinated their surprise arrivals and left Eve out of the loop.

"Yeah, Char, *real* thoughtful!"

Sawyer's promiscuity with both sexes.

"Oh, he's so evolved, so open minded—no, he's a slut!"

Luke always talking down to everyone and overexplaining everything.

"Eve!" her mother had screeched. "Stop it!"

"Shut up! You love this! You love this because you've never fucking liked me! You've always just barely tolerated me—well, guess what!? Now you don't have to pretend anymore!"

Her father had slammed his hands onto the table and shot out of his chair.

"That's enough!"

The rest had been a blur. Incoherent swearing as she'd lurched from the table. Luke had intercepted her as she'd skulked to the living room, placing a gentle hand on her shoulder.

"Hey—"

She'd batted it away and staggered off. Eve had passed out in bed and awoke around four-thirty in the morning, her head a throbbing mess, her words echoing. She'd stuffed her clothes into a suitcase and slipped out before anyone had awoken.

That was the last time she'd seen her family. It would be the last time. No turning back.

The bus banked right. The main thoroughfare leading to her apartment eclipsed, replaced by a new road. She couldn't help but think everything happened for a reason, even though she knew it wasn't true. The probabilistic nature of the universe meant any and all things were always possible. What actually happened was out of any one person's control. But what she'd done had set the stage for her to move forward, unencumbered.

* * *

"You said you met with Dr. Talbot yesterday." Callahan glanced from her notepad.

"Saw him," Simon answered. "Didn't meet with him."

"Do you meet with him?" she asked.

"Not typically, no."

"That would violate protocol," McCrae muttered behind her. He'd been milling between Simon's rock displays in an effort to keep out of the way, but continued to interject, to her annoyance.

"Is there anyone who does meet with him?" Callahan asked. "Colleagues, friends?"

"There's a group of guys his age," said Simon. "Steiner, Quigley, Patel."

He waved a finger as Callahan jotted down the names. "I know what you're thinking, but here at Pierce Technologies we pride ourselves on the utmost confidentiality and security."

McCrae grunted.

"And what about security breaches?" asked Callahan.

"It would've been brought it to my attention," said Simon.

"Nothing unusual?"

"Well, there was a power outage about a week ago—"

"What?" McCrae asked.

"It wasn't just us." Simon put his hands up. "The whole area went down. Our backup generators kicked in—that's why I didn't consider it a problem."

"Any idea what caused it?" she asked.

Simon shrugged. "Line failure."

She'd taken an inventory of the surroundings and her subject since she'd arrived. He was accommodating and upbeat. Too much so. In her experience, a person could only sustain an affectation for so long. Now that she'd lulled him well into a monotonous interview, it was time to test his front's integrity. Among the geological specimens, Callahan focused on a glossy black sphere inside a small glass cube on Simon's desk.

She pointed to it with her pen. "Is that obsidian?"

Simon's head snapped in its direction before a casual pivot back to her. "Oh, no—it's actually made of sand and water. A Japanese art form called *dorodango*."

He leaned on the edge of the desk. "Once you master the technique, it's proof that with a little practice and a little patience, you can achieve perfection if you're willing to get your hands dirty."

"So, it's a shiny mud ball."

"Well...yeah."

She eyed him, skeptical. He didn't seem like a brilliant genius. But maybe that was the game. Her phone buzzed.

"Excuse me." She turned away, answering the call. "This is Callahan."

"It's Mel. Can you hear me all right?"

"Yeah, what do you got?"

"A scale-model '98 Plymouth Voyager with a flat tire," answered Agent Melinda Masuda.

"A what?"

"You know how this case already had a weird *X-Files* vibe?"

"Yeah," said Callahan. "Classic or reboot?"

"I'm thinking classic. Monster of the week. Possibly a two-parter."

"I'd watch that." Callahan nodded. "Any special guest stars?"

"None yet, but..." A creak and whine on Masuda's end of the line. Desk drawer?

"What's that?"

"Hang on." Masuda muttered over the crinkle and flip of pages. "Nope—global conspiracy episode. These look like Russian ciphers. You need to get down here."

Callahan glanced at Simon, reconsidering his obliviousness as his eyes lit up with the anticipation of a golden retriever.

She hovered the phone away from her ear. "Thank you for your time, Dr. Pierce. We'll be in touch."

She hurried out.

Simon stepped away from the desk. "You know I didn't have anything to do with this."

"Well, I'd like to believe that, but..." McCrae punctuated with a slow shrug.

"General." Simon turned his back, side by side with him. "If it wasn't for me, you wouldn't even have those fragments—"

"All the more reason you'd feel entitled to one."

"Well, if you mean because I did in a few hours what the Army Corps of Engineers couldn't do in days, I can see where you might come to that conclusion."

McCrae scowled. "And Pierce Technologies's rights to retain research are at the discretion of the DOD."

"I'm speaking to you as a fellow man of science. You and I, everyone in that tunnel, knew we found something—" Simon peered over his shoulder, mindful of the agent guarding the door and the half-dozen more outside the office.

"We don't know what we found," said McCrae. "Still don't."

"See." He smiled. "You do understand."

"I understand you're running a business."

"I'm a scientist first. I have to know, and I want to help—"

"The project is on indefinite hiatus."

Simon grinned. "Any way I can."

* * *

Agent Reid Dempsey sighed. He checked the time on his watch as the potbellied property manager led him to the apartment. He'd already been delayed ten minutes while the manager had verified his badge with the local office.

"You're too young," the manager had said in a thick Armenian accent. "How do I know you're not some actor pretending to be an agent?"

Bad enough he'd been tasked with following up on the least probable suspect. Rookie assignment. Kincaid's car wasn't in her space. The faster he could confirm she'd just slept past her alarm, the sooner Callahan would issue him a new directive.

Two heavy knocks. "Hello? Anybody home?"

No answer. The manager unlocked the door with a grunt.

"Ms. Kincaid?" Dempsey stepped inside.

The book shelf appeared to be missing several volumes, the shade askew on a lamp in the corner. Short stacks of books and mail. Then there were the strange piles of rocks and twigs and acorns, some with feathers. He wasn't sure what to make of those. Or the hole in the ceiling, the fan leaning against the couch.

"Fuck is this?" the manager groused.

"Didn't tell you she was remodeling?" Dempsey scanned the kitchen.

No crumbs on the counter. Not even by the toaster. Spotless compared to the rest of the place. He stepped closer, tilting down, and discovered a hole in the bottom of the cabinet. He opened the cupboard, several broken glasses inside. Didn't make any sense.

"What are you looking for?" the manager asked.

"Don't know yet." But something had happened. An altercation, maybe?

"Then you have no right to be here."

Dempsey pulled on a pair of gloves.

"I am American citizen—I know my rights," said the manager. "This is unlawful search."

One of those guys. Best not to debate with him.

Dempsey gestured with an open hand to the messy conditions. "More like a wellness check. When was the last time you saw her?"

"Well, I, eh—don't usually. I'd have to ask the girls in the office."

"Could you do that for me? Please?"

The manager bobbed his head.

"Ms. Kincaid?" Dempsey headed to the bedroom.

Same disorder as the living area. Inside the closest, several empty hangers divided up the clothes. The shoes below were most organized in the front, pairs arranged side by side, as though the heap behind them didn't exist. A small travel suitcase leaned against the wall.

Another scan of the room. More books. Clothes on the floor. The top of the dresser had a small pile of smooth river stones and a pine cone. Nails in the wall. Pictures had been taken down. The bed disheveled. Something had been laid on top of the comforter—a box or a suitcase. His eyes followed the creases to the corner of a smartphone.

* * *

Callahan stepped into the lobby when her phone buzzed. "This is Callahan."

"It's Guzman." A husky man's voice answered. "Freitas is gone. Landlord says there was a van here last week. I've got to get their number because this carpet looks immaculate."

"Track them down," said Callahan. "See if you can get any phone records for Freitas."

"On it."

She hung up the call, striding past the quartered-off area outside where Forensics examined the blood stains. So far, no body and three employees unaccounted for. The code book Masuda had found at Talbot's gave them some direction. Though not a hopeful one.

"Callahan!" an agent called out from behind her.

She glanced over her shoulder, slowing her pace to let him catch up. "What did you find?"

"Not much. But there's about three minutes of footage missing from last night. Power went out and the system reset."

She stopped dead, facing him. "What?"

"Yeah. Whole area's down. This building's running on back up."

With no apparent outage at Pierce Technologies, it hadn't occurred to her that the utility workers on the north side of the building were restoring power. Had the previous outage Pierce mentioned been somebody's test run? If so, those three missing minutes were crucial.

The line foreman, a towering man with a trimmed beard, led her from the transformer to the back of a service vehicle.

"Lines just snapped," he said. "I mean, there's no way anybody could get in there, not that you'd want to."

He held up the old cable. The end was pulled apart like taffy. Her eyes narrowed, unable to conceive of what could have exerted such force.

The foreman nodded. "Craziest thing is...second time we been called out to fix it."

4

(pink)

Eve nudged open the restroom door with her hip, carrying a couple bags of O'Tasty Burgers, and locked it behind her. She inspected the counter for dampness and put them down. She rested her purse on the back of the toilet and pulled out the armored car, settling it inside the sink. The two men leaned out, haggard from their experience as cargo.

She grinned, raising an eyebrow. "Crazy morning, right, guys?"

They answered with vexed, surly glares.

They hate you.

"Sorry, sorry." Her smile faded. "Here, I—I got you some food."

She shrank the bags, using her fingernails to make a delicate drop onto the roof.

"All right, I'm going to grab coffee and figure some things out."

The younger man shook his head. "Look, if we're going to be hostages—"

"You're not hostages," she said. "I didn't know you were in there."

"We're going to need to know your name."

"No. No names."

"Yes. Yes, names. We'd feel better with names. I'm Troy and this is Kevin. And you are...?"

"Uhh." Her eyes darted around. The Coleman sink. Goji hand soap. A FreshPine paper towel dispenser. "Uhh, koh, uh, go-jah, pine?"

"Are you trying to make up a name based on stuff you see around you?" Troy asked.

"No," she answered in defiance, then conceded. "Yeah."

Someone outside tested the door handle. *Knock, knock.*

"Be right out," Eve answered. She turned to Kevin and Troy, quieter. "We've got to go."

Troy folded his arms. "Not until you tell us your name."

Impatient knocks. Time to leave.

"It's not up for negotiation," she whispered. "We need to go."

"Just make up a damn name," said Kevin.

"I tried that."

"No," said Troy. "I want to know her real name."

"She doesn't want to tell you," said Kevin.

Pounding on the bathroom door. Any longer and they'd get the manager.

"You're leaving in the next ten seconds whether you like it or not." Eve's loud whisper rasped. "Either you're coming with me or I'm flushing you."

Kevin snatched the paper bags. He and Troy dipped into the truck.

Thank god. She blew a long puff.

Eve nestled the vehicle back into her purse. She checked her reflection and tuned the dial. The blast tingled inside out as she rose to six feet, the upper limit of what she estimated could pass for normal. Any larger and her head and facial features might appear unnatural. She smirked, steadying her breath, invigorated by the sensory amplification. Maybe she didn't need to leave the country. Maybe she could hide in plain sight. A bigger, better version of herself. She stuck the *modifikator* into her jacket and lifted the shoulder bag.

No sooner did she unlock the door than an irate woman pushed past her.

"Stuff goes right through you, doesn't it?" said Eve, regretting it instantly.

* * *

To Eve, downtown was a sprawling outdoor mall. Lots of people. Lots of activity. Road noise, chatter, random car honks and blaring music. All of it brighter, louder, more real to her than ever before. Head on a swivel, she carried herself with the stilted pace of a harried robot, clutching her bag, certain everyone was watching her. She slowed, fearing for Troy and Kevin's safety, and hoping she hadn't scrambled their brains.

Deep breath.

"Remember," she whispered to herself, "nobody sees you. They see some tall blonde lady."

She ducked into an upscale coffee shop on the corner and approached the counter, the barista greeting her with a smile. She ordered a coffee, paid cash, no hassle.

"Love those boots, by the way," said the barista.

"Thanks."

The guy walking in liked what he saw as well, and smiled.

They bought it. They all did. This was her now. A new tingle. Emerald and royal purple.

She exited the coffee shop, pausing to secure the ill-fitting lid on her cup. A small radio-controlled car stopped at her feet. Her eyes slid over to the street vendor selling the red, yellow, and blue toys at a kiosk. One of the men sat in a director's chair on his phone. The other stood, talking to a customer.

She checked the car below. The colors were off. Close enough to be mistaken for one of theirs. And then there was the little dark bead on the windshield.

A camera lens.

The car zipped away from her and toward a couple of guys in khakis and plaid shirts. Too engrossed in conversation, they didn't notice the toy parking under their chairs. Luke had warned her about using public Wi-Fi. Hackers could setup malicious hotspots or break into networks and eavesdrop on data, stealing credit card numbers and banking information.

Maybe she could still get start-up money.

Eve snapped the lid on, acting as though she was on her way. She circled the patio, slinking behind a column, and dropped into a seat in the back corner.

* * *

Back at Pierce Technologies, a broad-shouldered agent with a square-jaw and crew-cut interrupted Simon and McCrae.

"Dr. Pierce, we're going to need your phone and laptop."

Simon blanched, then recovered. "Why not just cut off my hands and remove my tongue?"

"That something we can do, Hargrove?" asked McCrae.

Simon flashed a smile. "I have a meeting with the investors in a few minutes. Isn't there an exception?"

"We don't keep them," said Hargrove. "We just image the devices."

"See, but...my presentation's on there. Can't I just give you my phone for now?"

"That's fine."

"Not a word of this" —McCrae pointed a threatening finger at Simon— "or I will have you arrested for interfering in a federal investigation."

"Of course."

Simon handed over his phone, closing the door behind them.

He lifted the laptop lid. The videoconference software was still open, his meeting with Chang logged in its code. Deleting it was more incriminating than letting it stand. The connection history was just that —history. Known only to those who lived it and up for interpretation. After all, two plus two equaled five if you looked at it right.

He signed in, the shareholders already waiting.

Simon smiled. "Good morning, everyone."

Nods and smiles from the nine people in the gallery.

"Well, I don't know about you, but my schedule filled up quickly today," said Simon. "So I thought we'd jump right in."

More nods.

Simon double-clicked. The screen was consumed by the yellow-and-green Pierce Technologies logo, fading into the stars and panning across the asteroid belt.

He pitched. "The future of Pierce Technologies is the future of mankind. And mankind's future is out there—space. Mining asteroids."

A pan to Earth.

"Let's face it, this planet is dying."

Dead fish washing up on shore.

"Our resources are running out."

Wind blowing across endless desert.

"And the sooner people realize that, the better off we'll all be. But the problem is getting off this godforsaken rock."

Clips of twentieth century rockets launching.

"Petroleum-based propulsion systems are inefficient for both escape velocity and space travel. So Pierce Technologies isn't just going to provide mining equipment, we're going to pioneer the development of fusion plasma engin—"

"Whoa, whoa, whoa," a bald man spoke up. "Wait."

"Yeah, hang on," said a platinum-haired woman.

"Oh—is the connection bad?" Simon asked.

"Could you close this for a second?" the man asked.

The presentation closed, revealing the gallery of faces again.

The bald man leaned in. "You can't do that."

Simon grinned with defiant optimism. "Yes. I can."

"No—you're known for building laser cannons and shopping them as weapons for the military. And let's not forget our disastrous foray into the surgical market. You are not the person to put a fusion reactor on a launchpad and there's no country in the world that's going to let you."

"Not yet." Simon waved a finger. "But I can, and they wi—"

“That’s the other thing,” said the bald man. “If you do, I’m out.”

“Yeah,” said the platinum-haired woman. “That’s not what I thought this was going to be. I can’t support this.”

The gallery came to life with shaking heads and folded arms.

Who were these people again?

His smile didn’t waver. “I’m talking about innovation. The future.”

“You are innovating,” said the platinum-haired woman. “That’s what the public-private partnerships are for. Less risk, and it benefits both parties.”

The bald man nodded. “And if someone like Marty Glick gets one of these space projects up and running, we can jump on board with that.”

“Oh, I love Marty Glick.”

“He’s the best.”

“He’s delightful,” said Simon. “And we could sell him plasma engines.”

“We have no foothold in that sector,” said the bald man. “It’s a waste of money.”

Shareholders. No vision beyond quarterly earnings.

“And a dangerous liability,” said the platinum-haired woman. “I’ve heard enough. I mean, unless there was more to this—we did cut you off there.”

Kincaid’s research proposal. That always shut them up.

Simon didn’t blink. “Just a photonic microprocessor for a quantum computer.”

The gallery perked up, intrigued.

“See, now that,” said the bald man. “That’s in our space.”

The platinum-haired woman nodded. “That I can get behind.”

* * *

Simon strolled out of his office to find McCrae gone. He handed off his laptop and smartwatch to the box-headed agent without a second thought.

“Should have these back to you before the end of the day,” said Hargrove.

“Sure, whatever you need.”

Hargrove handed Simon his phone. “Don’t know if Agent Callahan mentioned it, but while the investigation is ongoing, we’re advising you and anyone in your household suspend all social media activity. You know, prevent any possible leaks.”

“Well.” Simon smiled. “The people in my household might need some convincing. Is that something I can get in writing?”

“Not to worry—an agent’s already been sent to speak with them so there's no confusion."

His phone vibrated. A text from Valentina.

`I'm sorry. It's over. I can't. I just can't.`

Simon's smile stayed steadfast. "Would you excuse me?"

He strode out of the executive offices, past the elevators and toward the restrooms. He banked right to a narrow side hall. It was a floor planning oversight, but it created a little-known private lobby of sorts, out of the way of foot traffic. Someone was already using the nook. Simon hovered at the corner, eavesdropping.

"They were asking about Freitas," Deepa whispered. "I don't know. I don't know that either. That's supposed to be your job. Look—I can't talk right now. They're all over the place."

Simon rounded the corner, pretending he was immersed in his phone.

Deepa bumped into him.

"Sorry," she said.

He smirked. "Can't let anybody know about our secret."

"What?"

"Our secret spot." He pointed with his thumb.

"Right." She nodded. "Sorry—I have to get back."

She hurried off. Simon dialed Valentina. The pickup was immediate.

"Didn't you get my text?" Her words were rapid-fire, lit by an Italian accent.

"I did, but...is this about the role-playing thing?"

"No—well, a little."

"Look, I think once you just find a character you enjo—"

"It's not about that, okay? I cannot survive without the social media. Is my whole business, it's my life."

"But it's not forever. Call it a detox. We do it togeth—"

"No, no, n—"

"Then we come back—"

"I can't, okay?"

"Talk about mental health and all that crap. You get a bump in follow—"

"I can't. If I'm not posting, I am poof—I disappear. Okay? I'm sorry. It's over."

In times like these, he recalled his parents' divorce. His father's numerous girlfriends. His mother's remarriage. Relationships were a revolving door, nothing more.

"Simon?"

"Well." A toothy smile rose. "Best of luck to you, then."

He hung up, grinning from ear to ear.

* * *

Dempsey shut the car door and entered a gray area. Nails in the wall. Sanitized kitchen. The closet picked through. Strange vandalism. Enough reason to believe Kincaid had skipped town and wanted to make it look like someone had ransacked the place. A warrant could take hours. By then, she might be out of the country.

Kincaid's phone was an older model, lacking security features. He held down the buttons to power it down, then opted to restart it in safe mode. Not full access, but enough. Scant call history. Dormant social media apps. Texting had dropped off, too. The most recent from someone named Georgie. Dempsey traced the number to an address in an affluent suburb several miles south.

A half hour later, he pulled into the driveway of a huge contemporary house. A woman with thick brown hair in pigtails and a baby on her shoulder peered out the large front window.

"Thank you, Dr. Parker-Preiss," he said. "I really appreciate it. I just need a couple minutes of your time."

"Well, good," she said with a faint Appalachian accent. "That's all I got."

He followed her in. Children's toys littered the floor, scattered under the coffee table and across a sectional sofa. She lowered the child into a pink pack'n'play nearby a standing desk and laptop.

"So if I can ask." Georgie folded her arms. "What did she do?"

"Like I said on the phone, I can't get into details—we just need to know where she might be."

"She really doesn't get out much."

"Okay, well, if she wanted to get away for a while, where do you think she might go?"

Her eyes popped open. "Oh, crap—yesterday was her birthday, I didn't even think about it."

"Well, you're busy." He gestured to the workstation and toys. "Anybody she would've gone out with?"

The corner of her mouth turned down, guilty. "We all kind of stopped hanging out with her. I think I'm the only one who still talked to her. I mean, I've known her for years, but...she just became a miserable person."

Maybe he'd misread the apartment. Maybe what he'd seen was Kincaid's depressive slump.

"When did that happen?"

"It's been years."

"And what's her state of mind now?"

She blinked. "Her state of mind?"

"Yeah." He shrugged. "Like, what do you think she might do if she was upset? Or maybe under a lot of stress?"

"Oh god, did she leave a note?"

"What makes—"

"Is that why you're here? Is she dead?"

"No. No, not that we're aware of. I'm just—where do you think she might have gone?"

"Well, now I'm thinking she might have driven off the Crest Highway."

"Why would she do that?"

"Because she can't let anything go."

5

(red)

Eve twirled the empty coffee cup with her middle finger. For a half hour, the radio-controlled car stopped under the chairs of unsuspecting customers. After parking for several minutes, it rolled away, aimless until it found a new target.

Suspects thinned out, leaving two. A man in a blue dress shirt and gray slacks packed up and stood. That left a pasty guy wearing a varsity jacket and expensive high-top sneakers. The toy car rolled under his chair. He picked it up and shoved it into a backpack decorated with patches and emblems of superheroes, video games, and anime characters. He stowed the rest of his gear and slung the backpack over his shoulder.

"Hang on, guys," Eve whispered to her purse. "Might get rough again."

She followed him down the block. Her mind went to *The French Connection*. He crossed the street, and she stayed on the opposite side, parallel with him, letting the distance between them grow. She jaywalked, slowing to a wander and glancing at signs as though she was lost. The geek checked over his shoulder and rounded a corner, his pace quickening. Another check behind and he bolted.

Eve sprinted, her longer stride closing the distance. He could have a gun, or a knife. But he didn't seem like the confrontational type.

He ducked into an alley.

With a touch more effort, she was upon him. Her hand clamped onto his shoulder. She spun him around—his eyes aghast, mouth agape.

"What were you doing with that car?"

"Yo, I don't know what you're talk—"

"Getting credit card numbers? Hacking people's bank accounts?"

"I wasn't doing noth—"

She released his shoulder. "Just tell me."

"I don't know what you're talking about."

"Look, I won't tell anyone, I just need some money."

"What are you, a drug addict?"

"No, I—You think I'm a drug addict?"

"You just chased me like six blocks."

She tilted her head. He had a point.

"So, you're not a cop?"

"No, it—"

"Help! This lady's crazy! Help!"

"It's not what you think," she rasped. "Just hear me out—"

"Help! I need help!"

"Shh! Stop." She dug into her jacket. "Shut up."

You suck at New Year's resolutions, too.

"Yo, somebody—"

The bright flash quieted the geek. He looked puzzled. Maybe wondering why the zap from the taser hadn't hurt. Then, panic set in. He craned his neck higher and higher. He dashed away.

A futile effort.

Eve knelt, reaching a cupped hand. He stumbled onto her fingers. She scooped him up, raising him to her face.

"Keys, now."

He dug into his pocket.

She floated him toward a plastic soda cap. "In there."

He leaned to the edge without taking his eyes off her.

The *modifikator* had no effect on the bottle cap as she returned the keys to normal.

"Where do you live?"

* * *

McCrae jumped out of a Humvee, barreling past the black sedans surrounding Talbot's house and across the lawn.

An agent put up a hand, stepping in front of him. "Sir, you—"

"The hell I can't." McCrae snarled.

"General." Callahan's brisk glide swept McCrae along, away from the agents and toward a van parked on the curb.

"Nice little disappearing act you pulled."

"We go where the investigation takes us."

His voice lowered. "Just got a call from Colonel Saeng on base. They found Lieutenant Reynolds in his quarters. Looks like he took a cyanide pill."

"Let me guess—he was a security officer with top secret clearance."

"He was."

She leaned in. "We recovered a Russian codex from Talbot's basement."

His face crinkled, fury settling into grim concern. "How's that possible? The Bureau ran a full background."

"Talbot's a British citizen, never popped up on their radar. There's no telling how long he's been working for them."

"Goddammit," McCrae grumbled.

She dug into her jacket, taking out a small plastic evidence bag storing a little glass vial.

He squinted at its contents. A thin, pale sliver with a frayed node at the end, stained with reddish-brown patches.

"What is that?"

"We think it's a woman's forearm. Possibly Irina Talbot's."

The ridges of his brow collided and the tiny limb came into focus, leaving him slack-jawed.

"You didn't know it could do this?"

What he did know chilled him to his core. The fearsome crack. Intense bolts of power ripping apart everything in their path. Steel and cement fused together. He considered the fragment coming into contact with an electric charge outside of the lab environment. Now he questioned how much Talbot had hindered their progress. And what his real intent was.

He tore his gaze from the vial. "We knew it was reactive to energy —"

"So this isn't part of the project?"

"No, ma'am."

She tucked the bag into her jacket. "That the truth or just what you're telling me?"

Anger filtered down his face, evaporating with a heavy sigh. "We told you the truth. We don't know the full extent of what it can do. And I guarantee neither does whoever has it."

* * *

Eve hustled up the stairs of a brick building to the third floor and unlocked apartment 309 (blue-green, black, brown). The studio made her old place seem massive. Every possible video game console and its corresponding accessories covered the coffee table, couch, and cabinet under a wall-mounted flat-screen while action figures, toys, spaceships and plastic swords populated the available space. Posters of superhero movies and anime characters plastered the walls.

"Oh god," she muttered.

She tossed the keys onto a fold-out breakfast table mounted to the kitchenette and found a cooking pot for the armored car. Troy and Kevin peered out as she pulled a colander from the cupboard.

"Sorry, guys, it's for your own good." She flipped the colander upside-down over the pot.

Eve took another pass of the place. Renovated building. Gentrified block. Those gaming consoles and their gear added up. She leaned over to examine a couple pieces of opened mail on the desk. His name was Eugene Hughes—and he'd paid off his student loans.

All modern capers needed a tech whiz. Jim Belushi in *Thief*. River Phoenix in *Sneakers*. Pretty much everyone in *Hackers*. But the movies never detailed what these people were doing. She'd read about programming language in college, but hadn't programmed anything herself. Maybe with a little persuasion, Eugene would get on board.

"You're Wanda—just play the part," she whispered. "Play the part."

She returned to the kitchenette, reaching into her purse and unzipped the inner pocket of her shoulder bag where he rested among her tampon supply.

She prompted him to climb onto her fingers, and then lowered him onto the table.

He leaped away, clutching his phone and backpack. "Please don't kill me."

"Killing you doesn't help me." She sat. "If you would have just listened—"

"I-I—I told you I don't have any money."

"Yeah, because you're spending it on toys. Yet somehow you managed to pay off your student loans in record time."

He frowned. "All right, it—it's a fake hotspot. I get banking information, passwords, credit cards...sell them on the dark web. But I didn't get anything from you—you didn't have a phone."

"Shit." She gasped. "My phone. It's—suitcase? Right? Yeah. I think. Yeah."

Nice method acting there. Really staying in character.

She shushed herself, scowling.

He studied her with apprehension.

"All right." She sighed, scratching her forehead. "You have any cash?"

"No, it's a digital wallet, and you're right, I spend most of it as soon as I get it. But you could probably rob a bank with that thing."

"Yeah, already tried something like that—I was really hoping for something with more anonymity."

"Well, what do you know about cryptocurrency?"

"That it's totally traceable once you spend it."

"Actually, there's ways around that. What about ransomware?"

Her jaw tightened. "I don't have time, so unless you know where I can get my hands on someone's computer—"

"My boss," he blurted out. "He makes bank and stashes half of it in crypto. He's always talking about how Neptonium's going to take off one day."

Her eyes lit up at the prospect of liberating herself from this trail of disasters. After swiping his boss's crypto, Eugene would help her navigate the dark web and buy fake identification. Her captives would never know her new disguise. A quick wipe down of the truck to clean off her fingerprints, and she'd return them to normal in the desert with no way to trace anything back to her.

She'd be free. Free to experiment with the fragment, validate her theories, and shove it in her old college professors' faces. She'd accept an honorary doctorate. She'd credit the hapless Russian spy and reveal her harrowing tale. The audience's stunned silence would erupt with momentous applause. Any and all charges dropped against her. She'd be hailed a national hero, a savior of human civilization worldwide, and forever as an icon of science.

Eve snapped back to the present. Eugene was staring up at her, quizzical.

She wasn't sure how long she'd zoned out. "You ever been to his place?"

* * *

Dempsey followed up with the forest rangers. No crash reports. They issued a bulletin for available personnel to scour the winding sixty-six miles of highway. An hour later, he walked into the FBI building, headed for Callahan's office. He'd made a bold move, but once she heard his reasoning, she'd agree it was the right one.

She crossed paths with him, carrying a cardboard box.

"Reid," she said. "What's the matter, you don't call anymore?"

"Got Kincaid's phone."

Her eyebrows rose.

"Looked like she fled, so...I improvised."

Tension pooled in her lips. Expected.

"Interviewed a friend of hers who's known her for years. She thinks Kincaid committed suicide."

Her face didn't change. But he hadn't gotten to the good part yet.

"So, Kincaid's college boyfriend died from a car accident. Completely derailed her. She never finished her doctorate—"

"Stop."

Uh-oh.

He blinked, meeting her gaze.

Her eyes melted bone. "You are not the Lone Ranger. Don't ever do that again."

"But you should've seen her place—"

"I would have if you'd taken pictures and sent them to me. Then I could have gotten a warrant to authorize cracking a civilian phone."

His mouth hung open, lips searching for words.

"We follow the rules because if we don't, people won't trust us. Without rules, anyone could do whatever they want. And that sounds good, until you realize what it really means."

"Understood."

"There was urgency to find a suspect; you made a decision. But you should have gone through me."

"Okay, I didn't mean—it won't happen again."

"It won't." She turned aside, prompting him to follow.

Two-week suspension, at least. Or she'd have him re-assigned. Getting kicked off a case like this would send his career trajectory straight for a cubicle in Des Moines.

He rushed alongside her. "But I do think it's her."

"And I think you're going to re-evaluate that. What did she drive?"

"Two thousand-two Corolla. Silver. Why?"

Callahan stopped at the doorway to a conference room, checking the box. "Hey, Mel—you got a silver '02 Corolla there?"

Masuda and Guzman sat at the conference table, dozens of miniature vehicles divided among them, reviewing the details of each one in evidence binders.

"No, but check this out." Masuda held up a little red car. "A 1962 Alfa Romero Sprint. They only made like seven hundred of these."

Guzman perked up. "Ooh—I'll trade you for a '57 Cadillac DeVille."

"No way."

"All right, all right." He reviewed his stockpile. "The DeVille and, uh...a '92 Mustang."

"What am I going to do with that?"

"Callahan. Masuda's hogging all the luxury cars."

"Cut it out," said Callahan. "Feel like I'm running a goddamn daycare."

"What is all this?" Dempsey asked.

"Everything we recovered from Talbot's basement." Callahan

shoved the box into his hands. "Need to verify the plates and follow up with the owners."

"Owners?"

"Wait until you hear what we found in the cat room," said Masuda.

Callahan sighed. "Sixteen years in federal law enforcement and now I'm chasing mad scientists."

"Evil, Soviet mad scientists," Masuda corrected.

"Thanks, Mel," said Callahan. "I'll try to put that into an official government document so it doesn't sound insane. You two can fill him in on the rest."

She took a half step and turned to Dempsey. "Oh—and let's put out a missing person's for Kincaid."

It gave him hope. She'd considered some part of what he'd said reasonable.

Callahan strode off down the hall.

Dempsey scanned the box's contents, disappointed. "Aw, nothing but pickup trucks and mini-vans."

Guzman and Masuda shielded their collections from his envy.

6

(royal blue)

Eve enlarged her suitcase, revisiting her black clothing. She riffled through a box of Eugene's cosplay items, swiping a balaclava and black gloves. She grabbed a shoulder sling bag hanging on a hook and emptied out the headphones and cables.

Great heists always assembled a team. The brains. The muscle. Getaway driver. An acrobat. She didn't know anybody like that. And she couldn't trust anyone. She'd have to do it all.

But you suck at everything.

Besides, heists were notorious for double and triple crosses. Bad enough the whole thing hinged on Eugene. Doubt fluttered inside. Periwinkle and coral.

"This is going to work," she whispered. "It's going to work."

At 10:00 p.m., she drove Eugene's red hatchback across town. She turned up the satellite radio report of an extreme terror threat. The FBI had grounded all flights statewide and closed the border. Though they didn't say it on the news, by now the government knew Talbot was missing and who he worked for.

Mexico was no longer an option.

Maybe she could hide at Eugene's for a couple days.

She rolled into a revamped neighborhood full of polished store fronts and curated graffiti murals. Cameras on every corner. Probably on every building. The street was quiet. And dark.

On Tuesdays, Zach Milner hosted a gaming tournament at his

penthouse catered by a local taco truck. Savory wisps of carnitas haunted the block, prompting a whimper from her stomach. She snuck around the back of an adjacent apartment building, pulling on the gloves and balaclava. Eve crept along the wall, then tilted around the corner to scope out the security cameras.

She hovered in the blind spot and slid the *modifikator* from the sling bag. A flash, and she rose few more inches. With greater reach and better vision, she tuned the dial and bent around the corner, striking the camera overhead. It shrank, snapping off the wall. Another blast, another camera broke from its support, this time from Milner's building.

According to Eugene, Milner left the veranda door unlocked for the smokers. Most everyone cleared out by eleven thirty, leaving Eve a narrow window to slip inside.

"All right, get in, get out." She pocketed the *modifikator*, pulverizing the miniaturized cameras on her way to the fire escape.

Eve leaped into the air, grasping the lowest rung with ease, expecting the ladder to drop the rest of the way, but it remained locked in place. And so did she.

She strained to lift herself, not taking into consideration how much more mass she was carrying despite her lean frame. The damn linguine. She hung, her shoulders searing.

She rasped, reaching overhead. "Oh god, oh god."

The triumph of her hand clenching the next rung dissolved with each subsequent reach, a ferocious battle with gravity, until she relieved some of the burden by securing her left foot on the lowest bar. With a clumsy swing of her right leg, she anchored her heel on the edge and made an awkward clamber onto the platform.

"All right." She gulped for oxygen under the window of the second floor apartment. "After lab...home gym."

She slinked up the wrought iron staircase. The windows were closed, but the occasional curtain was open. She dashed by, keeping her footfalls light as she raced up the next stair.

She reached the rooftop.

Voices above grabbed her attention. She dropped onto her haunches.

Eighteen inches of thick stone parapet separated her from financing her new life. Her jaw clenched. Rust and charcoal. Terror tingled from her sternum to her fingers and toes. Her breath shortened, and she stiffened. Rust and charcoal wilted into dingy purple and gray, dragging her down with them.

"What am I doing?" she whispered.

This was a terrible idea.

"I'm not a thief. Well—I guess I am..."

Just not a good one.

"I'm going to get caught. I—I can't do this."

A whiff of tobacco. Then, a guy's voice.

"Yeah, but, sometimes you just want a real cigarette, you know?"

"Yeah, that's why I bought the hand roller," another guy answered.

They couldn't be more than a couple feet away. Their voices were clear and crisp. She peered over the parapet.

Three of them, all dressed the same. Skinny jeans, thick-rimmed glasses, and bomber jackets. Ten yards away. Her amplified senses made it seem like they were closer. She smiled. She'd forgotten the new, improved version of herself. Old Eve couldn't have pulled this off, but New Eve was an unstoppable dynamo.

The door closed behind them. No beep, no chime. The alarm was in silent mode. Eugene had told the truth. Their heads filtered past the window, disappearing into another room. She glanced at the camera mounted above the entrance, then to the windows on the left.

That darkened hall led to Zach's office.

In and out before eleven thirty.

Eve skimmed over the ledge, onto the roof, and pulled out the *modifikator*. She crouched, sprinting for the door, tripping over her own two feet and landing flat on her face.

Super graceful, you unstoppable dynamo.

Twelve guys huddled around the wall-sized screen inside didn't react. They were too engrossed in the action of DeathRage 3. The last two players were locked in an intense battle for supremacy.

Eve remained flat, balancing on her elbows and knees in a clunky commando crawl across the veranda. She rose, backing against the wall alongside the window and peered in as they cheered. The rest of them wore outfits similar to the guys she'd seen earlier.

"It's like a cult." She adjusted the dials.

She pointed the *modifikator* at the camera above, shrinking it a touch smaller. The power light dimmed off. She twisted the door handle. Unlocked.

Eve slid inside, targeting a camera at the end of the hall.

"Ohhhhh!" The guys hollered, startling her into the air. The thump of her landing was masked by the boom and bass of the game's detonations.

Further into the hall, she shrank the next camera and clutched the first doorknob. Locked. She lowered the dial and aimed. But instead of just the knob, the entire door shrank off the hinges, screws and bolts popping and flying as a barrage of bullets and explosions erupted.

"Ohhhhhh!"

Dim light from the hall revealed an office decorated by pictures of nude women with human faces and robotic bodies, aside from their most feminine attributes. She shuddered in disgust, and pointed the *modifikator* at a camera in the corner, rendering it inoperable. Fanfare from the living room. The battle ended. Eve swiped the laptop, finding its bag under the desk. She opened the desk cabinet—a small safe inside. Words floated from the living room.

"All right, guys, got an early day tomorrow."

"All right, bro."

No extended chilling or chatting. Out of time, she blasted the safe.

"Make that money, buddy."

"Thanks, Zach."

The front door's lock clacked. She swung around. Beeps as the alarm set. She hung in the dark about to make a break for the veranda door, when a shadow hit the wall. It grew more concentrated as it neared. She tilted back, into the dark.

He twisted the bolt on the veranda door and turned around. Then paused. The office door was open. Or missing.

"You dicks. I don't know how you did this, but—" He flipped the light on, startled by the towering figure.

She hit the dial button.

* * *

Eve dropped from the fire escape onto the asphalt.

With a relieved huff, she pulled off the mask. "Didn't go exactly to plan, but at least I—"

She locked eyes with a young woman with coiled hair in lavender sweatpants holding a trash bag on her way to the dumpster.

Idiot! She can place you at the scene!

They stared at each other, motionless. Eve reached slow into the sling bag. The young woman ditched the trash, turning to run.

But Eve was a quick draw now. A burst of light, and the young woman disappeared.

* * *

Eve returned to Eugene's wearing the blonde wig and back to six feet. She lifted the colander off the pot. With two fingers and a light touch, she scooped up the young woman.

"I cannot tell you how sorry I am about this." Eve lowered her into the pot.

"Oh my god." The woman's eyes goggled. "Please don't eat me!"

"It's not like that," said Eve. "It is *so* not like that. You were just at the wrong place at the wrong time."

The woman shivered, glancing at the three guys and the bank truck. "What is this?"

"Tell her you name," Troy said.

"Janelle," she said. "My name's Janelle Sinclair."

"Dammit, Troy," Eve griped.

"What's that do?" Janelle asked.

Kevin sighed. "He thinks it makes her have to care about us. You know, like when you name a pet or something."

"Is that what this is?" Janelle's face sank. "I am nobody's pet!"

"No, no—you're not," Eve said. "This is all temporary."

"I know you keep saying that like it's supposed to be comforting," said Troy. "But it's not."

They were frightened and powerless. Pale mauve. She knew it all too well.

Eve huffed. "I'm going to fix this, okay? I just need to figure some things out. In the meantime, you need to hand over the guns."

Kevin folded his arms. "No way."

"You can have them back when I let you go."

"Look, we're trained and cert—"

"And I'm trying to keep everyone alive, all right? It's bad enough I'm leaving Janelle alone with all of you."

"What's that supposed to mean?" Kevin asked, offended.

"It means I have a very strict believe-the-accuser policy." Eve nodded to Janelle. "I've got your back, girl."

Janelle gazed up with a disbelieving grimace.

She hates you.

Eve frowned. "Just hand them over."

Troy and Kevin tossed their tiny firearms onto Eve's waiting fingers. She dropped them into a plastic lid and tilted her hand back into the pot.

"Eugene, let's go."

He planted a cautious foot onto a finger, testing it before climbing aboard. She lifted her hand. He fell onto his rear and scuttled to the middle of her palm.

With her free hand, she flipped the colander back over the pot.

Eugene clambered onto the table.

Eve reached into the sling bag for Zach. She unzipped the main pocket and dug around for the laptop. Next came the *modifikator*. She restored the laptop and opened it, pushing hair out of her face, the bobby pins tugging her scalp. Frustrated, she pried them out, tossing the wig aside.

"All right." She plopped into the chair with a heavy sigh. "What's the password?"

"No," Zach answered.

"What?" she asked, drained and impatient.

"The drive's encrypted," he said. "Without it, you can't get in."

She glared through heavy eyes, tongue pressed against the roof of her mouth.

"Dude," Eugene muttered. "What are you doing?"

Zach ignored him. "And if you kill me, you'll never get in."

"Eugene." She pressed her fingers into her temple. "Can you hack this thing?"

"No," he said. "The drive's locked out."

Zach folded his arms. "Are you ready to have a real conversation like adults where we talk about what we're looking for in this situation and negotiate a deal?"

She growled a sigh. "What do you want?"

"Oh—well, I'd like to go back to normal." Zach clasped his hands. "And, I'm also interested in that technology you have there."

Her eyes glazed over.

"So maybe I'd consider this as a down payment in our new partnership."

"Partnership?"

"Yeah. Fifty-fifty. All right, maybe more like sixty-forty since I'm putting up the investment." He reconsidered. "Seventy-thirty."

"Hey—I'm the one who found the damn thing."

"Wait—you didn't even invent it?"

"Well, no, but I figured out th—"

"So, you stole that, too?"

"Well, not exactly, I mean—it wasn't my fault."

"Oh, of course not." Zach smirked. "Never is. Classic underachiever. Just like my older brother. That loser's been working the same dead-end job for years and does nothing but complain about it. Same story for you, right? Crappy job, no friends, can't get a date to save your life?"

Wow, it's like he can see inside you.

Eugene's eyes begged him. "Dude."

Zach shook his head with a dismissive glance. "Let me guess—now you're on the run, and whoever's chasing you—"

"You don't understand," said Eve. Pale mauve clouded her vision.

"Don't want to know." He put up a hand. "They're going to catch up with you eventually. Point is you're making desperate moves because you've got this little voice inside saying you're in over your head—and you should listen to that voice."

He's a dick, but he's right. I keep you safe.

She slumped, eyes lowering, spotting the safe in the bag. Her lower jaw slid right and left. She plucked out the safe.

"What you need is legal counsel," said Zach. "And I can help with that. All we need is to negotiate a deal—at my normal size—in an attorney's office so we can talk about how we're going to market this thing."

She enlarged the safe halfway.

Zach gestured to it. "I see limitless applications in commercial logistics. We can cut freight costs to almost zero."

Eve stood, tossing the safe onto the floor.

"Where—where are you going?" he asked as she walked away. "Where is she going?"

Eugene shrugged. She returned from the closet with a hammer.

Zach backed away. "What are you doing?"

"Yeah." Eugene trembled. "What are you doing?"

She reared the hammer back. The guys cowered. She struck the safe with a pop, splitting it apart, and let the hammer drop.

Zach and Eugene stood, apparently thankful they hadn't been pummeled.

Eve sifted through the contents, selecting a notebook with a dark blue cover and discovering four hardwallets. She enlarged the loot and sat, resting the *modifikator* beside the laptop. She thumbed through the notebook and smirked, raising an eyebrow. She typed in the password.

The laptop booted up. "I'm not looking for a partnership."

She double-clicked a VPN icon, selecting the VPN-over-TOR option.

"All right, Eugene, I need your Wi-Fi password and some help getting a new identity, or several new identities."

"Dude, don't help her," said Zach.

Eve shook her head. "You don't really have a say in—"

"She needs you."

Eugene wasn't so sure. His focus shifted to Eve.

"Eugene."

"Don't do it, man."

"*Eugene.*"

"Don't do it."

"I just saw a dozen guys that looked like the both of you. I will totally find someone else."

Zach shook his head. "She's bluffing. Women don't have the same killer instinct as men."

Eve glowered.

"Don't do anything until you can get something from her."

"All right, that's it. You have till the count of—"

"Shut up." Zach turned his back on her. "Don't listen to this stupid bitch. You've got to show her—"

A flash from the *modifikator*.

Eugene blinked, frantic as he checked the world around him. He gazed down.

Zach was an eighth of an inch tall, his shouts inaudible. Eve dropped her elbow onto the tabletop with a thunderous pound and leaned forward.

"Password is *G* as in *golf*," said Eugene. "The number six, hash-tag, *E* as in *echo*..."

His panic faded as she questioned him. Software was his domain, yet Zach's harried attempts at getting their attention were a reminder not to screw with her.

Eugene seemed to warm to his role as guide through the dark web. "You can't just jump right in. I mean, it's easy to get what you need, but that's the problem."

They scoured marketplaces, scrutinizing sellers and researching their alleged sources, finding several promising ID's, most of which they determined were scams or clever traps by the FBI.

Hours later, three viable options remained, each from a different seller. She had no choice but to spend the extra five grand a-piece to overnight them to Eugene's.

Once they finished, she restored Zach to two and half inches and carried them to the pot.

"Hey!" Kevin said as she removed the colander. "It's freezing in here!"

"Yeah." Eve yawned. "That's because you guys are really small. I mean, honestly, I have no idea how you're breathing or digesting food right now."

"What?!" asked Janelle.

"Well, all of this is physically impossible," she answered. "I think it might have something to do with this field, but I've already said too much and it's late, so let me shrink you some blankets."

"You can't leave us in here," said Troy.

"Yeah," said Janelle. "You said you were going to fix this!"

They all hate you.

Eve held her palms up. "All right. I will—just get in the truck and turn the heater on until I figure this out."

She flipped the colander over the pot, biting her lip. She had no idea how to fix it.

Oh my god—now you're the weirdo keeping shrunken people in their basement!

"No." She shook her head, wishing it wasn't true. "No, I'm not."

Yes, you are.

But she couldn't let them go. Not yet. Troy and Kevin would run to the police. Eugene knew too much at this point and, considering his own crimes, would probably work out a plea deal. She'd broken into Zach's place and stolen his life savings. And she'd kidnapped Janelle because she was a corroborating witness.

The feds were monitoring airports and the border. Probably not just in California. And she had no idea if the Russians were tracking her. She needed more time.

Her captives—er, guests—traveling companions? They needed safety, protection, comfort. And maybe...tens of thousands of dollars each in hush money? If she could invest Zach's crypto, maybe she could earn enough to pay them off and pay him back. No harm, no foul.

But they couldn't stay in a cooking pot. They needed the comforts of home. Luxury. And fast.

* * *

Darien felt the silky skin of Cassidy's leg slide over his. Her fingers danced across the rich golden buff of his toned chest as it heaved. He pulled her close and she nestled into him, hovering in the wake of shared euphoria. He closed his eyes, absorbing the long wisp of her breath fluttering along his neck as she kissed it. The entire house vibrated, then shook with violence. She clutched him as he sat up, cradling her from whatever threat there might be.

The motion stopped.

"Just an earthquake," he said.

She nodded. "Guess so."

A heavy boom jarred the house. Another boom, picture frames hurtling off the walls.

"The hell was that?" she asked.

"Aftershocks?"

A tremendous rumble, and the foundation quivered. The house rocked and pitched, flinging from the bed at the mercy of unknown forces.

Eve hoisted the shovel load, scooping up the miniature house. A five-bedroom in a row of show homes outside of an incomplete development on the edge of the city. Several yards away, a severed water main sprayed into the night. She slid the chunk of earth holding the house into a sturdy cardboard box resting in the open hatchback.

* * *

An hour later, delirious with fatigue, Eve cleared away the appliances in the kitchenette's limited counter space. She enlarged the house to a suitable size for her captives—about as long as Eugene's microwave and almost too deep for the narrow counter.

Upon removing the colander, she found they'd taken her advice and retreated to the warm refuge of the armored car.

"Okay, everybody buckle up and hang on."

She placed it inside the cardboard box.

The vehicle doors opened, and everyone climbed out.

"All right," said Eve. "There's no running water, but I shrank a couple of porta-potties so that'll have to do for now."

"You stole a house?" Kevin asked, disapproving.

"I didn't steal it. Nobody owns it yet, therefore it's open game."

"The people who built it own it," said Troy.

"Are you going to nitpick, or are you going to live in the damn house?" Eve asked.

"It's a stolen house!"

She pulled a hand down around her neck. "You said you were cold. I'm giving you shelter—what more do you want from me?"

The front door opened. Two little people peered out.

"Oh, what the fuck!?" Eve threw up her hands, tearing her fingers through her hair.

"Oh my god," Cassidy yelped. "What is this? Where are we?!"

Eve glared. "What are you doing in there?"

The strapping young man with mussed dark hair stepped forward.

"We're real estate agents," said Darien. "And, I—I'm cheating on my wife."

"You have any referrals?" asked Eve. "I might be in the market for a new place."

7

(gold)

Early the next morning, Dempsey and Masuda headed to the A/V department and knocked on the door to bay three.

Callahan's head poked out. "Come on in."

She rolled back inside on a swivel chair. She'd conquered the playback station as her new workspace. It was littered with notepads and pens, empty water bottles and beef jerky wrappers. Three monitors displayed footage from eighteen different security cameras at Pierce Technologies.

"You been here all night?" Masuda asked.

"No, just since four." Callahan focused on Dempsey. "Kincaid's involved, but not how you think."

Callahan cued up the footage.

"Watch." She hit Play.

Dim and grainy video of Talbot seated on a bench, facing the building.

"He's been there for two hours, on his phone," said Callahan. "Or, pretending to be on his phone."

Talbot sprang from the bench, dashing off camera.

"Right there." Callahan pointed to camera eight. "He sees her from outside."

Her finger slid across the screen to camera five as Eve walked through the lobby.

"He runs to the transformer on the north side of the building, and..."

Black.

"So, she's our stain," said Masuda.

Callahan swiveled around. "Haven't been able to get DNA from the blood samples. But, they did find a hair matching Kincaid's in his living room."

"I'm telling you," said Dempsey. "She went back to that apartment."

"Someone went there," said Callahan. "We don't know the timeline or how she's connected."

"She's been trying to move into research for years," he said. "Maybe Talbot promised her something, or—"

"Or she's cat food."

"She wouldn't have known about the code book."

"Possibly," said Callahan. "We still don't know what happened to Freitas. And it turns out the Talbots had more than Lieutenant Reynolds helping them. Corporal Bower came forward. He said they'd convinced him Russia's more aligned with American family values, traditional marriage, stuff like that."

"Wow." Masuda's voice croaked.

"So they knew who to target," said Dempsey.

"Yeah." Callahan nodded. "By the time Bower realized what was going on, it was too late. Talbot told him they'd kill his whole family."

A knock at the door. Guzman entered, notepad in hand.

"Morning, everybody." He closed the door. "Liking the new office, Callahan."

"Thanks. What do you got?"

"Turns out Freitas is Macanese. Also goes by the name Heng Luo."

"That mean he's got two different passports?" asked Callahan.

"Flagged them both." Guzman nodded. "He spent time at this Chinese company, Baolei, which was investigated a few years ago, banned here and in Europe for reverse-engineering several products."

Callahan's brow crinkled. "Macao's not really nationalistic, though."

"Which is why I'm thinking they have something on him or he's indebted somehow."

"What's his activity?" asked Callahan.

"Email's dull, phone records are clean, probably had a burner. Frequented two restaurants in the area—both are now closed. Looks like they invested a lot into a serious IP theft operation." He tilted his chin to Masuda. "Could really use your expertise on that, Mel."

"I'll do it for a '91 Acura NSX."

He broke into a smile. "Done."

* * *

Eve cobbled together new identities using wigs and Eugene's cosplay collection, touching them up with photo-editing software. Bringing them to life in person was a little more challenging. She refined the sophisticated metropolitan persona in Diane Cernik with a dark chestnut wig, worn up, and rectangular eyeglasses. She stayed five foot ten, sticking with pencil skirts and heels, fitting attire for Diane's role as senior executive assistant to reclusive businessman Avery Devereux, another identity she'd forged in order to create a network of shell companies to launder Zach's Neptonium. Devereux's image had been fabricated using a random face-generator website, so Diane was his only connection to the real world.

After a couple nights in a shabby motel, Diane's astute professionalism lapsed as she gawked at the vaulted ceilings and panoramic windows of the penthouse showcased by the building's sales manager. It rivaled Sawyer's loft overlooking Times Square.

"The property is move-in ready. Twenty-four-seven concierge. Full kitchen. Balcony terrace. You have the only access to the roof. All the windows are smart glass which regulate temperature as well as your view."

"It's perfect." Eve gasped a breathless grin before regaining her composure. "Mr. Devereux will take it. And the floor below. He likes his privacy."

A day and half later, deliverymen were hauling in furniture and boxes while her efficient alter ego hunted more property on a headset.

"That's too much. You have anything smaller? Like three thousand square feet? Uh-huh. Okay. And what's the difference between that and the month to month? I see. Well, I have to go over a few things with Mr. Dev—You know what? Let me get the address."

Eve scribbled on the back of a receipt. "Definitely by the end of the week. Thanks."

She hung up, turning to the workers as they passed. "What's everybody want for lunch?"

* * *

Pleasant tones of harp music from a sound machine roused her the next morning. Eve rolled across the California king mattress. She outstretched her arm past an ornate box resting on the nightstand. Her fingertips touched the window pane. The frosted glass became clear, revealing the city skyline. She smiled and tapped it again. The glass turned opaque.

She traipsed through her palace in the sky in leggings and a tattered Nirvana T-shirt. Her fingers ran across the bamboo fiber sofas and sustainably sourced teak furniture to the mouth of the kitchen as the coffeemaker percolated to life. From there, she breezed onto the terrace, taking in a view of the city and the mountains beyond. Her smile widened, and she was overcome with joy as she planted her palms on the parapet. The *modifikator* had already changed her life for the better. Sort of.

Coffee in hand, she glided to the guest room.

The miniature house resided on a chunk of earth inside a large, clear plexiglass box on a sturdy table. An architect lamp over the box's lid warmed the roof. She'd left a wide green space behind the house with miniaturized grass and shrubs. A boulder sat alongside the garage and insulated pipes ran to the building from a water tower in the backyard.

Outside the box, a little standard electric motor plugged into the wall outlet spun the turbine of a miniaturized generator. The transmission line ran through a hole drilled into the box, buried in the earth.

She leaned toward the box with trepidation. "Good morning, everyone."

A tarp lay across the roof with the words *Thank You* painted on it.

She restrained a smile, biting her lip. They didn't hate her. Eve stepped away, pleased with her new life.

* * *

Inside the house, things were not so idyllic. Everyone gathered at the long table in the dining room.

"All right," said Kevin. "Since our captor's not playing with a full deck—"

Cassidy lurched forward. "That is sexist and offensive."

"Please," said Janelle. "That woman is out of her damn mind."

"Look, I know it sounds bad," said Troy. "But she told us she was running from the government and the Russians."

"Well, maybe it's true," said Cassidy. "I mean, she has a machine that shrinks things."

Zach scowled, arms folded. "She talks to herself constantly."

"Most geniuses do." Darien shrugged. "Einstein did. Freud did. Beethoven supposedly had whole conversations with himself."

"Or," said Cassidy, "she could be having a mental health crisis."

"And how are we supposed to talk her down?" asked Janelle. "Without making things worse?"

"You can't," said Eugene. "She's super paranoid about everything."

"Then maybe she's really protecting us," said Cassidy.

"But she's got millions of dollars now," said Kevin. "Why're we still here?"

Cassidy shrugged, tossing her honey-colored hair over her shoulder with annoyance.

"Well." Darien sighed. "She is keeping us alive."

Janelle scoffed. "For now."

"With my money," said Zach.

"All right, all right," said Troy. "Can we all agree we need to figure a way out of here?"

"Yeah, okay—*how*?" Zach glared at the ceiling before meeting eyes with Troy. "We're stuck in a box. Our phones are useless, and so far, the only one who gets any time out of here is Eugene. Are we really going to rely on Eugene?"

Eugene sat up. "Hey!"

"Well, hang on," said Janelle. "Maybe we should."

"Thank you," he said. "Wait—for what?"

"As our informant," she said. "So we can come up with an actual plan."

"No," said Eugene. "What if she figures out I'm spying on her? I don't want to end up in a petri dish or something."

"Well, you get on her good side so she doesn't suspect anything," said Janelle. "Tell us what you see. Try to get whatever you can out of her."

"No, no way." He shook his head. "I'm not doing it."

"Great idea, Janelle." Zach raised his hand. "All in favor of making Eugene our informant..."

Everyone but Eugene raised their hands.

* * *

The hum returned, louder, as Eve's gigantic face hovered above the city. She reached down with her thumb and forefinger to pluck a building from the cluster below, still too far from her grasp. The illusion broke, the hum halted.

She pulled her fingers away and backed from the ledge, trying to make sense of the noise and dramatic loss of depth perception. It was as if her whole reality had changed. She took a breath and headed back inside, distracting herself with an errand.

A visit to the potential warehouse for her lab provided Eve the opportunity to test-drive a more practical identity—the muscle. Or if things went to shit, another alter ego to throw off the authorities. Planning ahead was key. People in real life never had enough forethought.

She'd purchased an impeccable auburn wig to replace the one from her costume bin and added glasses with cardinal frames. At six feet, she felt more capable of handling herself as she walked the cracked asphalt on the industrial block. She dug into the pocket of a burgundy vegan leather jacket, glancing at the scribbled address, 2394 (yellow, blue green, brown, pink) 37th (blue green, gold).

She scanned the buildings, perking up at a nearby argument. A man and a woman.

"No!" The woman's voice.

A car door slammed.

Eve hurried around the corner.

A guy held a woman by the wrist. He had heavy stubble, and slicked-back hair. They stood alongside a red convertible, the woman clutching a guitar case in her other hand. She jerked away from him, her tousled hair chasing her movements. Her locks were accented with a stripe of lime green, another purple, another cyan, and beads threaded into yet another.

"Diego, stop!"

"Hey!" Eve blurted out.

They turned in her direction, the midday sun back-lighting the towering figure before them. Diego let go of the woman's wrist.

Eve neared them. "What's going on?"

"We're having a discussion," he answered.

"I wasn't asking you." She pivoted to the young woman who gazed up at her with a mix of relief and admiration, speechless.

"All right, I know what it looks like," he said. "But you don't understand—"

"He lied to me," said the woman.

"I did not lie to you. This is a legit studio." He presented the dilapidated concrete building behind him.

The young woman turned to Eve. "I gave him a five-hundred-dollar deposit and he expects another thirty-five hundred for this."

Eve glared at Diego as he sputtered. "It's just not—don't judge a book by its cover."

"All right." She sighed. "Give her the money back."

"Okay." Diego smiled. "We can all go in there, and you'll see—"

"Give it back." Eve stood straighter. "Now."

Oh yeah, real smart—what if he has a gun?

"Look, lady," he said, losing his patience. "It's a misunderstanding. You had no reason to butt in, so you can butt out."

He nudged his fingers into Eve's shoulder with a little shove.

Blazing crimson. She imitated the same move. "You butt out."

Her nudge sent him tumbling backward off the curb, off his feet, smacking his head against the bumper with a gong. She hadn't meant to shove him hard.

"Oh shit!" The young woman's jaw fell.

Eve gaped. "Okay—I did not mean for that to happen."

"No, yeah—it was an accident."

"Yeah, I mean, clearly—"

"And he pushed you first."

"Yeah."

Their eyes followed the contortion of his body to a splotch of blood on the bumper.

"Diego?" The woman ventured. "You all right?"

Eve shrugged, trying to convince herself. "I'm sure he's fine." She backed away, considering running and contemplating if she had to burn the identity.

The young woman leaned the guitar case against the car and knelt by his side. She pressed her fingers into his chest a couple times and then slapped his face.

"He's breathing." She dug into his jacket. She pulled out a check and tore it up, pocketing the pieces.

"You know," said Eve, "you could've stopped payment on the check."

"You can?"

"Yeah."

"Damn." She stood. "Thanks, by the way. I'm Quinn."

"Kira."

Dumbass.

"Look, I don't want to get you in trouble, but we can't just leave him like this."

Eve bit the side of her lip. "This his car? He have an alarm?"

"Yeah."

"Grab that."

Quinn hoisted her guitar. Eve stomped her boot heel into the driver's side door.

Bleating honks rang off the pavement.

The two women ran, ducking around the corner and past another block of warehouses. Quinn struggled to keep up. Eve slowed to a stop once the alarm faded.

"Don't know about you." Quinn caught her breath with a smile. "But I could use a drink. And I think I owe you one."

The offer took Eve by surprise. She needed to protect her identity, but they'd become partners in crime. The sparkle in Quinn's aqua eyes was a mix of adoration and mischief—the way Charlotte used to look at her when they were kids. And Georgie had dodged Eve for so long, the sense that someone wanted to hang out with her seemed impossible to pass up.

Totally possible. Ditch her.

"Sure." Eve shrugged, nodding. "Okay."

You don't know this person. It's like you want to get caught.

Quinn pulled up a ride share. In twenty minutes, they arrived at a saloon outside the Arts District. The Golden Stallion. Quinn greeted the bartender by name. The woman had a shaved head adorned with piercings, her arms decorated with tattoos. She plunked down two glasses, filling them with tequila.

Eve eyed the liquid, apprehensive, as Quinn recounted her story of meeting Diego.

"I swear to god they see a guitar and a pair of tits, and they think I'm an idiot. Then I fall for something like that...I just feel so stupid."

"You're not stupid." Eve shook her head. "People take advantage of...well, everyone. People take advantage of everyone."

Quinn nodded, raising a shot. They clinked glasses, downing them.

"I like to believe there are good people in the world with good intentions," said Quinn. "Or, at least they'll come through and do the right thing, like what you did."

"Oh, no." Eve winced, her throat burning. "Please don't tell anybody what I did."

Quinn smiled. "It's okay. I didn't get a good look at whoever it was that helped me. You and I met here."

The bartender refilled the glasses.

"Shitty thing is I have to crawl back to Carmen and Erica and tell them they were right."

"Went solo, huh?"

"Sort of." Quinn raised the glass. "Here's to going it alone."

"Hang on a sec." Eve held up a finger. "I don't really drink like this anymore—cut back a little while ago. You may not think so now, but, trust me, it catches up with you."

Quinn's face scrunched. "You can't be that much older than me. What are you, like, thirty-two?"

Eve paused, checking for sarcasm. "You're my favorite person in the whole world right now."

She clinked her glass against Quinn's and they downed another shot.

Quinn wiped her lip. "What were you doing out there anyway?"

Crap. The warehouse.

"Uh, looking for a job, which wasn't there." She shrugged. "Guess we both got scammed."

The bartender poured another round. Eve snatched it up, desperate to change the subject.

"To getting scammed." She lifted her glass.

"Well, if you need a job, I work part-time at this non-profit, No Nukes Now."

"Kira" did need a realistic cover. And it was a job she believed in.

Eve smiled. "That sounds perfect."

"Awesome. Oh—well, do you have any accounting experience?"

Her smile dimmed. "Yeah. A little."

An afternoon of day drinking evolved into a hunt for the best tacos in the neighborhood, then on to another bar for beers. At the third bar, Quinn ran into several friends, giving Eve the chance to thank her and head home for the night as the younger woman showed no sign of slowing.

The rail station was a couple blocks away. Thirty minutes later, Eve staggered into the penthouse.

She popped open the clips and pried off the wig, setting the eyeglasses alongside it on the entryway table. She stripped off her jacket, sweating from booze, and tossed it onto a chair.

She chugged a glass of water, basking in the chill of the refrigerator before refilling it at the dispenser. New friend. Day drinking. Potential new job at a place making the world better. Her life hadn't been filled with this much promise and fun since college.

Eve held the icy glass to her forehead and teetered into the sunken living room, tilting down to press the remote on the coffee table, eager for distraction and hoping to catch the late show. But programming had reached the absolute bottom. Celeb Talk.

"Looks like it's trouble in paradise for tech wizard Simon Pierce and fitness model Valentina Calavicci," said the gossip queen with frosted hair. "Earlier today ValCal updated her status to single and posted hashtag Better Days Ahead."

"Couldn't have happened to a nicer guy," Eve toasted the news, guzzling water as they tossed to commercial.

An anchor for the local station delivered a news brief. Crime and zoning laws. And then, Eve's company ID photo.

She choked.

"Tonight, the FBI is asking your help finding a missing woman."

She backed away, stumbling over the ottoman and landing with a heavy thud. Water spilled across the carpet.

"Eve Kincaid is thirty-seven years old and stands at five feet four inches tall. She's an employee at Pierce Technologies and was last seen in the San Fernando area."

She propped herself up.

"If you have any information regarding her whereabouts, please call the FBI hotline at the number you see on your screen."

Eve flew into her bedroom, hyperventilating. She paced, wringing her hands, future potentialities spinning in a warped mishmash of color and terror.

"Oh my god, oh my god, oh my god—what am I doing? I can't do this, I can't do this—I've got to get rid of this thing."

Her head whipped to her reflection in the full length mirror.

It answered, calm. "You can't."

"What?" she asked herself. "Why not?"

"You can't get rid of it," her reflection answered with composure. She stepped closer. "What are you going to do? Put all those people back to normal? They'll call the cops. Then they'll find you for sure. And what about the guy you knocked out today...?"

"Oh my god—shut up!"

"What about all the great stuff you wanted to do?" Mirror Eve asked. "Saving the world, remember?"

She stared into her own eyes, the faint hum filling her ears again, growing louder.

"All you've been doing is running and hiding," said Mirror Eve. "Is that what you're going to do for the rest of your life? Run and hide?"

"No." Eve's voice dropped. "They're going to hide from me."

"That's right." Mirror Eve grinned.

The hum reached crescendo as she neared her reflection. "And no one's going to ignore me or dismiss me or make me feel like I'm not good enough. Ever again."

8

(purple)

The taste and sensation of burnt carpet filled her mouth. Her head throbbed, eyes pulsing inward to escape the light. Every twenty minutes she fled to the bathroom, her intestines twisting into balloon animals. She sipped water, unable to stomach coffee, but in urgent need of caffeine.

"You shouldn't have drank like that," she scolded. "You know better."

Eve stood before a wall-sized whiteboard, overwhelmed by her own formulas. Queasiness churned her insides as the colors shifted up and down and back and forth. She turned aside, the motion stopped. She needed to figure out what the fragment was doing at the quantum level. But her brain and body weren't cooperating.

"Maybe another binder?"

Transcription required a different focus. The process was enough of a distraction and this particular binder detailed Talbot's assignment. He'd referenced something called "Mobius" which had blunted the disc cutters and burnt out the gears in the boring machines. Pierce Technologies's laser cannons had proved disastrous. The object had absorbed the energy, refracted and amplified it, causing the tunnel to collapse. Only a handful had survived.

Simon Pierce had been brought in to engineer a solution. Over several days, they'd excavated the tunnel and drilled around the Mobius to remove it. Once free of the bedrock, the object had produced a signal. A low, continuous resonant frequency.

She recalled the hum. Was that it? It couldn't be. How? Was it some residual—maybe due to exposure to the air?

The military had wanted to study the material, so Pierce had tested several approaches using sound waves to cleave off a portion. He'd devised a powerful, concentrated acoustic beam which had succeeded in separating several pieces. After that, the signal had stopped.

"Weird," she muttered. Had the fragment been signaling the Mobius? Or another fragment? How many were there?

Talbot's notes made no further mention of it. Only that the military couldn't reproduce the sound.

It wasn't clear if the next part was for headquarters. The military called the project Cactus Whistle, the base of operations nicknamed the Litterbox. The password was *Andalusia*, though since the project had been compromised, it had probably changed. Six days a week Talbot had driven to an airfield, boarded a small passenger plane, and flown to a location in the desert. He'd had limited knowledge of the chain of command. His only point of contact had been Lieutenant Colonel Das.

Talbot had insisted to his superiors that security measures had made it impossible to smuggle the fragment out of the country. However, he'd devised a way to remove it for short periods without arousing suspicion. Thanks to assets on base, Talbot could swap out the fragment with a piece of obsidian for eighteen hours every two days. He'd used the knowledge gleaned from the project to experiment on his own and transmitted some of his progress to headquarters. He'd convinced Irina that, for the first time, they had leverage over Moscow and as soon as he figured out how to transmute elements, he'd have enough to pacify them. Though the arrangement had appeased his superiors for a time, they'd grown impatient.

Poor Irina. Eve remembered the stone she'd placed over the spot she'd laid Talbot to rest, a patch of earth under the bushes outside her apartment building.

What if the FBI found the stone? A hair? A fleck of her skin?

Idiot. You should have shrunk him with your car.

"Stop." She shook her head, pushing the thoughts away. She'd insulated herself enough. Planned ahead. Or had she?

Desperate to occupy her mind, she returned to the binder. Talbot had dreaded the idea of handing the fragment to headquarters—not for fear of getting caught, but losing access to it meant he'd never learn its true nature. So he'd maintained he was on the verge of a breakthrough, though nothing in his notes hinted at anything conclusive. While the military had experimented on it using electrical and magnetic fields, Talbot attempted to regulate the rate and amount of particle transmission using something less conventional: tritium.

Eve tossed aside the notes and grabbed the binder of schematics. She flipped through the pages, pulling out several, and unfurled them. Sure enough, the *modifikator* had been designed around a homemade tritium battery. She abandoned the designs, swinging around to the equipment she'd stolen from Talbot's basement. One she was sure was a spectrometer. Another had a wand wired to a mainframe with a small monitor—a scintillation counter. She plugged it in and removed the *modifikator*'s cover. The purple holograph glinted as the wand passed over the fragment.

No reading.

Her brow lumped forward, perplexed. Where was the radiation?

She needed to study the fragment itself, but her life now depended on it remaining in the *modifikator*. Frantic yellow-orange squiggles rose up at the thought of losing it if she took it out. The tritium battery was at least a starting point. If she could continue his work, applying her theory, she might be able to create and control different distortions. Then maybe she could prove they were reproducible. Build a lexicon.

Colors floated and streaked by as she switched between her calculations, notes, and the blueprints, jumbling into new patterns. But nothing definitive took shape. She needed to test the action between the tritium and fragment.

Talbot's notes said the Mobius amplified energy, but the fragment wasn't behaving the same way. If there was a field, how would it react to another radioactive material? If her theory was accurate, and the field was stable, it should generate same effect.

Household sources scrolled through her brain. Her eyes darted to the ceiling. No smoke alarm. But there was one in the guest room.

* * *

Inside the miniature house, Janelle sat at the breakfast table between Eugene and Troy with her coffee and bran flakes. They exchanged awkward glances as rumbles approached. The rumbling intensified, plates and glasses shaking in the cabinets. The house jostled. They ducked under the table.

Cassidy screamed as she and Darien were flung to the carpet in the hall.

"Is this going to happen all the time?" asked Janelle, standing. The table and her clothes were drenched in milk and coffee.

"What do you think?" Zach entered the kitchen in boxers and a T-shirt, and scratched himself.

"Hey," said Janelle. "House rules are clothes in the common areas."

"Yeah, dude," said Troy. "I don't want to see your junk. Put some pants on."

"Who really cares?" Zach asked.

"I do," Janelle and Troy answered.

He grumbled, turning around. Another violent jolt sent him to the floor.

Cassidy and Darien were pinballed against each other and the walls. Rapid quakes shuddered the house, lessening as they grew more distant.

* * *

Eve hurried into the office and grabbed the aloe plant off her desk. She returned herself to normal, then shrank the plant a few inches. She pried open the cover of the fire alarm. Using a screwdriver, she tore open the gold foil surrounding the sensor, exposing the radioactive isotope inside and hovered it close to the aloe. Closer. Closer. The plant and its pot began to shrink.

She pulled the alarm away and it stopped. Closer, it shrank. Away, it stopped.

She brought the alarm closer to it again.

An awed smile formed, her eyes alight with possibility. It was a field. And it could be shaped with a fundamental force.

Blasting the fragment with energy generated a catastrophic reaction. But with beta decay and a regulated electric charge, the ionized particles enabled irregular blip-*pilb* projection. A distortion field. Elementary particles were being told to do contradictory things and also what they knew was still true. If she was right, the effect Talbot stumbled upon could be one of countless possible distortions.

Was there an order to them? And how to test it? Maybe her formulas could act as guide if she used the *modifikator* as the baseline.

She broke from her thoughts, the plant now a dot on the desktop.

* * *

Back inside the miniature house, Darien and Cassidy staggered into the kitchen.

"The hell was that?" Darien asked.

"Don't know." Kevin leaned in the doorway. "She ran in and ran out."

"This cannot happen every day," said Janelle. "Mornings are my sanctuary."

"Yeah, same," Zach muttered, taking a seat.

"Okay," said Cassidy. "So, there's no way to communicate with the outside world?"

Eugene shook his head. "Our phones can't connect to the satellites."

"I would say maybe wireless," said Zach. "*But we're trapped in a box.*"

"All right, all right, look," said Troy. "There's a satellite uplink in the truck. You think we can use it to boost the signal on our phones somehow?"

Eugene glanced at Zach for confirmation. "Well, yeah."

Zach's head bobbed. "Yeah, that could work."

"You guys know how to do that?" asked Darien.

"Well, not off-hand." He shrugged. "I figured we could look it up on the internet."

Dumbfounded silence swept the housemates.

"The internet?" asked Janelle.

"Yeah," Zach answered. "Oh. Yeah, I guess not."

"And you two are supposed to be the smartest people in here?" she asked.

"We're screwed." Cassidy threw up her hands. "We're screwed."

Darien rubbed her back.

"Everybody just relax," Zach said.

"Do not tell me to relax." Cassidy restrained her urge to strangle him.

"D-Man," said Zach. "Get a handle on your woman, all right?"

Janelle sat up. "Oh hell no."

Cassidy seethed, hand on her hip. "Excuse me?"

"I do not own or control her," said Darien. "So, I'd sleep with the door locked from now on if I were you."

Troy snickered, shaking his head at Zach. "Dude..."

"Not making any friends today, pal." Kevin smirked.

Zach leaned back. "Everybody be cool, all right? My place has a security system. The police are probably reviewing the footage as we speak. If you just have patience and a little faith, they will track her down."

* * *

Detective Paul Russo examined the terrace door, running his fingers through his coarse salt-and-pepper hair. No forced entry. No marks. No stains. He sneered, clicking his tongue, and crouched, careful of his lower back. Screws and bolts, splintered wood. He scooped up a couple of each and stepped into the office where his partner, Detective Allegra Velez, stood with her hands on her hips, scrutinizing the pornographic androids decorating the walls. Her ombré hair brushed the shoulder of her leather jacket as she turned to him.

"Can you explain this to me?" she asked.

"No," he answered. "I like my women a hundred percent human."

"That's why you're one of the good ones, Paulie."

"Yeah, tell that to my ex-wife."

She smirked.

"See the bolts?" he asked.

"Yeah. They ripped it off the frame."

"It don't make no sense."

"No door. No blood. No sign of struggle." She pointed to the open desk cabinet, a faint outline of dust around a clean square area. "Looks like there might have been a safe in there. And there's no computer, so I'm guessing they took that, too. But for some reason, left all of this priceless artwork."

Russo smiled. "So they wanted whatever was on the computer."

"And Milner? And his safe?" Velez squinted. "We sure this guy's really missing?"

"Stop looking for the quick solve."

"I'm considering all the possibilities."

"You just want to beat Lam in that competition you two got going."

"I'm not worried because it's inevitable that I win."

"Please. The two of you should just—"

"Don't." She pointed at him.

Russo put his hands up. Their gaze shifted to the desk. A young woman sat dissecting one of the security cameras.

"Well, hate to say it." Tanya huffed, pushing curly locks over her ear. "But these are fried. I mean, it's like there was a power surge but nothing else was affected. It's weird, the cables don't fit the ports."

Russo shrugged. "Maybe cheap knock-offs?"

"Maybe," said Tanya. "I'll get a better look back at the station."

* * *

Simon skimmed the subject line of Chang's email. In the best of times, dealing with Chang might be controversial. At this point, it'd be downright suicidal. He really wanted that favor, though. He glanced at the *dorodango*.

Patience.

Simon closed his laptop, smiling.

He stepped out of his office. Hargrove and Agent Durbin—a potato-headed man with a potato-shaped body—had commandeered a pair of desks, their laptops open, talking more than typing.

"Hey, saw the news about your girlfriend," said Hargrove. "Tough break."

Simon's smile didn't waver. "You win some, you lose some."

"Yeah, but what a loss," said Durbin.

Simon shrugged. "Well, there's more important things than having a hot, European fitness model for a girlfriend."

Durbin and Hargrove checked each other. Durbin shook his head. "I can't think of any."

"So are you guys going to be here much longer?" Simon asked.

Hargrove sneered. "Tired of us already?"

"Oh, no, you can play solitaire to your heart's content," said Simon. "I just figured there would be more for you to investigate."

"We're here as a security presence."

"And this area right here"—Simon grinned, circling his hand—"has never felt safer. Thanks, guys."

He strode out of the executive offices, catching the elevator before the door closed. Deepa was already on board, ill at ease.

"Thanks," he said. "Had to get out of there. Needed some fresh air, you know?"

She nodded. "Yeah."

The doors closed. The elevator shifted down. Simon glanced at her. "I'm sure this has been difficult."

"Oh, no, it's just—concerning..."

"Well, I mean, you and Freitas were friends. Finding out he's missing must be troubling."

"We weren't close." She shrugged, shaking her head. "I just knew him from acquaintances."

Simon nodded, slow, allowing the silence to linger. The doors opened. He snapped his fingers and pointed. "Forgot my phone."

She smiled, relieved. "I'll see you later, then."

Deepa stepped off the elevator. Simon checked his watch. Eleven fifteen.

He rode up to the executive floor, passed Hargrove and Durbin without a word, and closed his office door. He studied the personnel files for Bhandari and Freitas. Although Freitas was several years older and they didn't share any previous employment history, Bhandari had provided a recommendation letter on his behalf. More troubling, Freitas had long gaps in employment. Not quite incriminating.

Simon grinned.

Not yet.

9

(brown)

No Nukes Now resided in an outparcel overshadowed by larger buildings, with its own fenced off parking lot. Eve cringed at the cubicles behind the reception desk as Quinn led her inside. An older man, sunburnt with a shock of white hair, crossed paths with them.

"Mr. Fisher," said Quinn. "This is my friend Kira. She's here about the accounting job."

"Larry Fisher," he said.

Eve shook his hand. "Nice to meet you."

"You a basketball player? Volleyball?"

"Oh—no, I'm super uncoordinated."

He chuckled. "And honest. I like that. So, what do you know about the anti-nuke movement?"

"Well, I believe in it now more than ever. I mean, if I could, I would just shrink all the nuclear weapons so they could never hurt anybody."

"That is idealistic." He smiled, wagging a finger. "And I appreciate that. We're committed to a global moratorium on the construction of nuclear weapons by any country—no exceptions—and the dismantling of nuclear stockpiles."

"Right, because nuclear deterrence is like an addiction," she said. "We have to break the cycle."

Larry nodded, beaming. "Come on, Kira, let me show you around."

They toured the back offices and break room. Though quiet and austere, it wasn't stifling. People smiled at her, and each other.

Larry introduced Eve to Barbara, the head of accounting, a cheery brunette who would be on maternity leave soon. Barb asked her about her previous experience, leading to an impromptu interview with Larry jumping in—

"Quick—what's the square root of negative one?"

Shocking pink.

"That's the unit imaginary number," said Eve. "Because there's no real number having a negative square."

Unsure, Larry and Quinn deferred to Barb, who nodded. "You should probably hire her."

Last stop was a back room full of server racks and computer parts. Maps dotted with red circles lined the walls along with Cold War anti-nuke propaganda. A tall, wiry man with thick-rimmed glasses sat a computer, irritated with their presence.

"And this is IT," Larry said. "Powell here is our tech guru."

Powell gave a halfhearted wave.

"What are all the maps for?" Eve asked.

He sat up, enlivened. "Undisclosed nuclear silos."

Larry was about to dissuade her from asking a follow up, but—

"If they're undisclosed, how do you know about them?"

"Freedom of Information Act." Powell turned to the maps. "Mostly from the Cold War. You'll notice a lot are in Canada—part of a secret program started in the sixties to expand American dominance called Beef Mountain."

Quinn snickered under her breath. "Beef Mountain?"

"The rest are new installations that, technically, the government was never supposed to build and can't acknowledge their existence. That's an even more classified program called Backdoor Ram—"

"Okay." Larry guided them toward the door. "Tour's over."

"Wait," said Eve. "I want to hear about that."

Quinn smirked. "I'll explain it to you later."

How did this guy find secret military installations?

They headed down the hall. Larry excused Powell's paranoid theories, and then himself as he ducked into his office for a meeting.

"So, what do you think?" Quinn asked.

"Well, yeah." Eve shrugged. "I mean, if they'll hire me."

"I think you're a lock." She nodded. "Want to go out and celebrate?"

The tang of cottonmouth and burn of sour stomach still lingered. "Well, I kind of have some stuff to do."

"Oh, it wouldn't be until later. I know this great place—I'll text you around eight."

Tantalized by the morning's breakthroughs, Eve didn't want to lose momentum. But she didn't want to blow off her new friend either.

Autumn gold and sky blue drifted by. The playful glimmer in Quinn's eyes reminded her of Charlotte taking her by the hands, dragging her toward the Steel Phantom roller coaster.

She'd just have to exercise a little more restraint. "All right, sounds good."

* * *

"There's a gap between the lid and wall," said Troy.

"It's, like, a centimeter," said Zach.

"A centimeter's a lot to us!" Troy implored the others for support.

Breakfast dishes remained on the table. Conversation had devolved into debate.

"So," said Zach, "you're going to scale the wall and then repel down the other side?"

"Yeah." Troy nodded. "And then the table."

"And then what?" He counted on his fingers. "You need supplies, food and water, more rope. You don't know what's out there."

"What's your point?" Troy sighed.

"You've got to carry all that over the wall," said Zach.

Kevin sat forward. "I say we dig a tunnel. There's no bedrock here."

"And what happens when you get to the plexiglass?" asked Zach.

Kevin shrugged. "Figure it out when we get there."

"And then what?" asked Zach. "Where are we going? We don't know."

"At least they're coming up with ideas," said Cassidy. "Instead of shooting them all down."

"They're terrible ideas!" He shrugged, snatching a champagne bottle.

Janelle huffed, shaking her head. She turned to Eugene. "All right, so that's what you need to figure out. Where are we going?"

"Well." Eugene reached the across the table for a notepad. "I can draw some of it right now, from what I remember."

"And" —Troy pointed to him— "we need to know where she keeps that thing."

"I think the tunnel's our best option," said Darien.

Troy shrugged. "Climbing over the wall's faster, though."

"Then we've got to wait for her to take off the lid," said Kevin.

"And get her to keep it off," said Darien.

"Also you." Janelle pointed at Eugene.

"What?" His voice cracked. "Why?"

"You're already out there," said Janelle. "Distract her."

"I don't see why we can't just guilt-trip her into letting us go."

Cassidy picked up a champagne flute. “I mean, she’s obviously trying to buy our affection.”

“Yeah,” said Zach. “And you’re welcome for those Christian Louboutins. That’s my money she’s spending.”

Cassidy smiled, smug, sipping her mimosa.

“Problem is,” said Kevin, “she’s never around.”

Janelle nodded. “Which I’m thankful for.”

“Oh, she’s totally avoiding us,” said Cassidy. “I’m telling you, we ask for more stuff, talk about how it reminds us of home, it’ll screw with her brain.”

“No,” said Zach. “We don’t want her brain more screwed up than it already is.”

“*Pffft.*” Cassidy muttered. “Like you know.”

“Oh, I do,” he said. “We’re guinea pigs to her. The crazy shit hasn’t even started yet. I’m talking next-level mind games. We’re living like kings now, but then she takes it all away. Wakes us up in the middle of the night, forces us to fight to the death over food. You just wait.”

* * *

Eve returned to the penthouse and her whiteboards with a clearer head. She focused on the colors, shaping them with Talbot’s insights, and then allowed them to drift. Consumed by her kaleidoscopic vision, she lost herself in them. Hours passed until her phone buzzed.

Emma in HR at No Nukes offered her the job. She’d send an email with all the documentation.

The room had dimmed. The frosted windows had darkened. She still had to change.

Eve seized a pen and scribbled her brainstorm. Her refined formula had the advantage of taking into account real-world phenomena. But she still needed to determine its color expression—the transmutation—in order to define the field. Like anything else in the natural world, it should have fallen into a spectrum. Though the range would be greater than anything in classical physics.

Below the formula, she dashed off a rough sketch for testing her hypothesis. She could build on Talbot’s design, but it would be challenging since she had little engineering experience. She sighed and jotted down research topics. Among them, electronic hardware and circuitry.

* * *

Eve had expected a trendy downtown bar, not an hour’s drive south. But according to Quinn, people who waited in line for a bar were losers. The dive's pine wood-paneled walls, concrete floor, and near emptiness when they arrived suggested otherwise.

"This is one of my favorite places," said Quinn. "Check this out."

She hurried Eve to an antique jukebox.

"All original vinyl." Quinn gushed. "I mean, we probably won't hear anything on it tonight, but, it's a frigging time machine."

Eve nodded, not getting the allure. They passed a worn billiard table to a cluster of modern arcade games.

"I rule this shit." Quinn pointed to the flashing floor-panel lights of the *Dance Party Apocalypse* game. "*Interstellar Acid Nightmare* is my jam!"

"Mm-kay," Eve muttered.

She's way too cool for you. You're old and out of touch.

At the bar, a craggy-faced man with a silver ponytail dried out glasses with a rag.

"This is Sid—he's awesome," said Quinn. "Sid, this is my friend Kira."

Eve nodded. "Hi."

His eyes hung on her.

He knows you don't belong here.

"He likes you," Quinn whispered, grinning.

"Uh-huh," said Eve, unconvinced.

Quinn hopped onto a stool.

"What'll it be, sunshine?" Sid doled out coasters.

She swiveled to Eve. "I don't know, what are you in the mood for?"

"Uh, well." Eve smiled. "Not tequila. How about bourbon? Neat."

Sid bobbed his head to a private melody, picking up glasses. "Got a preference?"

"Johnny Drum, if you have it."

Eve sat. Glasses filled. Quinn hoisted hers with gusto. "To your new job."

She gently lowered Quinn's wrist. "You don't pound this."

Sid nodded. "She's right."

Mystified, Quinn mirrored her delicate sip. But that was the extent of Quinn's moderation.

Next was a shot. And another with the first people who sat at the bar. Quinn's voraciousness swept her along and Eve lost count as the place flooded with the wildest artists, musicians, and dancers mingling with truckers and cowboys, a women's roller derby team, and a motorcycle gang. Quinn had taken her to the coolest party she'd ever been to—the underground—alive with a pulse and energy of its own, the sense from somewhere in its roiling depths the next music icon would bubble to the surface.

The speakers juddered and quivered, vibrating the wood panels. Eve couldn't see straight. People and faces reverberated, unsure what was in her field of vision or her mind's eye. How was she even getting drunk? Her cells should've been too large—no—not now. She wouldn't remember even if she could figure it out.

Quinn ordered another round. Eve considered pretending to down a drink by tossing it over her shoulder, but it was near impossible not to douse someone behind her.

A couple guys homed in on them. Drowned out by the noise, they repeated pick up lines louder, the wit diminishing each time.

The guy with a sideways baseball cap leaned toward Quinn. "Screw me if I'm wrong, but haven't we met before?"

Before Quinn answered, Eve spouted off. "Oh—halametis ordle flarg."

"Flarg!" Quinn latched onto the game. "Elo peddle meta-shan."

"Kota goja pine." Eve turned to the guy. "Elo peddle meta-shan?"

He and his buddy with spiky hair and frosted tips backed off.

About to burst out laughing, Quinn grabbed Eve's wrist and led her to a high-top table in the corner. Quinn said she'd met many—probably too many—guys here before, but she wasn't ready. She griped about her ex.

"So, I thought everything was good. Got a little more serious, spending more time there, and it's just easier to keep an extra set of clothes and a toothbrush, you know?"

"He thought you were planning an invasion."

"Well, that's just it. I told him flat out: I'm not moving in. Like, rent for the three of us at this place is unreal—I mean, I don't even want to tell you because you'd kill me to get on the lease."

"Don't know about that," Eve mumbled.

"Serious. But, anyway—Kyle starts with all these rules about everything, and I'm like, okay, you know, he's lived alone, he's got his own thing going on—"

"Set in his ways."

"Right. No big deal. But then, it's like he's arguing with me about everything. We had this fantastic day. Drove up to Ventura, went to the beach, winery tour in Santa Barbara, had sex in the back of his car—all the stuff you'd imagine would be great and then it really is. And then, we're not back more than five minutes, and it's an argument about dinner. And, I think, one of my shoes wasn't where it was supposed to be...? Anyway, he stepped on it and that set him off. He was just looking for anything to push me away, but the second I put my hands up and said I was done, he was in love with me again."

"Poor guy."

"What about poor me?"

"Well, yeah, but he was the one who was scared."

"I terrified a grown man? You mean he was scared of commitment."

"No, he probably really liked you and he was scared of messing it up."

"So, he sabotaged everything?"

"Well, yeah."

"That's—How is that not being scared of commitment?"

"It's not the commitment part." She shrugged. "It's when it ends."

Quinn lost herself in the beads of condensation rolling down her glass. Eve sipped her beer, drifting back to a similar time with Gideon.

She'd been twenty-one. They'd been dating for months, spending most of their time at her place since her roommate was never around. Eve had her own rules. The bathroom was sacred. Gideon had had a toothbrush and toiletries but his toothbrush its own holder, his toiletries their own box. No showering together. If someone was in the shower, no one could use the toilet—under any circumstances. Clothing was mandatory. Eve never walked around naked even though she was alone most of the time. Nudity was for sex only. And sex was only in a bed. Her's or Gideon's. No hotel beds, motel beds, no beds at friends' places. No couches. Sex required advance notice, at least a day. And she never asked or initiated.

"Am I driving you crazy?" Eve had asked, opening the dishwasher.

"No." Gideon had pulled out the lower rack. "Why?"

"I'm trying not to ruin this, but—I feel like I am."

"You're not." He'd smirked, plucking out a couple plates. "If anything, I'd say you're really good at setting boundaries."

"Well, the last guy I went out with said I was too needy, and—it's not you; I just don't want to mess anything up. But I feel like I'm messing it up by trying not to mess it up?" She'd winced as the plates clanked together in the cupboard.

"I get it." He'd shrugged. "I mean, it's like we're walking this tightrope together, and, I don't want to make us fall, and you don't want to make us fall, so we're trying to hold each other up and not look down —"

"What if I already looked down?"

"Doesn't matter." He'd shaken his head. "It was a terrible analogy—it's not life or death. I like being with you."

She'd smiled. "I like being with you."

"Then there's nothing to be afraid of," he'd said, a crafty smirk rising. "So...you want to fool around?"

"No. How about tomorrow at this time?"

He'd chuckled, checking his watch. "Yeah, that'll work. Okay, so, for dinner I was thinking chicken tikka tacos. Now, keep in mind, I haven't perfected the recipe—"

"Hang on." Her had eyes lit up. "I rolled all the change today, and I was thinking sushi."

"Ooh—yeah."

"We could go to Pagoda or Hiroyuki's, or—" She'd become more animated as she'd described it. "Or, there's this new place with this big ass aquarium that winds through the restaurant and divides up all the tables."

"So that one?" he'd asked through a smile.

She'd grinned with an emphatic nod.

This was the Eve he'd known and loved.

"You wouldn't happen to have grabbed—"

She'd stuck out a paper menu.

"How could you possibly ruin anything?"

At some point, Quinn had launched into her break-up story. Eve wasn't sure when she'd started paying attention again, but Kyle and Quinn were locked in an all-out, knock-down bout leading to a harrowing car chase spanning the city, and most of the day, screaming and shouting obscenities at each other outside their respective apartment buildings. Later, in the middle of a public park, they'd briefly reconciled before the toxicity of the rancor between them dissolved the last of their good will. They parted as strangers, taking their individual lots of property and returning to their lives with the memory of someone who might have loved them.

The music cranked up way too loud. Eve could only make out syllables as Quinn shouted across the table, tears streaming down her face, drunk and heartbroken.

Eve didn't know what to say, so she got up and hugged her.

Quinn squeezed Eve's shoulders, her faint words cutting through the decibels. "Sometimes I don't think I've ever been in love, just chasing some dream that doesn't exist."

Eve couldn't imagine Quinn hadn't ever found love. It did exist. Eve had tasted it. It just wasn't meant for people like her.

They'd taken a road trip to Aberdeen to visit Gideon's parents. Spent the morning at Lake Sylvia hiking a trail and swimming. They'd returned in the afternoon, taking separate showers, Eve in the hall bathroom and Gideon in his parent's bedroom. She'd been nestled under a thick brown quilt in the guest room as he'd tiptoed in.

"Ooh that's a great idea," he'd whispered. "I could use a nap."

He'd closed the door so as not to wake her. He'd slipped under the blankets, folding his hands behind his head and stretching his back. His eyes had closed. Her hand had slid into his shorts.

Gideon's eyes had popped open. "Oh my god—what has gotten in you?"

She'd met him with an impish grin. "Nothing yet."

He'd chuckled. She was never this forward. And this had not been an approved bed.

A knock. Eve had flipped the quilt over her head. Gideon had cleared his throat as though awakened.

His mother had peeked in. "Sorry—didn't mean to wake you."

"It's all right. We were just, uh, taking a nap," he'd said as Eve had stroked him below layers of blankets.

"We were thinking dinner around six. Your dad wants to show off the grill."

"Sounds great," Gideon had managed. "Thanks, Mom."

"Sleep well."

The door had closed. Eve had sprung from the covers, nose to nose with him. They'd stifled their laughter, eyes locking, and leaned in to—

Eve awoke in bed, sweating from booze. She was alone in the dark, the auburn wig still fastened, her scalp aching. She pieced together the end of the night. They'd paid their tab, tipped too much. Eaten something deep-fried from a truck. The aftertaste did not leave a favorable clue. Quinn took a ride share home. Eve shouldn't have driven, but a ride share would've logged Kira Sloane's destination as downtown. She couldn't risk linking aliases. But Kira probably had too many attachments already. Eve needed an identity Eugene hadn't seen. The complications of her situation tormented her.

She wiped sticky drool from her face. Her boots were still on. She reached back to the pure dreams of Gideon and the lake, but didn't want to sully them with the way she was now. They were gone. All gone.

10

(silver, black)

"Hard truth," said the peppy young woman who went by AngDroid. "It won't be perfect on the first try. You'll probably use too much solder or too much heat or have insufficient wetting. And that's *okay*. Keep practicing until you're comfortable with the soldering iron. Or watch the next video and learn the magic of *de*soldering."

Eve hit Pause and checked her circuit board. The melted blob of silver had leaked into one of the traces. Her other attempts had the appearance of knobby tree trunks bent by a storm.

It's not perfect. You're a failure. Everything you do is garbage.

She chucked the board of botched connections against the wall. It dropped onto a pile of others outside the trash can.

AngDroid's online library of instructional videos were straightforward, and she was so energetic, it was the only thing motivating Eve. The sensation of a thick rubber band wrapped around her head throbbed.

"This is hopeless." She tore open a new box. "I don't know what I'm doing. I can't do this. You suck. I suck. Idiot."

The grinding churn in her stomach didn't help. A sour belch rose up as her phone vibrated. Quinn wanted to meet up for lunch.

"Oh god. This chick's going to kill me."

She considered not answering. But she hated when people did that to her. Old Eve would hide. Not New Eve.

* * *

She hoped the Garden Variety Cafe was a vegan joint specializing in Vitamin B-infused wheat grass smoothies. But Eve walked in to find Quinn pulling a strip of fried bacon out of a Bloody Mary.

"You look like shit." Quinn smirked. "Nothing a little hair of the dog won't fix."

Eve dropped into the booth. "What if it was a mutt?"

"That's what the bacon's for." She pushed a Bloody Mary toward her.

Eve eyed it with nausea. She grabbed the glass and sucked down a third of it, surprised how the savory salinity masked the alcohol.

"Look, you're really cool," Eve said, wiping her mouth. "And I have fun hanging out with you, but could we do other stuff besides get wasted all the time?"

Quinn snarled, glaring at the ceiling. "Oh god, not you, too."

"Other people say you drink too much?"

"Well, no. They just become 'sober-curious', which is a bullshit, half-assed way of saying *sober*."

"There's nothing wrong with being sober."

"No, but why curious? I mean, if that's what you want to do, just do it. Stop pretending you might want this other thing when you really don't—"

"Are we talking about someone in particular?" Eve asked, conversation-curious.

"Yeah, Carmen and Erica. But they weren't really drinkers to begin with. I mean, Carmen was a band geek whose parents wouldn't let her take the bus to competitions. They'd drive her and follow the bus. And Erica went to this Christian summer camp until she was, like, twenty."

"All right, well, I was a dork in high school. And, when I got to college, I partied a little too much—"

"That's what I'm saying, and you turned out fine."

"No—I flunked my sophomore year, lost my scholarship, and had to reapply. Didn't make getting into grad school easier either."

Quinn retreated to her drink. Eve chewed a bacon strip before taking a long sip. It was easing her hangover.

"It's just that..." Quinn sighed. "We went on this incredible tour last year. Started in Seattle and worked our way down the West Coast until we ended up at that place I took you last night. It was hard, but it was fun. Or, at least I thought it was."

The brightness in Quinn's face dimmed. "When we got back, we had some extra cash and I was ready to write an album, do more shows. But they never had time. Then Carmen told me she was taking a promotion. And Erica said she wanted to focus on her day job. I guess they realized music wasn't for them, and...they didn't know how to tell me."

Quinn somehow managed to sip her drink down to the bottom as she spoke.

"And this solo thing is scary. I mean, it was supposed to be us, you know? Now it's like I have this vision, that I'm over forty, no offense—"

"Not there yet," said Eve. "But thanks."

"Sorry. And I'm still singing in bars, just trying to make a name for myself. Working with random people, trying to get that feeling back, when it was the three of us. You know how many solo acts like me are out there? Some woman and her guitar? Shit, I might as well play in the park. Probably where I'm going to end up."

"Well, getting obliterated all the time isn't going to help."

"I tried. You saw what happened with Diego—"

"No, you were taking a shortcut. When do you practice or write music?"

"Well, mostly weekends." She shrugged. "I mean, during the week I get home at, like, six, and I don't always—"

"And then you go out at, like, eight?"

"Well, yeah."

"All right, I'm not letting you do this anymore."

"Excuse me?"

"This." Eve waved a hand in front of Quinn's face. "This bullshit."

Maybe it was the stabbing pain in her skull or she'd caught a second buzz, but the same fire that lit had Eve on Thanksgiving burned again.

"What you're doing is the worst kind of procrastinating," she said. "You're avoiding writing music, which is what you claim to want to do, but you're spending most of your time getting wasted and recovering from it. In the meantime, you're afraid of not making it, but you're not doing what you need to do in order to make it. And then when you don't do what you need to do, it just feels further and further away, and you feel worse. So you go out and get drunk to stop feeling like crap again."

Quinn's jaw jutted out. She clearly wanted to be angry, but Eve described the insidious cycle with such precision it was undeniable.

"I know that's hard to hear," said Eve. "But if it's what you really want, you have to go get it. It's not just going to happen. No one's going to hand it to you, and it sure as hell isn't going to be at the bottom of a bottle."

"Another round?" their waitress asked, passing the table.

"Yes, please," said Eve.

"Yeah, thank you." Quinn nodded.

"And," Eve added, "two waters."

Quinn returned to her. "But what if I can't do it? What if it never happens?"

Tears welled in Quinn's eyes, reminding Eve of a five-year old Charlotte who'd scraped her knee. Rosy pink and amber. She had kissed the wound, and Charlotte had thrown her arms around her.

"You'll know you actually went for it instead of drinking yourself stupid," said Eve. "And, I don't know—maybe you get a new band, people you click with. But in order for that to happen, you've got to put in the work. Or else you'll never find them."

Quinn's jaw tightened, fighting back tears.

"I know you're scared," said Eve. "I was, too. That's why I think I hid for so long. From everything. Don't do that. Don't do what I did. Because it takes a long time to come back."

Quinn sniffled, smiling. "I am so glad I met you."

Eve wiped the corner of her eye. "I'm glad I met you, too."

The waitress returned, setting drinks in front of them.

Quinn raised her glass. Eve lifted hers.

Clink.

* * *

Eve redoubled her efforts with the soldering iron, the next practice board better than the last. She let the iron cool before switching out the tip, and reviewed another AngDroid tutorial. Each one added a new skill, a new dimension of understanding. She broke for dinner, watching more tutorials and sketching designs for her own project.

She moved onto the terrace, etching her own circuit boards by dunking them into a plastic tub filled with ferric chloride. With gloved hands, she lifted them out and polished them clean with acetone. Though they were copies of boards she'd printed on paper from templates online, they provided a foundation to craft her own hardware. Back at the drafting table, she worked into the night, updating her design, incorporating new elements and knowledge. She could see where she needed relays, capacitors, inductors, resistors, and transistors.

The following day with a clear head and fresh coffee, she tinkered well into the afternoon. Her designs manifested as a framework of switches and knobs centered around the *modifikator* itself, mounted between the charge of an adjustable electric current. She toyed with the knobs, altering the frequencies entering the *modifikator*'s field and logging the settings on a notepad. Once she'd logged three dozen settings, she hauled in a couple fire extinguishers.

She placed an orange on a pedestal in the path of the *modifikator*'s antenna. Then turned a knob down on the rig and flipped a switch.

"Okay." She mumbled. "Matter or energy? Matter or energy?"

A press of the dial button and a blast hit the fruit. The orange lost integrity, melting.

Eve gagged, revolted, as the viscous liquid dripped off the pedestal. She flipped off the switch. She noted the result then sopped up the mess with a towel. She set down a fresh orange. Another scan of her log. There was no way of knowing the order of her hypothetical spectrum. She suspected it wasn't linear, probably multidimensional.

She dialed the knob to the higher end. Flipped a switch. Pressed the button.

The orange sucked into itself, rippling the space around it, and disappeared in a tiny spark.

"Oh shit!" She stumbled backward.

Stupid fuck! You created a black hole!

Heavy sheets of chartreuse and nickel closed in.

Pressed against the wall, she snatched a flashlight off the desk. She leaned over and slapped off the light switch. The room went dark. She whipped the flashlight's beam back and forth over the platform. No perceptible warping of space-time. The light zipped across the wall.

Oh, yeah, real scientific!

"Well, I don't know! How am I supposed to test that?!"

Throw something at it!

She flipped the lights on.

Eve reached into the sack of oranges and lobbed one, underhanded, at the pedestal.

It sailed over, free of gravitational tugs, and thumped onto the carpet.

She checked the dosimeter hanging around her neck. It hadn't spiked. No X-rays. Judging by the fact she was still alive, no gamma rays. The Geiger counter produced nominal ticks. And no heat from Hawking radiation, although, it was a rather tiny black hole.

"It's gone."

She scribbled in her notes.

Unlike a real black hole which would swallow more matter and grow, she speculated the distortion black hole could only grow if it received more radiation. Once the black hole evaporated, the distortion field resolved. What was more exciting, she'd stumbled upon a new way to study gravity—possibly quantum gravity—and potentially reconcile some of the most vexing issues in physics.

Well, once she'd figured out how to do it safely.

She planted the tossed orange onto the pedestal and reconfigured to a mid-range setting. A blast struck the orange. It didn't change. Smoky wisps rose off the pedestal as she reached for it. Her fingertips seared—"Ah, fuck!"

The orange rolled onto the carpet, a trail of fire igniting in its wake.

"Shit, fuck, fuck, fuck!" She dashed to a fire extinguisher.

Eve fumbled with the release lever as the cascading flames spread. Foam sputtered and sprayed from the nozzle. Thick plumes of steam filled the room.

With a pair of tongs, she set the orange onto the pedestal and rushed to adjust the knobs and switches to their inverse settings. The blast hit the orange. She waved her hand, clearing the air. Unsure, she grabbed the fire extinguisher and poked the orange with the tongs. It dropped onto the charred carpet. She scribbled the results into her notes.

Another setting, another blast. Eve reached out with the tongs; the ends passed through. Puzzled, she used her fingers—her fingertips disappeared inside. She jerked her hand away, then tried again, her fingers disappearing into the ghost fruit. Baffled, she checked her notations, then set the knobs to their inverse and hit the dial button. She reached for the orange, touching the bumpy peel this time. She was overcome with breathless, giddy laughter.

Eve tuned the knobs and switches, and fired. The orange vanished. She reached for the pedestal, surprised by the thump as it landed on the floor. She fumbled across the carpet and grasped the invisible fruit, captivated as she squeezed it. She returned it to the pedestal. A tune of the knobs, a flick of a switch, and the orange became visible again.

The next blast made the orange as hard as a diamond, so dense she dented the desk by striking the fruit against it. More adjustments and the orange levitated off the pedestal. It floated past her attempts at grabbing it. And higher. The ceiling fan blades whacked it into the wall. After anchoring it with string and another tuning, the beaten fruit dropped to the floor.

New settings. A powdery energy charged the fruit. She scooted away, seizing the Geiger counter. She waved the wand. The orange overheated and burst into flames. The spike in the counter's read-out dropped, the radiation either diffusing or becoming too energetic to pick up. She snuffed out the flames with a fire extinguisher and checked the dosimeter, the levels still well below the acceptable limit.

Next setting. The antenna charged before emitting a powerful white-hot blast, blowing apart the orange and burning a hole in the wall. The faint hum droned in her ears. She hit a switch, opening the circuit. The hum stopped. She closed the circuit again and hit the switch. No hum, but another blast shot through the hole.

She scanned the singed peephole with the Geiger counter. Little or no radiation. The readout waned.

But that energy couldn't be so harmless, could it?

Unless, the distortion field's dissipation returned particles to their natural state. Like the black hole. Radioactive, but not. Real, but not real. The field encapsulated the effects. In which case, lower-density substances might be at the mercy of the distortion once they were within its boundary. Was that how the miniaturized people were breathing? How she got drunk? And could a distortion field be distorted? How much could it be shaped?

She returned to the testing rig and placed a fresh orange on the pedestal.

* * *

If she'd learned anything from her experiments, it was that she needed a proper lab that wasn't near her living space. Eve stopped for lunch and left a message for the Realtor as Diane. Devereux wanted to close on the warehouse this week. After that, she grappled with ethical considerations on her way to the pet store. She returned twenty minutes later with a new test subject. A small tortoise.

"Sorry, buddy, but I didn't think I could catch a mouse."

She bit her lip, checking the notes. Eve tuned the knobs and hovered a finger over the button. The blast hit the tortoise. It fled into its shell. She propped up a lettuce leaf alongside it, waiting for it to re-emerge. The poor thing chomped at the leaf in vain, its entire head passing through before rearing back in confusion. Eve blasted the lettuce, and the tortoise withdrew into its shell. She waited. The creature poked out its beak, then stretched its neck. The intangible tortoise ate the intangible leaf.

Eve gazed with an awed smile.

The two fields interacted without conflict and with recognition.

She turned a knob up a degree and zapped the lettuce, slightly increasing its density. She pushed it closer to the tortoise, her finger passing through and hitting resistance inside. The tortoise, however, continued to eat.

She reset the knobs and returned the tortoise to normal.

Eve flipped through her notepad of settings and corresponding effects. Sometimes they were indiscernible, requiring more advanced diagnostic technology she didn't have, which she noted as *no perceptible change*. The more volatile settings she'd marked with *Do Not Use!* Distinct blocks of settings had emerged. The most consistent and stable affected matter, but a handful on the edges produced energy effects.

She paced the room, clutching the notepad, the soaring excitement of her breakthroughs overshadowed by the reality of her situation. She couldn't run out into the world with her formulas, declaring proof of concept, revealing her discoveries. The government would throw her into prison where she'd be the perfect target for Russian agents. If they could infiltrate a top secret military base, they'd figure out a way in there. She needed protection. She needed goodwill. She needed people on her side.

Nobody likes you. They never have.

Maybe they'd like her if she benefited the world. Eve flipped through her list. Aside from enlarging herself to fulfill her ecological fantasies, none of the other effects were useful for saving the planet. Maybe except for creating gigantic trees. But could the roots absorb nutrients from the soil? And she still wasn't sure how gaseous exchange operated in size-altered organisms. Her mind flashed to a global catastrophe of ginormous oxygen molecules suffocating the planet.

She shook off the scenario.

The black hole effect was promising. The distortion field might allow her to manipulate gravity in ways which would otherwise violate physics. If she could gradually warp space-time without reaching black hole level, it might make time travel possible. Then she could go back and undo her mistakes. But the effect was too dangerous to reproduce. For now. Her mind wandered, consumed with the tantalizing possibility of stopping Gideon.

"But then, I'd never get the *modifikator*. So, I'd have to go back, give myself the fragment, and all the knowledge to build a time machine, but that would only create an alternate timeline dependent on my timeline for its existence, in which case—no, nope. Stop."

She blew out a long puff and dropped into the desk chair.

"Other ideas. Carbon-capture converters. Lossless energy transmission." She skimmed her list. "None of which I can do with any of this."

To study the imperceptible and volatile effects, she'd need much larger and more sensitive equipment. And more power than she could generate in the penthouse. Probably more than she could use in the warehouse without drawing attention. Based on Talbot's notes and her own experimentation, she theorized exposing the fragment to higher forms of ionizing radiation would cause wild fluctuations in the fields—more intense effects, less control. A field might rupture or never form in the first place. Or it might distort reality in some other unpredictable way.

You're not smart enough for this.

And she didn't have inexhaustible funds. What she needed was another jackpot or a steady income. More than a part-time gig at a nonprofit. And she still intended to pay back Zach.

She stared at the tortoise as it chomped on lettuce, her focus dissolving.

"How am I supposed to save the world?" she muttered.

The world needed a replanting of its rainforests en masse. A total halt to deforestation. Complete suspension of fossil fuels. People were all too aware of the most direct, drastic measures and still didn't implement them. Too much sacrifice, too much change. Even if she got their attention—which would be easy if she was gigantic—they'd never agree to it. Her mind leaped to the end of her daydream—the nuclear warhead. No telling what such a high level of ionized particles would do to the field...or her.

And sure, ripping coal-fired power plants from the ground would be as satisfying as pulling weeds, but then millions of people would be without power. Maybe if she was gigantic, she'd gain enough attention to protest companies. She could demand they change their production practices and supply lines. But people already protested, and those supply lines still ran products.

She was still only one person.

The fact was Big Business ruled the world. Their money, their policies, their products—and people bought those products. An insidious cycle. She had to beat them at their own game. Replace them.

She needed a commodity.

Eve scanned her list. The powdery energy distortion. The setting sat on the edge of the volatile range, so she'd need the warehouse to test it further. But if she could temper it, she could alter an ordinary object with the effect. Figure out how to harness the power, convert it into electricity. Enough for massive particle-detecting equipment. Or a house. Or a city.

But she was no salesperson. Not a people-person.

Barely a person-*person.*

And not a scientist.

And nobody likes you. They'd never listen.

Eve wilted.

She'd need to surround herself with renowned backers. People like Simon, but not Simon. Then the government would see she'd mastered the fragment's violent reaction to energy and used it to better the world. They might even invite her to continue her research on the fragments. Everyone would love her.

Until they found out about your houseguests.

A cold lump formed in her chest. Glaucous blue dulled into charcoal.

"No." She swallowed. "I just need to make sure they're alive and happy and...pay them off."

A clean-burning fuel would be insanely profitable. It would also put most of the energy sector out of business. Oil nations would put a bounty on her head. The US government might set their sights on her. Maybe even partner with Russia. Then they'd take the *modifikator* away. And her theories. No one would ever know they were hers.

She was still hiding. Still running.

Eve bit her lip, twisting the flesh through her teeth. She'd never get the fragments. Or figure out the Mobius.

"Make them hide," she whispered. "Make them run."

The hum droned in her ears.

If she couldn't make people like her, maybe she could turn the people against *Them*. After all, people knew what needed to be done. Maybe she could nudge them in the right direction. Turn consumers against Big Business, against the power in their homes. Citizens against their own countries, against their own armies. Then, when she stepped out of the shadows and debuted her wondrous technology, the solutions to all of their problems, they'd love her.

She sat up with a start, rifling through her notes.

If she could exploit the reliable effects, make them accessible, she'd be able to walk through walls or become invisible. And it might help if she could block ionizing radiation. She was her own heist crew, with the exception of Eugene—and she'd know if he double-crossed her. She could plot every angle. Create an inescapable trap for the world which would only pull tighter.

Colorful puzzle pieces linked together before her eyes. She flipped to a new page, scribbling ideas from her mental tempest. If she wanted full comprehension of the distortion fields, she needed other fragments. They were probably still locked away at a military base. But she could do so much more now with the fragment she had.

Since Talbot had slacked off in his spycraft, the next best source of information was Pierce Technologies. Hacking wasn't an option as the government would be monitoring their network, and anything worth keeping might already be in a secure drive offline. Unless Simon had his own personal copy the feds didn't know about.

"Which he totally would."

Eve shopped for radiation suits online. Disappointed with the selection, she explored textile manufacturers, hoping to design her own. That led her to developments in radiation proofing, at which point she modified her search for manufacturers of smart materials with specializations in fabrics. One such company fit. Molykule.

A job for Diane.

"Hi, yes," she spoke into the headset. "It says you can weave material with varied specifications. Could you create something like a bulletproof radiation suit?"

"We can," the support rep answered. "But it is on the pricier side. What do you need this for?"

"How do I put this?" She sighed. "Mr. Devereux, he—he wants to be prepared for a post-apocalyptic world blanketed in nuclear fallout with hordes of survivors fighting each other for food and water."

"Ah," said the support rep. "So, the usual."

"Yeah. So cost is secondary to him." Eve sketched out an arm cuff design on a notepad. "If I gave you our measurements, could you give me a quote?"

"For the both of you?"

"Oh, yeah—pretty sure if he dies, I'm buried alive with him. And this will be a rush job. He just watched a documentary on Chernobyl."

Her next calls were similar, casting Devereux as a paranoid germaphobe and weaponizing his reclusive persona for the most extreme contingencies.

"Yes, I'm interested in commissioning a doomsday bunker," she said. "No, we don't have a plot of land yet. I'm just trying to get cost. Uh-huh. No. We're not interested in a community. We want to be as far away from everyone as possible. I can hold."

Next she needed more money. She switched tabs on her browser to a page entitled "Crypto Trading for Beginners."

11

(sterling silver)

Simon sailed into the lab in a sterling-silver suit and tie. This morning marked the culmination of months of work and hundreds of millions of dollars. The launch of Pierce Technologies's Fusion Power division. Simon had devised his own specialized laser array unlike other inertial confinement projects. Smaller size. Less start-up power. Greater amplification. Once the board got wind of its success, they were sure to fall in line.

Simon slowed to a stop, savoring the majesty of his brilliance.

"Dr. Pierce." An older scientist with dreadlocks approached him, tablet in hand.

"Dr. Bennett." Simon's smile glinted. "Ready to make history?"

"Well, I have some concerns."

"There's nothing to worry about. You're going to push a button or two; it'll be fine. Look—Dr. Vandekamp can do it if you want."

A young woman turned to them, quizzical. "Well, I—"

"See?" Simon glanced at Vandekamp. "Way to be a team player. Thanks."

Bennett sighed, presenting him the tablet. "That's not what I mean. It's the unconventional arrangement of the laser array—"

"But that's the point. Amplifying each successive cycle."

"Yes, but we didn't test that."

"That's what we're doing now."

"I meant in the lab."

"What do you think this is?"

Bennett inhaled slow, then exhaled. "That would be an incredible amount of ener—"

"It's a fusion reactor!" Simon grinned. "We'll be lucky if we get one one-thousandth of what we put in."

"I understand that, but if you look at my calc—"

"You only get so far with calculations." Simon waved off Bennett's words. "If you want to figure out real-world problems, nothing beats good old-fashioned trial and error."

"Please take a moment to consider the design may not have enough safeguards if we succeed in generating the amount of energy you're talking about."

"Dr. Bennett." Simon paused, thoughtful. "I hear your concerns and appreciate your input. You're a valued member of this team, and I couldn't have done any of this without you." He pivoted to the lab. "Let's fire this baby up!"

The technicians scrambled to their posts. Muffled whirs rose into a heavy vibration as the lasers on the other side of the wall revved. The technicians shouted confirmations back and forth. Simple facts, nothing more. They watched the four screens overhead. Inanimate pipes and tubes. The beam fired. Everyone fell silent. First amplification. Second amplification. Third amplification. Fourth amplification. The beams reached the target chamber, converging on a deuterium-tritium pearl several millimeters in diameter.

A bestial rumble quaked the room. A white-hot flash filled the screens as the chamber burst. The laser array arms collapsed. Twisted metal flew into the cameras. The video feed cut out. The resulting explosions were muted by layers of rock. The metallic whine of sirens blared. Thin wisps of smoke leaked in from the adjoining wall.

Simon leaned over the rail, white-knuckled. "What was the efficiency on that?!"

Frazzled, Dr. Vandekamp scanned the monitor. "For—forty-eight percent."

"Forty-eight percent!" Simon turned to Bennett, ecstatic. "You believe that!? That's monumental for a first-run!"

Bennett shook his head. "But the entire unit's—"

"So we build another one!" He raised a triumphant finger. "A better one. Better lasers. Bring us up to a ninety-six percent. Maybe more. That's progress."

"But this whole thing cost—"

"That's for me to worry about," said Simon. "Eventually we're going to take all this and condense it into—well, the size of something you could fit in the back of a truck. Dr. Vandekamp, email me those specs. Thanks—really appreciate it."

He snapped his fingers and pointed at the ragged scientists as though they'd won a championship together. "Great work, everybody! Let's get a cleanup crew in there, all right?"

Smoke filtered into the room as Simon exited the lab.

* * *

A half hour later, Simon stepped onto the executive floor at Pierce Technologies. He slowed. Two more agents were chatting with Box-Head and Potato-Man. A hefty man with a thin mustache-goatee and a young woman with jet black hair. More friends.

"Dr. Pierce," she said. "Agent Melinda Masuda. This is Agent Manuel Guzman."

Simon smiled. "Oh, are you here to pick up the boys?"

She smirked. "We need to ask you a few questions."

"Well, I thought Agent Callahan gave an exhaustive interrogatory."

"And we have more. Different, other, better questions."

"Better questions?" he asked, cheerful. "Fantastic. Right this way."

He strode into his office. Guzman closed the door behind them, while Masuda took immediate note of Simon's desk.

"*Dorodango*." She pointed to the sphere.

She didn't possess Callahan's detachment. She wanted him to know she was clever.

Simon grinned. "That's right."

"My uncle's obsessed with it. Like an addiction. We're really worried about him. You should watch out."

"I'll keep that in mind." He nodded, inviting them to sit. Should be fun.

"I'm fine," she answered.

Guzman stood behind a chair, taking out a small notepad and pen.

The big guy was quiet. Conscientious. A bloodhound. Callahan had sent them for a reason.

Simon sat at his desk.

Masuda paced, pausing to inspect a large chunk of turquoise. "So how extensive was your background check on Dr. Freitas?"

"That's more of a Human Resources question," said Simon. "I know my name's on the building, but I don't make all the hiring decisions."

"Except you signed off on his hiring." She stepped to a jagged piece of malachite.

"Possibly. Would've been years ago."

"Two years ago. Were you aware he's a native of Macao?"

"No." Simon shrugged. "But my understanding is Macao's a special administrative region and not subject to Chinese law."

"True." Masuda nodded. "Unless, he worked in mainland China for several years under the name Heng Luo and didn't disclose that."

Chang had already infiltrated the company. Quite flattering, really. And advantageous in this situation.

Simon didn't blink. "Well, that would be troubling, wouldn't it?"

Guzman looked up from his notes, Simon acknowledged him with a raise of his eyebrows.

"And who would have handled background checks at the time?" Masuda examined the dinosaur egg.

People don't like people smarter than them—makes them feel inferior.

"Susan Schnichtner," he said. "Would you like to speak with her?"

"No, that's all right. So, you don't remember an email asking her to fast-track Dr. Freitas?"

"Afraid I don't."

"Any idea why you'd do that?"

He shrugged. "Mining operation in Utah...?"

"South Henry Mountain," she said, facing him.

He snapped a finger and pointed. "That's the one."

"How well do you know Randal Chang?"

"I know he's a successful entrepreneur based in Hong Kong."

"I meant your personal relationship with him."

"We spoke briefly at a tech conference last year."

"And what was the substance of that conversation?"

"Trivial?" Simon snickered. "Hi, *how are you*, small talk."

"Are you aware Randal Chang owned a company Heng Luo worked for in mainland China—I'm sorry, Frederico Freitas worked for in China?"

Simon shook his head, pleased his answer was genuine. "No, I wasn't."

"So last year was the first time you met Randal Chang?"

"Well, no. We'd run into each other before, would've been years ago."

"Years ago as in when Freitas was hired, or years ago before that?"

Thinks she's so clever.

Simon didn't flinch. "Before he was hired."

"You have any recent contact with Randal Chang?" she asked.

"I spoke with him the morning this whole kerfuffle started."

Guzman checked Masuda's irritated expression.

"And what did you discuss with him?" she asked.

Simon leaned forward, elbows on the desk. "He offered the possibility of shifting production to one of his facilities."

"And," said Guzman, "you didn't think it was a bad idea to talk to somebody who may have ties to the Chinese government?"

"Well, obviously if I had known...something...was missing at the time, I wouldn't have spoken to him." Simon shrugged. "But, otherwise, he was just a business person asking me a business question about my business. I didn't think anything of it. I mean, I'm more of a scientist, really."

Dumbfounded, Masuda and Guzman stared back at his vacant, easygoing smile.

"You know, now that I think about it," said Simon, "Freitas had a recommendation letter from Dr. Bhandari, but I'm not even sure how they know each other."

Masuda's eyes slid to Guzman.

Simon watched her lips tense in frustration. His hint was too convenient—yet too suspect to ignore.

She sighed. "And where is Dr. Bhandari?"

Simon checked his watch. Eleven a.m. "Should be in her office. Fifth floor."

"You have a copy of this letter on file?" asked Guzman.

He nodded. "HR would have it. I can take you down there."

Simon stood, ushering them out. He tapped his smartwatch as they turned their backs, dialing his direct line. His desk phone rang.

"Oh." Simon pulled back. "That's one of the investors—forgot about that."

He turned to his secretary. "Sasha, could you escort Agent Guzman to HR and Agent Masuda to Dr. Bhandari? Thanks. I have to take this."

Guzman met Masuda's aggravated scowl with a subtle wave, cautioning patience as they followed Sasha.

Simon slipped into his office and closed the door.

He picked up the phone, pretending to be on a call. "Hello, this is Simon Pierce." He smiled, checking his smartwatch as he spoke. "Yes—yes, of course, I remember. Uh-huh. Well, I was under the impression that fell into the discretionary budget and we could—ah...I see. Isn't there some sort of tax write off or something? Uh-huh. Uh-huh. Well, you know, we can make an event out of it, if that's what needs to happen. Tell you what—let me talk to Marketing, and let's see what they come up with. Yeah. No—no, I totally understand. No harm done. I'll let you know. Alright. Talk to you later. Bye."

At eleven ten, he stepped out of his office.

"Well, that went better than I thought," he said to Hargrove. "They're not back yet?"

It was obvious to Hargrove they weren't. "No?"

Simon nodded. He sailed toward the elevators and banked right, counting his steps into the nook. He stopped to gaze out the window, and stuck his hands into his pockets.

Deepa rounded the corner, then backed away. "Sorry."

"Oh, no, it's fine." He faced her. "You already talk to Agent Masuda?"

"Agent Masuda?"

He nodded. "She's looking for you."

"Did she say why?"

"Something about Freitas, and a recommendation letter? China?" He shrugged. "I don't know."

Panic filled her eyes.

"Deepa, if there's something wrong..." Simon tilted his head, offering a compassionate ear. "I'm sure if you just explain it to them—"

"You don't understand," she said in a hush.

"About what?" The elevator chimed behind his words.

"The...the whole thing." Deepa struggled. "My partner, she—she didn't know. We were just trying to make connections, network. They wanted to know what we were working on, and they dumped all this money in front of us, and—our student loans were gone. I mean, do you know what the average salary is for a geologist!? Then they were like, *Help us get this guy hired,* and I was like, *Sure!* You have to help me. We didn't know what we were doing. It was a mistake. We just made a bunch of mistakes."

Deepa turned, meeting eyes with Masuda.

"Of course, I'll help you," Simon said with a toothy smile. "Any way I can."

12

(silver, yellow)

Russo and Velez huddled at their desks amid the din of the bullpen.

"All right, so we're sure they used the fire escape," said Russo.

She sipped her coffee. "Explains how they got the cameras out the wall."

"Then why leave the ones at Milner's place?"

"Maybe that flash?" She shrugged, shaking her head. "But if they fried the security system, why not do the same thing downstairs?"

He grunted. Velez fixated on her coffee. Silence conquered their brainstorming session.

"You two look like you could use a break." Tanya strolled in with a laptop. "DMV came through with the traffic cams."

"Thank god," Russo muttered.

She pulled up a chair between them and pointed to a blurry image on screen. A blonde woman with glasses, frozen in time as she pulled a hoodie over her head, exiting a back alley.

"Holy Christ," said Russo. "She's got to be like seven feet tall."

"Maybe it's the angle," said Velez.

"Nah." Russo shook his head, pointing. "See that window? It's eighty-four inches from the ground."

"And how do you know that?" asked Tanya.

"Drive-by shooting when I first moved out here, before they prettied up the neighborhood. Had to give testimony on that one."

"Can you bring it up any more?" asked Velez.

Tanya frowned. "That's the problem with these street cams—great coverage, not so great resolution. And it's dark."

She hit Play. The woman disappeared around the corner.

"Somebody must've seen her," said Russo.

The video played on. A little red hatchback pulled out of the side street and sped off.

"Like that guy," he said. "Can we get the plate?"

"Maybe the next intersection—hang on." Tanya sifted through the footage.

She brought up the video, zooming in on the hatchback's bumper, illuminated by the street lights.

"That's Eugene Hughes's car," said Russo.

"Who?" asked Tanya.

"A no-show at Milner's little get-together." Velez rolled back to her own laptop.

"He's missing, too," said Russo. "Couple detectives at Olympic are working that one. Ain't done much better than we have."

"So, Milner and Hughes faked it?" asked Tanya.

"Maybe," said Velez. "Looks like Porter ran his plate yesterday."

The detectives hustled downstairs and caught up with Officer Porter, a lean guy with a trimmed fade.

"Yeah," he said. "Took a statement from Terrence Moss. Said he'd been talking to his girlfriend on his way home from his shift at L.A. General. He was like five minutes away when she hung up to take out the trash...never came back. "

"And he didn't see anybody?" asked Velez.

"He got home, she wasn't there." Porter shrugged. "He waited a couple minutes, tried calling her, and when she didn't answer, he went downstairs."

"You get a warrant for the building's cameras?"

"We did," said Porter. "But the footage cuts out around eleven-ten. And the camera was gone. Like somebody ripped it out the wall. That's why we pulled the traffic cams and got your guy's name."

"Got a case number?" Russo asked.

"Yeah." Porter thumbed through his notepad.

Thirty minutes later, Velez and Russo returned to Milner's building and stalked through the alley. Velez crouched, squinting at a tiny pile of broken metal and glass, unrecognizable traces of the camera's housing. She gathered up as much grit as she could with her gloved thumb and forefinger, dropping it into a plastic bag. She stood, finding Russo peering into the dumpster.

He hopped off, dusting his hands clean. "Got to check with sanitation, find out when they pick up and where they drop."

Next stop was Eugene's, a half-hour across town. The detectives handling the case granted them access to the apartment, eager for any new information.

"The kid's mom called it in." Russo perused the posters and action figures. "Santiago says somebody wiped the place down, especially the kitchen."

"Yeah, they never get everything," Velez muttered.

"Well, Forensics only found one set of prints."

She scanned the floor and crouched, running gloved fingers across the carpet. A thin golden strand twisted around her fingertips they passed. She lifted the blond hair and stood.

"See?" She pulled an evidence baggie from her jacket.

Russo mugged, impressed, and scanned the room once more. "He's got quite a collection."

"Looks like my teenage cousin's bedroom." She sealed the bag. "Maybe whoever this woman is seduced him, and he spilled his guts, you know? My boss is rich—I know where he keeps everything."

He picked up the notice from the desk. "Loan's paid off. Kid was making money. More than an entry-level gig."

"So maybe he had something on the side." Velez regarded the gaming consoles with more suspicion. "And he was afraid of hanging onto the money so he spent it as soon as he got it. Maybe whoever he was involved with got out of control."

"Maybe."

A thin crust on the Formica countertop near the stove caught Velez's eye. She squinted, leaning in to identify it.

"What's that?"

"Don't know." She reached out a gloved fingertip. Could be drugs. She dug into her jacket and produced a small vial, filling it with whatever bit of the substance she gathered.

She faced him, considering their revisit of the crime scenes.

"Thing is," said Velez, "she's the only one leaving the alley."

Russo nodded. "Yeah, hope you brought a change of clothes."

"So, she carries Milner's body down the fire escape?" She plugged a stopper into the vial. "And a computer and a safe? I mean, even if Hughes was helping her—"

"Well, all right, maybe he was already downstairs," said Russo. "And he killed Janelle Sinclair."

"And Mystery Amazon Woman kills him?"

"Yeah."

"So she leaves three bodies in the same dumpster? And when she walks away, where's the computer? Where's the safe?"

"All right, so, maybe she hands it off to someone else."

"And where'd they go?"

"They, uh—stay in the building?" He shook his head, aware of the theory's inadequacy.

Velez smirked. "Well, at least she'll be easy to spot."

* * *

Zach stepped over chunks of broken foundation as he made his way into the den. Mounds of soil were piled in the corners. Eugene, Darien, and Troy were fighting to pull Kevin out of the hole they'd dug in the floor. All of them were filthy.

He folded his arms. "What happened?"

"Tunnel caved in," said Troy.

With a final heave, they brought Kevin above ground. He spat and coughed dirt.

"We just need—" Darien panted "—to reinforce it. You know, like an old mine shaft."

Zach snickered. "You're not digging into the earth's crust. You basically created a sinkhole under the house."

"You serious?" asked Kevin.

"Yeah." He nodded. "The soil's too loose. I mean, there's no rain here, but you should still probably fill this dirt back in."

"Could we..." Eugene chuffed. "Do that...after a break?"

* * *

Eve devoted her day to etching circuit boards, soldering connections, and wiring the foundations of the arm cuff. She'd studied where to put potentiometers and varistors to regulate voltage. Integrated circuits at key junctures would add functionality.

Hours passed until she checked the clock. She'd skipped lunch and needed to grab a bite before Quinn's show. Anxiety and low blood sugar shivered her belly. Meeting Quinn's friends. After seeing the crowd at the roadhouse, she figured they'd be avant-garde. And she'd been too drunk the day they'd met to remember the people at the third bar. She'd left without talking to anyone.

Had that been rude?

Yes.

They thought she was aloof?

They think you're a snob.

Her reflection warped in the chrome rim surrounding the magnifying glass with the lamp's glint. Her nose was too pointy, her face too drawn. Like a witch. Maybe burying it behind glasses and fake hair wasn't enough.

What did Quinn see?

An ugly, stupid, loser freak in a wig.

She blew a long, stilted huff. Dread sank its chartreuse and purple claws into her thoughts.

"No." She scooted back in her chair. "She wouldn't hang out with me if she didn't like me."

She wants to make fun of you with her real friends.

"No, no—she likes Kira."

If she finds out you're lying, she'll hate you.

"Then she won't." Eve stood, then turned off the lamp and soldering iron.

All the parts were there. She didn't want to start assembling them and run into issues with only a couple hours to work. Tomorrow's project. A full day dedicated to her masterpiece.

* * *

On short notice, Quinn had secured a venue. It was a cozy tavern with wood tables and chairs in little alcoves. The modest stage in the corner was a single step above ground level. Eve arrived after seven-thirty, her strained eyes still burning. Middle-aged regulars mingled. By eight, a younger crowd moved in. Couples and foursomes. From her bar stool, Eve could tell Quinn's music was background noise as televised sports and loud conversations took precedence.

"We can't put on the jukebox?" a guy asked.

"Not tonight," the bartender answered. "Sorry."

Eve cringed. Quinn's guitar work was excellent, her voice spot-on, even the mic was at the right level. It was the songs. They were good, but Eve didn't recognize any of them. And a couple were really sad. A meager round of applause followed Quinn's announcement she was taking a break.

She met Eve with a grim scowl.

"You're doing great." Eve gave a thumb's up. "You sound amazing."

"This was a terrible idea," Quinn muttered. "They're not even paying attention. That's worse than being booed at."

"I mean, I don't know any of these songs." Eve shrugged.

"It's all original stuff." Quinn picked up a beer.

"Oh—well, I figured your friends would be more supportive."

"I really didn't tell anybody else."

Her relief was short-lived. "Well, why not?"

"They just know me differently, and, I'm trying something new."

"Why didn't you put a band together first?"

"I told you—it was supposed be us. And it didn't feel right to play our songs with other people. Then it was too short notice, and—I don't know." Out of habit, she downed her beer. "This was a bad idea."

Eve took the empty glass from her. "Okay, it's just different. And new. So it's a little scary. Just—play stuff they know."

"That's what I was trying to avoid," Quinn whispered. "The girl playing cover songs on her acoustic guitar."

"Well," Eve whispered. "You...are that girl playing her acoustic guitar."

"It's like I'm starting all over again."

"It's just a step. A necessary step. It's not forever. It's the beginning of a new, different Quinn." Eve nodded with reassurance. Sparkles of gold, mint, and pink. Charlotte.

Quinn sighed, begrudging. "Any requests?"

"I'm a sucker for Fleetwood Mac." She shrugged.

"Me, too." She smiled, stepping away.

"She's cutoff, by the way." Eve said to the bartender as Quinn took the stage. "Just give her water."

A familiar riff vibrated the air, accompanied by it's infamous bassline. *Rhiannon*. The chords echoed. The chatter fell out of the room. Heads turned to the stage in disbelief as Quinn's voice haunted the tavern. A trio of rowdy college guys sitting at a booth were quieted, the biggest of them captivated. His skinny buddy teased him and the husky guy silenced him with a backhand.

The next round of applause was louder, exuberant. Quinn's eyes met Kira's. The rock star wouldn't give herself away with a smile, but her friend did. She demonstrated range. The Allman Brothers. Nirvana. Queen. Dolly Parton. Prince. The crowd had requests. By the end of the night, she had a jar full of cash.

The husky frat boy approached as Quinn unplugged the amp.

"You've got an incredible voice," he said.

"Thank you." Quinn nodded.

"Selling any CD's, or you have a website?"

"That's a work in progress."

"Cool. I'm Wes, by the way." He pointed to the amp. "You need any help?"

"No, we're good." Eve stepped in.

"This is my friend Kira." Quinn smirked. "And sometimes bodyguard, sometimes roadie."

"Bodyguard, huh?" Wes's skinny friend joked. "Let's see what you got."

He put up his fists like old-time boxer. Eve poked a finger into his shoulder and sent the kid stumbling into the chairs behind him. A tickle of satisfaction rose up. Bubbles of deep blue, pink, and green.

He steadied himself, standing. “Yeah, so, I’m going to go.”

The kid staggered away. Kira eyed Wes.

“Should probably go help your friend,” she said. “Seems kind of drunk.”

“Yeah.” Wes focused on Quinn. “So, you doing more shows any time soon?”

“Well, I don’t have anything lined up yet, but, I might be back here.”

“Cool.” He nodded, wobbling on his heels at Eve’s gaze. “All right, well, I’ll be on the look out. Good luck.”

He walked off, shoving his hands into his pockets.

“Why’d you do that?” Quinn asked with a quiet smile.

“Oh, I’m sorry,” Eve answered with thick sarcasm. “Were you actually interested?”

“No, but it’s, you know—you’ve never wanted to date a musician before?”

“Oh.” Eve scoffed. “Okay.”

“It happens a lot, and”—Quinn shrugged—“he’s not the worst guy who’s ever tried.”

“He’s practically a child,” she said in a hush.

“Maybe to you,” Quinn said with a playful smirk.

Eve gasped with a chuckle. “You bitch.”

* * *

The timer had shut off the architect lamp above the mini-house hours ago. The housemates had settled into bed. Darien and Cassidy had taken the main bedroom. Troy and Eugene shared the second, Kevin and Zach the third, leaving Janelle with her own room.

The guestroom door creaked open. Rays of blinding light flooded the house’s windows, broken by Eve’s encroaching form and the gentle tremble of her steps.

“Oh god,” said Eugene. “What do you think she wants?”

“I don’t know, dude,” Troy answered. “Just relax.”

The housemates held their breath as she neared.

“This is how it starts, man.” Zach muttered. “Waking us up in the middle of the night with all kinds of crazy shit.”

Kevin answered with a deep snore, unaware of the situation.

The lid lifted from the box, shuddering the house.

“Janelle?” Eve whispered. “Can I talk to Janelle?”

Janelle stared at the ceiling, intense light bleeding through the curtains. “Oh, what the hell is this?”

“Sorry, everybody,” Eve mumbled. “I know it’s late.”

Janelle slid on a pair of slippers. She opened the front door, shielding her eyes.

"Sorry, sorry." Eve whispered, closing the door behind her.

The room dimmed, and Janelle lowered her hand. Eve was still in Kira's clothes, minus the wig and glasses.

"You requested my presence," said Janelle.

"Yeah, you said you were in marketing?"

"Marketing analyst."

"You know anything about the music industry?"

Janelle sighed, coarse. "I know it's highly competitive."

"All right, I know somebody, and they're really good. And, I want to help their career. Like, make them a star. How do I do that?"

"Well, there's no formula. I mean, record companies dump millions of dollars into talent, and even with all their metrics and data, sometimes it doesn't matter. You never know what's going to catch on."

"This will. What do I need to do?"

"Well, they need a demo. Doesn't have to be studio quality, but it does have to be an excellent sample of what they do. Take that to a producer—a real producer—not somebody who's going ask for a whole bunch of money upfront, make a bunch of promises, and not deliver."

"So I've heard."

"You're better off finding a consultant. And, you know, your friend might have a modestly successful career." Janelle shrugged. "But the odds of becoming rich and famous aren't great."

"No." Eve nodded. "She's a fucking rock star."

13

(silver, blue green)

Though Talbot's notes said he'd removed the fragment from the *modifikator* on a regular basis, Eve didn't want to disturb whatever delicate balance he'd created between it and his homemade betavoltaic battery. Plus, her calculations were based off the testing rig and different charges running through the *modifikator*. Her solution was much the same, with the *modifikator* acting as a component which could be inserted to or ejected from the arm cuff's housing. She figured once she obtained more knowledge, more fragments, she'd have more freedom to experiment. After testing connections and individual mechanisms, its own set of dials and switches, Eve set the cuff onto the desktop.

She slid the *modifikator* antenna-first into a special slot in the housing. It locked in place and she closed the cover. She rested the cuff on her left forearm, pulling the latch closed, and it clamped shut. Her belly tingled and tightened. Electric blue and white.

You don't know what you're doing.

She swallowed a deep breath. "This is going to work. It's worked before. There's nothing to worry about."

Another deep breath, frigid air coating her windpipe.

She turned the dial and clicked the switch into the first setting. Eve pressed the button, a blast coursing through her. The initial rush of adrenaline subsided. She didn't feel any different. She reached a hand out. It passed through the office wall. She yanked it back, the fluid sensation of her particles flittering back to her. Filled with nervous joy,

Eve stepped through the wall. Drywall and stud molecules filtered through her. It reminded her of sticking her head out a moving car. Her particles rushed up behind as she drifted away from the wall and into the bedroom.

She couldn't celebrate. Changing was one thing—changing back was another. Throes of anxiety wobbled her insides.

Relief as her finger touched the dial button, solid to her. She turned the dial and switches to the return position and pressed the button. Another blast. She reached out her hand, placing it on the bedroom door and slapped the surface with triumphant gasps.

Eve rushed back to the office to review her notes and adjust the settings. She hit the button and stepped toward her phone, checking for her reflection. She was invisible.

"Oh, yes—yes," she whispered. But she couldn't see the arm cuff, her hands or any other part of her. "Oh, no—oh, fuck! Fuck!"

She made a frantic scan of her notes. Then she hovered her thumb and forefinger in the general area where she suspected the dial button still was. With a feather's touch, she detected the dial on the cuff.

"Uhhhhh—okay, okay, so—so it was two down, so it should be... three clicks up and one-quarter turn."

She dialed the setting and pressed the button. Visible.

"Oh, thank god," she gasped. "Okay, got to remember that—whatever clicks I am away from neutral position. Should probably build a fail-safe."

She recalled an invisible super-dense orange she'd created earlier. She'd want to test such a function before attempting to layer fields on herself. She took off the cuff and reviewed her schematics. Since she'd taken AngDroid's advice and left room for upgrades, a fail-safe wasn't too difficult to install.

AngDroid's videos played in the background as Eve soldered.

"Time to level up your make!" AngDroid announced.

"Seen it." She muttered, clicking Next.

"And now," said AngDroid, "something a little different. More of a PSA, I think. I've gotten lots of emails from makers asking the best ways to attach magnets to their heads. Or in their heads. Or implanting them in their bodies along with chips, sensors, and antennae. So, this episode, I'd like to discuss actual bionics and why, maybe, DIYing this isn't such a great idea."

Eve got pulled into AngDroid's lesson on transhumanism. She sprinted across the internet for brain-machine interfaces. To her disappointment, there were no homemade options. The technology was still in its infancy, confined to research, though loads of papers had been written. Universities the world over were exploring applications and limitations. Eve watched people with robotic prosthetic arms and legs, students wearing caps dotted with sensors controlling quadcopters in flight.

"Award-winning research at CalTech has led to a promising prototype for a groundbreaking brain-to-machine interface."

Eve gawked, entranced, as they demonstrated how it integrated with any system.

"Designed by researcher Shadi Al-Sana, the breakthrough surpasses current technology developed by a dozen other universities and even the U.S. military. Although funding has been pouring in, researchers caution the design is still just a prototype and wouldn't be commercially viable for several years."

Eve hit Pause. "But I want it now."

Her eyes lowered to the arm cuff. It would be a serious upgrade. Sneaking into the university could be practice before infiltrating Pierce Technologies. And if she couldn't find the prototype itself, then maybe she'd get the schematics.

* * *

Lamp posts illuminated in staggered order across the university campus amid the dusky haze. Few students and faculty roamed the paths. Eve lingered in the gathering darkness of the parking garage, dressed like a motorcyclist. Black from head to toe. Gloves and boots. She'd picked up a sleek helmet with an opaque full-face visor from a shop north of the warehouses. The dealer had told her they were only made and sold in India, and the visor had night vision. Though dubious at the time, she found the clarity impressive as she slunk behind a row of shrubs. She pressed the button on the arm cuff. Violet, then blue.

Invisible. No shadow under the lamps.

She checked over her shoulder, hurrying onto the path, and stumbled into a bike rack.

"Shit." The bicycles jostled.

A college guy looked up from his phone. He glanced around.

Eve froze, watching him. She edged away from the bikes and bumped into a lamp post with a gong. The light trembled.

The college guy's eyes widened, and he backed away.

Eve dashed off.

She trekked across the campus, up the steps of a stunning building of copper and mirrored glass, still gleaming aqua in twilight. She turned the dial again. With a press of the button, she became intangible and phased through the doors.

She stepped into a pristine lobby of white marble and bamboo paneling. She checked the directory posted on the corner as two professors walked right through her. Eve reached a door at the end of the hall and passed inside.

Computer stations, patient beds, electrophysiology rigs, oscilloscopes, sensory equipment, and a variety of neurological monitoring devices filled the lab. But no prototype. She phased through an adjoining door. Inside, an engineering lab. The prototype rested in a heavy-duty hard case. Though no more than a collection of wires, it had been placed with care. The top portion was an EEG net. Silver orbs for sensors were netted together with sturdy mesh. The wires connecting it flowed into a series of longer cables with port connectors at the other end.

Better than schematics.

She hit the fail-safe and, with a flash of sepia and myrtle, returned to a visible, solid state. Eve closed the case's lid and snapped the clasps shut. She turned the dial and set the switches, then shrank the case to an inch and a half. She stuck it into a leather pouch on her hip as the door to the engineering lab swept open.

"How'd you get in here?" a woman demanded behind her.

Eve swung around. The young woman from the video, her big brown eyes a mix of shock and annoyance.

Damn. She already had seven angry mouths to feed.

What's one more then?

Eve aimed the arm cuff at her.

Shadi turned to run. The blast struck her. With each step, escape grew further and further away.

* * *

Forty minutes later, Eve was in her home office. She enlarged the hard case to normal and set it aside. She opened another pouch and prompted Shadi to climb onto her fingers.

"Go ahead." Eve nodded. "It's okay."

She lowered the terrified woman onto the desk.

"This, this isn't possible." Shadi goggled at her new surroundings.

"And yet here we are." Eve smiled, ruffling the hair in the back of her head.

"What are you going to do to me?"

"Oh—no, nothing—I'm not going to do anything to you. I just need your help merging your machine with this."

She held up the arm cuff.

"No." Shadi's eyes blazed with defiance. "I won't."

"Really? It would be a lot easier if you said yes."

"Oh, so now you're going to hurt me?"

"Well, no, but I mean—I don't want to. I'm not going to..." Eve sighed, distracted by a low, grinding hum. She checked over her shoulder, and the noise vanished. A little tickle inside. Waves of indigo, pink, and green, a flash of crimson. Frustration. This little person was getting in her way.

Eve returned her attention to Shadi. "You're not the only one working on this. I promised I wouldn't hurt you. I didn't say anything about them."

Shadi's mind filled with the faces of her fellow researchers. People she'd worked with for years. Teachers, partners, friends—at this point, family. "Fine. I'll do it."

"See?" Eve cocked on eyebrow. "Easy."

She glimpsed the equations on the white boards. "You're clearly an intelligent person. This prototype could help millions." Then she spied the burnt patch of carpet.

"It will." She nodded. "And a lot sooner than a few years."

Shadi found Eve combative at times, refusing to explain her creation in detail, or the suit it was being stitched into, and only revealing hardware specifications when necessary. But Eve was full of questions. She wouldn't pick up the soldering iron until Shadi alleviated her doubts. They worked late into the night.

When they finished, Eve interrogated Shadi on the prototype's functionality and operation, logging her answers and reviewing them. She asked more questions, and scribbled more answers. Once satisfied, Eve stood and left the room without a word. She returned moments later, setting the back of her hand flat against the desk.

"Thank you, I know that was a lot."

Shadi stared at the open palm, then up at her. "What are you going to do with me?"

"Taking you some place safe. It's okay."

"No." She backed away, glancing about for options to run.

"All right—this is me being polite. I could just pick you up."

Reluctant, Shadi climbed into her hand. A rush of air washed over her and Shadi steadied herself with each jostling footstep.

Her expression curdled at the sight of the house. "What is this?"

"You don't want electricity and running water?" asked Eve.

* * *

Troy, Eugene, and Zach were playing video games when the house rumbled with their captor's approach. They hit Pause. A heavy gust. The lid.

"Ohh no." Janelle groaned from her room. "I am not doing this every night!"

The knock at the front door puzzled the guys. So did the distinct thunder of the lid and the woman's fading steps. Everyone was awake now—except for Kevin who had to be prodded.

They sat Shadi at the dining table, brought her water, and offered food before she recounted her story.

"She somehow broke into my lab, stole the brain interface, and forced me to merge it with her shrinking machine."

"Yeah, that's a little bit of a problem for her," said Zach. "Taking other people's shit."

"It isn't hers?" she asked.

"No."

"Are you sure?" asked Shadi. "She seems to know how it works."

"We don't know." Troy shrugged. "Maybe she invented it and the company was trying to take it from her?"

"Wait a minute." Kevin turned to Shadi. "You're an engineer. Can you figure out a way to use the satellite uplink in the truck to boost our cellphone signals?"

"Dude," said Troy. "She just got here."

"You want to get out of here or what?" asked Kevin.

"I want to get out of here." Shadi nodded. "Can the truck connect to anything?"

He shook his head. "Not since it's been shrunk."

She sighed. "Well, then it's doubtful we could use it. Our devices simply don't have the power to connect to the satellite network."

Dejection swept over the housemates.

"But," said Shadi, "we might be able to use the truck's antenna to amplify our ability to connect to wireless, provided we have a strong enough signal."

"I know her Wi-Fi passwords," said Eugene. "I helped her configure like three VPN servers."

"For what?" Zach asked. "Why would anybody need that?"

"I don't know." He shrugged. "They're all for different phones. She's got, like, a platinum subscription."

"Whatever, doesn't matter," said Zach. "We're still in a box."

"Right," said Shadi. "About how high would you say those walls are?"

"To us?" Kevin pondered. "Thirty-five feet, maybe?"

"All right." Shadi quieted, working out the situation. The housemates fixed on her in anticipation of a revelatory plan. All except for Zach, who stood gobsmacked that this newcomer had become their savior.

"If we can get one of our phones out of here," she said. "We could use it like a satellite."

"Great plan." Zach gave mocking applause. "All right, so, that's not going to work."

"*Shut up, Zach,*" said the other housemates.

"Let her finish," said Troy.

"If one of us has Wi-Fi tethering," she said. "We can use that to connect. And it would be better if we could get it into the air, like with a drone."

"Exactly," said Zach. "And where are we supposed to get a drone from?"

"Didn't we just tell you to shut up?" asked Janelle.

"Yo, dude," said Eugene. "I got a remote-control car. Maybe you could re-purpose that?"

"Maybe," said Shadi. "Let me take a look at it."

He rushed to his bedroom.

"Once it's in the air," said Shadi, "we'll have to line it up with the antenna, that should get us a signal on our phones."

"Yeah, it'll be full of interference," said Zach.

"It's better than nothing," said Troy. "And all we need to do is call nine-one-one."

"Will they still be able to trace the call?" Darien asked.

"I don't know." Shadi shook her head. "At the very least, they might be able to approximate where it's coming from."

"Doesn't matter," said Janelle. "We'd be talking to the police. You know, the people you said would figure out where we were if we were patient?"

Zach fold his arms. "It hasn't been that long. Few weeks, maybe."

Eugene returned with his radio-controlled car, placing it in front of Shadi.

"Will they even understand us?" asked Cassidy. "Or are we just going to sound like mice to them?"

Kevin shrugged. "Might be better if it sounds like a prank call."

Shadi examined the radio-controlled car. "Why does it have a camera?"

All eyes turned to Eugene.

"You little scumbag," said Cassidy.

"No! No," he said with a nervous smile. "It's not what you think. I—I needed it to see."

"See what?" asked Janelle.

"When I was driving it around."

She folded her arms. "Taking your nasty ass pictures."

"No, I swear! I was just using it steal bank information, which probably...doesn't sound better."

"Are you kidding me?" asked Zach.

"Well, you paid us shit."

14

(silver, pink)

No Nukes Now was all about fundraising. Larry spent his day in meetings talking to lobbyists. Quinn sat in a cube farm with a dozen other people, making scripted calls from lists of potential donors. Eve shadowed Barb, learning the fundamentals of annual filing and reporting. It was a little more daunting than the repetitive data entry she was used to. Didn't help Eve was distracted by daydreams of her completed super-suit.

Lucky for her, Barb required several breaks. On one such occasion, Eve grabbed another cup of coffee, and stole away to IT.

Remember, don't be you. Be Kira.

Powell raised his eyebrows. "Can I help you with something?"

She pointed to the wall. "Your maps."

"What about them?"

"Well, you didn't really explain how you found those spots."

"Yeah, Larry doesn't like it when I—I shouldn't have said anything, all right?"

"Well, you can't do that." She snickered. "Because now I want to know."

He shot her a skeptical scowl. "You really want to know?"

"Yeah. I mean, it didn't sound like you were making it up."

He hesitated to answer.

"And it wouldn't surprise me if the government was lying about the number of nuclear weapons in its stockpile."

"All right," he said. "But don't tell anybody. Especially Larry."

"Of course." Her eyes lit up. "It's top secret."

She pulled up a chair as he minimized several windows and opened a new browser, revealing for an instant his desktop wallpaper—a series of jagged limestone pillars stretching to the horizon.

"The Tsingy de Bemaraha."

"Yeah," he said surprised she knew of it, and the correct pronunciation.

"It's on my bucket list."

"Same." He nodded, regarding her a little higher than before.

She hid a curious smirk. Eve would've suspected his bucket list consisted of Los Alamos and the Bermuda Triangle.

A satellite map of the earth appeared. Powell zoomed down to the western part of Nevada.

"So, it's pretty easy," he said. "We'll start here because this where a lot of known air force bases are. When we zoom in, we can see most of it. Obviously we can't see everything, but from what they show us and what they don't show us, we can see how they alter the satellite images."

He zoomed in further, circling the cursor around nearby pixelization. "There. I mean, it doesn't look like anything—it's desert, right? But we know the base is there, so the satellite captured something they had to erase."

"I don't understand—so, you're just looking through hundreds of thousands of acres for pixelated squares on a map?"

"Well, no." He snickered, pulling out his phone. "That would take forever."

He thumbed through the phone's browser, pulling up a tab for a message board. The FoilHat Collective.

"That's where these guys come in. They drive out to some place they suspect is—something—and drop the coordinates online. Like this one."

He tapped a message with the subject line *Tower 82* (purple, taupe, yellow) and entered the coordinates into the map.

"This is, supposedly, the premier testing ground for the most advanced aircraft the US has developed over the past forty years. Not more than sixty miles from downtown. And if we zoom in—"

The map's resolution refined.

"We get this."

East of the mountains, craggy red earth. Portions faded to a dull pink, devoid of buildings, unnatural in their shape. The irregular spots appeared organic, until Powell zoomed in closer and the detail in the surrounding areas betrayed their camouflage. The irregular portions had been pixelated.

"And that's it." He shrugged. "All you need is a few former officers paranoid about the threat of nuclear war or worried about some people having too much power, and they drop little hints."

"Wow. Not even the government can quarantine the past."

"Nice Pavement reference." The corner of his lip rose. "I must've listened to *Crooked Rain* till I wore out the cassette. Oh—well, do you know what cassettes are?"

He's being polite. He knows you're ancient.

"Yes. Unfortunately." She nodded.

"Well, I mean, you've got to admit, there was something fun about making mix-tapes."

A flutter of pastels—pink, blue, and yellow.

"Yeah." She smiled. "Yeah, there was. Hunting for songs on the radio..."

"For hours." He grinned. "And trying copy cassettes when you didn't have a dual player?"

"Yes! I had to hold my sister's Hello Kitty tape player next to my stereo."

"It taught us ingenuity." He chuckled, then shook his head. "Yeah, but my *Crooked Rain* tape—that was the Christmas I asked for a CD player. Think it started my obsession with technology."

"When did the obsession with missile silos start?"

"Chasing a UFO with my best friend's girlfriend."

"See—that's another story you just can't start and not finish."

"Kira," Quinn's voice piped.

Startled, they turned to find her standing in the doorway.

Quinn smiled. "Just wondering if you wanted to grab lunch, unless you already have plans?"

Her eyes sparkled in amusement as Eve and Powell fumbled, refusing to look at one another.

The flutter of pastels was squelched by a thick, charcoal fog.

Eve folded her arms. "Oh, uh—I—"

"Yeah, I usually eat at my desk." Powell shook his head.

"Thanks." She stood. "That was really interesting."

"Sure—just a...weird, little trick."

"Yeah." She backed away. "I'll have to remember that one."

She hurried past Quinn as Powell closed the browser and retreated to his work.

* * *

Shadi spent the morning sourcing items for a homemade soldering iron. The home improvement supplies Eve had left them for repairs provided her with everything else. She commandeered the dining room table, capitalizing on the overhead lighting, and dismantled Eugene's radio-controlled car as the basis for a drone.

After some trial and error, and the sacrifice of a couple electric toothbrushes, she rigged a set of rotors. But the limitations of the remote control wouldn't allow for the additional channels necessary to steer. She slumped in her chair.

"It's not going to work, is it?" Zach sipped from a beer bottle.

"It'll get into the air," she said. "It just won't go anywhere beyond that."

"So I can have my toothbrush back?"

"That's not helpful," said Troy.

"It was a stupid plan, okay?" said Zach. "Let's say she comes in to get Eugene—which, by the way, she hasn't done in ages. We've only got like eight seconds between when she leaves and comes back to put the lid on."

"Well, yeah." Troy nodded. "Eugene's got to turn that eight seconds into sixty."

"Yeah, and once again, we're putting our faith into someone who folds like patio furniture."

"Wait a minute." Shadi sat up. "That pervert put a camera in here—maybe I can use the channel."

Revitalized, she delved back into her project.

* * *

Callahan took pride in the fact that Assistant Director Osgood didn't make frequent appearances in her office. But this morning, he'd invited himself in and shut the door.

"We need a body," he said. "Or a direction. We need—"

"The fragment." She nodded.

His face was still youthful, but the pressures of the job were obvious by his thinning hair.

"No hits on the border?" he asked. "Nothing from TSA?"

"No, sir. But most likely scenario, Talbot went rogue."

"And killed his wife? Forgot his code book?"

"Reasonable if he was in a hurry. And maybe she wouldn't go along with it."

"Kelly." He sighed, dropping into a chair. "People up top, they're telling me, *find it or get out of the way*."

She glanced at the vein bulging on his forehead but focused on his eyes.

"They're not going to steamroll us," he said. "They are going to remove us."

There wouldn't be much opportunity for federal law enforcement dismissed from their posts. Much less if the fragment was used in a terror attack or resurfaced in the form of a new weapon.

"We need to show them something," said Osgood. "The longer this thing is out there...well, I won't be sleeping—I'll tell you that much."

"We've considered the possibility." She sighed. "He made himself small. In which case, there's much less chance he could use the fragment for something destructive."

He blinked. "That doesn't make me feel better. And that's not going to pacify Garza. I mean, we've been given unprecedented resources—"

"Resources don't matter if we can't detect him."

"Well, you need to detect something." Osgood huffed, standing. "Something for them to chase down. Even if just gives you and your team more time."

He reached for the door knob. "Garza wants an update at seventeen hundred. Send me whatever you've got at sixteen."

"Understood."

He opened the door and walked out.

Callahan's mind filled with calamities. Her team getting fired. A shoot-out between Russian agents in downtown Los Angeles. An explosion wiping out city blocks. Her hazel eyes fixed on a picture on the opposite wall—wild horses running across an endless expanse of prairie, mountains in the distance. It wasn't that she didn't care. It was that at some point, caring got in the way of doing. The potential lives at stake depended on her clear head. It was the only way to save them.

The knock at the door didn't register.

"Got a minute?" asked Guzman, with Masuda beside him.

Her focus shifted, accepting their presence. "Yeah."

They sat in front of her desk.

"Okay," said Callahan. "So what happened with Bhandari?"

"Full confession," said Masuda. "Handing over trade secrets regarding government projects to a foreign adversary. Mostly stuff about rare earth deposits and new ways of extracting them, but nothing fragment related."

"Her partner worked at the Jet Propulsion Lab," said Guzman. "Gave away some pretty sensitive information to a Chinese handler. Good news is handler was intercepted at the airport."

"They have anything on Freitas?"

Guzman shook his head. "Claims no connection. As does the Chinese government."

"Of course," said Callahan. "What are the odds the Chinese and the Russians were working the same target?"

"Pretty good." Masuda nodded. "We're thinking Pierce mentioned something to Chang. Maybe to brag, maybe entice him into some other business deal—"

"And the Russians were already running a deep infiltration," said Guzman.

"But the Chinese wouldn't just pull Freitas," said Masuda. "We think he was trying to work Talbot, unaware Talbot was a spy."

"Left eight messages on his phone," he said.

"Jeez."

Masuda smirked. "Desperate, right?"

Callahan leaned back in her chair. "When was that?"

"About a month ago," Guzman answered. "Over the course of a couple weeks."

Callahan's gaze floated to the ceiling. "There were two power outages at Pierce Technologies. And you said a van cleaned out his place the week before."

She dropped back to Earth. "We need to check the video."

They returned to the audiovisual bay and pulled up the footage from the week before Talbot's disappearance.

Callahan scrolled through the timeline. "So, let's say Talbot agrees to meet Freitas on the campus. Let's him know in-person, doesn't text."

"Freitas wouldn't do that." Masuda shook her head. "He'd try to go some place public, where they could talk, drink, build rapport before he convinces him to hand over data."

Guzman shrugged. "Maybe he takes what he can get."

Callahan waved them over.

They crowded in, focusing on the grainy footage of one camera angle. Nighttime. Freitas loitered by a bench. The footage dropped out.

"Now Talbot's free to do whatever he wants," said Callahan.

She fast-forwarded three minutes of blank screen until the footage picked up again.

"And...nothing."

She rewound the footage. Freitas searching, then black. Rewind. Freitas. Fast-forward. Black. The corporate park reappeared.

"Wait." She hit Pause.

She rewound again, scanning back and forth across the different camera angles. She hit Play and pointed to a middle screen. A parked car only visible by the glint of its headlights reflected off a lamppost.

"There."

Another fast-forward. Black. The images returned, the vehicle was gone.

"What kind of car did Freitas drive?"

"An RS7," Guzman and Masuda answered.

They rushed downstairs to the evidence lockers. Boxes of shrunken vehicles remained stored in bins. Guzman heaved one off the shelf and popped open the latches. Masuda reached in and plucked out a steel-gray vehicle, turning it forward and backward, aware of a shifting inside. She held it to her ear and shook it.

She flipped the blade of a pocket knife and dug the tip into the trunk, prying it open. Fine grains trickled out. Sand and kitty litter. She tilted the car over, dumping the rest onto the shelf. A tiny, desiccated human body spilled into the pile. The clothes were rumpled and dusty, his skin taut.

"So Talbot got Freitas." Guzman muttered.

Masuda glanced into the bin. "We should probably check the rest of these, huh?"

* * *

According to Quinn, the spot down the block was cursed. In thirteen months, it had been a burger joint, a French bakery, and a poke bowl place. Now it was Fit to Be Thai. She and Eve sat in the back corner, alongside the windows facing the street.

"I swear I get the same table every time," Quinn said.

"Maybe it's you." Eve scanned the menu.

"Is it? Am I a restaurant-killer?"

"Well, you certainly have the opposite effect on bars."

Quinn chuckled.

"Which reminds me." Eve lifted her eyes. "Do you have a demo?"

"I do." Quinn hesitated, leery. "But I'm working on a new one. Why do you ask?"

"Just curious." She shrugged. "You know, in case I run into a music producer or something."

"Don't. Don't do that."

"I'm trying to motivate you. I don't know how all this works, but at the very least, it would be proof you're writing songs. So whenever you're happy with it, I'd really like a copy. You know—keep you honest."

"All right." Quinn glanced at her menu for a few seconds before she couldn't resist. "So, what's up with you and Powell?"

The center of Eve's chest tightened. A scramble of hot-orange squiggles and obnoxious magenta flashes. She'd had been sworn to secrecy. And there was something with Powell. But the idea of anyone getting close to her already filled her with angst. The added complications of her various alter egos twisted her up her brain.

"Nothing. I asked him a question, and—we were just talking, that's all."

"Don't get all flustered." Quinn delighted in her discomfort.

"I'm not getting flustered. Why're you making this into something?"

"I'm making conversation."

Eve leaned back. "I'm not looking for anything serious right now." She tried focusing on the menu, but glanced at her friend.

"Doesn't have to be serious." Quinn's eyes flared as she shimmied playfully. "You can just have fun."

"I'm not having fun. Nothing fun, nothing serious. Will you just drop it?"

"Jeez." She reared back. "No reason to get all pissy."

See? It's you. Nobody likes you.

Eve traced bits of color from the prices, fretting over what lie to tell.

"Everybody gets a little nervous when they're attracted to somebody," said Quinn. "It's kind of a relief to know you do, too."

"Well." Eve huffed. "Great you think that, but it's just that, I'm—"

A loser? A freak? Liar? Thief. Killer. Kidnapper. Basket case. Pick one. They're all accurate.

She wrestled with what she could say and not jeopardize her alias. Then Gideon filled her mind's eye—followed by the eight shrunken people living in a stolen house in her guest bedroom.

"I'm weird. Like really, really weird. Always have been."

"You're kind of weird." Quinn shrugged. "But so is Powell. And who wants to be normal anyway? Normal's boring."

"Normal helps you get along with people."

"Then you and I are the right amount of weird."

How dare she. Those sparkling aqua eyes. The cute upturned nose. She could make any funky hairstyle or offbeat outfit look good. Just like Charlotte.

"No, you're—" Eve sat forward, preparing her case. "All right. Most little girls want to be a ballerina or a princess for Halloween. I wanted to be a silk moth."

Quinn stifled a laugh. "Why?"

"They were my favorite thing. They're fuzzy and—I just liked them. And my parents were trying to reason with me: do you want to be a fairy or a pixie or butterfly? *No, I want to be a moth.* So they made me this costume out of this plush fabric with extra arms, and wings which were like a cape, because—well, silk moths can't fly."

"They can't?"

"They've been domesticated for over three thousand years. It's been bred out of them."

"Oh."

"Yeah. And they sewed this bonnet with antennae made out of pipe cleaners and put these big, black, round eyes on my head. It was my favorite costume for years. Sometimes I wore it around the house I liked it so much."

"Okay?" Quinn chuckled. "That sounds adorable."

"Yeah, except you're not seven and didn't go to my elementary school. Phillip Farbman told me I looked stupid. And Jenny Wheeler said I was ugly. And when I told them it was a bug they—she and her friends threw all the candy they didn't want at me and said I was gross. When you're a kid, everybody tells you to be yourself. But that's bullshit. You can only be little bits of who are."

"Oh, come on," Quinn shook her head. "Kids are mean. And they don't know shit about the world."

"Well, yeah." Eve scoffed. "I don't care about Jenny Wheeler. Or Tommy Gordon. Or Tiffany Ippolito graffitiing up my locker—it's the past."

Their voices had faded long ago, but their words hadn't. She spoke them in her own voice. Every moment of every day. Stupid. Ugly. Unwanted. Worthless. Behind her every thought, behind her every action. An insidious cycle.

"Doesn't sound like it is," said Quinn. "Is that what you meant by hiding?"

"A little. Maybe. Mostly a career thing."

"Okay." Quinn leaned forward. "As someone who gets up in front of people and risks embarrassing themselves all the time, I can tell you those people don't matter. What matters is the amazing person you are today."

She means Kira.

Eve sighed, peering out the window. She spotted a dour man in a dark blue sedan staring at her from the across the street. Their eyes met. His expression didn't change. Ice-cold white flashed in her vision. He shifted into Drive and pulled away.

Her gaze drifted back to her friend.

"So in a way," said Quinn, "those jerks helped make your awesomeness possible."

"Huh." She smirked, considering her fortunes. "I guess so."

Quinn rocked her shoulders in a jig, pleased she'd lifted her spirits.

Eve watched her mini celebration. "No, but seriously, I'm not in any place for a relationship right now."

Quinn slouched, rasping an irritated growl as she glared at the ceiling.

"What? I'm not."

She smiled. "Just be open to it. Don't hide your awesomeness from the world."

The world would only get bits of it first.

"Okay."

15

(silver, red)

Barb's training devolved into office gossip, complaints about pregnancy, and mindful Do's and Don'ts of their shared workspace. Eve's mind slid back to her new suit. How would it work? Would it work? Were the connections good? Was there something she'd missed? Had Shadi lied to her?

She and Quinn left the building at five-thirty.

"You better be working on that demo," Eve warned from across the parking lot.

"I am!" Quinn grinned.

"I want a copy! I'm serious!"

Her friend shook her head, getting into her car.

The creeping sensation of eyeballs tugged at Eve. She checked over her shoulder. Across the street, the dark blue sedan she'd seen at lunch. The same dour man. She got into the hybrid, watching in the rear-view as Quinn's little sea foam-green car puttered out of the lot.

Probabilities spun. The FBI would've approached her, maybe surrounded the building. But how the hell would the Russians—

Hot yellow.

"Oh, shit." Her chest clenched. "Could be coincidence." She started the engine and backed out. "Maybe he works around here."

But as she drove down the block, the sedan threaded through traffic, tailing her. She couldn't go home. And she couldn't go to Kira's.

Eve hit the accelerator and sped through in the intersection. He followed, cutting off a passing city bus. She pulled onto the freeway, careening between cars and trucks. The sedan coasted behind, zipping through traffic.

Had to be Russian. The feds would've set up a blockade.

Fear and adrenaline. She found an opening and veered across three lanes. She slid within centimeters of other drivers and triggered a symphony of car horns before exiting into an expensive neighborhood. A sharp right, then a sharp left. The tires screeched as she raced down the block.

A faint squeal, then a zigzag of headlights before they roared up behind her. The residential street offered no cover. Eve ran a stop sign, seconds from smashing the front end of another car as she swerved out of the way. She jammed on the accelerator and shot past the homes like a Formula One racer.

Police sirens blared. Blue-and-red lights flickered in her mirrors.

The squad car zoomed alongside the Russian. The officer inside signaled him to pull over. He shot away from the cop and through the intersection, an SUV crossing in front of him. The dour man cut the wheel hard, tires shrieking and rubber burning as he skidded. His car spun out of control.

Eve glanced at the near miss in the rear-view, slowing as she turned off the main road. She cruised the side street, searching for a secluded park or a clearing or some place without any homes or cars or pedestrians, but there were too many goddamn people everywhere.

"First thing I'm going to do is bulldoze this entire place." She pounded a fist on the steering wheel. "Three million acres of nature preserve!"

She navigated the maze of twisty streets, finding salvation in an undeveloped lot in a cul-de-sac. She drove onto the grass, between a cluster of trees to a patch of thick scrub and turned off the headlights. Eve reached into the glove compartment, taking out a small plastic caboodle which held a miniaturized spare car—a sporty black coupe—and wig. She slid a slim case from inside her jacket and took out the *modifikator*.

Darkness shaded the neighborhood. Not wanting to wait any longer, she shrank the hybrid and picked it up. Blue-and-red lights flashed. She ducked down behind the shrubs. The squad car slowed. A beam from a flashlight whipped back and forth across the trees. She held her breath. The light shut off. The car crept along the curve of the cul-de-sac, checking the driveways. She watched the squad car sit at the stop sign for a solid minute before the cops drove away.

She restored the coupe to normal-size along with the wig.

Headlights. She ducked behind the car. A vehicle parked in a driveway up the street. Not the cops or the Russian. She crept out.

Today was too close. They could go after Quinn for leverage. But the dour man had kept his distance.

The street cams.

He didn't want to be identified either. If the Russians knew about Kira, they'd been to her place. But she was never home, so they wanted to find out where she was going. And if the FBI was investigating, the Russians couldn't risk any more exposure while they tried to recover the fragment first.

Eve smirked. He must've been frustrated as hell to chase her like that.

Inside the coupe, she swapped out wigs. The car crept out of the brush and with a couple bumps lumbered onto the pavement. Houselights illuminated as she backtracked to the freeway. Police tended to the SUV in the intersection. No sign of the blue sedan. He must've gotten away.

* * *

Eve pulled into the high-rise's private garage and parked the coupe in her spare space. Once home, she changed clothes, scarfed leftover pad Thai, then grabbed the miniaturized hard case containing the suit and left again. With the Russians closing in, the suit would make all the difference in her survival.

She arrived at the warehouse in Diane's luxury electric vehicle a half-hour later. She paced the block, pausing to listen. Dark and quiet. She shrank the car and pocketed it.

With a clunk, the warehouse's rear door unlocked. The initial creak of its opening swing faded. She reached for one of the thick switches.

A single row of lights revealed the wide industrial space. Horizontal awning windows high above and a large overhead door secured shut with a steel latch. She locked the rear door and dug into her pocket as she stepped across the gritty concrete floor.

Eve enlarged the hard case and took out the suit, ducking into a little office space in the back corner. She stripped down to a sports bra and compression shorts. She slid her legs in, pulling the suit up the length of her body. The material was thin yet dense. The mix of polymers, carbon fibers, and bismuth oxide for radiation proofing created a mottled appearance. Reminded her of a black rustic moth. The designers had taken breathability into account, giving what she expected to be a formfitting garment more mobility and a less oppressive feel.

She slipped her arms through the sleeves and zipped up part way, making sure none of the wires had come loose or twisted leading up to the sensor cap dangling off her shoulders. She spread the cap's clamshell-like EEG net and let it close. The sensor orbs pressed through her hair and secured into her scalp. She zipped up the rest of way, then opened the panel on the arm cuff. The *modifikator* locked inside, and she latched it shut.

Eve dropped her folded clothes into the top portion of the case and skimmed Shadi's instructions, beginning with the most basic controls. She ran through the actions, motions, and sensations necessary to turn the dial in her mind.

It remained motionless. She studied the arm cuff, concentrating on the movement required in her right hand to use the dial button. Still nothing. With a coarse grunt, she glared at the dial, all her mental powers focused on willing it to move. Lightheaded and winded, Eve huffed in frustration.

This isn't going to work. What were you thinking?

"What *was* I thinking?" she whispered.

The first time she'd used the *modifikator* on herself, it was...green, purple, blue. The dial ticked up a notch. Startled with a spark of excitement, she considered whenever she reduced it was blue, yellow, silver. The dial rolled down. Green, purple, blue. It rolled up.

Her tongue curled outside her lip, pinned against her teeth as she focused on the cuff's switches, the different effects they represented. Like when she'd made herself intangible for the first time and it had felt —gray, purple, gold. The switch clicked into first position.

She chuckled in stilted gasps. Red, yellow, white. More clicks. Second position. Violet, blue, scarlet. *Click, click.* Third position. Orange, scarlet, brown. Fourth, then fifth, and back up again, clicking away until she reached neutral position, infinite black.

She stopped the exercise, returning to the dial button. It rolled up and down with ease. She mixed the mental commands, running through different settings in awe of its intuitiveness. In minutes, the brain-machine interface had taken the arm cuff she'd only practiced with for a few days and stitched together linkages with the particular nuances of her mind. When Eve considered her laborious learning curve putting the cuff together—

Shadi's a genius. Unlike you.

Red spikes and waves of magenta crests.

The clicks stopped.

Eve seethed, inhaling deep, and blew out her jealousy and resentment.

With a clearer head, she considered the mental process for pressing down on the button without touching it. Familiar with the settings, she tuned them to the return position and stared at the dial button intent on its function. The right index finger—no—a sensation. Not of the machine, but the satisfying sometimes terrifying push of the button and the knowledge something extraordinary was happening. Electric blue, white, silver—the dial button's actuator quivered.

A jolt shot through her. Eve dropped to normal size.

"Holy shit." She gasped.

The real tests. Green, purple, blue. Another jolt coursed through her.

She enlarged, rising more than ever before.

Forty feet in height. No labored breathing. No cardiac strain. She felt heavy. Mighty. She lifted a foot, taking a single step forward, her movement more consequential. Another step. She wanted to push down the walls. Breathy laughter escaped her smile as she glanced up at the rafters. She wanted to find Jenny Wheeler and Tommy Gordon and fling them over the neighborhood. Pick up the Russian's car and shake him out of it. If this was forty feet, what would four hundred feel like? What about four thousand?

Green, purple—the dial rolled up and up.

"N-No, no, no, no." She dialed it down with her fingers and pressed the button, returning to six feet. "Got to watch that."

What about the other controls?

She spied a cinder block in the corner and carried it to the middle of the room. She pointed the cuff—green, purple, blue—and enlarged the block to the size of a small house.

Orange, scarlet, brown. Clicks, then a jolt. She didn't feel any different. It should have made her super-dense. Harder than a diamond, stronger than graphene.

Eve stepped up to the wall of concrete, tapping her finger against the rough surface. She reared back a fist and with a jab dented the block. No pain, just the shattering of rock under her knuckles. She punched with her left, then right, then left, over and over and over, boring a hole. The low hum filled her ears, droning deeper until it growled like an engine. She was strong. Impervious. Powerful.

Gray, purple, gold.

She stepped forward, walking through the cinder block. Her atoms slipped between the concrete's molecules. She was a dense fog flowing through denser grains. She feared she might lose herself or have an errant thought and be fused with the block. But her form persisted. Airy, yet intact.

She reached the other side, her particles zipped up behind her. Like a refreshing, rushing spray—but she was the spray. She walked backwards, flittering out the other side, her particles snapped back into place. The blips and *pilbs*—the information—kept them linked and organized. Brown, green, gray. *Click, click.* Her solidity returned.

She stepped forward, halted by an excruciating tug at her heel. She turned around. Her left ankle had fused into the cinder block, boot and all.

"Oh, shit—shit!" She took a breath. Gray purple— "No—okay, think about this..."

If she went intangible again, the concrete atoms could end up becoming part of her heel.

Infinite black.

A jolt and she stumbled forward, her boot squeaked against the floor.

The cinder block had reduced to normal. She dug into the boot, squeezing her ankle with her fingers. Flesh and tendons. Like the black hole, once the field resolved, the particles returned to their original state. Though relieved at the moment, she considered the unpredictable effect a nuclear detonation might have on a distortion field. Or an accidental X-ray blast.

Future experiments.

Red, yellow, white. She floated from the ground. She twisted about, rising higher and higher, to the ceiling. She braced along the metal rafters. The relentless effect soon had her backed against them. Blue brown black. She fell, sailing face-first toward the floor. Red, yellow, white! She hovered inches above the ground, rising once again. Blue, brown, black. She dropped onto her knees and stood, gasping.

She raised her arm and took aim at the cinder block. Yellow, green, pink. More clicks. Energy charged at the end of the cuff. A white-hot orb shot out with a sizzle. The ferocious bang sent hot-orange chunks flying.

"The hell was that?" A man's voice. Outside.

Eve froze. The hum stopped.

She shut the case, shrank it, and scooped it up. Eve dashed to the door and flipped the lights off, holding her breath. The faint sputtering of an idling engine.

Violet, blue, scarlet—invisible. Gray, purple, gold. Another jolt. She walked through the wall.

Outside, a large man with a fat-face stalked the alley. A leathery guy in a sleeveless jacket approached him from the other end.

"Yo."

Fat-Face turned around.

"Lights must be on a timer." The leathery guy tilted his head at the windows above.

The fat-faced man jimmied the warehouse door's handle. Locked. "All right."

She followed them to the moving truck parked in front of the warehouse across the way. Two more guys loitered behind the truck. A bulky man with a thin mustache and sleepy eyes stood by the driver's side. While the others dressed like they were going to the gym, he wore a white button-down shirt, open at the collar, and a black suit jacket.

"We good?" he asked.

Fat-Face nodded. "Yeah."

The bulky man rapped his knuckles on the driver's window. The engine cut out. The two guys in the rear rolled open the doors.

Eve backed away as they pulled out a loading ramp. Whatever they were doing, they didn't want witnesses either. Which meant it wasn't good. At least they'd left her warehouse alone.

Next time, she'd have to be mindful of her neighbors. She sprinted off, slowing near a loading dock several warehouses over. It took her another seven blocks before she found a suitable place to switch back to normal, change clothes, and enlarge a car without being caught on camera.

* * *

Though they disliked most of Zach's suggestions, the housemates warmed to the idea of a taco-night video game tournament. Anything to break up the days and loosen the tension of waiting for a chance to call for help. They gathered in the living room, competing in four-player rounds of *Go-Kart WarZone X*.

"In your face, bitch!" Cassidy taunted as she blew Zach's cart off the road with a hood-mounted grenade launcher.

Janelle cackled at his virtual demise.

"Okay," said Zach. "You don't even know what you just did."

"Uh—yeah I do," said Cassidy. "I annihilated you."

"You're a button masher," he said. "You have no idea—"

"I don't need to know," she said. "All that matters is I kicked your ass."

"All right, give it up." Troy reached for Zach's controller.

He huffed, handing it over.

The game's jaunty theme music was undercut by muted thunder. More. Louder. Game play stopped. The telltale rumble and whoosh of the lid lifting ruined everyone's buzz.

"*Eugene.*"

"Ohhhh god." He tensed, fingers digging into the couch's armrest.

Janelle leaned over with an encouraging pat on his knee. "Your time to shine."

"Can't you tell her I'm asleep?" he asked.

"*Eugene!* Where are you?"

"That's a big negative, ghost rider." Zach took a swig from a beer bottle.

"Don't listen to him," said Troy. "You've got this. There's nothing to worry about. Just keep her talking—don't give her the chance to think about anything."

"What if I run out of things to say?" Eugene asked.

"You won't because you've got this."

Shadi picked up the improvised helicopter along with Eugene's laptop. "Everyone get your phones. First one who gets a signal, calls the police."

Eugene peeked out the front door. Her waiting hand rested on the ground, palm up.

"Get on. I want to show you something."

"Well, we're kind of in the middle—"

"Get on."

Eugene stepped into her hand, regretting the two beers he'd had. The others crowded by the sliding glass door. She lifted him and turned away.

"We're clear," said Kevin.

They rushed out the back, Troy sprinting to the armored car.

"All right." Shadi set down the helicopter. "There's no gyroscope, but, there's also no wind—well, there is, but it's the air conditioning and it's above the threshold of—"

"Yeah," said Zach. "We've all watched you try to fly this thing."

"I can get it vertical," said Shadi. "But I need someone to keep the tail steady."

She held out a string.

"How did this become my job?" he asked.

"You're the only one who got captured without a phone."

"Bullshit." He snatched the string from her hand. "I don't get any eye protection from this floating blender you created?"

She chucked a pair of plastic safety glasses at him.

He caught then and grumbled, pulling the elastic over his head.

Shadi knelt, swiping through the menu options on the phone duct taped to the helicopter. She flipped open Eugene's laptop. "Everybody stand back."

She stood as the helicopter's propeller spun. It whirred, flitting side to side, and lifted off the ground. The slow, uneven ascent swung into a wide loop. The housemates scattered, ducking, as the propeller sliced through the air.

"Sorry." Shadi dashed aside, steadying the laptop.

The helicopter wobbled erratically, bending a wild curve.

"Oh my god." Zach dropped to the dirt. "Just land it."

"Pull the damn string." Shadi backpedaled.

The housemates cringed as the main rotor listed to one side, winging the craft on a perilous downward arc. Zach flopped onto his back to dodge it and yanked the string, correcting the tail end. The helicopter wavered back and forth, rising higher.

* * *

Eve set Eugene onto the desktop and pointed to the laptop's screen.

"Took your advice and got into cryptocurrency," she said.

The dashboard page totaled her holdings close to eighteen million dollars, the current value of Neptonium hovering somewhere around twelve thousand.

He gaped. "What the hell?"

"Well, I bought up all the Neptonium I could, then invested in a mining operation started by this reclusive millionaire, and the value sky-rocketed. This is the last chunk of it I'm about to cash out."

"Holy crap."

"Yeah, so, you're kind of on my good side." She reached for the mouse, the faint rev of an ignition behind her words. Eve turned her head aside, unsure if it was the strange hum she associated with the fragment or something else.

"Well," Eugene blurted out. "So, you're saying I get a cut?"

She faced him, soured by the question, and clicked Sell.

* * *

Back at the miniature house, Troy backed the armored car into position, guided by Kevin.

"This isn't going to work," said Zach. "It doesn't have an external dish."

The phone's display illuminated. The housemates raised their devices, swaying in search of the helicopter's blessing.

"I got it," said Cassidy. "I got it!"

"Me, too!" Darien grinned. "It's connecting! It's taking forever, but it's connecting."

* * *

"So, where are these rigs?" Eugene asked. "Bulgaria? Kazakhstan?"

"Yeah, I don't know." The woman shrugged. "That businessman might be pulling out soon. But I was thinking we could put our heads together on a new project."

"Uh, a—a new project?"

"Yeah. I mean, I can trust you to keep your mouth shut, right?"

"Yeah, you-you—you can trust me."

"Good. Because I'd hate for you to be on my bad side again."

"That's nowhere I want to be." His stomach bubbled with beer and fear.

She bent over, hands braced on her knees. "So when I put you back, what are you going to tell everyone?"

"Well, what—what do you want me to tell them?"

The woman smiled. "That I need you to help me build a mining rig."

"Okay." He nodded. "I can do that."

"Oh—just a sec." She straightened up, turning away. "Forgot to put the lid back on."

He couldn't let her leave.

"Wait." Eugene called out. "So—so what are we using? GPUs or ASICs?"

She swung around. "FPGAs. They're better for the environment."

"Well, I mean, on the whole, crypto mining is not great for the environment."

"What's it matter?" she whispered in exasperation. "We're not actually building anything."

* * *

Shadi had gotten into her groove with helicopter. To her surprise, Zach had shut his mouth and gotten into his own rhythm guiding the tail end with the string. The variable was Eugene. No telling how long he could keep her busy before one of their phones connected.

"Mine's out," said Darien.

"Mine was," said Cassidy. "It's coming back up."

Janelle and Kevin were still hunting for signal bars.

Cassidy's connection held. She swiped to dial out as rumbling footsteps shook her to her core.

"Nine-one-one, what's your emergency?"

A giant fist clamped around the helicopter, crushing it to pieces. The woman opened her fingers, parts raining down on the little people as they fled to the house.

Shadi ran toward the sliding glass door. A hand slammed down like wall in front of her, blocking her path. She broke in the other direction—met with the opposite palm. The two hands closed in on her.

The woman scooped her up, lifting Shadi to her face.

Shadi stared into the giant, gray eyes as they burned with

resentment and hostility. She trembled with such terror it was impossible to stand. She wanted to cry, but was well beyond tears.

"Hey!" Kevin protested. "Leave her alone!"

"Yeah," said Troy. "We put her up to it!"

"Kevin?" asked the woman. "Troy! Really? I thought we were cool."

"What part of this is cool?" Troy asked.

With a harsh sigh, the woman lowered her into the enclosure. Shadi scrabbled from her knees to her feet as the other housemates joined her in the yard. She gasped in deep breaths. Her clarity returned, and she anchored onto the conversation around her.

"All right, look," the woman said. "Nobody's thrilled with this situation, but it's the best—"

"What happened to letting us go?" Kevin asked.

"Well, yeah," she said. "Eventually. But, I'm not there yet, all right?"

"All right," said Kevin. "When do you think that might be?"

"I don't know." The woman folded her arms. "Look, I don't want to give you some time frame and then blow past it and then you're all mad at me for that. I don't know how long certain things are going to take. It's more about phases. And right now, we're just finishing up Phase One."

"So what phase are you thinking then?" he asked.

"I don't know." She shrugged. "End of three...? Beginning of four?"

"And how long is that going to take?" asked Janelle.

"Could be a few months?" She looked askance. "Maybe a year."

"A year!?" Janelle cried.

"We have lives and families!" Kevin roared.

"You don't think I know that?" she countered.

"I don't think you do! I've got a wife and three kids—"

"And this is temporary," said the woman. "Why do think I'm trying to make it as comfortable as possible? I buy you whatever you want—shoes, clothes, jewelry, booze, drugs—other stuff. You name it. I give it to you."

"None of it means anything without the people we love," said Kevin. "Don't you have somebody—don't you have a family? People you care about?"

Shadi watched the woman's jaw move, but no words came out. And something was happening in her eyes. Her focus seemed to shift—

"No, she doesn't!" Zach derided.

"*Zach.*" Janelle rasped, scolding.

"Look at her face!" He pointed. "She doesn't have anybody. That's why she doesn't care."

"I care!" she defended. "I care so much! You have no idea how much I care."

"All right," said Kevin. "What about your family?"

"Well, I don't...really...talk to them anymore. But that's none of your business, and—"

"Sure sounds like our business," said Kevin.

"Do you want to talk about it?" Cassidy ventured.

"No!" She bristled. "This isn't therapy."

"I mean..." Cassidy shrugged. "It could be if, you know, if you think you need it—"

"No—oh my god—I'm not doing this! I don't have to do this. You know why?" She grabbed the lid. "Because I can do this."

"Wait!" Janelle stepped forward. "What about your music friend?"

"That's—I should have never asked." She sighed. "But I was drunk—Look, you will all be very happy when I let you go, and I will let you go. But you need to be patient and...stop doing things like this."

She secured the lid onto the box.

"Good try, babe," Darien said, rubbing Cassidy's shoulder.

"I think I can get her," Cassidy nodded. "That music friend Janelle mentioned—"

"I don't think so." Shadi shook her head. "I'm not a psychologist, but something in her eyes, when Kevin asked about her family. Like it triggered something. A memory, or...she was envisioning something."

"Like her murdering all of them?" asked Zach.

"No," said Troy. "She said her mom didn't call her for her birthday. So she's just not talking to them."

"Not talking to them?" Zach pointed to the lid overhead. "Or putting up imaginary walls so she doesn't have to face the truth she killed them?"

"Maybe." Shadi nodded. "Maybe she's convinced herself that's what happened in order to not think about it."

"Yeah," Kevin muttered. "Like believing spies are after her."

"What do you think it means," said Darien, "when she said we're all going to be very happy when she lets us go?"

No one answered. But after her encounter with their captor, Shadi didn't want to find out.

* * *

Eve returned to the office. Eugene stood at the edge of the desk.

"Bad side again?" he asked.

"Neutral."

He nodded.

"What do you know about botnets?"

"I've built a few." He shrugged. "Just messing around, you know? They're usually pretty simple."

"These aren't going to be simple."

She planted her hands on either corner of the desk, looming over him. "And you don't say a word to anyone in the house. You understand?"

"Yeah." His head bobbed. "Yes, yeah."

16

(silver, royal blue)

Despite her exacting specifications, Eugene and Eve created several basic bots in an hour. He instructed her alongside the laptop while she typed. Their bots were good, but basic. She wanted them to post in different languages, interact with other botnets they built, and maximize their behavior to appear more human. Eugene suggested a herding program, but Eve wanted to tweak that, too, with additional layers of stealth and control. Both exhausted, she told him to sleep on it and returned him to the house.

Eve took a five-hour nap. By 6:30 a.m., she was parking an SUV behind the loading docks of a commercial building in Santa Clarita. She hiked up a forested embankment and made herself invisible. Another half-mile trek up a hillside and across the lawn, and she passed a handful of FBI agents on security detail outside Pierce Technologies. She'd debated sneaking into Simon's home in Santa Monica, but figured storing classified information at Pierce Technologies allowed Simon plausible deniability.

Simon arrived around seven in a tailored pewter suit and sapphire tie.

Eve hurried behind him—gray, purple, gold. And glided through him as an agent opened the door. While security waved Simon through the metal detector, Eve sidled along the farthest wall. She rejoined him as he entered the elevator lobby.

Brown, green, gray. *Click*. A man in a sweater vest glanced to a man wearing a bow tie, unsure of the sound's source. A woman in a cable knit sweater and slacks turned in his direction, also aware of the noise. He shrugged.

They boarded the elevator. Eve slipped in. She found a spot against the wall in the back as they sorted themselves. Three more people rushed to the closing doors. Bow-tie guy held them open.

Eve tensed as they crowded in. She stepped aside to avoid bumping into anyone. They pressed the buttons for their respective floors. Two more people piled on and Eve's mind shifted to gray, purple, gold. *Click, click*. Sweater vest stepped through her.

The doors shut. The elevator rose. But she didn't. She sank through the floor. Her relative position in the plane of reality had been disrupted. A complication she hadn't considered. Intangibility silenced her scream as she hurtled down the shaft and into the earth below.

Brown, gre—wait, infini—*No!* Red, yellow, white!

She hovered in the dirt and rock on a slow ascent, filtering through the concrete foundation into the shaft until she reached the elevator stopped on the fifth floor. The last two passengers, Simon and Sweater Vest, waited for the doors.

Blue, brown, black; brown, green, gray. Clicks. Her invisible boots thumped onto the floor. Simon and Sweater Vest turned around while Eve caught her breath in stifled, controlled gasps.

"Huh," said Simon. "Maintenance should probably have that checked out."

They stepped into the executive floor. Eve shadowed Simon, the low-pile carpeting leaving no trace of her steps. She'd only been in Simon's office once, when she'd first been hired. His desk was different. And he'd added more rock displays. Two agents inspected Simon's office for bugs, signs of tampering, examining the corners, under the desk, the chair.

The block-headed agent took out Simon's laptop. "Has anyone had any contact with your computer aside from you, Dr. Pierce?"

"No one's touched it but me." Simon smiled. "Brought it home last night and here this morning. Same as yesterday and the day before."

Irritated, the agent handed over the laptop.

"If you could close the door on your way out," said Simon. "That'd be great."

The door shut.

Simon lingered, listening. He gripped both sides of the laptop bag's backing, bending it to reveal a hidden zipper. An ultra-thin laptop slid from a hidden panel. He stepped around the desk and sat, reaching into a side drawer for a wireless mouse. He opened his work laptop and rested the ultra-slim one inside.

Eve hung over his shoulder while he entered the password:

Bh8P$f3Z (indigo, light orange, dark purple, violet, emerald, pink, aquamarine, yellow)

Her focus drifted as she mouthed the series of colors in repetition. Her eyes shot back to the screen in time to catch a glimpse of his desktop wallpaper—an ancient map of Hollow Earth. Simon logged into a VPN, opened a browser, and signed into a secure email server. He deleted several messages from months ago. She didn't catch more than subject lines before they were erased. She hoped they weren't fragment related.

A knock. "Dr. Pierce?"

Simon hit an icon on the menu bar. The screen locked, displaying the yellow-and-green Pierce Technologies logo.

He smiled. "Yes?"

The block-headed agent stuck in his head. "Some of the agents can't access the building—their key cards aren't working."

"Well, that's an IT issue."

"But we need your sign-off."

"You have my permission." Simon grinned with a gracious sweep of his hand.

"We need you to be there."

"Of course. Of course you do."

Simon left the room. The rounder agent took a post guarding the door.

Eve leaned over the laptop. The problem wasn't the password but the inability to see her own fingers. She poked at each key, struggling to use Shift, and then Backspace until she got the combination right. The display reverted to the Hollow Earth map. She found the touchpad much easier and clicked the search bar, careful as she entered a familiar term: *Talbot*.

The document results were localized in one folder. She clicked on a couple files and skimmed them.

Cactus Whistle.

Eve rummaged into a pouch on her hip for a thumb drive. She fumbled sticking the invisible drive into a port. She right-clicked, copying over the entire folder. Paranoid, she vacillated between the door and the screen. The estimated completion time fluctuated. The rounder agent folded his arms, peering over his shoulder. His eyes settled on the dinosaur egg. Then, he turned around. She held her breath. His head swung side to side, surveying the room. Voices approached.

"Appreciate it, Dr. Pierce."

The rotund agent faced forward.

"Well, next time you can just ask IT," said Simon. "Pretty sure you guys aren't going to steal anything."

"We prefer to go through protocol. You're the original sign-off."

Eve canceled the download and yanked the drive from the port.

"I'm giving you permission." Simon smiled, reaching the doorway. "Forever and all-time. I trust you aren't a security risk."

She closed the folder and locked the screen.

"Thank you."

"You're very welcome."

Eve stood back, holding her breath as Simon sat. The agent closed the door.

"Thanks," said Simon.

She blew a long, quiet exhale as he logged back in.

He deleted a couple more items and signed out of his email. He double-clicked a 3D modeling simulator.

Eve crept closer. Several blueprints and schematics popped up in a side-bar on screen. The main window filled with a sprawling floor plan. A building with several dozen different pipes running through rectangular blocks leading to arms focused around a center core. Twelve tubes ran above it, feeding into three silos. A fusion reactor.

Simon tweaked a few elements, altering their assigned values, and saved the changes. He opened another project. These designs concentrated into the base of a long cylinder. After modifying a couple values, he hit Save and selected Run from a drop-down menu. A progress bar popped up as the program rendered.

The simulation opened.

Beams fired through the tubes, amplified by each successive pass, converging on the core. The reaction ignited. The shell around the core illuminated green, collecting tritium atoms. Energized particles siphoned into the silos above, igniting the cylinders' bases. One launched.

The other two flashed red. The reactions burst in their bases and shredded the core's shell below, scattering tritium everywhere. Hazard symbols populated the surrounding area inside concentric orange rings.

The simulator charted the remaining rocket's trajectory with a black line within a range of several blue ones.

To Eve's horror, the plasma engine cut out.

The simulated rocket plummeted into the middle of Lancaster. It slammed into buildings and shattered apart. More concentric orange rings mapped the potential fallout of the demolished engine. The prevailing winds blanketed the desert and Edwards Air Force Base with radioactive particles.

"Still better than last time," Simon muttered. "Got to be a way to weaponize that."

Eve backpedaled. The heel of her boot bumped into the wall.

Simon turned around and stood.

She edged away as he pushed aside the vertical blinds. He must have assumed a bird had struck the window.

No smear of feathers. His smile sank.

The desk phone lit up. Sasha. "Dr. Pierce?"

He leaned over and hit the intercom. "Yes?"

"There's a representative from the power company here to see you."

"Be right there." Simon turned off the intercom.

He closed the rendering program and transferred the wireless mouse to his work laptop. He snapped his personal laptop shut and slid it into the secret slot. As he zipped up the bag, he paused, turning in Eve's direction. His eyes lingered, probing the air. Robotic.

She stared into his hollow pupils, expecting him to see her.

He finished zipping up the bag, shoved it under his desk, and walked out. The round agent resumed his post at the door.

She had no idea if and when he'd return. Or if he'd re-open his personal laptop. And there was no soundless way to unzip the bag. She could make it intangible, but if by chance she dropped it, it would fall to the center of the earth. Stealing or sabotaging it risked hinting at her presence. The data could be backed up on an external drive. But that meant breaking into Simon's home. Considering her track record, probably not the best move.

Eve huffed in aggravation. The only way to stop him was to create a new energy source before he did—a truly clean one. Gray, purple, gold.

The rotund agent stepped into the room, checking around.

Eve strode right through him and out of the executive offices.

She rode the elevator, solid and invisible, awaiting its return to the lobby. Someone got off on the third floor. Curious, she followed—gray, purple, gold—passing through the door into her old department.

Same faces. Same conversations. Someone new at her desk—a young woman with thick brown hair tied back and bright brown eyes. Her was cubicle decorated with photos of puppies and kittens, friends and family.

Eve stopped short.

No concern for her disappearance. No memorial. No vigil. Whatever personal items she'd had were either confiscated by the FBI or tossed into the trash. Aside from her calendar and coffee mug, she knew there was a small branch from a ponderosa pine with two cones. She ruminated over which fate it had suffered.

Greg stopped at her replacement's cubicle. "Hey, great work on those status reports, Lana. Couldn't have done it without you."

Eve had worked this stupid job for seven years and Greg hadn't bothered to acknowledge her birthday. She dashed through the cubicles and stuck out a foot as he passed—brown, green, gray.

He buckled forward, landing face-first onto the floor. Gasps. Everyone shot out of their chairs.

"Oh my god!"

"Are you all right?"

To Eve's astonishment, they rushed to his aid.

"What happened?" Lana helped him up.

"Don't know. Guess I tripped over my own feet," he answered. "Looks like I won't be on *Celebrity Dance-Off* any time soon!"

Laughter. Relieved, genuine laughter.

It's you. Nobody likes you.

No—they didn't like Old Eve. And New Eve had more important things to do.

***

By mid-morning, she was back at her home office, disappointed with the trove of documents. Most were incomplete, registering as corrupt when she tried opening them. The rest were fruitless. Redacted scans. Boilerplate memos. Email chains from government officials amounting to bureaucratic fluff. A single text file, however, proved far more valuable.

Much like Talbot, Simon had chronicled his involvement. Bullet points evolved into narrative paragraphs, reading like the early draft of a memoir.

- *11/7/2016*
- *Lt. Colonel Luisa Fernandes, Army Corps of Engineers*
- *tunnels outside Black Mountain, western Nevada*
- *Three weeks in, the Corps struck impenetrable strata. Their attempt at pulverizing it with a Pierce Technologies laser cannon resulted in an aberrant explosion and catastrophic collapse of the tunnel. General Russell T. McCrae had been tasked with determining the cause and assisted the rescue mission. Within hours of receiving his assignment, Gen. McCrae contacted me for a full elucidation of the laser's design and operations. Destiny. Some people call it fate. Cynics would say it's coincidence. Personally, I believe momentous events involve momentous people because they've put themselves in the position to have momentous things happen.*

"Oh god," Eve muttered.

After helping the Corps dislodge the mysterious object, it and Simon had been brought to an undisclosed base. The Mobius produced an audible, resonant frequency which Simon had deduced could be used affect the material where brute force and energy could not. Once Simon had succeeded in cleaving pieces from the Mobius, he was escorted onto a small passenger plane and flown to a regional airport.

He'd paid attention to the terrain, highways, and landmarks on his trip back into the civilian world. His best guess was that the Mobius was hidden away at a military base somewhere west of the Mojave. Though he couldn't speculate for national security reasons, it hadn't stopped him from making several references using cardinal points.

But this was Simon Pierce. Half of it could be bullshit.

Eve opened a GPS map on her laptop. Using Powell's method, she zoomed in and scanned the vicinity. She found pixelation and zoomed out. Swaths of barren dunes. Thin dirt roads running to them. The colors matched the desert's reddish hue. But the trails stopped, the details wiped from the terrain.

Geometric shapes emerged. She printed a hard copy and enlarged it with the *modifikator*. With the map tacked to the wall, she charted Simon's hints with a red marker, circling the area.

She sifted through posts on the FoilHat Collective's message board for mentions of "Litterbox" or government research west of the Mojave. A FoilHat named "Agent86" had driven out to a stretch of dunes, discovering a fence marking the edge of military property. Along with the location's coordinates, Agent86 had included a photo of a sign reading *No Unauthorized Entry* with a pair of Humvee's racing up behind. The coordinates fell within the red circle.

Agent86 suspected the military had used thermal imaging, hence the vehicles already en route when the picture had been taken.

Eve stepped back, lost in the map. Even invisible, they'd detect her a football field away. An attempt during the hottest part of the day might limit her heat signature, but if they used such technology on the outer perimeter, they'd employ more rigorous sensors on the base itself.

She folded her arms, gnawing at the side of her lip, puzzling over how much intangibility might conceal her. In that state, her molecules didn't interact with matter at the same level, but they weren't gone—she still had a surface, though diffused. Infrared thermography could detect gas leaks, so they might identify her movement as a cooler patch shifting through the landscape. Or pick up a hint of the distortion field. No telling how the military would react to such an anomaly. She'd have to test it.

Her mind sprinted in another direction.

"If I can figure out which airstrip they're using, I could shrink, become superdense and invisible, and stowaway on the plane—but none of those flights would be registered. So I'd have to stake out the airstrips at every regional airport. That's if they're still flying to the base..."

She paced as her mind leaped further.

"But even if I infiltrate the base, anything caught on camera floating with my invisible hands will get me surrounded, so then I'd have to blast my way out."

She blew an unsettled puff, dragging fingers through her hair. "Okay, let's think about this. Been really good not killing anybody, and... these are soldiers—our soldiers. Home turf."

Eve plopped down at her laptop. "There's got to be another way."

The more she explored the FoilHat board, the more she became convinced the fragments and the Mobius were secured underground. But maybe not at the same base. Everything topside might be a decoy, empty buildings setup for appearances, the actual entrance hidden among them.

Her mind wandered to the most extreme, blunt solution. At hundreds, if not thousands of feet tall, superdense, invisible, she could uproot an entire base with her bare hands. She'd still have troops to deal with, but maybe not any bloodshed. A stunt like that would not endear her to the military or the American public.

"All right, let's call that Plan F." She twisted side to side in the swivel chair. "So...focus on the clean-energy angle. But if I file patents that's going to draw attention, and the government starts snooping around, and—"

She sat forward.

"Why can't I snoop on them?"

She scoured the internet for the barest threads of McCrae's career. His commands had been sporadic, three or four-year blocks followed by gaps of the same amount of time. His last command had been in 2012, but according to Simon's notes, McCrae had accepted the project at the end of last year. She didn't want to risk investigating him, even under one of her aliases, but maybe she could convince the conspiracy yahoos to do it for her.

She created a FoilHat account and pasted a link to McCrae's bio page, along with a comment:

Pretty suspicious job history. Sounds like he's got a second home @Area51

"No, that's stupid. Idiot." She folded her arms with a huff. "I don't know, I don't know what people want."

She stewed over the words, unsure how much blood to drip into the water. Part of her thought it didn't take much for the FoilHats to speculate. But the geeks among them could be quite discerning. Connoisseurs of intrigue who poked holes in fake moon landing theories.

She bit her lip. Something had to pique their curiosity. She had to sell it to them. A notion that she knew something they didn't. She deleted her previous sentences. Her next attempt was short, crisp, with more dramatic flare:

On good authority, THIS is the authority.

Post.

* * *

Eugene slumped on the couch while Zach navigated the fantasy role-playing game *FireLance: Endless Dynasty*. Kevin slouched at the head of the dining room table, resting his chin on one hand. His gaze was distant, as though he were faced with an impossible decision. Troy sat to his left, hunched over a copy of Steppenwolf. Janelle sauntered in from the kitchen. She set down a triple-decker sandwich of ham, turkey, bacon and cheddar while balancing a margarita in her other hand as she sat.

"That doesn't seem very healthy," said Kevin.

"It's multigrain bread." She shrugged, taking a sip.

The dull silence broke with the chirps and moans of Cassidy and Darien down the hall.

Shadi stormed out of her bedroom. "Do we really need to hear that all the time?"

"Everyone copes differently," said Troy.

"Yeah." Zach smirked at Shadi. "If you ever want to blow off some steam, just let me know."

Her eyes and nostrils flared. "Never going to happen."

"You say that now." He shrugged. "But, give yourself a couple months."

She growled, shuddering, and turned toward the kitchen. Shadi spun around, pointing to Eugene. "Wait—she's got you working on a mining rig. You'll have internet access."

"Well, not exactly," said Eugene.

"No," said Zach. "You'll have internet access."

"With a humongous keyboard and her looking over my shoulder the entire time." Eugene sat up. "What am I supposed to do? Log into my email and tell my mom I'm being held captive by a neurotic giant?"

Zach scoffed. "First person you contact is your mom—pathetic."

"My mom's the first person I'd contact," said Troy. "I'm sure she's worried sick. I missed Easter. That just doesn't happen."

Janelle shook her head. "Terrence must be losing his mind."

"My youngest turns twelve this weekend." Kevin nodded. "Oldest is off to college in a few months."

"How many altogether?" asked Janelle.

"Three girls." He sighed. "Can't imagine what Jeanie's going through right now."

"There has to be some other way," said Shadi.

Zach paused his game with a snide turn to Eugene. "What do you know about crypto mining that she can't find online?"

Shadi folded her arms as Eugene's mouth hung open. Kevin leaned forward. Troy closed his book.

"Well, you know." Eugene fumbled for an answer. "Hash rates and...block-chain."

"Eugene." Janelle scowled. "Is there something you want to tell us?"

He shrugged, hoping his voice didn't crack. "No...not really."

"Dude," said Zach. "You were supposed to be our informant! We all agreed—"

"I didn't agree!" Eugene pointed to himself. "You're not out there alone with her, all right? I have no idea what she's going to do from one minute to the next! She swore me to secrecy, and if she finds out she's going to kill me."

"Oh my god." Zach craned his head back. "No, she won't."

"She can get rid of me whenever she wants! And then she has you or Shadi, or she'll kidnap somebody else!"

"We're not going to let that happen," said Troy.

"Oh, yeah?" asked Eugene. "What are you going to do? With your tiny muscles? You're going to stop her? Really?"

"Nobody's going to tell her anything," said Troy. "We're all on the same side here."

Eugene squirmed, squeezed by the pressure of everyone relying on him and the penalty he'd suffer if their captor discovered he was a spy. She seemed to have a pathological dislike of spies. At the same time, he didn't want the others to think he was a coward.

Shadi approached the couch. "Eugene, we're all scared and we all want to escape, okay? What are you really working on?"

He heaved a harsh sigh. "Bots. Like, whole botnets."

"Robots?" asked Kevin.

"An internet bot," Zach answered. "It's a program that does the same thing over and over. You connect a bunch of them—that's a botnet."

"She wants social media bots that coordinate with each other," said Eugene. "Within the group, and other botnets we're making."

Shadi and Zach exchanged glances, puzzled by their mysterious captor's interest in the virtual space when she had such a powerful way to alter the physical world.

"And she wants them in different languages. Mandarin, Russian, Hebrew, Hindi, Urdu, Farsi—I'm supposed to be figuring out how to increase the randomness of their behavior but still maintain the schedule she wants."

"What do you think she wants to do with them?" asked Shadi. "What's the messaging?"

"I don't know." Eugene shrugged. "She won't tell me. But, whatever it is, it's global."

"All right!" Zach clapped his hands. "Daddy's got this!"

"Just spit it out," said Shadi.

Zach stood. "We can't make some obvious S-O-S, right? But, we can Trojan horse a code that leads back to her. We create a security flaw that will give someone else access to her system, and that's where we put our distress signal."

"But you said we don't know where we are," said Janelle.

"Ah." Zach raised a finger. "That's why Eugene is going to expose her actual IP address."

"I'm not going to be able to do that." Eugene shook his head.

"You're not going to," said Zach. "You tell her what to write and she'll put it in there."

"Dude," said Eugene. "She's not going to fall for it, okay? She's not stupid."

"Dude, trust me—"

"You've been wrong about everything! Why would I listen to you?"

"Well," said Troy. "Normally I'd agree, but..."

"Yeah." Shadi nodded. "This might actually work."

Eugene glanced over at Kevin and Janelle, both in agreement with them.

"Yeah, sure!" He threw his hands up. "None of you are risking your lives on a suicide mission!"

"I know how you feel." Shadi knelt alongside the armrest nearby him. "When she picked me up, I didn't know what was going to happen. Just that she was angry and I was completely helpless."

He folded his arms, refusing to meet her eyes, and withheld the urge to cry.

"But if you pull this off," said Shadi, "she won't know what hit her."

"Yeah." He muttered. "And if she finds out, neither will I."

"She won't," said Zach. "Tell her it's a security patch—"

"No, nothing like that," Shadi warned. "Blend it in like it's something she asked for."

"We'll go over it a few times." Zach nodded. "Get it down pat and just feed it to her."

Eugene's eyes darted around, checking the faces of his fellow housemates, all of them eager to be rescued.

He swallowed hard. "You sure this'll work?"

Zach smirked. "It'll be all the attention she doesn't want."

* * *

Velez and Russo answered a call on a daytime B&E in the Broadway district. Once again, there wasn't much to go on, and they had to wait for street-cam footage.

"Lam is two solves ahead of me already," Velez griped as they waited at the window of a food truck.

"This one's easy," said Russo. "Soon as we get the footage, this guy's dead to rights."

"We're halfway through the month and I'm losing ground," said Velez.

"What happened to it's inevitable you win?"

"Damn Milner case threw me off." Velez took the adobo wraps from the vendor and handed one off to Russo.

Raucous cackles distracted her.

Down the block, a tall redhead with glasses and her friend with colorful stripes in her hair were window shopping.

Velez elbowed Russo, pointing with her chin. "Hey, check it out. Who's that look like?"

He searched, aimless, until he spotted the redhead. "Don't know. Who?"

"Our Amazonian burglar. Burglamazon."

"Is that what we're calling her?"

"That's what I'm calling her."

"She ain't tall enough."

"Maybe it was the shoes."

"She's robbing a place in six-inch platforms? Please."

"I don't know, something about her..."

He took a second look and shrugged. "Kind of."

Velez raised her phone as Russo took a bite out of his wrap.

"What are you doing?" he asked with a mouthful.

"Block for me." She hovered the phone's camera above his shoulder, snapping a shot of the women.

"You're not seriously—"

"Yeah, because asking people on the street if they committed a crime always gets a straight answer."

She lowered her phone, checking the image.

Russo turned aside, fuming in a whisper. "Look, the Milner case is cold—"

"Not cold." She shook her phone. "Still working on it."

"This ain't how we solve it. We got no evidence on that lady—come on."

Velez stuck out her jaw, stung by the critique. "Can we at least wait till we hear back from Forensics before we toss it into the freezer?"

"Fair enough. But you got to delete that." He took another bite.

She grumbled, thumbing to the picture, selected Delete, and—hit Cancel. She pocketed her phone.

"I'm telling you," said Russo. "Burglamazon will turn up."

* * *

Since Eve hadn't been sure how long her caper at Pierce Technologies would take, Kira had requested the day off. Quinn was already off, so they had met for lunch in the theater district. After a couple Bloody Marys, they wandered Broadway buzzed. While it was fun, Eve didn't want to risk losing the rest of the day or night.

"Okay." She checked the time on her phone. "You have songs to write. And I need to not be drunk any more."

"Or." Quinn raised an eyebrow. "Maybe you're not drunk enough."

Eve's mind drifted afar, considering the possibility "No, no." She waved a warning finger. "I have things to do."

"Yeah, like what?"

"Like..." She blanked for an excuse. "I—I can't remember right now."

"Bet a little whiskey would help."

Eve snickered. "In my mind, you have a theme song."

Quinn chuckled. "What? What is it?"

"Shimmer."

"The Fuel song?" Quinn squinted.

She flinched. "What's Fuel? No—Throwing Muses."

"What's Fuel?" Quinn's face twisted. "And, who?"

"Are we still having the same conversation?"

"I don't know? Who's Throwing Moses?"

"Muses. I thought you were a musician?"

"Ouch—because I don't know some obscure band?"

"They're not obscure. Kristin Hersh is a musical genius. So is her sister who was in The Breeders back in the day—you know, the Cannonball song?"

"Okay." Quinn's head bobbed, recalling the tune. "So what's the other song about?"

"It's about her beating a bunch of guys in a whiskey drinking contest."

Quinn tittered. "All right, let's do that. We can talk music while I put some guys to shame."

"No, no." Eve put a hand up, grinning. "Stop. I need to go home, and so do you."

Her friend glared skyward. "Oh my god—it's like hanging out with my mom."

"Don't ever say that again," she said through a laugh. "Or I'm taking you to Twelve Step."

"It's one day. And, we're already kind of drunk."

"I want you to be happy, and you won't be happy if you wake up tomorrow and realize you could have written a brilliant song two friends talk about twenty years from now."

Quinn shook her head, still smiling. "You suck so bad."

"I know." Eve chuckled, nodding. "I do."

They parted ways at the rail station. Eve hopped the line toward Kira's, figuring the walk to her apartment would be sobering. She still had to deal with the dour man. Find out if the Russians were staking out Kira's place.

She stepped off the railcar. A man in a khaki coach jacket and dark jeans sat on a bench in the middle of the platform. His gaze swept the length of the train before meeting eyes with her.

"Kira." He smiled as she neared.

She kept walking in spite of the hot yellow gathering in her periphery.

He stood. "Kira Sloane. You and I have a mutual friend."

Eve slowed, studying the boyish face as the breeze rustled his grayed brown hair. It wasn't the dour man. And he didn't have an accent.

Her brow wrinkled. "I'm new in town. Barely know my boss's name."

"You're a terrible liar." He smirked. "Lucky for your boss, our friend doesn't want to draw any unnecessary attention."

"All right, I don't know who you are." She stepped away. "But if I see you again, I'm calling the cops."

"Not with that fake ID."

Slate and vermilion blocks clustered in her vision.

She stopped dead, her lungs empty. "I don't know what you're talking about."

"Look." He shoved his hands into his jacket pockets. "I don't know all the details, I just know you stole something. They want to meet with you, tomorrow night. Pico Station. Eight o'clock."

"I don't know what you're saying."

He leaned back, amused. "Sure. Okay. Our friends don't like it when people steal from them. They don't deal well with that. So the fact they want to meet means whatever you have is valuable, and they want it back."

The deep hum welled inside her, resonating like an approaching train.

She stepped closer, pointing a fierce finger. "Come near me again, you'll find out why I'm still alive."

She heard the words after she spoke them, surprised they were hers.

"Hey." He put his hands up. "After this, I don't know you. Eight p.m. tomorrow. Pico Station."

He backed away and boarded the railcar, the doors shutting behind him. A revving whir and the train sped off, the hum fading with it.

No need to go to Kira's. She checked over her shoulder and left the platform, marching six blocks to a public library where she exited the restroom as Diane.

Scenarios consumed her on the way to the penthouse. The *modifikator* was the only thing keeping her alive. Once they had it, she was useless to them.

Worthless.

If it came down to it, she'd have to leave Kira behind. And Quinn. A deep sooty pit of dread opened up inside, pale purple and pea-soup green.

Eve wrung her hands and paced the living room. Was the FBI still looking for her? If the Russians were this close, how much further behind could they be? And what about the police? Someone was investigating the disappearance of the armored car and two guards. And the other disappearances across the city. Had she covered her tracks well enough? Would they detect a pattern?

With Kira's identity in jeopardy, her fallback plans were disrupted. Diane had secured a plot of land for Devereux's bunker, but its completion was months away. She needed the power source in order to save the world and herself. But that meant keeping her nosy neighbors away from her warehouse—

And what about your houseguests?

"No—no, I've got that covered—"

You can't trust them. They don't like you. Nobody does.

"They're not going to say anything."

What's to stop them from taking the money and ratting you out anyway?

Her fingers tore through her hair. She pinned her wrists against her forehead.

Then everybody will know what a horrible freak you are.

She gasped, choking on the cloud of sepia filling her vision.

Everything you do is wrong.

"No, no, no, no, no, I just need more time." She zipped back and forth across the room. "I need—I need—Fuck!"

Space and time. Both out of her control.

But she had the suit now. And with it, she could run and hide and evade in ways she couldn't before. She could attack. She could manipulate.

Her pace slowed, breath easing into her lungs. "Wait..."

The man at the station didn't know what she had, only that she'd stolen it. Maybe the dour man had been tasked with delivering the same message. They both had approached her during the day. They knew what she had was dangerous, but no one had told them why. Talbot's notes said he'd withheld details from Russian intelligence. He'd told Irina he'd had leverage. Maybe he hadn't told them about the *modifikator*. Maybe the puzzling formulas had been enough.

But, hadn't they noticed her height? Maybe they'd chocked it up to boots or lifts, an inconsequential detail they overlooked as part of her alias. Their mission was to recover the material.

How many operatives would they send after her?

How many could she get?

The low hum returned. Handing over a spy or two to the government could bring her within reach of the Mobius. Prove her allegiance. At worst, they were leverage.

She turned to the balcony terrace, considering its unused real estate. An herbaceous garden with a decorative in-floor pond. And then there was the vacant apartment below. She grabbed a notepad and pen, scribbling a shopping list and sketching out plans for a new residence.

17

(silver, gold)

After a shopping spree for home goods and a stop at the pet store, Eve scoured the internet for real estate. She combed interactive maps, surveying properties, and jotted down the most promising targets. She evaluated the neighborhoods and circled a six bedroom in West Hollywood with a little saffron pool house.

Her next project required the television. She'd memorized a kickboxing workout DVD ages ago, but hand-to-hand combat with professional foreign agents required more rigorous training. She settled on three apps: an in-depth Krav Maga instruction, a Wing Chun virtual trainer, and another for kung fu. An enlarged spent paper towel roll with broken chopsticks stuck through it served as a makeshift wooden dummy. Between sessions, she rehydrated and shopped the internet for more supplies—another plexiglass box, board game pieces, and lots of sand. All rush delivery.

She wiped sweat from her neck and picked up the remote.

"There's no way I'm going to remember all this," she mumbled.

She pressed Play, tossing the remote onto the couch, and dropped into her stance. Eve copied the movements of the instructor—sweeping her left foot, then right foot, following their hand motions and kicks and jabbing the air.

Though longer sessions, the kung fu app was more approachable. Two instructors executed the forms, a man and a woman. Afterward, they sparred to demonstrate real-world functionality. She positioned her mock wooden dummy diagonal from the screen, eyeing their movements while punching and kicking.

* * *

The erratic temblors rumbling throughout the afternoon troubled Eugene as Zach coached him at the laptop.

"The hell is she doing out there?"

"Who cares?" Zach answered. "Focus."

"This isn't going to work. She's not going to fall for this."

"She doesn't know what she's looking at."

"Not entirely, but—she's reading up on it and she's got some kind of photographic memory."

"Eidetic memory." Shadi sat at the dining table with them. "There's no such thing as true photographic memory."

"Sure, fine, whatever," said Eugene. "She can remember shit. And if I put it in there, she will look it up."

"Which is why we're doing this," said Zach. "Your delivery has to be like, *This is nothing*."

"Maybe we should convince her to switch programming languages," said Shadi.

"No," said Zach. "That's a huge red flag."

The sliding glass door rolled open and Troy entered, shirtless and sweaty, fresh from a run in their extensive backyard.

Shadi followed his bare chest as he headed down the hall for a shower. "Well, I'm just saying, we have to...be able...to...the, um..."

Eugene and Zach glanced over, catching the glisten of Troy's back.

"*Shadi*," Zach said with annoyance.

"Hm?" She awakened.

"All right." Eugene stood. "I need a break."

Janelle pushed open the kitchen door with a sterling tray of fresh baked chocolate chip cookies. "Good, because I've run out of counter space in there."

Zach tugged Eugene's arm. "Sit down."

"I need to think about something else for like an hour," said Eugene.

"You want to learn how to bake?" Janelle set the tray onto the table. "Keeps your mind off shit."

"I don't want to think at all," said Eugene.

Kevin wandered in from the garage. "Ooh—cookies."

Shadi reached for one and Janelle swatted at her hand with the oven mitt.

"You can't have those," she said.

"Why not?" Shadi pouted.

Janelle frowned, guilty. "They have lard in them."

"Why would you even make something like that?" Shadi asked.

"It's the recipe I know. And they don't come out the same with vegetable shortening."

"See!" Eugene pointed to Janelle. "That's regular memory! There's no way she's not going to notice me doing this shit!"

"Sit down." Zach ordered. "It'll be fine."

"No," said Eugene. "We need another plan."

"What you need is a crash course in sales." Darien sauntered in with Cassidy. "And I don't mean to brag—"

"Oh, it's okay, you can brag." Cassidy smiled. "We were the top performing real estate agents in our territory, three years running. Seven of them were murder houses and one was a meth lab."

Eugene put his hands up, shaking his head. "No, no, no, no, no, no, no, no."

"He's broken." Zach leaned back. "You broke him."

Eugene clasped his hands together. "Yo—if I'm going learn anything from you two, it's going be how to pleasure another human being."

"*Eugene*," said Cassidy. "Thank you."

"I know." Darien smiled. "Sales seems both easy and mysterious."

"You don't understand," said Eugene. "She's not wired like a normal human being, all right?"

"Totally get it," said Darien. "But in our line of work, you have to learn how to get along with everyone. It's not about personalities, it's about the deal. And we're going to get you the confidence you need to close this one."

"It's sick," Eugene muttered, "But I actually believed you when you said that."

Darien nodded, spreading his hands. "And I can teach you how to do the same thing to everyone, all the time."

"What are we talking about?" Troy walked in, pulling on a fresh T-shirt.

"Trying to give Eugene confidence." Zach sighed, pinching the bridge of his nose.

"Dude," he said. "You're making it more than it is."

"Easy for you to say," said Eugene.

"No, no," said Troy. "We're all in this together. We all want the same thing here. We want you to succeed, dude. Let us help you. You take a little advice from everybody, piece together what works for you, and know that you've got this."

Eugene's face brightened, a boost in his spirit.

* * *

The rumble of Eve's activity ended, but Eugene was too busy being bombarded with advice to notice.

"Honesty is the best policy," said Darien. "Except when it's not. Which is why it's so important to sound honest. And you do that by connecting with someone."

"Even if you don't like them," said Cassidy. "Or have nothing in common with them."

"We're not in the business of selling so much as we're in the business of people," said Darien. "The key is to be interested."

"Specifically, you need to identify what they want," she said. "People won't tell you because they're afraid to admit it or they're distrusting or they're poor, but they'll let you know in subtle ways. It's your job to pick up on their cues and let them know you're the one who can give it to them."

"And you don't just say it flat out." Darien smiled. "It's a game, right? You do this little dance, have some fun. And the two of you...get what you want out of it."

He turned to Cassidy, her eyes ready to meet his. They kissed and groped each other as though Eugene wasn't there.

Zach's advice wasn't much better. "You have to show her you're the alpha."

Eugene leaned forward, elbows on the table. "All right. How do I do that?"

"By demonstrating your power and control in the situation."

"But...I don't have power or control—"

"Right. You just act like you do."

Eugene's face twisted. "What?"

Zach pressed his hands together, aiming at him. "Alphas dominate whatever situation they're in. You have to be the master at all times."

"There's no such thing as an alpha," Shadi said from behind him.

"Of course, coming from a woman." Zach muttered. He raised his voice. "Ever hear of the alpha-wolf?"

"It's inaccurate." She neared the table. "In fact, the man who developed the theory has been trying to get the publisher to retract the study for decades."

"Okay, so what makes them dominant, then?"

"Nothing. He realized they weren't observing dominance so much as a negative reaction to captivity. In the wild, wolves organize familial packs based on their personalities, age, condition—and they breed regardless of hierarchy."

"And only alphas breed. Survival of the fittest."

"All wolves can breed," she said. "And *fittest* means *best suited to the environment*. Think about it—if only the top ten percent of any species reproduced, there would be far fewer plants and animals and people on Earth than there are."

"No, they're just betas and sigmas, and—"

"Those aren't real things," said Shadi. "It's a myth perpetrated by guys like you to make yourselves think you're better than everybody else."

"Well, wait," said Eugene. "You really didn't dominate anything last time. And the first time, she just made you smaller."

"Oh, yeah? Want to see me dominate this conversation?" Zach held up both middle fingers. "When you're ready to get educated, come find me. I might consider helping you."

He stormed off, and Shadi sat down. She expounded the neuroscience of fight-or-flight response, the mechanisms of fear in the brain, and how human beings operated using a system millions of years old for modern-day scenarios without a prehistoric parallel. Though exhaustive and informative, it offered Eugene no comfort.

Troy sat down.

"All right, yo, lay it on me," said Eugene.

"First off," said Troy, "you're not fooling anybody. Want me to be real with you? You need to be real with me."

He puffed up about to defend himself, then deflated. "All right, I'm not even from L.A., I'm from San Bernardino."

"Doesn't matter." Troy leaned forward, elbows on the table. "You know what you got that nobody else here's got?"

Eugene shrugged.

"Knowledge and power."

"What the hell are you talking about?"

"See, your problem is, you're looking at everybody else. But this is your territory, man. This is your universe. That's why I say you've got this. You already know all this shit."

"Okay, sure, but—I don't have any power in this situation."

"Look, look—she listens to you. And it's because she knows you're scared—"

"That's what I been saying! What if she finds out I lied to her?"

"Let's be objective," said Troy. "Why are we all still here?"

"I...I don't know." Eugene shook his head. "I really don't."

"Because she's not a killer. She wouldn't be doing all this to keep us alive." He tapped a finger on the table with every word. "And you know this shit."

Each tap imbued Eugene with invincibility. Until the tremors of each nearing step shook down the walls he'd built up over the past few hours, leaving him bare and exposed. A heavy gust. The lid lifted.

"*Eugene.*"

He floated down a procession of assurances, nods, and a hearty slap on the shoulder by Troy. The front door closed behind him.

* * *

"You shouldn't have told him she won't do anything," said Kevin.

Troy shrugged. "She won't."

"You didn't run to help me because you thought she was harmless," said Shadi.

He pursed his lips. "Important thing is getting it done. If it means taking his mind off his fear, so be it."

* * *

Eugene stood alongside the laptop as the woman's fingers flitted across the keyboard, taking dictation. He was doing it. He was actually doing it. Like Zach told him. Like Troy said he could. He was going to be a hero. The hero. But then, she paused, her eyes scanning the screen.

Eugene imagined the worst—

She squinted. "What is this?"

"It's what you asked for—"

"You lying little shit!"

He imagined her fist slamming down, annihilating him in a burst of blood splatter.

"Eugene?"

He stared up at her, blank, still consumed by the vision of his demise.

"You were saying?"

"Uhhh. Yeah. You know—I-I don't think this is going to work. I mean, what you're asking for...I don't think this is it."

"Oh," she said, disappointed.

"Yeah, I'm sorry, but—"

"No, it's—it must be really hard to do this without the internet. How about we search right now and brainstorm?"

He leaned back, unprepared for diplomacy. "Uh, okay. Yeah."

"Let me pull up this site I found—you can tell me if I'm on the right track."

Eugene breathed deeply. His knees were still ready to give out under him.

"This is the guy I been reading," she said. "He's kind of an asshole, but—well, here."

The web page loaded. He recognized it. A dark-web hacker forum. She scrolled down to a long post.

"Oh, no—he's good."

SvenData. Hacker. Nihilist. Might've been Scandinavian, or was at least hiding out there. If she was taking lessons from SvenData, at some point she would've discovered the security flaw.

"Awesome," she said. "Okay, so, can we incorporate some of this?"

Darknet architecture. She already wanted to mask the code, encrypt whatever else she could. Now she wanted to modify their bots' programming with protective layers based on SvenData's designs.

"Uh, well, I—I'm still not sure what you're trying to do. I mean, I thought these were social—"

"They are."

His relief melted. With her every keystroke, he helped erase her fingerprints, making it harder for anyone to find her. By the time he walked through the front door, the knot in his chest was so tight he expected his heart to stop. He was no hero. And more afraid of admitting it to his housemates than he was of her.

Zach and Troy were playing *Go-Kart WarZone X*. Their eager faces asked all the questions.

"It's done," said Eugene.

They sprang from the couch.

"Holy shit," said Zach.

"I told you—you got it." Troy pointed at him. "I told you."

"Yeah." He nodded. "You did."

Maybe he could blame Zach.

18

(silver, purple)

Fog lifted off the bay. The sun warmed the coastline. Simon had taken an evening flight for a breakfast meeting with Marty Glick, a puckish little man, well into his fifties. They sat at a polished outdoor café on the Zeugma campus while employees in polo shirts and chinos passed by.

"Now, I haven't had eggs like that in quite a while." Simon pushed his plate aside. "You know, a lot of people think eggs Florentine is attributed to Catherine de Medici, but—"

"That's a myth," said Marty. "It was actually a police commissioner a hundred years or so later who fabricated the story that she'd brought a team of cooks with her."

Huh. Simon's head ticked to the side. "That's right."

Marty lifted his coffee mug, appearing amused. "Delamare, I think his name was."

"So, have you given any thought to my proposal?" Simon asked, fixing a cuff on his platinum suit.

"I have." He took a sip from his mug. "And, it's a no."

Why did they always have to be so difficult?

Simon smiled, baffled. "I don't understand. It fits into your whole long-term plan. Mining asteroids. Self-sustaining cities in space. The future."

"Yeah." Marty's blue eyes lingered. "You know why I created Tmesis?"

What is this game?

Simon's brow clenched, but he kept a bemused smile. "No?"

"*SpaceQuest 3030.*"

"I remember that show—Kronut! And Lieutenant Bort."

Marty nodded. "It was only on for a year and a half, and clearly a knock-off of better sci-fi, but I loved it. The ship's computer was so intuitive it was like its own character, not just some machine they asked questions or barked orders at. That stuck with me. I wanted to recreate that for people."

Simon nodded. In his youth, he'd dreamed of Agartha, and all the wondrous lands and creatures inhabiting Hollow Earth. Nevertheless, at a young age, he'd known no such place existed below the surface, just layers of molten rock surrounding an uninhabitable core.

He wants something. He's just taking the long way round.

"Well, I'm sure millions of people would be surprised that the operating system they use everyday has its origins in a cult TV show." Simon leaned forward, straightening his amethyst tie. "That vision, that same future—"

"The future I envision, people work together," said Marty. "It's not about one person. It's a collective effort. Everyone is there for everyone else."

"Right, sure, yeah. And it's the two of us. Working together. What's the problem?"

Marty leaned back. "I don't want to work with you."

"Why?" He grinned. "I'm brilliant. You're brilliant. We both have fantastic hair."

He set his coffee mug down, focused on Simon's unwavering grin. "You know, one of my hobbies is human behavioral psychology. I mean, if you're going to build cutting-edge AI, you need to know what people are thinking when they interact."

"I collect rocks." Simon's head bobbled.

"See, I can't get a good read on you, and partnerships require trust."

His mouth drooped but didn't erase the smile. "You don't trust me?"

"Never have," said Marty. "Don't you think it's odd we're meeting out in the open?"

Simon shrugged. "Figured it's a nice day."

"I don't want to be alone in a room with you behind closed doors."

He reared back, chuckling. "What do you think I'm going to do?"

"I don't know." Marty shrugged. "What do you want to do now that I've told you'll never get what you want?"

Bash your skull in. Skin you alive. Incinerate your body with a particle accelerator.

"Even if you were the only option," said Marty. "I wouldn't go into business with you."

The edges of Simon's smile rose again. "I don't know what you're talking about."

Marty stared back at the hollow expression.

"Okay. Well." He checked his watch. "I have another meeting, so, good luck with your fusion missiles."

"Rockets."

"Sure." He stood, taking his coffee mug.

"Good luck building a future nobody wants." Simon shrugged. "They did cancel it, after all."

Marty walked off.

* * *

Masuda sat between cubicles, tilted back in her chair, and flung a stress ball at a ceiling tile. A thump, and it sailed back into her hand.

"All right, " she mumbled. "So, no other bodies."

"Except for the one in the cat room." Guzman pulled up a chair.

"Right." She flung the ball into the ceiling. "And Forensics determined the fingerprints matched Irina Talbot's."

"All right—why kill her?"

The ball snapped into her hand. "I don't know, he...he double-crossed her."

"Double-crosses his wife and partner?"

"Yeah—because...the sex isn't good any more, and he has a magic rock now."

He snickered. "How does that change anything?"

"I don't know, I'm just spit-balling here," she said. "They've grown apart, because—at first it was exciting and passionate, you know? The thrill of the two of them against the world, leaning on each other. But now they're trapped in this rut where he's in the basement every night and she's alone upstairs guarding the house, and he's pretty sure she's cheating on him with the yoga instructor but he can't prove it or hire a private investigator because—"

"He's a spy?"

"Right." She flung the ball at the ceiling. "So he's resentful of his fake job and his real job, and with his fake relationship and his real one, so he starts plotting his escape from the four concentric circles of the hellish Venn diagram his life's become. Enter Kincaid. Someone with a mountain of resentment and pent-up ambition. And they connect."

"Then why's he collecting all the cars?"

"That I don't know." Another fling, another thump.

"Mel." Callahan stepped out of her office. "What have I told you about that?"

Masuda sat up. "It helps me think."

"Does it?" asked Guzman.

Dempsey strode in, shaking a VHS tape over his head and grinning. "I got it."

"So you weren't on suspension?" Masuda asked. "You went back in time?"

"No," he said. "Well, sort of...Just—come on, you need to see this."

They headed down to the audiovisual department and popped the tape into a VCR.

"All right," said Dempsey. "So, this bank truck goes to a shopping mall—"

"Sounds like the start of a terrible joke," said Masuda.

He held up a finger. "Except it doesn't leave."

The tape played. A closed-circuit camera captured the missing armored car's arrival, outside a shopping plaza. It parked behind the building. Cut to the next camera angle, obscured by tree branches. A flicker under the foliage, on the pavement. Cut to another angle.

A small, dark figure ran across the parking lot, a black mop of chaotic hair unleashed from the hoodie.

"The hell is she thinking?" asked Masuda.

"That she's going to take a bunch of money," said Guzman.

Dempsey nodded. "The cops have been working the angle the two guards stole it—"

"So Kincaid has them, too?" asked Masuda.

"Maybe." He shrugged. "If not, might be hard to find their bodies."

"Oh." Masuda waved a finger. "It can be done."

"All right," said Callahan. "So what do we have in terms of tracing the cash?"

"No luck." Dempsey sighed. "Only a small fraction of it's logged, and none of it's been spent."

"Then we still got no way to find her," said Guzman.

"Yeah, we do," said Callahan. "Dempsey's got the right idea."

"Are you serious?" Masuda gaped with a tentative smile. "Are you saying what I think you're saying?"

Callahan nodded. "We're going to *X-Files* the hell out of this thing."

"Yes!" Masuda clenched her fists in glee.

"Strange disappearances, bright lights in the sky, suddenly haunted places, weird smells—from now on we're chasing all the crap nobody else will touch."

* * *

The flight from San Francisco was less than an hour and half. Simon took a car service for a relaxed ride to Pierce Technologies, arriving in the afternoon. Plenty of time for a scheduled restroom break and the usual security protocol with Hargrove and Durbin.

Once settled into his office, he opened his work laptop. The first of his emails was an invite to an impromptu meeting from the shareholders.

Simon clicked the link and logged in.

He grinned. "Good afternoon, everyone."

Nods and mutters.

"I'm going to cut right to it," said the bald man. "The FBI officially informed us about the security breach—"

"Ah," said Simon. "Then you know I can't comment on it."

"Yes," he answered. "They made that much clear."

"Well, if this is in order to assuage your fears, let me start by saying —"

"There's also the other matter of the accident," said the bald man.

"What accident?" asked Simon.

"At the Workshop? Where you conducted the test of an experimental fusion reactor that we all agreed was not part of our long-term strategy, and you neglected to tell us you'd already built?"

Simon smiled wider, spreading his hands. "We'd already spent so much time and energy—"

"And money," he said. "And five people were treated for smoke inhalation in an experiment in which several researchers said Dr. Bennett repeatedly warned you was not safe."

The promise of profit is all they care about. Remind them.

"You're focusing on the negative," said Simon. "It was successful. And once we iron out the design, we'll be on track—"

"No, we won't," said the platinum-haired woman.

"—to have the most efficient fusion reactor on the planet."

"We discussed this," said the bald man. "And you acted in direct violation of this board."

Bunch of nothings who bought themselves the illusion of importance.

"It's my company." Simon chuckled.

"It's because of this and other concerns—"

"What concerns?" He lit up.

The platinum-haired woman sat forward. "You met with Randall Chang. Who is under investigation by the US government."

"Yeah. Investigation," Simon said with an airy shrug. "They haven't found anything yet."

She winced in disbelief.

"For those reasons and more," said the bald man. "We've called a vote to remove you as CEO."

"I have all the controlling shares." Simon grinned. "I'll create a new board."

"Simon." A bearded man waved. "You lost that when you agreed to be publicly traded."

"There's no way I would have done that."

"As your general counsel," said the bearded man. "I can say we explained it to you in detail, and you said it was fine."

In order to get the investment. Shit.

"That—that can't be right." He continued smiling.

"It's the legal agreement which formed the board," said counsel, circling his hand. "All of these people. You were fine with it."

They got lucky. They're still just parasites. Let them think what they want.

"So," said Simon. "We all understand there's been some misunderstandings—"

"A majority of us believe you are ineffective in this role," said the bald man.

"I am not only effective, I am essential. If we can just take—"

"We're not saying you can't be involved in some other capacity that contributes to the success of the organization," said the platinum-haired woman.

"My capacity is ownership, operation, and innovation at Pierce Technologies because I built this co—"

"You built a laser cannon," the platinum-haired woman said. "And in order to get them mass produced, we invested the capital. You didn't create it out of nothing. And you didn't do it by yourself."

"None of you"—Simon chortled—"did anything."

"All in favor of removing Simon Pierce from the position of chief executive officer," said the bald man.

"Aye!" the board members responded.

"All opposed?"

Simon sat in silence, staring at the screen. His expression was blank. His eyes, his thoughts were elsewhere—chopping the heads off these worthless bags of worm food while they begged for mercy.

The board members glanced about, unsure if his video feed had frozen.

"Simon?" asked general counsel.

A gradual return to reality. The edges of his mouth curled up, his faced brightened. Smiling.

"I've decided to take a sabbatical," said Simon. "A well-deserved break in order to recharge, reassess, realign. Get back to my roots, you know? Inventing. Creating. Innovating. That's where I belong. Not in some office, behind a desk. It's burning me out. I think it'll be better for everyone. Really."

* * *

Kira left work at five thirty. The identity which she'd intended as a fallback had gone from an existential threat to fueling her plans. The Russians meant leverage. No Nukes meant access to an established network.

No strangers surveilling from across the street. No cars following her. As an added measure, she'd rented a private garage. A little concrete building no bigger than a small house nestled in an industrial neighborhood. She swapped out vehicles, changing into Diane, and drove to the high-rise in her luxury electric car.

In the hour's break at the penthouse, she put the finishing touches on her plan, tended to her new pets in the pond, and reviewed a map of the area. For dinner, she reheated her attempt at recreating Gideon's kale-and-paneer casserole (still couldn't get the spices right) before driving back to the rented garage. She switched into Kira and drove the hybrid to a park-and-ride lot at a rail station several blocks away. From there, she took a circuitous train ride to Pico Station.

Eve stepped onto the platform, the bustle of the street behind the ringing bells of the railway signals as passengers boarded. She hung back, scanning faces for hints of recognition.

"All right, this is easy," she whispered. "You do this without thinking about it all the time."

A metallic hiss and the train sped off with a whir. Her head swung side to side as she glided the length of the track. She reached the metal gates leading to the street and stopped.

Was this a trap? Or had she been stood up?

She turned around. A beefy man in a windbreaker appeared from around a kiosk sign, his stern gaze locked on her.

The thrill of fright and excitement—electric blue and white—sent her hurrying down the stairs. The man followed. She rushed down the block, round the corner, glancing over her shoulder. He wasn't more than a few steps behind. She turned on her heel, darting into a wide alley between buildings and reached into her jacket. He chased her into a narrow passage.

Her path was blocked by a dumpster. Eve spun around.

Winded, the man held up his hands, taking an extra second.

"I am here to deliver message," he said. "Your brother, Luke. His wife. Their new baby."

Not what she expected. She choked, tormented by the memory of swatting Luke's hand away. Laurel green grayed into desert sand.

She swallowed hard, forcing the memory down, trying to sound tough as possible. "You go anywhere near my family and I will literally shit all over the Kremlin."

That did not sound the way you thought it did.

"Two days," he grunted. "Give us what we want and they live."

Her eyes burned with guilt and fury. Laurel and crimson. She was ready to lunge at him.

He nodded, reading her face. "I am just messenger. We know material is dangerous. You will put it in box, put box in travel bag, and wait on bench at Pico Station for contact. You know him. He drives blue car. Tomorrow night. Eight o'clock."

He turned aside to leave.

"And that's it? You're going to let me walk away?"

He sneered. "I told you, I am just messenger."

He headed out of the alley. Now was her chance.

"Yeah?" she asked, louder. "You going to tell them what I said? If they go near my family?"

He stopped, peering over his shoulder to answer. A flash filled his vision. His legs wobbled as the ground shifted. His eyes refocused, spots mottling the rising world. The heavy clomp of her steps jarred his senses. He ran for his life, looking back as she closed in at astonishing speed, reaching out her hand. The sensation of falling overtook him again as he dropped through a drain grate, screaming as he plummeted.

"No!" Eve slammed a fist onto the asphalt. "Dammit."

She blasted the grate, shrinking it away, and dialed the *modifikator* to neutral before shoving it into her jacket. With her phone's flashlight, she peered down the length of pipe. Endless darkness. Even if he survived the fall, the rats would get him. She turned the light off.

Luke. Gemma. Christopher. Of course they'd pick them. Charlotte was at an United Nations clinic in East Africa. Sawyer had given a TEDTalk last year and was too prominent. And neither of them had kids.

She stuck the *modifikator* into its case and stood. Eve marched out of the alley and several blocks until she found a cellphone store crammed between a Whirl'd of Smoothies and a shoe store. She bought a burner phone and set it up outside. There were only three voice-changing apps available for the model, so she installed the highest-rated one as she walked the street, settling on a secluded space between an apartment building and a New Age temple.

She selected a man's voice. Her fingers dialed through the color sequence. The first ring, her insides rattled. With the second, every muscle tensed.

"Hello?"

"Uh—yes," she said. "Good evening, Mr.Kincaid. This is Agent... Armstrong. I'm calling about your sister—"

"Have you found her? Is she okay?"

Her throat closed. Her mind spun. They'd talked to her family. Questioned them. What had they said? Were they listening?

"Hello? Are you there?"

She swallowed.

"We needed to inform you, um—" She hesitated, then sputtered and fumed, the software distorting her voice like a warped digital banshee. "You're dead! Your whole family's dead! We're going to kill you!"

She hung up and popped out the battery. She shoved the phone into a trash can as she hurried back to the rail station, confident the FBI would protect her brother's family.

* * *

After a stop at the garage and another identity change, Eve returned to the penthouse with enough time to retrieve Eugene. They dove right into coding and logged a solid hour of work.

"Whenever I see that string"—she pointed at the screen—"The word *piddlewomp* pops into my mind."

"What?" He chuckled, peering over his shoulder at her. "What does that mean?"

"It's a made-up word." She shrugged. "But it just pops into my head."

He snickered, regarding her with more curiosity. "So, um, what were you like in high school?"

She typed away, giving him a side-eye. Faded plum boxes, sage green puffs, and chestnut-brown rays. "A dork. Kind of a misfit. There were only like five of us."

Eve had been so sure Neal had had a crush on her, but he's asked Clarissa to prom, so Eve said she had the flu and hid in her room for three days.

"What about you?"

"Pretty much the same," said Eugene. "I mean, before that, I really didn't have any friends."

"Yeah," she muttered. "I've never been good at that either."

He nodded, facing the screen again. She checked the time in the corner and bit her lip.

"Wait." Eugene pointed. "That's a miskey."

"Yep, thanks." She backtracked, correcting the error.

"Well, I don't know about you." She mustered a yawn, stretching. "But I am beat. I think this is a good stopping point."

"Uh, sure," he said. "You're the boss."

She set her hand palm side up alongside him.

"You want to hit Save first?" he asked.

"Oh—yeah, that would be good."

* * *

Diane's E-V circled the warehouse. Convinced the block was empty, Eve parked and shrank the car. Once inside, she hit the lights and locked the door behind her. With long sweeps of the side of her shoe, she cleared the floor of cinder block chunks. She enlarged a couple cases and changed into the suit. The radiation proofing would protect her if the other precautions failed while developing her clean energy source.

She unpacked the second case, enlarging the items. First, a specially designed plexiglass box with a small port built in the front and a hatch on the side. Next, her testing station, upgraded with better switches and knobs. A personal dosimeter. A Geiger counter. A package of potassium iodide tablets. A folding table, notepads, pens, two fire extinguishers, and several copper cylinders. She enlarged the plexiglass box until its walls were a foot and half thick and made it superdense.

A truck growled outside.

Eve held her breath. Doors slammed shut. Muffled words. She listened, squinting, trying to deduce their activities. After sustained silence, she picked up the testing rig and slid it into the mouth of the giant box's port.

The warehouse's door handle wiggled.

Who the fuck were these guys?

She spun around, grabbing her helmet, and dashed to the door. She slapped the lights off. The door handle juddered, halting with a frustrated final clunk.

Violet, blue, scarlet; gray, purple, gold.

Eve passed through the door.

"What are you doing?" A lion-haired man approached the fat-faced one.

"Who sets a timer for nineteen past the hour?" asked Fat-Face.

"Maybe it's slow?" Lion-Hair shrugged.

Fat-Face scanned the ground. He pointed to tire marks leading out of a puddle. Lion-Hair nodded. They turned, heading for their warehouse.

Brown, green, gray.

Upon hearing the click, the men checked over their shoulders. More clicks. They lingered, glancing at each other as she aimed.

A flash—and the dumpster alongside them shrank down to a couple inches. In the darkness, it might have looked like it disappeared.

"Yo, dude, yo," Lion-Hair mumbled.

"You saw that, right?" asked Fat-Face.

"Yeah, man." He backed away.

They took off running.

Scaring them off wasn't enough. She needed them to leave her alone. They wouldn't go to the authorities, but what if they told their boss? What if the boss had a police officer on the take? Like in *Asphalt Jungle* or *Serpico* or *Training Day*?

Eve raced after them, taking aim. "N-No, no, no."

She phased into their warehouse. Fat-Face and Lion-Hair were carrying a table toward the door. Three other guys stood at long tables dividing up plastic bags filled with white powder.

A drug operation.

She had to hand these guys over to the cops—no, the cops would tell the FBI about a super-powered vigilante. Capture them and then make it look like a rival gang had torched the place.

Fat-Face and Lion-Hair braced the table against the door handle.

The bulky man stood from a card table, glaring. "The hell are you doing?"

Fat-Face struggled to catch his breath. "Th-There-There was something out there."

Click, click.

Lion-Hair checked Fat-Face. "You hear that?"

"It's in here, man," said Fat-Face. "It's in here!"

"What is?" asked the bulky man.

A flash sparked behind the lion-haired man. The crate behind him shrank to a pellet. He spun around. The men pulled their guns.

"What is going on?" asked the bulky man.

"We were checking the block," said Fat-Face. "That warehou—"

Eve's fist popped him in the nose.

Fat-face recoiled, catching the blood as it dribble from his nostrils. An uppercut knocked the wind out of the lion-haired man. The two men flailed, taking haphazard swings as she unleashed the fury of her invisible fists. Fat-Face made a desperate two-handed shove.

She landed on a wooden crate. An accidental tap of the return setting, and she popped into view—visible, normal. A pang of fear—hot yellow and tangerine—the settings clicked out of position.

Orange, scarlet, brown. Ultradense.

They opened fire. Bullets ricocheted off her, flying into crates, into the drugs. One struck Lion-Hair in the temple. Another went into Fat-Face's chest. He flopped onto a mound of packages, motionless, while Lion-Hair slumped to the floor.

"Stop! Stop!" the bulky man demanded from under the cover of the card table.

They relented.

Her words were muffled by the helmet.

"What?" one of the gun men asked.

"Sorry!" Eve flipped up the face mask. "That wasn't supposed to happen."

"Shoot her in the face!" the bulky man ordered.

Before she could speak, the nearest gunman fired a round.

"*Ugh!*" She winced at the heavy snap. The bullet bounced off, skimming the ear of the furthest gunman.

"Ah, shit!" He grabbed the searing, bloodied cartilage.

She dropped the visor and pointed the arm cuff. Blue, yellow, silver. With a blast, she shrank the trio while the ringleader raced for the door.

Green, purple, blue. She enlarged to thirty feet, dropping the heel of her boot in front of the exit to cut him off.

Eve knelt, demolishing the table full of cash with her left knee, and wrapped her fingers around him. Blue, yellow, silver. She reduced to six feet, and stuck the ringleader into a pouch on her hip. She flipped up the visor in a frantic search for the others.

Movement in the corner of her eye. "No! Come back here!"

Two three-inch men fled to a corner, taking cover behind shelves of cleaning supplies.

"Shit!"

On her hands and knees, she scoped out the crevices between boxes, trying to gauge their hiding spots.

"All right, look, guys, I know this seems bad, but coming with me is a lot bet—"

Screams, and a tiny man ran out, chased by a pair of thick brown rats, one of them with bloodstained jaws.

"Oh god!" Eve lurched backward, scrambling away in disgust. She placed a protective hand over the pouch on her hip, where the ringleader banged against the leather.

The rat was too quick. With a snap, it snatched the man's leg, carrying him off as it darted away with its compatriot. She shoved boxes aside, clearing her view of the back wall. Blood splatter, remnants of clothing. A tiny shoe with a torn ankle stuck out.

Eve stood, grumbling, and scanned the ground. Fat-Face's body lay atop the packages. A splotch of gore on one of them. The last tiny man had been crushed by the collapsed table as he'd tried running.

She glanced at the wall-to-wall carnage. "Nice one, Eve."

She raised her arm. Yellow, green, pink. A white-hot ball fired and the drugs burst into flames. As she'd suspected, they'd disabled the sprinkler system for fear of ruining their product. The crates and boxes were next—yellow, green, pink. The conflagration spread through the warehouse.

Gray, purple, gold; violet, blue, scarlet. She vanished into the night.

* * *

In less than an hour, Eve arrived at the penthouse as Diane. She slid the leather pouch onto a high table and walked off to put away the suit.

Once the motion stopped, her restless captive used a large knife sheathed on his ankle to pry into the leather. He struggled to puncture it, hacking away until the blade snapped off the hilt. Tremors. The rumble intensified. A violent jostle. The button rivet popped. Light poured in and he rushed out.

"Stupid *puta*," he said. "You think you're getting away with something, huh?"

"I had a completely different plan for tonight, thanks, before your lackeys started snooping around. But I guess I don't have to worry about that anymore."

"What are you talking about?"

"Well, you know, after they put out the fire, the police are going to find two guys with bullets in their heads from, presumably, their own crew."

He folded his arms. "Yeah, except I told my boss about your warehouse, the lights shutting off."

Her lips rumpled, forehead puckering.

"Why do you think I had Tiny and Marcos checking it out? Lionel knows there's something going on, and they're going to look there first."

She sucked her teeth with a slow nod. "Okay. Okay. So, a trade. You give me information, and I give you protection. New identity, new life, million dollars to start over."

He scoffed. "I pull in five times that a year."

"Really?"

"Yeah. I'm what you call upper management. So, if that's your best offer, you can shove it up your ass."

"I am twenty-nine times your size," she said, as though the precise number would sway him.

"Yeah?" He sneered. "So what? What're you going to do?"

"Sorry?" Eve squinted at his insolence. "I was expecting at little more humility seeing as how I just wasted all of your friends."

"Wasted?" He chuckled. "Let's just say your execution was lacking."

"All right." She balked. "I'll...crush one of your legs with my thumb. Shatter all the bones and turn the muscle into mush—well, then, I'll need to make a tourniquet so you don't bleed to death—"

He grimaced. "What are you talking about, tourniquet?"

"Well, I need information—"

"Take your million and leave the country. Because they're going to come for you. And they won't stop till you're dead."

Great. That's all you need. Drug dealers hunting you down.

And another captive who didn't respect her. Eve scowled. She didn't have time to hunt for another warehouse. She had to create her clean energy source.

"You won't do nothing." He snickered, then beat his chest. "Not afraid to die. Not afraid of you. Stupid bitch."

He's right. You're weak. Stupid. He can see right through you.

She snatched the little man and stood.

"Hey!" His voice faded with the natural swing of her arm.

She remembered Talbot's body. The cats fighting over Mrs. Talbot. The rats from earlier in the night. She didn't need to do anything drastic.

She carried him to the kitchen counter. With her free hand, she removed lilies from a vase, tossing them onto the countertop.

He splashed into the cold water inside the long glass cylinder.

"If you don't care," she said. "You can just sink."

He obliged, resting on the bottom with his arms folded.

Eve sat at a bar stool and folded her arms. They locked hard stares. He turned bright red. Then purple. He kicked off the bottom, rocketing up, and broke the surface, gasping for air as he thrashed.

"What's the matter?" she asked, deadpan. "All you have to do is stop swimming."

"You don't got the balls!" His thin voice echoed. "You're dead! You hear me?!"

"Yeah?" Her faint smile lifted with derision. "Who's going to kill me? You? Your gang you're never going to see again?"

"I'm going to rip out your tongue before I put a bullet in your head!"

"Imagine that—big tough guy like you dies in a glass of water. Want me to tell them it was half full or half empty?"

She figured it'd be easier to keep afloat at his size but not freeze to death. He must've had the same idea. Something in his face changed. He panicked, arms and legs paddling. His fingers scrabbled for traction on the slippery wall.

Eve stood from the bar stool, hands together in prayer. "Well, I'm going to let you be at peace, so..."

"No! *Hey!* Hey! You're not a killer!"

"You don't know anything about me." She stepped back and away.

* * *

Her distancing rumbles filled him with angst.

This was where he was going to die. Not in a bloody shoot-out with the police or a rival gang, but in a vase on a woman's countertop.

The water grew heavier. Colder. The burn in his muscles no longer a source of heat but a stark reminder he hadn't conserved his energy. His heart beat out of his chest. Slow death. Hypothermia and drowning. Pain on top of pain.

A thick white cord appeared. He clutched it with numbed fingers, looping it around his wrist and arm.

She lifted the length of butcher's twine, raising him to her face.

She smirked. "Change your mind?"

* * *

Lit tea candles warmed her captive. She miniaturized towels, a table and chair, complete with silverware. He chowed down on curry chicken and whatever leftovers she found and reduced. She took notes as he spoke. He was Armando Cordero, formerly of the Pinoy Blood Crew.

"The P-B-C!" He coughed, still winded from his near-drowning.

She glanced up from her notepad.

He shrugged. "Sounded better when we were kids. We were bush league. Running drugs, keeping territory. Didn't have a lot of cred or numbers, so we linked up with this other crew. Cousins with some of our boys. But, you know, then the cartels got big."

"So you started working for them?"

"Nah." He wiped his mouth. "This Vietnamese gang is getting squeezed, too, so we start forming alliances. All over. There's a little scuffle over who's in charge, until Lionel steps up. Says he can get mass firepower. All handmade. He figured out how to scrapyard the metal, form the parts. Has, like, twenty guys assembling assault rifles. Hardest thing was getting the ammo."

She stopped writing.

"The cartels thought they were dealing with street hoods," he said with a prideful smile. "In a couple months, we blew them wide open, consolidated with the other gangs. After that, everything north of San Diego became the Badlands."

He lifted his glass and took a sip of wine.

"How do I keep them from snooping around?" she asked.

"You don't." He cleared his throat. "You got Lionel's attention. He's not going to stop until he knows who you are and what you're doing."

She grumbled.

"Between you and me," he said, "he's only half a brain. The other half belongs to his sister, Lida."

"And where's she?"

"Nobody knows. I don't even think she's in the country."

She flipped to a fresh page. "Okay—tell me about operations."

"Sorry, those are trade secrets."

"Not any more. Unless you want to go for another swim."

"No, thanks." He smirked. "Just ate."

"Don't screw with me." She sat forward. "You lie, and I will figure it out. Then you'll see what I'm really capable of."

He scowled. "I work distribution. We cut the drugs, weigh them. Portion it out. Get the money from dealers. Make sure it's all there."

"How many warehouses?"

"Dozens. You'll never find all of them. And Lionel rotates. He'll let something go empty for months."

"What about the money? How do you launder it?"

He frowned, folding his arms. Eve tapped her finger in front of his table, the hefty vibrations jingling the silverware and knocking over his glass.

"They use banks—not like real banks, but, you know, they all got fronts. Laundromats, dry cleaners, bars, one's a flower shop. Money comes in the back, goes out at the counter. They like mom-and-pop joints, so it looks like people might be living there, but really, it's so we can have cash available whenever we need it."

"And the banks don't move?"

"They do, but slow. Slower than warehouses."

Cut their cash flow. Expose their network to the police. And, depending how well-fortified each bank was, it might be good practice infiltrating a secure government facility undetected.

"How many guys to a bank?"

"None, if possible. Unless it's a drop night." He mulled the numbers. "Then, you got guys outside, couple more inside...including the captain and the banker? Four, maybe five. You can't just walk in there."

She smiled. "Yeah, I can."

Armando divulged specifics on several choice locations, a couple he'd managed for a time. The florist was considered a cushy assignment, low-profile on a quiet block. Out of the dry cleaners, only two were worth the trouble. Then there were the strip clubs, bars, food trucks, *taquieras*, and an art gallery in the middle of downtown. He told her when the big drops took place, where the guards posted, and about how long it took to log and flip the cash.

She carried him out the sliding glass door. Cool night air wafted over the terrace as Eve stopped at the edge of the pond. A small island rested in the middle, and on it, the little pool house she'd acquired. While not intended for him, it was meant for more dangerous houseguests.

"Pond's heated," she said. "The fish are Oscars. They're aggressive and think anything that lands in the water is food. Feel free to take any room you want. I'll be back in the morning for your list."

"List?"

"Yeah—groceries, toiletries, clothes, alcohol. Whatever you need."

She knelt, leaning across the water and pressing the back of her hand into the sand. Armando stepped onto the strange isle. Eve stood while he searched the dark, examining his new abode.

"Oh, and watch out during the day," she said. "We get a lot of crows."

* * *

The island shook as she departed. A sudden vicious swirl churned the black water, the edge of a fin breaking the surface. Armando turned back to the bungalow he'd been given. The sliding glass door rumbled shut. A breeze whipped over the terrace, chilling him. Better than dying in a vase.

19

(silver, brown)

Eve rolled out of bed after less than four hours. She clutched her coffee mug, skimming replies on the FoilHat message board. Her other fishing expedition. Most were snarky comments or cryptic inside jokes.

There was a red dot in the corner of her default profile icon. She clicked it. A direct message from another user, Don Rumata:

Not true. I knew the man himself. I worked on a guidance system under his leadership several years ago. No UFOs or dimensional portals. He doesn't have a lot of patience for bullshit but one of the best people you could ever work for. I remember he used to do crossword puzzles in pen, and sudoku before it was cool. A down to earth guy who conducts himself with integrity. Last of a dying breed. Big Saints fan and big fan of LSU, so by no means perfect ;)

She leaned back. Better than the other responses, though not as insightful as she'd hoped. She figured by now the FBI had a dossier on her. So she needed a dossier on someone close to the Mobius.

LSU and the Saints, so, maybe a Louisiana native?

Eve delved into public records and social media, supplementing her research with genealogy websites. He'd graduated from LSU in 1985. BS in electrical engineering, PhD in applied physics. ROTC throughout. Joined the military as an officer. Married in 1986 to Gloria Mendoza Avalos, divorced in 1988 and remarried in 1989 to Camille Duval. Divorced in 2006. Two children. Benjamin, born 1991, graduated from

MIT, working near Boston in cybersecurity. And Abigail, born 1993, in a graduate program at Oxford.

Eve winced. Younger and smarter than her, more accomplished. But too distant to be useful. More clues. Sudoku before it was cool.

"So," she whispered, "around 2004?"

She tried the search terms *McCrae*, *guidance*, and different years. A single photo of him appeared from 2002, in the out-of-print *Technology Today* magazine. The article focused on computer hardware tested by the military for a guidance system.

Who was he now? What did he regret? What kept him up at night?

His career arc emerged. She'd pieced together the commands, their locations. Denver, DC, Boston. Searches of his rank as major and colonel produced better results. Former colleagues and service members had pictures posted on social media. Weddings, birthdays, graduations, and rank promotions. At times, he appeared stoic, eyes adrift, mind elsewhere. Other instances he was engaged, happy. Eve compiled a list, noting the occasion, date, clothing, weight, hairstyle, and mood.

She stared at a cropped picture of the general at his son's wedding. The couple's first dance. He'd been divorced ten years by then. He'd immersed himself in work, more secretive projects. None with the publicity of the guidance system.

Brow pinched, she pulled the edge of her lip through her teeth.

Provided no suspicions surrounded her yet-to-be-created power source, contacting someone with his rank was out of the question. If Diane approached him, how long before the feds discovered she wasn't real? Each scenario played out in her mind. None ended well.

But he was a scientist. And his mission was to unravel the secrets of the Mobius—

Dots of coral and periwinkle.

What did they already know? What if they'd figured out more than she had?

Probably. You're not that smart. You're not special.

"No, my theory—"

Is childish and ill-conceived.

"But—but it works."

And Talbot had said the military used electromagnetism for their experiments. What if they'd seen the Mobius as an element? They'd wanted to exploit the energy properties. The security breach would have triggered a lockdown, a moratorium on the project.

If he was as reasonable as Don Rumata had said, McCrae might find her research valuable. Maybe enough to overlook how she'd arrived at it. They could bond over deep conversations about the nature of reality, the fabric of the universe. She couldn't help but think his pesky notions of duty and honor would get in the way.

Nobody—

"Yeah, I know. But they like it when I'm somebody else. So I just have to be somebody he likes."

* * *

"So how long you think before someone figures it out?" Darien asked.

Silverware clanked and dishes passed around as the housemates enjoyed a family-style celebratory breakfast of sizzling bacon, French toast, waffles, scrambled eggs, and batches of Janelle's fresh-baked blueberry muffins and banana-walnut bread over hot coffee and orange juice.

"Not too long." Zach passed a plate of bacon. "People are always taking programs apart. The government has whole divisions dedicated to malicious code and security flaws. Once they notice the bots' activity, they're going to investigate. And when they do..."

"Well, you know." Eugene shrugged. "It might not happen right away."

"Okay, not right away," said Zach. "But it gets the ball rolling."

"Well, she has all these security measures," he said. "So, it might take a little longer."

"That would make certain people work harder, dig deeper," Zach said, his patience thinning. "And when they see Canis Major-8, they'll know something's up."

"Why?" asked Cassidy. "What's Canis Major?"

"Me," said Zach. "I'm Canis Major. My Eight Pillars of Making That Money, Buddy?"

The housemates glanced at each other, baffled.

"Point is"—he huffed—"it's out there, and someone will find it."

"Eventually." Eugene took a sip of juice.

"Yeah, okay." He eyed Eugene with annoyance. "Eventually."

"All right, maybe this is totally stupid," said Cassidy. "But, should we try to fix ourselves? Like, put ourselves back to normal?"

Shadi shook her head. "We have no idea what she's done. It might be dangerous to tamper with whatever's keeping us like this. I mean, the equations I saw didn't make any sense."

"Oh, so you're a quantum physicist now, too?" Zach asked.

"No, jackass," said Shadi. "But I have some knowledge of quantum theory."

"Of course you do," he muttered.

"Well, if you think of the brain as a quantum computational organ," she said, "creating multiple associations and connections simultaneously, then you realize it would be helpful to understand how things can be zero and one at the same time, particularly in terms of consciousness."

"Go back a second." Troy leaned forward. "When you said 'keeping us like this,' what did you mean?"

"Well, in classical physics" —Shadi picked up a muffin— "In order to shrink something, you'd either have remove atoms or electrons from an object."

She pried off the muffin top with her fingers.

"Or squeeze them out." She gripped the paper wrapper and clenched her fist, soggy pastry and berries squirting from the top. "She's somehow avoided that."

Her demonstration dampened the mood.

"To do something like this," Shadi explained, wiping hand with a napkin, "would involve a quark like the Higgs-boson, which gives some particles resting mass. And, makes me wonder—what gives matter dimension in space-time? Or relative size?"

"There are particles for that?" asked Darien.

"I don't know." She shrugged. "I hadn't really thought about it until now. But she's done something to alter things at a fundamental level and somehow preserve other aspects of them."

"So." Cassidy pointed to the muffin mess. "That could happen to us, at any time?"

"There's nothing to indicate it would," said Shadi. "I just don't know how she did it."

"So, we need that machine," said Cassidy.

She nodded. "We'd need the machine."

"Yeah," said Zach. "Good luck with that."

* * *

Eight uncomfortable hours and three different airports later, Callahan and Dempsey landed with enough time to check into a couple rooms at a budget motel in Allentown and order pizza before they crashed for the night.

Bleary-eyed, Dempsey met Callahan in the parking lot the next morning.

She handed him a coffee. "Up all night watching pay-per-view?"

"No, the mattress was terrible. Yours was all right?"

"I don't sleep in a bed." She shook her head, sipping her coffee. "Slept in the armchair."

"You had an armchair?"

"Yeah. So, are you all right? Because I was going to have you lead."

"I thought I was on probation?"

"You are. Which is why you're leading."

He squinted, quizzical.

"Your angle was that Kincaid was a suspect. Now she is. I want to see if you can color inside the lines."

"Okay. I can do that."

"Let's see..." She stepped around the car to the driver's side.

"But just so we're clear," he said. "We're going in on this with a lie, right?"

She tilted her head in annoyance.

"We're telling them she's missing."

"She is missing," said Callahan. "And we're trying to find her."

They drove across town to the West End and beyond. Maples and elms forested the neighborhood. They pulled into the driveway of a craftsman-style home of stony brick and blue-gray wood siding. A dog barked from inside as they ascended the porch.

"We keep him in the other room whenever company's over," said Anne, leading them into the living room.

She was petite and slender. While her hair had dulled to silver, her magnetic blue eyes outshone Eve's gray ones.

Callahan assessed the room. The warm walnut sofas with billowy pillows and white duvets centered around the fireplace. She scanned photographs while Dempsey made small-talk about dog breeds.

A framed photo on the mantle. Eve as a geeky teenager, reluctant to smile while her younger sister's arms hugged her and their younger brothers. Another photo in a curio cabinet. The two boys played a game on the floor while Eve curled on the couch under a knitted quilt with a book, wearing a bonnet with pipe-cleaner antennae. Were it not for the resemblance to her mother, Eve could've been from another family.

Eve's father Noah walked in. Tall, lean, his hair faded to a sandy brown compared to pictures from years ago. Anne offered coffee and espresso, and biscotti, inviting the agents to sit.

"So." He sighed. "You here to give us the bad news?"

"Noah," Anne scolded.

"No," said Dempsey. "We're still actively working your daughter's case. Trouble is, we don't have enough good leads. We've been unable to locate her car, no financial activity, and no suspicious activity with her cellular service."

"What do you think that means?" asked Noah.

"We're not sure," said Dempsey. "That's why we're here. You know if she may have been involved in anything?"

"Like what?" asked Anne.

"New relationship," he said. "New business? Anybody she may have met."

She shook her head. "Pretty sure she wasn't meeting anyone."

"We really haven't spoken to her," said Noah, "since the holidays."

"She hasn't spoken to us," Anne corrected. "She cut off ties with us."

"Right." Dempsey nodded. "I know you already discussed it with Agent Barclay, but can we talk about Thanksgiving?"

Anne turned aside with a huff and a flip of her hand.

"She was drunk," Noah answered.

Dempsey shrugged. "We've all said things out of character when we've had too many."

He glanced at Callahan. Her eyes slid to meet his, equivalent to shaking her head. Dempsey's attention drifted to the couple, letting the silence hang.

"She was always quiet," said Anne. "But we figured if there was anything wrong, she would have spoken up."

"You know if there was something wrong?" asked Dempsey.

"Well," said Noah. "I mean, things didn't turn out the way she would've hoped—"

"That wasn't our fault," said Anne. "And lots of other people have setbacks."

Noah grimaced, discouraged from going to further detail.

"What about the accident?" Dempsey asked him. "Gideon's death hit her pretty hard."

"That was over a decade ago," said Noah. "And she got treatment. You're probably better off talking to her therapist."

"Unfortunately," said Callahan, "Dr. Moore died of breast cancer about three years ago, so any information you could give us would be helpful."

"We already talked to the other agents about this." Impatience rose in Anne's voice. "She was treated for depression and after a few months quit the meds and quit therapy. She didn't tell us at the time."

"And she didn't tell us about the doctorate program either," said Noah.

"You think she felt guilty?" asked Dempsey.

"Oh yeah." He nodded. "Lost her scholarship her sophomore year, and we had to pay for some things out of pocket."

"It wasn't ideal," said Anne. "But we took care of it."

"And I think it weighed on her." Noah shrugged. "So that, and not finishing her doctorate, especially when, you know, her brothers and her sister they...they went on, and—I think that might have been it."

"That's what set her off?"

"Yeah. She just bottled it up."

"You said you were sure she wasn't meeting anyone." Dempsey ventured to Anne. "Even though you hadn't spoken to her, what makes you say that?"

"She's just an antisocial person," she said.

Noah flagged a hand. "That...that's not—"

"Okay, I'd like that stricken from the record." Anne raised her voice. "I shouldn't have said that."

"We're not here to cast judgment," said Dempsey. "But that's a very specific term. Was that a diagnosis?"

"No." Anne's smile wrinkled with discomfort. "It's just—she wasn't typical. I mean, she wasn't killing animals or anything, but, you know, kids have personalities. Charlotte was the little princess. Luke was always logical, Sawyer was the adventurous one—"

"We thought she might be gifted," said Noah. "So, we had her tested. And she's not, or—they didn't think so."

"What made you think she was?" asked Dempsey.

"The memory game." Anne's smile widened, more genuine. "She seemed to know which cards were which before you could flip them."

"She would go into, like, these trances," said Noah. "You could see it in her eyes. Always working things out. Out loud sometimes. A lot."

Anne glared at her husband.

"Thought she might have an imaginary friend for a while, but, no." He smiled. "Just her. Having these whole conversations. Made it a little hard to make friends."

"You take her to somebody about that?" asked Dempsey.

"No." Anne leaned forward. "We spoke to her about it. A few times. That's all."

"Any idea what made her stop?" asked Callahan.

"Well, she never really stopped," said Noah. "Just in public. For the most part."

Callahan focused on Anne. "What made her stop in public?"

"Well, I think—there was a birthday party in the neighborhood." The woman squirmed in her chair. "She must have been seven or eight, and...I took her aside and told her, 'You're embarrassing your sister.' She seemed to get the message after that." Anne cast her eyes down. "I was trying to help her, make things easier..."

Callahan glimpsed at Dempsey, tilting her head toward the mantle. He caught the pictures over her shoulder. The radiant smile of the young woman with caramel hair.

He turned to Noah. "So, Charlotte was the princess. Sawyer was the adventurer. Eve was, what, then?"

"A bookworm." Anne answered. "And, maybe, more interested in the butterflies in the yard than other kids."

"And moths." Noah smiled.

"And flowers." Her eyes softened. "She loved the flowers when she was a little girl."

"She wasn't a bad kid," said Noah. "Just not—"

"Not what we expected." Anne confessed. "Not what I expected. I always felt like there was something she wasn't telling me. And when she said I never liked her—"

Noah reached over and held her hand.

"Is that what it was?" Anne asked him. "She thought I hated her?"

He shook his head with a whisper. "I don't know."

* * *

Dempsey scribbled into a notebook as Callahan drove to the airport.

"A resentful loner with dangerous technology," he muttered. "There's a movie I want to see."

Callahan sighed. "We're missing something."

"Yeah, a professional psych evaluation."

"Eccentricities don't make someone mentally insane."

"Thank god for that, right?"

The wheels groaned along uneven pavement.

He glanced at her. "Did I pass?"

She nodded. "Seemed like you might be able to work in a team. And you recognized nonverbal cues during an interrogation and improvised without prior instruction."

Dempsey shrugged. "Well, I did go to FBI school, so..."

"You have a knack for getting people to open up. That's invaluable."

He looked up, unprepared for the compliment.

"Well, thanks," he said. "You're good at cutting through bullshit, which—I don't think I've told you I really appreciate. And I'm sorry for creating more of it when there was already enough to go around."

"Glad we got that cleared up."

* * *

The next morning, Dempsey strolled into the office with a bag of pastries. Callahan's door was closed. Guzman poked his head out of a cubicle.

"I smell guava," he said.

"Good nose." Dempsey handed over the bag.

"The little place on Fourth?"

"Yep."

"Ohhh," Guzman growled heartily. "Read my mind."

Dempsey leaned into Masuda's cubicle. "She doesn't sleep in a bed?"

Masuda turned slow, tilting back. "She's got this huge papasan chair. Think of her more like a big cat that loves horses."

Dempsey puzzled over the analogy, unsure how to square it with his notions of Callahan.

"So, we almost had a lead," said Masuda. "Somebody called Kincaid's brother posing as FBI, then threatened to kill him and his family. They traced the call to a cell tower here in L.A., but it looks like a burner. Hasn't pinged since."

"Okay, so can we ID the buyer?"

"Paid cash. Tried getting the store's footage, but, they don't have any—"

"Wait, don't tell me—because the employees are stealing shit out the back."

"Probably."

"Great."

"But" —Masuda held up a finger—"Manny got a hit. These two real estate agents went missing weeks ago, and so did one of the show homes."

Guzman wiped his thumb across his mouth as he walked up behind Dempsey. "Got another one. This guest-house up by Melrose."

Masuda raised an eyebrow at Dempsey. "Want to come along for the ride?"

"He's with me." Callahan sailed out of her office. "Just talked to Hargrove—Pierce is packing up."

* * *

An older woman in a white lab coat pulled up the results on a flat-screen monitor as Russo leaned against the counter.

Velez rocked side to side and clapped her hands. "All right, this is what I been waiting for, Calderon. Let me have it."

"The hair is human." Calderon smirked. "But we couldn't recover any DNA. It does appear to be from a wig, though."

She brought up a window on screen for a side-by-side comparison with natural hair. "Small difference, but you can see how much thicker this one is than average."

"Any idea what might cause that?" asked Russo.

She shrugged. "Hair thickness varies from person to person. Given the color, this might have been more prized because it could hold up to processing."

"What about the powder?" asked Velez.

Calderon clicked to open another window, filled with boxy granules. "Very fine river sand. More than likely from a construction site, based on some other compounds we found."

Velez and Russo exchanged puzzled squints.

"Does it have any use in the kitchen?" asked Velez. "Cooking? Maybe cleaning a stove?"

"Not to my knowledge." She shook her head. "It's for masonry. Plaster."

Velez huffed, turning to Russo. "I'm going to lose to Tony Lam."

"It ain't over yet."

"Now the fun one." Calderon clicked open window displaying various broken shards and warped shapes. "We weren't able to identify this substance in any of the tests we ran. Where did you find it?"

"Behind a couple apartment buildings." Russo shrugged.

"So, it doesn't look like anything?"

"It's inert." Calderon gestured to the monitor. "Doesn't react to anything we expose it to. And as you can see, it doesn't have a uniform structure. I'd like to send it out to UCLA and see if their material sciences department can identify it."

A shred of hope. Otherwise, the case was on ice.

"Yeah." Velez nodded. "Let's do that."

* * *

Armando slept until late morning. The bed was more comfortable than he'd anticipated. He awoke to find a stocked pantry and refrigerator. Bread, eggs, butter, milk, soy milk. She'd expected guests.

The place reminded him of a beach house. Three bedrooms, two of them with two twin beds, and a den with a fold-out couch. The living room centered around a large flat-screen television and several shelves of an extensive DVD library.

A legal pad and pen rested on the breakfast table under a slow-turning ceiling fan. She'd been serious about asking him for a list. He couldn't understand why she wanted him alive. The second she set him free, he'd run to Lionel.

But she hadn't known about their operations. So who was this place meant for?

Unsure how the house was getting power, he ventured outside. The sun warmed the sand. He walked the perimeter, surveying the exterior and followed a series of wires running from the roof to a small metal shed with a red-and-white sign.

Danger: High Voltage.

He tested the handle and yanked it open. Heavy-duty deep-cycle batteries inside. Thick cables ran from the shed's roof across the island. Armando followed them to a fenced-off clearing dotted with more warning signs. A larger, prefabricated shed buzzed. She was some kind of scientist. And despite her clumsiness, the whole thing was well planned. He backed away from the mysterious structure and returned to the bungalow.

He enjoyed a breakfast of fried eggs and buttered toast. The coffee was superb. He contemplated his list of wants and needs, jotting them down as he idled. But as the coffee grew tepid, the comforts made him uneasy. That was what she wanted. To keep him well fed and complacent. Discourage him from escaping.

Like hell.

Armando wandered out the front door, past the deep impression left by her hand, and neared the pond's edge. No shells, but bits of gravel were revealed by the water licking the shore. He gathered up a few, then flung one out. It plopped into the surface, followed by a savage churn and the crest of a dark, ribbed fin. He chucked another stone, more to the right than the last. The fish raced to the impact. More excited. More fins. Another toss, and another. The fish rallied, the surface roiling before settling into choppy waves.

Armando returned to the house, mulling his imprisonment.

They were fish. How bad could they be?

He washed his dish and pan, placed them in the drying rack, and examined the narrow cupboard door. Moments later, he pulled a toolbox from the hallway closet. A minute after that, he unscrewed the hinges. He marched outside, nearing the shore with the cupboard door in hand. He flung it over the water, several feet to him, but no more than inches. A splash, and the water rippled. A vicious snap broke the surface, sucking up the door, and leaving a swirl of currents. A gush from below, and the water billowed with shattered wood.

Didn't take much to imagine broken bones in bloodied water.

A nasal caw jolted him from of his spellbound stare. He looked up to find a crow in mid-dive-bomb. Armando dashed across the sand, stumbling to the ground. The wide shadow and gust of wing flaps swallowed his entire world before returning to light. He sprang to his feet, running to the porch. He checked over his shoulder as the crow landed on the shore some distance away. The bird cocked its head, analyzing him.

The rolling rumble of the sliding glass door startled it into flight. The woman's approach trembled the water. She knelt on one knee.

"Sleep all right?" she asked.

He nodded, heart pounding. "Yeah."

"I'm here for your list."

"I'll get it."

He walked into the kitchen—a tremor shivered the ground. Armando tore the page off the notepad. He returned to find a small mailbox planted in the sand.

Armando made his way down the beach, irked by the way she studied him. He stuck the page into the box, closing the door.

She reached across the water as he backed away. The isle quaked as she lifted the mailbox.

"Should have most of it within a day."

"Thanks."

She eyed the bits of broken wood in the water. "Might want to be more careful."

The island trembled as she stood.

"I'll have to get a baffle now," she said. "The crows won't quit—they're too smart for that."

She turned on her heel, the quakes lessening. The rumble and boom of the sliding glass door closing was erased by the arrival of two crows on the parapet.

Maybe it was best to ride this situation out.

Armando backed off, retreating to the safety of the house to explore the DVD collection.

* * *

"Dr. Pierce." Callahan peered into Simon's office. His rock and mineral specimens were gone.

Simon looked up from a paper box and smiled. "Agent Callahan. Here to arrest another one of my employees for espionage?"

"Not today." She approached the desk. Dempsey strolled in behind her.

Simon snapped his fingers. "Maybe next time."

"Everything all right?"

"Fantastic, actually." He placed a ceramic mug into the box. "I'm indulging in a sabbatical. Regrouping. All these unnecessary complications, it's taken me away from the science, you know?"

"Really?" She smirked. "I heard you were removed."

"Difference of opinion." He smiled. "It's still my company. And I'm confident they'll come around."

She glanced at the desk. "Where's your shiny mud ball?"

"Oh—dropped it by accident," he said. "But I'll have plenty of time to make another one. Had a winter home built in Flagstaff a year ago and I don't think I've ever used it. Really looking forward to it. So, what brings you two here? Don't believe I caught your name."

"Agent Dempsey." He nodded. "Wanted to ask you some questions about Eve Kincaid."

"See, like that." Simon flipped a hand at him. "Answering the same questions over and over. It's maddening. I don't know how you ask them."

Dempsey smirked. "Well, the trick is to ask them in a different way. Like, you repeatedly rejected Kincaid's applications into research, why?"

"Seems more like something for the EEOC." Simon grinned. "But seriously, I can assure you, many women—of all different backgrounds—are accepted into research positions at Pierce Technologies."

"So why not her?"

Simon took a reflective breath, playing with a walking spiral toy before tossing it into the box.

"Research projects require teamwork. Didn't seem like she'd be comfortable voicing her ideas in a group."

"I'm sure there's plenty of other introverts working in research," said Dempsey.

"True." Simon dumped a tray of ballpoint pens into the box. "But I also learned a long time ago to distance myself from the unfortunate."

"What do you mean by that?" asked Callahan.

"You know, the unlucky. The miserable. They drag things down. They can't seem to get out of their own way, and they will impede your forward momentum." He raised a finger. "And, in effect—they impede progress."

"And when did you figure that out?" asked Dempsey.

Simon snapped a finger and pointed to him. "Back in high school. Alister Meeks. We should've been the best of friends. We liked the same shows, books, movies, games. We hit it off the first week in the same calculus class, got to talking about Agartha—"

"Excuse me—what?" asked Callahan.

"*Hollow Earth Chronicles,*" Dempsey muttered with a touch of embarrassment.

"Right." Simon nodded. "Next day, Alister brings in this lunchbox with a map of all the mythical lands on it, and the other kids just lay into him. It was at that moment I realized the danger of guilt by association. Never spoke to him again. Went off and forged my own way."

He spread his arms. "And here I am today. Unlike Alister Meeks, who's probably lived a mediocre life in obscurity. Don't know. Really haven't thought about him till now."

Dempsey and Callahan glanced at each other, disturbed by his callousness.

"So, you don't think it's possible Kincaid could have a vendetta against you or the company?" asked Dempsey.

"She very well may." Simon grinned. "I'm just saying there isn't a damn thing she can do about it."

* * *

After work, Eve rushed home and pushed the living room furniture to the wall. She connected a monitor and a storage drive to a thermal-imaging camera, then changed into the suit. She approached the camera —violet, blue, scarlet; gray, purple, gold.

She stopped and spun around. She took short steps, long steps, sprinted down the hall, twirled, jumped, hopped, and made a super slow pass in front of the lens. Brown, green, gray; pink, white, orange. She slid off the helmet and reviewed the footage.

"Okay, so they're going to notice that."

Although not apparent on the thermal level, when zoomed in, she did leave a strange blur. And changing her movement patterns didn't hide it.

Her brow pinched.

Eve brought the storage drive to the office, plugged it into her laptop, and studied the warped rippling—an elongated lump, rolling under the fabric of reality. She hit Pause. Her blur had no boundary, distinct yet fluid within the world around it. The particles were still interacting with another system, recognized but hidden.

A quick search and she downloaded an image analysis software. She ran frames from her test exercise through various filters, screening the images through ranges of contrasts, fluorescence, and different phase and particle levels. But the blur didn't reveal anything more.

"It blocks information...or the camera doesn't know how to interpret it."

She leaned back, forcing out a breath. Any abnormality at high-security location—especially where there already had been a breach—would trigger an immediate threat response. Her lips twisted, recalling the mayhem at the warehouse. She considered how the military would react to her presence. Soldiers would confront her in a narrow hall, firing M16s—

"Mm-mm." Eve shook her head. "No, no. No."

* * *

"Well, I guess that's it, huh?" Eugene asked.

"Oh, we're not done." The woman closed the botnet herding program. "Now I need ones that can make payments. Anonymously."

He shook his head. "That, that's not—"

"Small denominations. Twenties, fifties, maybe a hundred here and there."

"That's not possible," he said. "I mean—"

"Not yet."

"Sending money online is traceable."

"All right, check this out." She pulled up a new browser window. "There's this company in Panama—lets you send money with total anonymity. You can use a bank account, crypto, whatever."

"Yeah, until it gets banned here. Or they figure out a way to monitor their network."

"I don't need it forever—couple weeks. You think we could automate a bunch of bots to make transfers using their system?"

"Well, I mean, in theory, yes, but—why not just make one big donation?"

"It's not the same. Besides, I already do that for things like preserving the rainforests and preventing Arctic drilling and eliminating commercial plastic use."

Which was sort of true. It was just under Devereux's name.

"Donations under five hundred dollars don't have to be reported," she said. "But lots of anonymous ones would look bad, so, I was thinking we could pair the bots. One scours the internet for donor information and another applies it to online forms."

His brow and mouth wrinkled, full of questions he knew she wouldn't answer.

"Here, let me show you what I have spec'd out already."

She opened a file.

He squinted, scanning rows of code. His gaze widened in wonder. In a week or so, she'd learned to program based on patterns alone, then incorporated measures she'd picked up observing others. It wasn't perfect, but her comprehension was clear.

Captivated by her brilliance, he hesitated before turning around.

"This is really good."

"Yeah?"

"Yeah. All right, so, can you show me how the payment site works?"

Over two hours, they pieced together a design for their bots and troubleshot potential problems.

He caught her checking the clock.

"I think that's good for now," she said.

"You sure?"

"Yeah." She closed the windows. "And I wanted to give you something."

She slid open the desk drawer.

The tremble sent shivers up his spine. His eyes squeezed shut as her bunched fingers encroached, slow. The delicate landing vibrated the desktop. She left a gift-wrapped box at his feet.

Uncertain, he glanced at it, then at her. He knelt, cautious, and ripped into the wrapping paper, revealing a high-end virtual reality set.

Eugene tore away the remaining wrapping. "Holy crap."

"Sorry—I had to open it to set it up online," she said. "But I downloaded all the games for it. And it's yours to keep, you know, when you get out of here."

"I—I don't know what to say."

She shrugged. "You can just say thank you."

"I don't even know your name."

She bit the inside of her lip, eyes askance. Her eyes slid to him. "You can call me Selene."

"Can I tell everyone else—"

"No." She wiggled her hand. "Just between us, okay?"

He smiled. "Thank you, Selene."

She smiled, and set her hand down for him.

Eugene picked up the box and stepped aboard. The tingle inside wasn't fear anymore. He'd never felt so connected to someone he didn't really trust. But her touch was warm. Her presence, energizing. And she seemed to understand him in a way no one else did.

20

(yellow, black)

The spot north of the warehouses was a dead-end road with a view of the tracks. Eve suited up and shrank the car. Violet, blue, scarlet.

Invisible, she trekked several blocks to the warehouse. Gray, purple, gold. She passed through the wall. The space was as she'd left it. Brown, green, gray; pink, white, orange. She dug into her belt pouches and unpacked her experiment, enlarging then items on a folding table.

Ferocious pounds hammered the door. Startled, she leaped back. Miniature fire extinguishers clinked across the floor.

The door handle waggled with intensity.

She gathered up her equipment and reduced it, piling it back into the case.

Violet, blue, scarlet; gray, purple, gold.

She passed through the wall to eavesdrop.

A muscular man with a chin strap beard peered up at the light coming out of the windows overhead.

A thin man in a tank top rounded the corner. "They said it might be on a timer."

Chin strap checked his watch. "Almost a quarter past the hour."

Eve darted back in. Brown, green, gray. She shut the lights. Gray, purple, gold. She passed outside.

"I don't think this is it," said the thin man.

"Oh, so you think Armando had Tiny and Marcos killed? And burned all that product?"

The thin man shook his head. "I don't think this has anything to do with it. Maybe one of the cartels is making a move."

"Maybe this is their front."

The thin man shrugged. "Then why don't they come out and kill us?"

"That don't mean nothing. And you heard Lionel—he wants whoever it is."

They weren't going to quit looking for her. Not unless they had bigger problems. She could help with that.

Eve crept around the building. Parked in the street, a large four-door SUV. She stuck her head inside, checking for passengers, then backed out. Orange, brown, scarlet. She pulled a pen from a pouch on her hip and stabbed it into the rear tire. A loud pop and hiss. The car alarm blared. She wrenched the pen from the rubber.

The two men rushed to their vehicle.

Eve marched back to the dead-end by the tracks and enlarged a black sports car with tinted out windows.

The florist was the closet location. She weaved through side streets, heading south, and parked behind an abandoned building. Violet, blue, scarlet. She slipped out, walking two blocks to a nondescript two-story building nestled between a barber shop and nail salon. A man loitered in the lot between buildings, behind wrought-iron gates. Like Armando had said.

"All right," she whispered. "Infiltrate secret compound, undetected. Acquire portion of funds. Escape with funds, undetected. Alert authorities."

She took a deep breath, exhaling slow. "Try not to screw it up."

Bonus points if you don't kill anyone.

Eve crossed the street—gray, purple, gold—and passed through the door.

This place didn't specialize in bouquets, but functions. Bridal showers, weddings, quinceañeras. *Pay your deposit in cash, get ten percent* (silver, black, orchid) *off.* She peered between flower displays. A man in a tailored red track suit stood at the bottom of the stair.

Brown, green, gray. *Click.*

He perked up but kept his post. Frustrated, Eve rushed to the end of the aisle. Green, purple, blue. She rose to eight feet, then tapped her finger against the ceiling. Blue, yellow, silver. She reduced to six feet.

Tracksuit craned his neck, surveying the aisles. "Hey, yo, Zuke?"

A man's voice answered from the stairs. "Yeah, man, what's up?"

"Stay up there." Tracksuit pulled out his handgun.

He stalked through the middle aisle.

Eve sidled past him. She bumped a display. A plush bumblebee toy tumbled to the floor.

Idiot. Minus five points.

His arm snapped aside, aiming the barrel of his gun. He took out his phone. "Hey, Suzuki! Stay where you're at. Something's going on. I'm calling Mac—see if he's still alive out there."

"All right, man," Suzuki answered. "I'm calling the Cap."

So much for undetected. Minus ten points.

Eve leaned toward the bottom of the stairs. A trim man with a thin goatee was on his phone.

"Yeah," he said. "I don't know—he thinks something's going on."

Eve crept up the stair.

"He's calling him right now," said Suzuki. "All right."

He hung up then slid a handgun from under his belt.

She took another step. The floorboard creaked. She flattened against the wall and froze. Suzuki peered down the stairs. He pulled back. She held her breath as he turned around, helpless as his elbow bumped her rib.

Minus ten.

He spun around, startled. Eve slinked away as his hand reached out, probing the wall.

"Yo! This place is haunted!"

"What's up?" Tracksuit asked.

"We got a poltergeist or something, yo!"

"The hell is all this noise?" the bank captain groused, coming down the stairs.

He had the bearing of a pirate, complete with a patchy beard and horizontal scar on his right cheek.

Fantastic. Now everyone knows you're here. Minus twenty.

Gray, purple, gold. *Click.* He walked right through Eve.

Suzuki hunted for the sound. "You hear that?"

"What?"

"That, like—like, snap?"

"Old floorboards," the Captain answered. "This building's ancient."

Brown, green, gray. *Click.*

"That?" The Captain shrugged. "What do you want me to say?"

"Hey, I talked to Mac." Tracksuit neared the stair. "He ain't seen nobody, but this stuffed animal just fell—"

"The hell are you talking about?" the Captain asked. "Are you serious with me right now?"

Eve reached the second floor while they argued. Gray, purple, gold. She sailed through the closed door at the end of the hall.

An ordinary office, except for the duffel bag full of cash alongside the safe. An enormous man sat at a little desk intent on his laptop. He might have been well muscled in his prime, but his belly now stuck out like a couch cushion, the remnants of definition confined to his biceps.

Brown, green, gray. *Click*.

The banker lifted his head. “Boss man?”

He stood, closing the laptop.

One good shot, knock him out.

“Cap?” He lumbered toward the door. “That you?”

Eve reared back and jabbed a fist into his jaw.

“Ugh!” He winced.

Another jab, in the nose. He grabbed his face.

She launched into a flurry of strikes. A right then a left and right, a barrage of overhand rights, left elbows and left hooks, copying the forms she’d seen earlier in the day.

The banker withstood them all, swatting back, blood dribbling from his nose. Gauging the area of whatever was pummeling him, he grappled, clutching her left wrist and right arm. Alarmed by the contact, he flung her away like a pair of hot coals.

Eve hit the floor. She sprang up—orange, scarlet, brown.

He staggered toward the door. “Hey—”

Her arm hooked around his upper chest, trying to put him in a sleeper hold. He twisted and struggled as she dragged him backward. He trudged forward, wheezing, pulling her along. She yanked him back, harder. He hammered a fist into her invisible arm. Then, she felt him go limp. She released him and he toppled like an avalanche.

Pretty sure that was a heart attack. Minus a million points.

“*No*...” she rasped. “Dammit.”

She leaned over him. He was flushed but breathing.

Gasping for her own breath, she took aim at the duffel bag. Blue, yellow, silver. Eve sprinted across the room and snatched it, shoving the bag into a pouch on her hip.

“I told you,” said Suzuki. “Poltergeist.”

Suzuki and the Captain stood in the doorway. Eve glanced at the red speckles dotting her invisible figure.

“Poltergeists don’t want money.” The Captain pulled his gun.

Head-splitting pops echoed. Their bullets ricocheted off her. A stray struck Suzuki’s left shoulder. He took cover behind a filing cabinet. Eve wrested the Captain’s gun away then knocked him out with a right cross.

Tracksuit rushed in, his gun drawn. He reared back at the figure flecked with blood and lead dust.

Eve lunged toward him, sweeping his legs.

Tracksuit flopped onto the floor, the gun flying from his hand. He reached for the weapon—Eve kicked it away. He raised his hands above his head, surrendering.

“Hey! Checo!? Zuke?” Another man’s voice, somewhere downstairs.

She needed out, now. A flash of panic. Tangerine squiggles and fuchsia waves. The settings clicked out of position.

Eve pointed the arm cuff at the window. Yellow, green, pink. A ball of white-hot energy blasted the window apart, leaving smoldering edges.

The two men stared at her in the smoke as she lowered her arm.

Red, yellow, white. Eve leaped from the gaping hole, sailing upward in a long arc. Blue, brown, black. She dropped straight down and slammed onto the rooftop of the plaza across the street.

She pushed herself up from the shattered slates and turned around, the florist burning as a trio of sirens neared.

"God, I suck."

* * *

Back at the warehouse, the SUV was gone. Eve hit the lights on, then took aim at the door—orange, scarlet, brown—making it superdense. She pulled off the helmet. Refreshed by the cool air, her exhale became a hiss, annoyed by the condition of her suit. She took out the storage case and resumed unpacking. She enlarged the plexiglass box to an enormous size and made it superdense.

She popped open the panel on the arm cuff. No sound—she could increase her stealth by replacing the other mechanisms inside with quieter ones.

"Of course." She sighed, popping out the *modifikator*. "I'm so stupid."

After securing the *modifikator* in the testing rig, she slid the rig into the giant box's port. A hatch on it's side allowed her to place a copper cylinder inside on a small pedestal. She locked the hatch and returned to the mouth of the box, reviewing her notes.

She set the switches and dials to the proper frequency on the rig. Pulled back her hair and slid on the helmet. A push of the dial button. The beam struck the copper cylinder. It glowed orange with energy, turning yellow, then white. She yanked a cable on the front end. A thick panel of plexiglass dropped, closing off the chamber. The cylinder's charge increased, exploding in an intense fireball. The box held up.

Rapid ticks puttered from the Geiger counter she approached the box. They lessened, the readout lowering. The box's higher density seemed to block the cylinder's radiation. So far. She checked the dosimeter around her neck. No change. Smoke flooded out as she opened the hatch. Though charred, the mount had survived. Maybe something would go well tonight.

The warehouse's door handle clattered. Eve lifted the visor, peering over her shoulder. Murmurs of conversation outside.

She gritted her teeth. "Always when I'm trying to do something."

A hefty clunk struck the handle, the gong and recoil shocking the would-be intruders. She grumbled as she ejected the *modifikator* from the rig. Secured it into the arm cuff. Flipped down the face mask. Violet, blue, scarlet; gray, purple, gold.

Eve stepped outside. The SUV had returned with a new tire. It sat parked between her warehouse and the burnt-out one. A tattooed guy climbed out from the driver's seat. He followed another man wearing a beanie hat around the building. Eve crept to the corner.

Five men huddled around her warehouse's rear door, bickering over who was stronger and the proper use of sledgehammers.

She strode to the SUV and stuck her head through it. No one inside. She backed out. Brown, green, gray; pink, white, orange. Then she took aim—blue, yellow, silver.

She scooped up the toy-sized truck, marching to the intersection, and lobbed it into the air. Infinite black. The truck returned to normal and crashed into the pavement on its side with an echoing boom. The car alarm brayed, whinnying, and faded out.

Violet, blue, scarlet.

The men peered down the street and ran toward the wreck. Their silent shock gave way to confounded expletives.

"You were supposed to stay in the car!" said Chin-strap.

"Well, I'm glad I didn't!" said the driver.

"How did it get all the way over here?" asked Beanie Hat Guy.

The thin man shrugged. "Maybe somebody rammed it, or—"

"I didn't hear anything," said Beanie Hat Guy.

"Me neither."

"Yeah," said the thin man. "And if another truck hit it, how did it get on its side?"

Chin-strap put his hand on his hips, considering the lack of tire marks. "All right, it is kind of weird."

The men shifted, uneasy, scanning around them.

"So, how did it happen?" asked Beanie Hat.

"That—that's not important," said Chin-strap. "Right now, we need to get this thing out of here. Call Kenzo, tell him we need another ride and a tow truck."

"But Lionel said—"

"Did you not hear that?" He pointed to the wreck. "We're lucky the cops ain't here already. Tell him fifteen minutes."

They huddled, backs to each other, on guard for whatever may be lurking. Kenzo arrived fourteen minutes later in another SUV with a tow truck behind.

Eve watched, arms folded, as the men righted the SUV and hauled it onto the truck bed. They piled in and drove off.

Finally, she could get some work done.

She passed through the wall and lifted the visor, checking the time with an aggravated sigh. Another cylinder, another charge. Each successive attempt extended the cylinders' charge time, but she couldn't seem to prevent them from rupturing. She scowled at the sooty, char-stained box. The hatch was worn, leaking smoke. Two cylinders remained. Her notes devolved into frustrated scribbles.

"This isn't a real lab." She huffed. "I don't know what I'm doing. I'm not a real scientist. I don't even know what this stuff is."

She checked the clock.

Maybe Plan F wasn't such a bad idea—take all of the fragments in one shot. She could experiment in her completed underground bunker free of interruption. Find a temporal distortion effect. Once she harnessed it, she could unwind events in a series of paradoxes. Give herself the fragments, and the knowledge to use them so she'd never have to enact Plan F in the first place. But that was if she found the effect. If there was one. She'd still have to infiltrate a domestic military base. All manner of things could go wrong. And there was no guarantee she'd create a time machine before they caught up with her.

A harsh grumble scratched her throat as she checked her notes. The numbers and symbols lifted off the page in a swirl of color. She turned to the cylinders. Eve grabbed one and opened the hatch, finding the top hinge loose. She balanced the cylinder atop the blackened, melted mount and shut the door. While she maneuvered the testing station to line up with the off-kilter position of the cylinder, the cylinder rolled off, onto the floor.

"Fuck!"

Another balancing act. The cylinder rested in a delicate nook. She hurried to find the right tilt of the *modifikator* and set the dials. A quick study of the rig and she turned the primary knob down, just shy of the off position. She pressed the button.

A blast. The cylinder warmed to an orange glow. The reaction slowed. The cylinder tumbled off its precarious post. It rolled along the bottom of the box until it melted through it and into the concrete floor where it fizzled. With a loud pop yet weak burst, the cylinder cracked the ground.

She snatched the last cylinder. Balanced it in the same precarious spot. Adjusted one of the switches on the rig to a half position. No effect at first. Tiny dots of orange light began emanating from it.

More and more they coalesced, the powdery energy flowing steady. She waited, expecting an explosion, but none occurred. Stable.

Slow little dots of orange floated off, burning white, and vanishing into ether. She grabbed the Geiger counter. The hatch's top hinge snapped off as she swung it open. Low read out—0.01 millisievert. Equal to a dental X-ray. Yet far more energized. The foundation of her new power source.

The world's new power source.

21

(yellow, silver)

Eve returned to the penthouse with a new problem. How to capture the particles floating off the cylinder? Aside from the scintillation and Geiger counters, she'd added a drift chamber, a couple calorimeters, and X-ray and semiconductor detectors to her inventory. She'd figured out Talbot's modified spectrometer had been redesigned for high-energy ion detection. The other machine was his attempt at a glass Cherenkov detector—which didn't work. She cobbled together a Cherenkov detector of her own using the image sensor from a mid-grade digital camera and thin layer of magnesium fluoride. Despite her new equipment, she could still only guess what the particles were.

They emitted little or no heat, so they could be free neutrons. But they didn't produce radioactivity in surrounding matter. But they did carry a charge.

Eve puzzled over her notes. Her best guest was that the distortion field emitted some sort of in-between particle. A plasma-like substance which never reached the full potential of atomic excitement, suspended at an early stage of the process.

True cold fusion.

They'll think you're a crackpot.

She hissed.

If she wanted any credibility, she'd have to avoid such a term. She dove into an internet search. How did researchers capture energy from their own fusion experiments? No one appeared to have a great solution. Harnessing the immense power was one thing—maintaining a system which degraded over time was another. She slumped over the laptop, bracing her head with her fingers.

"So I need a technology that doesn't exist yet." She lifted her head. "But—none of this exists, so...there's no wrong answer."

No, dumbass, there's still a right answer.

Eve flinched at the scolding. She bit her lip, twisting the flesh through her teeth.

Proposed designs used intense magnetic fields coupled with massive cooling systems. Most were composed of conceptual materials. But her slow plasma didn't have an issue with heat. And if the particles weren't neutrons—or least, not behaving like them—maybe she could capture them without the complications of nuclear fusion?

Research and designs available online detailed experimental materials for ion capture. Panels of modified photovoltaic cells might work for a first run. She just had to prove it generated clean power and obtain it in a safe, practical way. And that her energy source wouldn't wear down materials the same. She grabbed a pen, narrowing down the most promising candidates.

Eve awoke, invigorated, on less than four hours' sleep. She stood at her laptop, sipping coffee, and reviewed the botnet.

Almost.

She slipped on the headset, shifting into Diane. She dialed Molykule.

"Mr. Devereux was so happy with the suits he'd like to order another of each," she said.

"Of course," answered the support rep. "I can put that in for you right now."

"And, do you make solar panels by any chance?"

"That's in our wheelhouse. We make a lot of those."

"We'd like them made out of a very specific film."

"Well, we already make a wide range of photovoltaic cells—"

"I don't think you make this one." She hovered the cursor over her email's Send button. "If I send you the specifications, could you give me a cost estimate? As a rush job?"

"Sure. Send it over."

Sent.

"If I can put you on a brief hold, I can put those numbers together for you."

"Of course."

Instrumental smooth jazz.

Eve turned to a stack of mounted servers. She flipped on the switches. Lights blinked and flitted, powering up. Back at the laptop, each server came online. The botnet beckoned. Once she set them into motion, there was no stopping.

"Ms. Cernik?"

"Yes."

"Just sent over the cost estimate. And, in talking with production, they don't think it would be a problem to have this done in a few days."

"Perfect."

She activated the first wave of bots. India and Pakistan. Plenty of time to monitor them and mediate their behavior.

* * *

"All right, so, I think I figured it out." Eugene forked a stack of pancakes onto his plate. "The bots are part of this, like, campaign to end nuclear weapons—maybe even nuclear power—all over the world."

"Well, that doesn't sound so bad," said Troy.

"Yeah." Cassidy set down a pitcher of orange juice. "I kind of agree with that?"

"What does it have to do with us?" Janelle asked in annoyance. "I mean, couldn't she let us go first?"

"Yeah," said Kevin. "Why go through all the trouble?"

"Well, think about it," said Eugene. "Think about all the countries that have nuclear weapons. Eliminating those weapons is a direct threat to their power."

Zach groaned. "Ohhhhhh no."

At first, everyone thought he'd spilled something, but an uncharacteristic quiet had overcome him.

"Okay," said Zach. "Just work with me on this—what if she's planning on using that device to make herself gigantic and the only thing that can stop her is a nuclear warhead?"

The housemates considered the possibility, exchanging unsettled glances. Except for one.

"That's ridiculous." Eugene shook his head.

Zach sat up. "Why else would she be trying to get rid of all them?"

He scoffed. "She's trying to help people—"

"Oh my god," said Shadi. "Maybe that's why she wanted my interface prototype."

"Why?" asked Janelle. "So she can shrink people just by thinking about it?"

"Theoretically, yes." She nodded.

"Or entire cities?" asked Cassidy.

"Well," said Shadi, "maybe. If Zach's right—"

"Guys," said Eugene. "You're jumping to conclusions."

"Are you kidding me?" Zach leaned against the table.

"She's not some evil, comic book mastermind," he said.

"Dude," said Zach. "You've got like Stockholm syndrome or something. Yesterday you were terrified of her, and now she's this great person?"

"Well, I've gotten to know her better," said Eugene. "And she wouldn't do that."

Disconcerted glances passed between them as Eugene reached across the table for the syrup.

"Troy said it himself." Eugene settled back into his chair. "Why are we all still alive?"

He awaited a response, and was met with blank expressions.

"Because she's not a killer," he answered. "She's not a crazy psychopath."

Kevin and Shadi glared at Troy.

"She's trying to end the threat of nuclear war," said Eugene "I'm talking global world peace. And that means taking on some of the most powerful people on Earth." He flipped a hand to Troy and Kevin. "Like the government, like the Russians. It's dangerous. So, she's taking precautions. She's protecting herself. And us."

He dug into his pancakes, satisfied with his argument.

The other housemates checked each other for confirmation. Eugene could no longer be trusted.

* * *

Eve downed her last swig of coffee and stared into the empty mug. She'd finished the pot, but always ended up having more at work while chatting with Quinn. They usually killed a solid twenty minutes in the break room every morning. Her smile weakened. Soon, if she was successful, Kira would disappear.

Unless you screw it up. Which you probably will.

A lump dried out her throat. A dull purple pit opened inside, followed by an uneasy yellow-orange squiggle. Were Luke, Gemma, and Christopher all right? What about her parents? How much did they hate her? How much did Charlotte?

She couldn't leave without taking care of Quinn.

Eve took a detour on the way to work. Famed music producer Lorenzo Leggono had a studio downtown. She walked right into the building like she had every right to be there, waving at the camera overhead as if to announce her arrival.

A young woman with supermodel cheek bones buzzed her in. As she got close, the receptionist frowned.

"Umm, do you have an appointment?"

"No." Eve smiled. "But I do have questions."

She smiled with distaste. "Well, you really need to make an appoint —"

"Does Mr. Leggono offer consulting services?"

"Yes, I do," answered a man with a Catalan accent.

Eve recognized the face from internet searches. The deep brown eyes. Olive skin. Long dark hair in a ponytail. He reached out a hand as he glided toward her. In the past, Eve would have looked to the floor, but now she met his eyes and shook his hand.

"Kira."

"Pleasure." Warmth radiated from his smile.

Her heart skipped a beat. The electric tingle emanated from her belly and unfurled in a starry-blue, wild-pink, and yellow-lotus nebula.

"Do you have a sample of your work?"

"Oh, no—this would be like a gift. For a friend of mine," she said. "I just want to help her with her craft."

"I see." His head rose and fell like a peaceful tide. "Normally my fee is twenty-five thousand dollars, but for you, fifteen."

Silver and red, amethyst-and-amber sunrise. "Thank you, that's very nice of you."

"Well, you're being very nice for your friend." He handed her a business card. "So, send me a sample of her work; I'll give it a listen. We'll set up a meeting and go from there."

* * *

After a grand-scale kitchen clean up, Eugene retired to the bedroom he shared with Troy for a session with the virtual reality system.

Troy poked his head in, making sure Eugene was immersed, and then snuck to the garage where the other housemates had gathered.

"You think he told her about the code?" asked Kevin.

"Oh, definitely," said Zach.

"I think if she knew," said Darien. "We would already know she knew."

"Unless they're playing some game with us now," said Zach.

"Or he never put it in there," said Janelle.

He gave her an affirming nod.

"Look, look," said Troy. "We've got to find out first. Everything else is speculation."

"Yeah?" asked Zach. "And how do we do that without him going back to her?"

Kevin's face scrunched. "We get him drunk."

"Or we drug him." Cassidy shrugged.

All eyes turned to her, bothered by the idea.

"Well." She folded her arms. "She gives us whatever we want, and I might have some...I'm trying to contribute."

Shadi raised her hand. "I think we need to try to get the device."

Zach snorted. "Impossible."

"It's really just a matter of getting over the walls," she said. "We're small and light enough where gravity won't have the same intensity if we jump off the table."

"Jump off the table?" asked Troy.

She nodded. "Plus we're landing on carpeting. It wouldn't be same impact as if we were normal sized falling from the same height."

"Even if that's true," said Zach, "we'd still have to climb whatever else is out there and we don't know where she keeps it."

"And," said Janelle, "we need Eugene to not know he's helping us distract her."

"All right," said Kevin. "Let's do some recon. See what we can get out of Eugene. See if it's possible to get over the walls."

"Well, what other tools are in the shed?" asked Shadi.

"What shed?" Kevin asked, quizzical.

"I thought that's where the propane tank was," said Darien.

"No," said Kevin. "Propane's in the fake boulder next to the garage."

"So what's in the shed?" asked Shadi.

"What shed?" Kevin asked in frustration.

The housemates filed outside, past the fake boulder and beyond, to a large shed resting in the sand.

"How did we not see this before?" asked Zach.

Kevin shrugged. "Maybe she just put it here."

"Well." Shadi surveyed the distance. "The boulder is blocking the view of it from the house."

"You think it's filled with spiders?" asked Cassidy. "Like regular-sized spiders?"

"Why would she do that?" asked Zach.

"Why does she do anything?" Janelle countered.

Kevin took a cautious step closer and rapped his knuckles on the door. He lingered, tilting an ear toward it. Silence. He leaned back, glancing at Troy.

It was Kevin's *can't-be-too-careful* look.

"All right." Troy picked up a length of rebar. "Everybody stand back."

He readied it like a baseball bat. Kevin reached for the door handle, checking with Troy once more. Troy nodded. Kevin turned the handle and yanked the door open. A wall of plastic tubs with a red-and-green ShelfStaple logo. Troy lowered the rebar, puzzled, and tossed it aside.

Kevin reached up, lifting the next highest tub. Troy shimmied out one below. He set it on the ground and tore the plastic ring off the top, popping off the lid. Inside were dozens of pouches of vacuum-sealed, ready-to-eat food.

"I've seen this stuff before," said Darien. "My brother-in-law stockpiles it. It's good for, like, twenty years."

Shadi considered the dimensions of the shed. "There's got to be enough in there for ten people for at least a year."

* * *

Eve slipped into No Nukes Now and darted past the cubicles. The door to Barb's office was closed. She headed to the break room for coffee. Powell was filling a cup himself from the single-serve machine.

"Good morning." He stepped aside to the cream and sugar.

"Morning." She picked up a coffee pod.

"That's...a really great jacket on you."

"Thanks."

Relief as the hiss and percolation of the dispenser ended the awkward silence.

"So," she said. "Any new conspiracies?"

"Well, actually, yeah." He smiled, stirring his coffee. "This newbie started a thread about this general, and—long story short—everything about this guy has been scrubbed from the internet."

"Really?"

"Yeah. His whole bio's gone. All the links about him that were active a couple days ago are now four-oh-four."

Pink, purple, black, purple, pink. A wormhole with bright pink trumpets on either end joined by shades of ever-darkening purple linked by a black tube. And also, for some reason, grape jelly and cream-cheese sandwiches on pumpernickel at the neighbor kid's house.

She blinked, returning to the present.

Powell smirked. "You really need that first cup in the morning, huh?"

"Or three. Yeah." Eve nodded, taking her coffee from the tray. "So, the FoilHats think they're being monitored now?"

He shrugged. "Well, they always think that."

"Hey, Powell." A woman from the cubicle farm leaned in the door. "Glad I found you. My computer isn't working."

"Have you tried turning it off and turning it on again?" he asked in a dull tone.

"Yeah, the screen's blue and it won't do anything."

Concern washed over his face.

"Excuse me," he said to Eve. "I need to take care of this."

Powell hurried out with the woman as Quinn sauntered in for a fresh cup.

"Morning," she said with a sly smile. "Late start today?"

"Missed the alarm." Eve's head bobbed.

"Snuck past me so you could talk to Powell?"

"That—that's not what happened."

Quinn raised her eyebrows. "Oh, no—I see how it is."

"There's nothing—"

"I was going to give you something," she said. "But now I'm not so sure."

Eve squinted. Was it Kira's birthday? Had she told Quinn her birthday?

Quinn whipped out a jewel case from her coat, the silvery disc inside glinting.

"Oh my god." Eve grinned, reaching for it.

She yanked it away with a smile. "You were avoiding me."

"I wasn't avoiding you."

Quinn handed over the jewel case. "It's only, like, six songs, but it's proof I been working."

Eve set down her coffee and flung her arms around her friend. "So proud of you."

"Well, you pushed me—repeatedly. And now I have more song ideas, so—I think I can really do this."

* * *

For lunch, Eve insisted they go to DeVour, an upscale restaurant wedged between expensive hotels. Towering windows poured sunlight on white tablecloths and sparkling marble floors. Men in suits with no ties, and bejeweled women in haute fashions, carrying their little dogs in oversized purses.

"We can go somewhere else," Quinn whispered. "I mean, we're not really dressed for this."

The painfully thin hostess didn't acknowledge either of them.

"Oh, don't worry about that," said Eve.

"And I'm strapped for cash this week anyway."

"This is on me." She turned to the hostess and smiled, speaking loud enough for people in the dining room to hear. "Excuse me. *Hi.*"

The hostess wrinkled her nose, passing a snooty look up and down at her.

"Yes." Eve nodded. "We're standing here. In front of you."

Without a word, the hostess took two menus and prompted them to follow. She led them toward a table in the back corner.

"Excuse me." Eve stopped the hostess. "We'd like to sit over there, by the window."

She pointed to a table overlooking the street.

"It's wherever we have space." The hostess shrugged. "And I'm afraid that table is—"

"Empty," said Eve. "And not reserved for anyone. So, we'd like to sit there, please."

Nothing was going to stand in her way. Not anymore. The familiar hum droned in her ears.

The hostess's apathetic gaze met the two infinitely black holes in Eve's eyes.

The hum grew louder. An overwhelming force thundering closer.

The hostess flinched. Her faux smile withered. "Right this way."

Quinn tried to hide a smirk as they sat. The hostess rushed off and they opened their menus.

"Okay," said Eve. "I have another surprise."

Quinn raised an expectant eyebrow.

She leaned in. "I hired Lorenzo Leggono to listen to your demo."

Quinn stiffened like someone had put a knife to her throat. "What? You did what?"

"Not the reaction I was expecting." Eve pulled back.

"I mean—how do you know it's really him?"

"I met him in person," she said with a wistful smile. "And let me tell you, pictures do not do him justice. But it's for real. He does consulting."

Quinn leaned forward, whispering. "Did you rob a bank or something?"

"No. And that's not funny." Eve pointed a warning finger. "I finally sold my condo."

Laurel green. She double-blinked to dismiss the color, hoping it wasn't a tell.

"What condo?"

"In Sacramento?" She shrugged as though it was common knowledge. "Where I moved from? There was a problem with the buyer and there was a hold...it's not important. Anyway, it went through."

Quinn's eyes narrowed, her jaw jutting out. "I can't— You can't do that."

"Yes, I can. It's a gift."

She sank into her chair, touched and confused. "Why're you doing this?"

Eve leaned in. Her folded arms braced against the table. "Because there's nothing worse than unrealized dreams."

* * *

Simon's winter home west of Mount Elden was nestled in a tight clearing surrounded by acres of ponderosa and pinyon pine. The nearest neighbors were miles away. Seven bedrooms, five bathrooms. Two huge, arched oak doors craned apart revealing a grand double staircase carved from monstrous slabs of basalt. A retreat to his roots. Back to science.

"Right this way, boys." Simon swaggered in, the ends of his steel-gray jacket flapping.

The movers followed him and slowed, unprepared for the interior. The floors made of long, polished beams of hemlock. The chandelier of longswords. The six suits of armor standing sentry within the curves of the carved stone stairs. The burnt tapestries embroidered in ancient elven language.

"Whoa." A rotund mover grunted.

Simon spun around, his yellow tie swinging, and beamed at the man. "Impressive, isn't it?"

He slapped a hand on the mover's shoulder, casting his opposite palm across the expansive room. "It's an exact replica of the Mountain King's hall from the fourth book of *The Hollow Earth Chronicles, The Stonehearted Symphony*."

"Wow."

"The staircase there? All cut from the same Scottish cliffside."

"Yeah, that—that's something."

"And those are genuine suits of medieval armor, sourced from historical societies all across Europe."

"Cool, well, I'd better get to work."

"Of course." Simon released him. "You'll have plenty of time to admire it on your many trips in and out."

The mover backed away.

Beyond the grandiose foyer, the house was more conventional. Simon found the residence well maintained by the caretaker in his absence. His only gripe was with one item—Qiopa, the virtual home assistant, powered by Tmesis. Glick's flagship gizmo. Probably spying on everything everyone said or did.

The primary unit had been installed in the dividing wall between the kitchen and living room. Simon ripped it from the housing, leaving the wires hanging. He wandered into the reception room, examining the circuit boards and processor. He could improve upon Zeugma's design.

"Dr. Pierce." A pair of movers hauled in a heavy-duty aluminum trunk labeled *Fragile*. "Where do you want this?

"Basement." Simon pointed. "And be very careful."

"Oh—and there's a zookeeper outside?"

Simon tossed the Qiopa unit onto the nearest sofa and sped to the front door.

A young man in a polo shirt and cargo shorts waited with a clipboard.

"Didn't give you any trouble, did he?" asked Simon.

The animal transporter smiled. "No, Jormanjur was very good."

"Jǫrmungandr." Simon corrected.

"Yurmandger."

"Jǫrmungandr."

"Yermajagar."

"Your-mon-gan-djur. Jǫrmungandr."

"Yurmagander."

"Close." Simon pointed to him. "You'll get it."

"If you could just sign here, Dr. Pierce." He handed over the clipboard.

Simon dashed off his signature and pointed. "It's these stairs on the left, first left, down the hall, last door on the left."

Several burly men in polo shirts and cargo shorts carried in a record-breaking reticulated python. Simon followed them upstairs, overseeing the delivery into an enormous terrarium. The transporters walked out while Simon's rotund mover-friend lingered, curious about the creature.

"Holy crap, that's a big-ass snake."

Simon folded his arms, smiling. "Twenty-three feet."

"Wow."

"I'm about to feed him in a little while if you want to stick around."

"Really?"

"Yeah. You can actually climb right in there, if you want."

"While you feed him?"

"Yeah."

Simon's unwavering smile unnerved the man. "I should probably—I've got to get back."

He hurried out of the room.

Simon leaned toward the glass. "Sorry, buddy. Maybe next time."

The movers cleared out after a couple hours, and Simon spent the rest of the day unpacking. Later in the afternoon, he called his father.

"You've reached Al Pierce of Pierce Motors, your place for the best deals on new and used cars. I'm glad you called and will get back to you as soon as I can."

Beep.

"Hey Dad, wanted to let you know I'm in town. Let's meet up for a drink later and catch up. Talk to you soon."

He hung up, confident his father wouldn't return the call until tomorrow. Simon thumbed through his contacts as he strolled to an open box. He pulled up his mother's number. Listed as Cindy Dunkelmeyer. Had been since he'd been in high school. A ring—

"Hi, sweetie, how are you?"

"Fantastic as always."

"My diamond Simon..."

"And how are you?"

"Doing really well. Except for my sciatica acting up again. Just getting out of work right now. Why don't you come over? Bill would love to see you. We usually go out for drinks with the Futtermans from down the street."

"Oh, yeah—Linda and Don."

"Yes! They're a trip."

"I remember."

"Have you talked to Ian yet?"

Why would he do that?

"No." Simon grinned. "Not yet. Lots of unpacking. I mean, barely got a chance to call you."

"Well, you should call him."

"I figured he's busy, with the...adopted llama farm."

"Rehabilitation clinic."

"Ah, that's it."

"You're always looking for opportunities, and this is a chance for the two of you to connect."

Avoiding the unfortunate was a constant battle.

Simon's smile twisted as he sucked his teeth, grinning wider. "Right. Guess everything happens for a reason."

He reached into the box, taking out small a bubble-wrapped package.

"So you'll give him a call?"

"As soon as the opportunity arises." Simon tore off the bubble wrap, a small cardboard box inside.

"Good," she said. "And who knows? Maybe after some long overdue bonding, a little of that diamond touch will rub off on him."

It would not.

"One can only hope."

"So, we'll see you later tonight? Around seven?"

"Let's say seven fifteen, seven thirty. Need to find places for a few more things."

They hung up. Simon pocketed the phone. He ripped the seam of the cardboard box. The *dorodango* from his office. Still intact. Still in its little glass case.

There was opportunity here. A chance to tinker. To design revolutionary fusion power, and plasma rockets, launching humankind into a brilliant future. And put him back on top. But he'd need a novel power source. He dumped the *dorodango* into his opposite hand and closed his fist, crumbling it. Clumps of dirt fell away as his fingers unfurled, a gleaming black crystal fragment resting in his palm.

22

(lemon yellow)

Eve waved goodbye to Quinn and got in Kira's hybrid. She glimpsed into the rear view mirror. The dour man. He'd traded his blue sedan for a silver sports car. Across the street. As usual.

He didn't dare wait outside the vehicle. Not since his partner had disappeared and Eve hadn't shown up at the drop-off. What did he want now? What were his orders? She could only hope the FBI had whisked her brother's family away to a safe house. She only knew the game she played with the dour man every afternoon on her way home from work.

The dour man crept up, two or three cars behind. He weaved in closer with the flow of traffic. So rote she assumed it was textbook. Not to say losing him was easy. He engaged with the city's heedless drivers with a fierce gusto and sporting combativeness, making it an entertaining challenge.

Her strategy relied on never pulling off the same exit. He never knew at which point she would veer across lanes and slip away. For her, it didn't matter. She could reach the waypoint garage from six different exits and a network of side streets. One night, she'd pulled off an exit five miles beyond any of the previous. Another time, she'd darted onto the first available off-ramp as he'd sped up, abandoning him in gridlock no more than a quarter mile from where they'd started.

Once in the garage space, Eve checked her vehicle for tracking devices. But never found any. She assumed her Russian shadow was still too wary of being caught on camera. And if she missed a tracker, she figured shrinking Kira's car nullified their ability to locate it.

Eve walked into the penthouse with a smug sense of satisfaction. She savored the waning adrenaline while shedding her persona. Priority number one was the bots. The little buggers were active but not as prolific as she'd hoped. Unattended, they'd sent dozens of messages but only infected a hundred or so machines.

She fiddled with their settings, about to save, and—hesitated. They'd garnered several hundred followers apiece. They maintained conversations without human participants questioning their authenticity. She studied the software's metrics readouts. Too many variables. Too drastic a shift or too ambitious, and she risked ending her anti-nuke campaign before it started. She needed to build momentum, a loyal following. And she had no idea how.

The bots seemed to have figured it out. So she let them be.

Instead, she activated the others. China. Russia. North Korea. Iran. Israel. The United States.

Dinner was a teriyaki-chicken rice bowl, then off to pick up Eugene. Eve stopped short, surprised to find him already on the front porch.

He waved, smiling.

His attention jolted her. Hot-pink-and-orange squiggles. She waved back, forcing a small smile, and lifted the lid. The front door opened.

"Hey." Kevin walked out, flagging a hand. "Wanted to talk to you real quick."

She set down the lid.

"So I was thinking of turning the garage into a gym. But I'd need some supplies—construction material, new tools, stuff like that."

"Hm." She folded her arms. Why were they so eager with her now? "Don't you already have tools?"

"Different kind of project. It's—"

"I saw what you did with the ones you have. Maybe I should take them all away."

"Well, I wouldn't." He shrugged. "I mean, things happen. You want to shrink a plunger every time a toilet backs up?"

She sighed. "Point taken."

"Which reminds me—water pump in the basement's making a noise. I should probably take a look at that."

"All right. Give me an itemized list of everything you need, and I'll review it."

"Thanks. I appreciate it."

"And I appreciate you taking care of the house."

"No problem...gives me something to do."

Maybe they were just bored. Stir crazy and tired of each other.

"Eugene." She set down her hand and he stepped on.

He gave Kevin a cavalier wave as she lifted him into the air. Kevin returned a slight nod.

* * *

Back inside, the housemates had already gathered in the dining room.

"All right," said Kevin. "Think as long as we don't ask for anything too crazy we should be okay."

"Well, what are we building?" Darien shrugged. "What's the plan here?"

"This may sound drastic," said Shadi, "but I think we need to consider a way to incapacitate her. Maybe even kill her."

"Hell yeah," said Zach. "Now we're talking!"

"Sign me up!" Janelle slapped a high five with him.

"Okay," said Cassidy. "And what happened to *If she's gone, we're stuck in this terrarium and we're dead*?"

"Well, hang on," said Troy. "She doesn't know we know. If we start asking for more nonperishables and stockpiling, we can double our supply."

"Probably should've been doing that anyway." Kevin shrugged. "I mean, she could slip in the shower and break her neck."

"That's my point." Cassidy sighed. "How long can we really survive without her?"

"Well," said Shadi, "provided we have enough food, it's making sure the water recycling system works properly. But maintaining it without her—you're right. Which is why I'd prefer to get the device."

"But like he said." Darien lifted a hand to Zach. "We don't know where it is." He turned to Shadi. "And like you said, once we have it, it could be dangerous. I mean, what if we end up blowing our molecules apart? We don't know how it works."

"It looks like she just points it at things and presses a button," said Zach.

Janelle nodded. "That's pretty much what I remember."

Darien threw his hands up. Cassidy huffed, folding her arms.

Troy turned to Shadi. "You were saying we're light enough where gravity won't affect us. How're we supposed to generate enough force to do anything to her?"

"Great question," said Shadi. "I was leaning toward something like the blinding of Polyphemus."

"The what?" asked Kevin.

"The cyclops from the Odyssey," Troy answered. "Odysseus plunges a wooden stake into his eye."

"Right," said Shadi. "Maybe something like a catapult, launch shrapnel into her face..."

"Okay." Darien rubbed his temple. "That sounds like a terrible idea. If we miss, we're just going to piss her off."

Zach nodded. "Which is why killing her really seems like the best option."

Cassidy put her hands up. "I don't wear fur, I don't eat meat, and I'm not going to kill somebody because they're keeping me in a box."

"All right," he said. "What about an explosive? We blow the lid off."

Kevin shook his head. "We risk blowing ourselves up."

"Can we combine these ideas?" asked Janelle. "Fire an explosive at her with a catapult?"

Cassidy recoiled. "*Janelle.*"

"What? I'm tired of this shit. I want to go home."

"Not sure how accurate a catapult would be," said Shadi. "We might be better off with a ballista—a giant crossbow. But instead of arrows, we use bombs. If we don't kill her, we'd at least blind her."

"Or piss her off," said Darien. "Can't we try to negotiate with her?"

"We're the hostages!" said Kevin. "We can't negotiate!"

"We have nothing to negotiate with!" Janelle argued.

"And she's crazy!" said Zach.

"And a thief and a liar," said Shadi.

Troy nodded, calm. "It is a waste of time."

"What's gotten into all of you?" asked Cassidy. "You're smart people, but you're jumping to conclusions. I thought we were getting information first."

"We can't trust Eugene," said Kevin.

"Well," said Cassidy, "let's at least confront her about the shed."

"You really think she's going to tell us the truth?" Janelle argued.

Darien leaned forward. "All we're saying is let's not give the person who's been keeping us alive a reason to kill us."

"Yeah, well, my vote is still for crossbow-bomb," said Zach.

"Well, you're an asshole," said Cassidy.

* * *

Eugene peeked over his shoulder with a wide smile. "You're making my job easy."

"Thanks," said Eve.

"You really are amazing."

Pink-and-orange squiggles.

She concentrated on the screen, unsure how to handle the compliments. His whole demeanor had changed. No more stammering. No fidgeting. She tried chalking it up to gratitude, but his eyes said otherwise. An uneasy lump formed in her throat. She'd never relied on feminine wiles.

You don't have any.

Such things were for women like Quinn or Charlotte who possessed effortless skill and grace.

Well, that, and you're nothing anybody wants.

Diane and Kira made her feel otherwise. But as Selene—without a disguise to hide behind—her awkwardness was exposed.

Face it, your best years were with Gideon. And you ruined that, too.

"I mean it," said Eugene. "I never thought of myself as an activist, but using what I know to make a difference ...I'm proud to be part of this. We're going to save the world! The others just wouldn't understand."

Her fingers stopped typing. She met his gaze. "You didn't tell them, did you?"

"No." He shook his head. "No, like I said, they—they wouldn't understand."

"Good. Because that's the problem. I'd like to start letting people go, but not if I can't trust them to keep their mouths shut. There's you, obviously, but I need you for a little longer."

"Of course," he said with an affectionate tilt of his head.

"Okay, so who else?"

"Well." He debated his words. "There really isn't anyone else...? I mean, Darien and Cassidy seem okay but they're shady. Zach's an asshole—you knew that—and he hates you. Shadi's pissed you stole her prototype. Janelle talks about publishing her memoir after you're in prison. Kevin and Troy, well—Kevin thinks the only way to clear their names is if you get caught. And Troy acts like he's Mr. Perfect all the time, so I can't imagine him not going to the police."

"He is kind of perfect," she muttered.

His brow rumpled, but he switched to a smile. "But, you know, that's why I look forward to working with you."

"I like working with you, too." She regretted the words the second they crossed her lips. "So, let's get back to it."

She resumed typing. His eyes again. Ogling her breasts. They must have seemed enormous. Desert sand rippled with tangerine zigzags. She tried not to squirm. Was this what Quinn and Charlotte dealt with all the time? Had she not noticed leering like that as Kira or Diane? Queasy, she focused on the screen.

Rose and crystal blue. It felt good, to be considered attractive. But it was Eugene. She hadn't thought of him that way, and—wasn't he scared of her? How had this happened?

Without her, he'd starve to death, freeze to death, die of

dehydration, or be eaten by some animal. But those realities didn't register to him. What was she was to him now that his fear had lifted? Still a powerful force, but not one he had a full appreciation for. Gideon might have been immature—downright horny at times—but he'd given her space. And time. He was about the only guy who'd done that for her. The others just applied more pressure. So she'd shut down. Leave. Never call again.

The things Gideon had adored about her hadn't only been about her body. How she always made lists out loud. Her fascination with barbules. The way she'd stop mid-sentence when an idea popped into her head. And he'd loved her ideas, the way she looked at the world. How she made everything strange and wonderful. What she'd loved about him had seemed endless. His playfulness. His ridiculous (yet tasty) culinary concoctions. His own brilliance in the way he could take an idea and run off in so many different directions and come back in an instant as though time had stopped. He could always brighten her day.

There would never be another like him.

Her fingers tapped the keys, but her mind seceded from the activity. Back to an overcast day years ago. The feathery layer of dewy Bermuda grass as she'd knelt.

I keep thinking, what if you're my soulmate? she'd said. There's no one else like you. At least, I haven't found anyone. But I've branched out. Met different guys. This last one...was a mistake—I don't know. You don't want to hear about that. Let's see, Georgie had her baby. Went over to her house, got to see everybody. It was like a reunion. They're all married, kids, careers. Don't know if I wanted all that, marriage...I just wanted you.

She'd stared at his headstone, as if it would answer.

A harsh breath had shot from her mouth. *I don't have the money to go back to school. I don't have the money for anything, and, I can't tell anyone because—I feel like such a loser. I need help, Gideon. I need—something? A sign. Guidance. Anything. Please.*

A cold, thin breeze had passed over. Not enough to move a leaf.

Of course. Her eyes had watered, and the world had blurred. *I'm talking to a rock. Because there's nothing. We're just tiny little specks on a tiny little planet existing for a split-second in a massive universe. I hate that.*

Her lip had curled with bitterness. *I hate it.*

Frustrated by the cruel joke of existence, the hum reverberated, so loud it reached across time. Across space.

There's nothing. Without this, there's nothing for you.

Eugene checked her face. "You all right?"

This is all you have.

She wiped her eyes. "Can't look at a screen for this long."

"Maybe it's too dim," he said. "You can make it brighter. I don't mind."

Don't stop.

She rubbed her forehead. "I think we need to stop."

Or it's all gone.

"It's only been, like, an hou—"

"I'm done." Her tone softened. "Let's just call it a night."

He didn't argue.

Eve removed the lid from the enclosure, and hurried to the office to fetch Eugene. When she returned, the housemates were standing outside. She laid her hand down, and Eugene stepped off.

"Is there a problem?" she asked.

"Don't know." Kevin shrugged. "Maybe you can tell us?"

"I'm not sure wh—"

"Look." Darien stepped forward with a winning smile. "There's some debate about—"

"We found the shed," said Kevin. "Full of food."

"What shed?" asked Eugene.

"Behind the fake boulder," Zach answered. "A year's supply for ten."

Eve folded her arms. "It's a precaution. In case something happens to me."

"See." Darien gestured between himself and Cassidy. "That's what we were thinking—"

"Yeah." Eve nodded. "You can only eat food if it's been shrunk. Same thing with the water."

She didn't want to confuse them with the details of her own digestion. The size difference of her enzymes was slight enough the effect was negligible, as she still got drunk when she was taller. But, not taking any chances, she enlarged her groceries to scale and ate most of her meals at home, with the exception of outings with Quinn.

"If something happens to me, and, for whatever reason, I can't get back here right away, I wanted to make sure—"

"We live for a year before we starve to death?" Zach asked.

"Dude, shut up," said Eugene. "She's thinking about our well-being."

"Why can't she just put us back?" Janelle challenged.

"Oh, well," Kevin mocked. "Why don't we ask her?"

"Okay." Zach shrugged, turning to Eve. "If you care so much about us, why not put us back?"

You heard Eugene. They can't be trusted. Everyone will think you're horrible. You need to save the world first.

"Because I'm not ready yet." Eve put her hands on her hips. "Right now, it's for your own good. And I don't have to answer questions from any you."

The hum growled between her ears, vicious now. Something disconcerted the housemates. Could they hear it?

"All right, look." Troy raised a hand. "Maybe if you just explained the situation to the government or whoever, they'd listen."

Then they'll take it away from you.

"It's not that simple," said Eve.

"But maybe they'd understand if you explained it to them."

And how many people are dead because of you?

"They wouldn't." She reached for the lid. "This conversation's over."

"Hey!" Zach stomped forward. "You can't do this to us!"

"I can do whatever I want!" Crimson-magenta shock wave.

The housemates toppled to their knees, hands clamped over their ears, reeling from the decibels echoing inside the enclosure.

"And you aren't going to argue with me about it."

She secured the lid. Laurel green. Guilty she'd lost her temper. She was sure she'd given them tinnitus.

The insidious cycle had begun. Gideon's headstone. The hum persisted, droning behind her thoughts as she readied supplies for the night's raid. The police needed to discover more than one operation, a pattern revealing the Badlands' money-laundering network. Maybe she could redeem herself as a crime fighter.

Everything you do is wrong.

* * *

Her ghostlike form had become natural. The refreshing sensation of her particles moving through something. To be unseen was comfortable. To find herself visible was a disappointing and sometimes jarring realization. But to walk down a street at night—passing through people and cars, inside and outside lights—not part of the world but in it, one with the very fabric of the universe, filled her with gratification. Silver, cyan, gold, and emerald. Like the first time she'd used the *modifikator* on herself. What if she combined them? The rushing thrill and soothing bliss. Unseen and intangible, expanding into the totality of existence...

Her musings evaporated as she neared a man with a shaved head standing guard at the back door. He was busy texting.

Invisible, she phased inside.

Another guy in the hall, also involved in his phone.

She strode down the length of the corridor.

Another man, arms folded, leaned against the wall.

She rounded the corner.

Another at the door leading to the laundromat.

Eve phased through him and the door. Two more men paced the darkened rows of washing machines and dryers. In her view out the windows, a man loitered outside. One more across the street, checking his watch.

She smirked.

They'd boosted security. She stepped to the front counter. Brown, green, gray. And lifted the receiver from the desk phone. Her fingers covered the earpiece as she dialed with her free hand. Nine (brown), one (silver), one (silver). The line rang.

A dispatcher's muffled voice answered. Eve pressed the hook switch and hung up. Brown, silver, silver. Eve bent down and with the lightest touch, laid the receiver on the floor. Gray, purple, gold.

She stepped backward, passing through the wall into the hall. She crossed the pair of guards. Around the next corner, a man with a horseshoe mustache stood guard. Eve phased through him and the door, into a cluttered back office. A lanky guy with wide gauges in his ears sat at a laptop while a man in a worn brown leather jacket zipped up a duffel bag. The safe had only a bank deposit bag left in it. They were clearing the place out.

And they were already on edge. She could run them in circles until the police showed up.

Eve backed out, moving to the end of the hall—brown, green, gray. She reached up and pushed a bottle of lemon-scented cleaning solution off a shelf. It thwacked against the floor, oozing neon-yellow goop.

Two men rushed toward the noise. Gray, purple, gold. She hurried into the back office. The safe had been closed. Orange, scarlet, brown. She held up a fist, swinging her knuckles backward.

Knock, knock.

The banker and his bodyguard glanced to the door, then at one another.

"Yeah?" asked the bodyguard.

No answer. He pulled his gun and sidled toward the door. Eve stepped aside.

"What do you want?"

No answer.

"Yo, Berto?"

The banker stood, pulling a handgun from under his belt. The bodyguard jerked the open the door. No Berto.

"All right, I'll go check it out."

"No, no," said the banker. "Call TJ, tell him to do a sweep."

Eve's lip curled as the bodyguard put a phone to his ear. Berto turned the corner.

"Where were you?" asked the bodyguard.

"Something fell," said Berto.

The banker's bodyguard huffed as he pocketed his phone. "Sweep the building."

Gray, purple, gold. She rushed through the bald guy guarding the back door and out of the building. Orange, scarlet, brown. She raced to the dumpsters, pummeling the side of them.

The rapid drumming startled the guard. He drew his gun, then his phone.

"Yo, there's somebody out here." He scanned the lot. "Yeah. I don't know—I didn't see nobody. All right."

He hung up, still searching. Two more men stepped out of the laundromat.

"Where they at?"

"By the dumpsters."

Berto hovered behind them. "Go check it out."

The three men wandered into the lot.

Gray, purple, gold. She ran to the back hall. Brown, green, gray. Eve flung an entire row of cleaning supplies off a shelf. Gray, purple, gold. She shot through the bodyguard as he ran into the hall. They were occupied. Now to incapacitate the banker until the police arrived.

The banker stood in front of the desk, gun at the ready, facing the closed door.

Orange, scarlet, brown.

The deadbolt's thumbturn snapped into locked position. The banker's brow rumpled. He pointed the handgun.

"Jimmy?" he asked. "That you?"

She stepped around him and slid his cell phone across the desk.

He reached back for it, still fixed on the door. He turned around for his phone, lowering the gun, and leaned over the desk.

Eve grabbed his wrist, wrenching his left arm around.

He twisted, panicked, unsure where to aim.

She clutched his other wrist, wresting the handgun from his grip. It clunked onto the floor.

"Jimmy!" His voice cracked. "Jimmy!"

She pinned his wrists against his back with one hand and muffled his hollers with the other, resisting the laughter bubbling up inside of her. He must've been terrified.

He fought harder, twisting and jerking about, exacerbating the unnatural bend of his arm.

She tightened her grip, the hum filling her ears. Control. She was in control. The colors seeped out of her—indigo, viridian, maroon—an overflowing well into the universe. Settings clicked on the cuff.

The door handle joggled. "Artie?"

"Mmm! Mmph!"

Her palm jammed against his lips. Couple more minutes and the cops would show up. A jangle. A key sawed into the lock. Cracks of pale mauve. Control over.

You blew it. Again. Time to bail.

But she didn't want to let go. If this was what she did—ruin things—why stop if she did it so well? The hum grew heavier, louder, into a deep growl.

Jimmy burst through the door. "Artie?"

Artie writhed, eyes begging.

"You all right?"

Two other guards rushed in behind Jimmy, mystified by Artie's contorted face. His nose, lips, and cheeks were smooshed.

Where the hell were the police?

"Think he's having a seizure," said Jimmy.

Artie shook, trying to direct them to the specter with his eyes.

Jimmy approached him. "It's all right, buddy, we're going to get you some help."

He reached for Artie's shoulder. His fingers bumped into something unseen yet solid.

Jimmy jumped back. "Whoa!"

"What? What?"

"He needs an exorcism! There's something in here!"

More guards filled the hall behind them.

She flung Artie into the nearest wall.

He flopped to the ground. The others kept their distance.

"Holy shit!"

She wanted control. Indigo, viridian, maroon. A dark aura radiated from within her, the growling hum in full force. What was this?

The men's faces slackened.

Green, purple, blue. She rose to eight feet.

A faint buzz filled the room. They searched for its source.

They were afraid.

Good.

Pink, white, orange. Visible.

They staggered back, gawking at her.

Eve's fist smashed into the nearest guard. His skull smacked into the door frame. Her elbow cracked into Jimmy's face. He toppled onto the duffel bag of cash. Two other men ran.

She charged after them and punched the slowest in the back. He went flying into the first. They tumbled over each other to the floor.

"The shit is this?" Berto stood at the end of the hall with two more men, guns pointed.

Powerful snaps rang out as the bullets bounced off her and into the walls. She stormed toward them—green, purple, blue—larger.

They dashed to the front of the building, slamming the door shut behind them. With a stomp of her heel, it sailed off the hinges and slid across the linoleum. The men swarmed through the rows of washing machines, desperate to escape.

She took aim. Yellow, green, pink. A ball of white-hot energy boomed, blowing apart a stack of dryers. The warped metal crashed through the storefront glass. Flaming hunks showered into the street. Fire alarms blared. Foam sprayed from overhead.

Eve clomped past the men cowering behind the machines and out of the smoking hole. The two guards tasked with securing the exterior dithered in the middle of the road. The growl and aura faded, replaced by approaching sirens.

She turned in their direction, brushing foam off her shoulder. Violet, blue, scarlet. She vanished. Red, yellow, white. She leaped into the air. Thin traces of foam rained onto the asphalt.

23

(yellow, blue green)

Eve sipped her morning coffee as she pored over the metrics. The bots had sent hundreds of messages, garnered millions of followers and infected thousands of computers. She aligned her chatbots in India and Pakistan, overlapping their messaging and contacts. Botnets in Russia and China had been driven into sleeper campaigns due to crackdowns by the respective governments. Iran and North Korea were engaged in a similar piecemeal blocking strategy, fighting to squelch them. She activated more in new locations, linking them with others around the world.

The United States and Israel remained fringe. The donor bots would kick them into gear, establishing a global movement. Not a simple fad individual nations could tamp down. Bigger. Everywhere. All the time. She entered a new phrase into the chatbots' vocabulary: *OneIsTooMuch*. It circulated through the network.

She minimized the windows. Time to send Lorenzo an email with Quinn's demo. She'd been meaning to listen to it herself. The ride into work this morning would be perfect.

She refilled her coffee and headed to the guestroom.

"Eugene." She pulled off the lid. "Come on, buddy, we've got work to do."

Groggy, Eugene rubbed his eyes. He slid on a pair of sunglasses, preparing for the screen's brightness as Eve sat at the desk.

"All right, I need this finished."

"Like, now?"

"You all want to go home, right? Well then, I need this up and running." She dimmed the display.

"We should be close," he said.

"It's the randomization I'm worried about."

"Shouldn't be too hard."

"You sure? They're still going to follow the herding patterns? Not just start donating more and more?"

"Yeah, I think the hard part's going to be linking them through the payment site."

She glanced at the time. "Can we do that in less than an hour?"

Stymied, Eugene's mouth hung open.

"*Eugene.*"

"Yeah—I mean, we could try."

They reviewed the latest lines of code. They tested different methods for routing payments. Eve never lost focus. No chitchat. If a method didn't work after a couple attempts, it was onto the next until they fashioned a solution.

Forty minutes later, a successful test run on a Save the Rainforest website.

"All right." Eugene smiled, triumphant. "That's it—we did it."

"Great job, thank you so much." She set her hand down for him.

"We're not going to turn it on?"

"I am. You need breakfast."

She lowered him at the doorstep, replaced the lid, and rushed out of the room. Back in the office, she changed the target website to No Nukes Now. A few clicks, and the donor bots filtered out into the world.

* * *

Cassidy and Darien crept into their bedroom to find Shadi on her knees, prying a baseboard with the claw of a hammer.

"What are you doing?" Cassidy cried. "This is a million-dollar house!"

"Well, if it's been reduced by the same ratio, it's only worth about thirty-five grand." Shadi yanked the hammer back, freeing the baseboard from the wall.

The others rushed toward the commotion.

"Shadi?" Troy asked in disbelief.

"I can't believe I'm saying this" —Shadi huffed— "but, Zach's right. She's not letting us go. And it's doubtful she'll give us what we need to assemble the crossbow, so I'm making do."

"That's not the right tool for that," said Kevin. "You're going to snap those in half."

"Kevin," Cassidy scolded.

"Anybody else hear a sound yesterday?" asked Darien.

"Before or after she blew out our ear drums?" asked Zach.

"Yeah," said Troy. "Like a vibration, or—"

"Or a buzzing." Janelle nodded.

Darien pointed to Shadi. "You said she hooked up her device to your...brain machine—"

"Brain-to-machine interface," she corrected.

"Yeah. That." He nodded. "What if, whatever that thing is, it's affecting us?"

"Sounds like a bunch of pseudo-science bullshit," Shadi answered. "So, unless you're going to grab a hammer and start pulling baseboards, get out."

Another *thwack*. The claw dug between the wooden slat and wall.

"I don't know," said Janelle. "I do have this brain fog lately? But I just been drinking more coffee."

"Well..." Zach shrugged. "I'll admit I am obsessed with killing her, but she did take all my money."

"She wasn't even wearing it!" Shadi protested. "There's no evidence for what you're talking about. The sooner we kill this lunatic, the sooner we get out of here."

Cassidy knelt alongside her. "Shadi, you are not a killer. You're just out of balance and need to realign your energ—"

Shadi scowled and reared the hammer back, threatening to swat the woman's head.

Mortified, Cassidy scrambled backward across the carpet and stood.

Zach eyed Darien with suspicion. "Why are you two so against escaping?"

"We want out of here as bad as anybody else," said Darien.

"Do you?" he countered. "You're the only ones consistently having sex."

"Yeah!" Janelle stepped forward. "This is like one big vacation for you."

"You all could be having sex, too!" Cassidy shot back. "Don't blame us for your lack of initiative. And Janelle—we invited you."

Stunned silence. Zach pivoted to Janelle. "What?"

Her brow pinched. "Why is that so hard to believe? And second, I don't answer to you."

"All right, all right," said Troy. "Fighting among ourselves isn't going to help anything."

"We're tired of being trapped here!" Zach threw up his hands. "And listening to them have sex all the time."

"Would that make everyone happy?" asked Darien. "If we just had an orgy? I mean, Cass and I been talking, and—"

The house shook. The lid was back on.

"Hey," said Kevin. "She left the lid off. She's getting careless."

"Okay," Darien muttered. "So maybe we can escape without, you know..."

"Nope. Bitch stole my prototype." Shadi took another whack farther down the wall.

Eugene leaned through the doorway. "What's going on?"

"Remodeling," Shadi answered, unsure how much he'd heard.

"Well, I wouldn't get too involved." He smirked. "Because she's getting ready to let us go."

Janelle folded her arms. "She said that? Just now?"

He nodded. "She said, 'You all want to go home? I need this finished.' Now she just has to make sure it works. So, I guess that's another thing Zach's been wrong about."

"You are so fired when we get out of here," Zach muttered.

Janelle scrutinized Eugene with a side-eye. "She say when?"

"Well, no, but—probably some time soon." He turned away. "Any pancakes left?"

* * *

Eve grabbed her mug and headed to the kitchen. Another hour before she had to leave for work. She refilled her coffee and glanced at a smattering of sudoku booklets. Didn't seem like a productive use of her time. Nor did the stacks of books on college football under them. It was the off-season. She'd been studying the previous year's highlights. Memorizing the names of players on the upcoming LSU roster. Absorbing decades of player line-ups, coaches, stats and scores. Numbers. Swirls of color moving through time.

But ingratiating herself to McCrae felt futile. His loyalty was to the government. Any interest he showed could be a ploy. Diane wouldn't bother with such a strategy. Neither would Kira. They didn't plot or plan, waiting for the perfect moment. They would go and get it.

Plan F had been waiting downstairs. If she wanted the fragments, maybe it was time to stop tiptoeing around and take them.

But epic heists required thorough examination of every detail. She took advantage of the spacious, twenty-four-foot length of living-dining area in the apartment below the penthouse. A shallow wooden frame, fourteen feet wide, filled the room. Its bottom was composed of layers of painter's plastic. Over the course of several afternoons, she'd filled the frame with sand and arranged a series of jagged stones on piles of gravel to represent the San Gabriel Mountain range.

She glued together game board pieces. Mapped them out on a grid. Then secured them into the sand at their relative distances to represent cities and towns north of the mountains, including Edwards Air Force Base. The desert was divided by thin-cut strips of vinyl tape to represent major highways. Clumps of rock and gravel marked lesser mountains. Little collections of plastic cubes denoted landmarks. Though it had taken hours, Eve couldn't bring herself to use the elaborate diorama for its intended purpose.

It had felt wrong. Rash. But after seizing control last night, not as much.

She took a delicate step into the giant sandbox. Her shoe crunched onto the mountain peaks. Gravel tumbled into the plastic pieces representing the edge of suburban Pasadena behind her. At her relative height of twenty miles, the San Gabriel range extended five feet in front of her, about sixteen miles. The entire box represented 3,728 square miles, much of it desert north of civilization. She scanned the three-dimensional map for a better starting point. A sparse patch northeast of El Mirage.

She tread across the mountains, losing her balance on the shifting surface. She caught herself—pink spirals and orange dots—a disorienting wobble. She snorted.

The whole thing was ridiculous. Standing in a giant diorama. And somehow incomplete. What would the peaks crushed under her feel like? Would she hear her own movement against the planet? Would it echo? She contemplated the thinness of the atmosphere. Would she have enough oxygen?

Eve blew off the questions, trusting in the distortion fields. They'd worked well enough so far. She had to focus on the heist. Starting in the Angeles National Forest would make things more complicated and erase the element of surprise. She took a step north, and her left foot landed in a crevice of the mountain range. She shifted on her heel, wondering how much the earth would rumble with the subtle turn, and set her right shoe ahead of the left.

Another step. Her left shoe cleared the peaks and landed in the desert. The slight drop put her off her footing. She stabilized, chilled by the realization that a misstep would annihilate anything under her. Just like Talbot. Except this time, it would be a little desert town. And that was only what she could see. A network of roads and farms spanned the region, but the scale eradicated their detail.

She blew a nervous puff from her lips.

This was her starting point. A two-hour drive to a dirt road off the 395 (blue green, brown, brick red). She took a cautious right step forward. Her left foot joined. Another step, coming to a stop before a strip of highway. Right, then left, plotting her way into the expanse. She pivoted to a tiny grid of a dozen white plastic cubes glued together in a space no wider than a soda can.

The base.

She squatted, careful not to shift on the balls of her feet. Her fingers dug into the sand around the cubes, unearthing a chunk of soil. The underground tunnels and chambers were represented by aluminum foil, pinched tight around stiff copper wire. A clump of dirt loosened, sloughing off, shedding crinkled foil with it. The poor souls inside would plummet to a horrid collision with the earth. Would the tunnels separate so easily? Below-ground structures must have steel supports. But gravity would win out.

She'd have to use two hands, treat it like a baby bird. She stood, lifting it to her face.

Simple as that, and the fragments would be hers. Invisible, she'd walk into the desert. A few steps to the east and she could plant the artificial root ball into a valley. The soldiers would defend the base. But she'd infiltrate it by shrinking down and becoming intangible. They'd secure the fragments. In the turmoil, she'd recover them, phasing out of the tunnels. Then she'd become ultradense. Surf down the crumbly slope. Have a car waiting in Barstow.

Though terrified, the soldiers would be unharmed. Their greatest loss would be the exposure of a secret military installation—and its inconvenient relocation. Reinforcements would come from Edwards Air Force Base and Fort Irwin. Fighter jets would do them no good, so they'd deploy troops from helicopters. Their confusion would be short lived. They trained for this sort of thing, relished it. Taking into account their loading and travel time, she estimated she had no more than ten minutes. She'd have to do it in under three.

Eve knelt and wriggled the model back into the dirt, patting the edges down and smoothing it out. She glanced over her shoulder. At this scale, the San Gabriel Mountains reached her shins. While laughable before, closer to the surface, the terrain had more life. She tried to envision the curvature of the earth. Would she see it? Feel it? Would it affect her balance?

Her eyes scanned the uneven cubes representing city limits.

What would those people think as they stared out the windows of their offices and cars?

Terror. Sheer terror.

How many would die of shock?

So? They don't care about you. No one does.

The hum rose in her ears. The scenario continued to play out.

With a single blast, she could vaporize the entire city. If she made herself superdense, no conventional missile could hurt her. Fighter jets could only swarm around her. The world would be powerless. A tingle emanated from her belly and brain meeting in between—electric blue into indigo—as the hum growled louder.

"Oh god." She recoiled. The sound vanished.

She stepped out of the sandbox. "All right—this can't happen."

But if it did, if it came to it, she'd be unstoppable.

You could do whatever you want, have whatever you—

"*No.* No. No."

Those couldn't be her thoughts. She wanted to restore the glaciers, heal the oceans, replenish the ozone layer, replant forests.

Disgusted, she banished the scenario and collected herself, heading for the door. Her plan would work. It wouldn't come to this. The world would praise her invention. She'd win over McCrae. The government would acquiesce. But in the back of her mind, the notion persisted—no matter what she did, no matter what she said, people wouldn't accept her.

They never do.

* * *

She finished a final dusting of make up and slid on the cardinal frames. Ready for work. A buzz on the dresser. Both phones rested side by side, identical down to the bamboo wood-grain cases. She picked up the Diane phone.

"Hello?"

"Good morning, Ms. Cernik," a man answered. "This Ramon Otero with the county fire department calling to inform you about damage to your property."

"My-My property?"

"Well, you're listed as the contact for the warehouse. Should I be talking to someone else?"

"No, I'm the right person." She glanced at the clock. Seven forty-five. "I'll be there as soon as possible."

She hung up, stripped off Kira's clothes and swapped them for the Diane outfit stowed in the garment bag. After a wig change and slight size reduction, she raced downstairs. Traffic already tightening, she fought through the congestion, zipping through lanes with such viciousness cars peeled aside to let her pass.

Eve slowed as she neared the building. Two fire trucks were crammed into the lane. The rest of the block was quartered off by yellow police tape. Firefighters trudged outside the blackened remains of the warehouse. The southwest corner had collapsed, the roof in shambles. Two walls remained standing, coated in soot.

Her experiment?

Aghast, she wandered toward a huddle of people. A young man with a sporty haircut in a polo shirt spoke to a rugged man in a blue uniform while an older guy in a suit and a young woman with ombré hair wearing a leather jacket listened in.

"Ms. Cernik?" The uniformed man raised his brows.

"Yes," said Eve.

"Ramon Otero. We spoke on the phone."

"What happened?"

"We're looking into that," he said. "Forensics found traces of C-4 and accelerants."

"C-4?"

The kid in the polo shirt stepped forward. "Hi. I'm James Cho, your insurance adjuster."

She shook his hand, ruminating over the C-4. Who'd planted it? The Russians?

"Just to let you know," said James, "your policy doesn't cover arson, even if it was done by a third party."

She waved him off, turning to Otero. "I don't understand...so somebody bombed the building?"

"Well, that's what Detectives Russo and Velez here are trying to figure out," Otero answered.

"There was a fire in the building across the way about a week ago," said Russo. "We have reason to believe it might've been gang related."

"Gang related?" asked Eve.

"You seen anything suspicious?" asked Russo. "Interacted with anyone in the area?"

"I've been here three times." Tension rose in her voice. "This being the third. We hadn't even started using it yet. I have shipments to cancel—or re-route."

Her tongue curled in her mouth. The Badlands. By now, Lionel had dug into who owned the warehouse. And he'd know a front when he saw one. Bastard had turned the cops onto her. The authorities would pry into Devereux's business operations.

Everything had to happen now.

James leaned over. "Well, there might be reimbursement if it impacts your busi—"

"You can't reimburse us for a product we haven't started making yet." Eve huffed, taking out her phone. "All right, I have calls to make... unless you need me for anything else?"

"Well, hang on," said Russo. "Has anyone made any threats? You have any creditors?"

"No. So, we have to ask permission before we buy another warehouse?"

"Is that what someone told you?" asked Russo.

"No, I'm asking," said Eve. "Is that what you're telling me? This city's got a racket and we didn't get the message?"

Russo shrugged. "Not that we're aware of."

"Excuse me," said James. "Just need a quick signature confirming you understand we're not going to pay anything out."

Eve scowled as James handed her a tablet and stylus.

"Ms. Cernik," said Velez, "you said your company was working on a new product. Is there anyone you might be in competition with?"

"No." Eve handed the tablet back to James. "And I can't disclose details since we haven't brought it to market yet."

Velez nodded. "You have any other properties in the area?"

Colors wafted by. Other addresses. "No—well, nothing like this. Residential."

"So, no other commercial properties?" asked Velez.

She shook her head with a shrug. "Not that I can think of at the moment."

The detectives glanced at each other.

"That all?" Eve held up her phone. "I need to get on this."

"Thank you, Ms. Cernik." Russo nodded. "We'll be in touch."

* * *

After a ferocious tear through the streets northbound, Eve pulled into her rented garage space. She changed clothes and cars, then battled every inch of pavement to park at No Nukes at nine fifteen. She checked the lot for late-morning stragglers as she held Diane's phone to her ear.

"Tamsin." She smiled. "Such an interesting name. Uh, my name is... Diane Cernik, and I'm calling from Lymantria Holdings. We've acquired a promising energy technology, and since Mr. Glick is a renowned futurist, we wanted to invite him to our premiere demonstration."

Tamsin was noncommittal, but agreed to forward Diane to Marty's voicemail.

Kira walked into No Nukes Now a minute later, waving to Quinn as she hurried past her cubicle. She stopped at the door of Barb's office upon seeing Larry.

"I can come back," said Eve.

"No worries," said Barb. "But you might want to grab some coffee. We've got our work cut out for us."

Larry grinned. "Donations are off the charts!"

"Oh, that's awesome!"

"Yeah, I wanted to talk to you about that." Powell careened in.

Eve stepped aside. "Morning."

"Morning." He nodded, but focused on Larry. "All these payments seem to be coming from the same network out of Panama."

"So?" Larry shrugged. "It's probably a campaign started by those anti-nuke protests in Pakistan. If people in some of these countries want to donate, they can't go through traditional means."

"But people in the United States?" asked Powell.

"I don't need to tell you there are people here who don't trust the government."

Powell couldn't argue. "Well, okay—"

"Yeah," said Larry. "We've raised almost two and a half million dollars already."

Crimson and chartreuse. Half the money she'd earmarked. She was going to kill Eugene. She'd specifically asked him—

Eve forced a smile. "I-I can't believe that." She backed away. "I'm going to load up on caffeine."

She hurried to the break room.

How fast could the donor-bots empty the funds she'd set aside? And what would happen once the payment network received transfer requests from an overdrawn account?

Eve jammed a pod into the dispenser and hit Brew. She checked over her shoulder, then pulled out her Diane phone. She could mitigate some donor bot activity, but if they continued to ramp up donations on their own, there was a problem with the software. With a few swipes, she reduced the amounts and lowered their frequency. She pocketed the phone and grabbed her coffee.

On her way to Barb's office, she crossed paths with Powell.

"Hey, Kira," he said. "Got another conspiracy for you."

Her Diane phone buzzed. Loud. "Sorry—I have to take this."

She ducked into the ladies' room. Eve rested the phone against her ear and shoulder, locking the door behind her. She checked the stalls for anyone else.

"Hello, Ms. Cernik?"

She smiled, keeping her voice down. "Hi—yes—this is she. Sorry. Just got on the elevator."

"This is Casey Nylund from Chris Yarrow's office returning your call. Ms. Yarrow's interested in reviewing your design as long as she's provided with a waiver."

"Oh—well, the inventor is not permitting us to—We'd be happy to give Ms. Yarrow a demonstration first, within our own legal parameters."

"All right. I'll have to get back to you."

"Thanks. Talk to you soon."

Eve hung up. She peered dismally into her coffee. Bringing it into the restroom disqualified it from consumption. She dumped it into the sink and tossed the cup, hoping to god Powell wasn't standing outside but desperate to know what he'd seen in the donations. She unlocked the door and rushed out, a half step from bumping into Quinn.

"What's the matter?" Her friend grinned. "Drop a stink bomb in there?"

"Uhh—yeah." Eve nodded. "That and I need coffee."

Quinn chuckled. "Well, I hope this isn't a bad time, but I need to talk to you."

The Diane phone vibrated.

Eve took a step back. "Um—I will catch up with you in a minute. Maybe two. Two minutes."

She dove into the restroom, locking the door behind her.

"You okay?" Quinn asked with concern.

"Yeah," she said through the door. "Just—don't really want an audience for this."

"Right. Sorry."

Eve whispered into the phone. "Hello, this is Diane Cernik."

"Hi, Ms. Cernik, this is Jayden returning your call from Mr. Borg's office. Mr. Borg wants to know what it is you're offering."

She spoke as if in a library. "A breakthrough in energy technology."

"Well, I mean, what specifically—"

"Look, I'm not playing Twenty Questions," she said in a hush. "If he's not interested, he's not interested. Sorry to cut this short, but I have to go."

She hung up, brainstorming the next tech mogul on her list if Borg declined. A notification popped up on her phone. The donation-bots were out of whack again.

"Shit."

She reconfigured the bots and pocketed the phone, then flushed the toilet for effect and washed her hands.

Walking into the break room, she found Quinn leaning against the counter.

"Doing all right?"

Eve cleared her throat. "For the moment."

She popped another pod into the dispenser.

Quinn smirked. "Sure that's a good idea?"

"I need it to live." Eve hit the Brew button.

"You're acting really weird today."

"I told you I was weird," Eve corrected. "This is normal."

"Why don't you just go home sick?"

"I'll be fine." She shrugged. "Bad take out, I guess. You needed to talk?"

"Yeah, so, I don't want to sound ungrateful, but I was thinking—could you maybe not give Lorenzo my demo? Or at least that one? I have some other songs—"

"Well, I already did."

Quinn's lips parted, horror-stricken. "What—when?"

"Well, I didn't have to physically give it to him. I just sent him an email."

"You...you have to tell him not to listen to it."

Eve snickered. "What's the matter? Is it all profanity or something?"

"No, I don't think it's—Wait—you haven't listened to it yet?"

Her guilty pause said it all. "Well—"

"Are you fucking kidding me?" Hurt consumed Quinn's face.

"Well, I haven't had the chance and I wanted to sit down an—"

"You're the whole reason I did any of this. How could you do that? I don't even—"

"It's not like I—"

"Forget it. I don't care."

Quinn stormed out.

About time.

Eve's insides collapsed, the dark blue walls in the deep gray well closing in on her, tighter and tighter, as she shrank smaller and smaller to fit inside. The light above would become a tiny pinhole and she'd return to the familiar black emptiness.

The final spurt of steam from the dispenser snapped her back to reality.

* * *

A quick trip into the city, and Simon purchased three more Qiopa models. After dismantling the first and dissecting it, he determined the best way to maximize the processing power was to route four of them together, wiping three of them of their operating systems and create a distribution cycle whereby the primary unit leveraged tasks to the others. Nothing like outdoing the competition to get the inventive juices flowing.

Zeugma had made the Tmesis software device-specific, so tailoring it to his design required more dabbling than he'd anticipated. He tweaked the operating system, and removed its pesky data collection. Simon tested his new virtual assistant, named for the aloof and ethereal oracle at the edge of the barren Wyvern Rift.

He walked into the foyer, grinning. "Jareima?"

"Yes?" A woman's voice answered in a Lebanese accent—same as the actress who portrayed the character in the film adaptation. "With whom do I have the pleasure of speaking?"

It was in character. Take that, Glick.

Simon chuckled, reigning in his delight. "Dr. Simon Pierce. But you may refer to me as *my lord*."

"Yes, my lord."

He clenched a jubilant fist. "How're you doing?"

"I am operating quite well, thank you. What is it you wish of me, my lord?"

"Jareima, we have a project which will require utmost confidentiality. Do you understand what that means?"

"Confidentiality. Marked by intimacy or willingness to confide. Something which is private or secret."

"Correct. Anything we work on in this house—particularly in the basement—is confidential. You understand?"

"Yes, my lord."

"Good." He secured the knot on his turquoise tie. "You'll be keeping a confidential log only I will have access to, understand?"

"Yes."

"It is to be kept only server partition D. Nothing in the cloud."

"Cloud access is off."

He snapped both fingers, pointing. "Excellent. Arm the security system, level one."

Triple beeps.

"And let's start that log right now. Begin with the date and time. First header, Dr. Simon Pierce. And...I will begin dictation."

"Ready."

"Late last year, I was called upon by an important client to assist in a project they could not complete on their own."

He walked to a heavy wood-paneled door with a modern lock and dead bolt. "Legal agreements prevent me from going into detail, but let's just say this was a monumental discovery."

He opened the door. Lights illuminated, revealing a long staircase to the basement. "Despite my cooperation, interest, intellect, and resources, my involvement was cut short." Simon descended the stairs. "No hard feelings—these things happen. Can you hear me all right, Jareima?"

"Yes, my lord."

"Fantastic." He opened the door below, lights coming up.

Gleaming white counters and steel racks hosted state of the art equipment. Computer consoles, servers, and every manner of scope and diagnostic unit. Adjacent to work spaces for soldering and welding stood three large stainless steel cabinets filled with an engineer's inventory. Three metal cases rested by the door. At the farthest wall, a huge steel and cement chamber with a viewing window of thick high-impact glass.

"Now, my interest in geology is well known," said Simon. "Being in the mining industry and traveling to exotic locations has afforded me the opportunity to obtain unique specimens, amassing a collection that is the envy of other rockhounds."

He took out a small, velvet ring box from his jacket. "And as it happens, I've come into possession of a truly extraordinary material, bearing remarkable resemblance to the aforementioned monumental discovery."

The fragment rested in a satin notch. "If it is indeed the same material—and I have good reason to believe it is—then my experimentation will center around controlling its unusual energy properties with resonant frequencies. Of course, since information was withheld from me, I know very little about said material."

Just enough of the truth. Ignorance would pave the rest of the way.

He opened the chamber door. The shard was dropped into a small compartment inside an electron probe microanalyzer. He exited and sealed the chamber.

"Based on cursory examination," Simon said as he stepped to the computer console, "my specimen appears to be crystalline. I suspect it's composed predominantly of carbon, making it nothing more than a black diamond, really. But a quick scan will reveal its true structure and composition."

He swiped through the analyzer's menu. The machine warmed up. Once ready, he hovered his finger over the button.

"If it is the same material, it might react to energy. However, a sample this small...I believe it would be negligible."

Electrons shot into the shard. A tremendous white bolt erupted from the fragment with a hellacious bang. The analyzer exploded. Smoldering parts smashed into the walls. The chamber itself split apart. Chunks of cement lay broken on the floor. Two overhead light fixtures had shattered, another dangled by a seam.

Simon ducked behind the console. Foam sprayed from above, quelling the fire.

"Simon," Jareima said, "you must evacuate."

He peered over the console. Smoke filled the lab. Thick froth buried his expensive, shiny equipment.

"You must evacuate, my lord."

A grin stretched across his face.

24

(yellow, pink)

For the first time at No Nukes, Eve felt like she was working. Barb sat back, letting her process the files and build reports. They broke for lunch. Eve revisited the donor bots and reined them in on her way to Quinn's cubicle.

But her friend wasn't there.

"She left for the day," said Quinn's cube mate. "Said she wasn't feeling well."

Eve's insides twisted.

See? It was just a matter of time.

Back to eating lunch alone. Like Powell. She headed for the IT room. He put down his sandwich, surprised to see her.

"Hey, sorry about before—it was important."

"It's cool." He shrugged. "I figured."

"And I—I didn't drink that coffee. I threw it out."

He snickered. "Okay."

"You really think there's a problem with these payments?"

"Well, they're all using this network called SPLNTR. It's not illegal—I've used it myself to see how it works."

She smirked. "Sure you have."

"Seriously. The Foil-Hats mentioned it and I wanted to test it out, so I sent money between a couple of my accounts. It's pretty airtight. There's no information from end to end. Now, in terms of what the network sees, I don't know. There must be some tracking. But I don't think they keep logs—which, I'm sure you know, isn't going to fly."

"Well, it's not completely anonymous." She shrugged. "I mean, we're still getting payment information."

"That's what bugs me." He wagged a finger. "If people are using the online forms, then why use SPLNTR?"

Inquisitive bastard. If it came down to it, she could find out where he lived using the payroll files. Bump into him by chance. Go on an impromptu date. Once she got him alone, it would be all over. But then she'd need another house.

"Maybe just some activist movement?" She shrugged. "Like Larry said."

"Maybe."

"All right, well, Barb's probably looking for me. I'll talk to you later."

She returned to the office, planting herself behind the desk. The second half of the day was nowhere as intense. Barb even let her leave fifteen minutes early.

Eve rushed to her car and dug into her purse. Quinn's demo. She'd shoved it in there after sending the tracks to Lorenzo with the intention of listening to it. At least she wasn't a total monster. She pulled out of the lot, checking the mirrors for her Russian shadow.

Unprepared for her early exit, the dour man sped into traffic only to get stuck behind a city bus. Eve queued for the on-ramp and slid the CD into the player. Diane's car didn't have such primitive technology, so this was her best opportunity to give it a listen.

Eve glanced at the track listing—which she hated to admit she hadn't looked at before. The first song was "Scarlet." It opened with a splash of guitar chords and the unexpected addition of furious drums. The lyrics told the story of being rescued by a fiery-haired superwoman who taught her how to believe in herself again.

"Oh goddammit, Quinn," Eve muttered as tears clouded her vision.

The next was "Love & Dread" about her break up with Kyle, which Eve also hated to admit she didn't remember in great detail. But Quinn had gleaned something from their conversation as the song resolved with her making peace with the matter. "Pacific Highway"—a song about her former band's tour and eventual demise, ringing with a sense of betrayal and loss as she ventured from gorgeous coastal forest to the emptiness of the desert. Each song was deep and personal. Maybe too personal to share with anyone else but Kira.

Eve turned down the volume and put the phone to her ear.

Right to voicemail. "Quinn, it's me. I know you're mad, and—in my rush to be helpful and do this great thing for you, I was careless and thoughtless and I'm sorry. Can you please call me so we can talk?"

She hung up, traffic taking priority, and pulled onto the exit.

* * *

Kira Sloane had lost her edge. He'd expected her to race off. But she didn't. Six car lengths behind, he followed her onto the off-ramp. Four blocks later, the hybrid entered the gates around a nondescript concrete building. He lingered in the plaza across the street. Fifteen minutes later, an expensive electric vehicle exited the gates. The windows were tinted. But based on the fact that Kira Sloane drove a hybrid, he followed it, taking down the license plate.

The E-V coursed through traffic until they reached the inevitable deadlock of the freeway. Once clear, the car inched into downtown and slipped into the private entrance of a luxury high-rise. Rather than waste time on a fruitless stake out, he rolled past the building and out of the city.

* * *

Eve stormed into the penthouse. She wrested off the wig, marching toward the guestroom. "*Eugene!*"

She tore off her glasses. "Get your ass out here—now!"

Eugene rushed out of the house. "What?! What happened?!"

"What do you think?!" She lifted the lid.

Eve carried him to the office, neglecting to cover the enclosure.

* * *

"Uh-oh." Zach mumbled, peering out the curtain.

"Okay," said Darien. "So how long you think before she comes back and kills us?"

Janelle folded her arms. "Hundred bucks says he didn't put it in there."

"I don't know." Troy sighed. "She seems pretty pissed."

"Forget about him," said Kevin. "This is our chance."

"We're not ready," said Shadi.

"There's a couple extension cords in the garage," said Kevin. "Maybe we can scale the wall or at least measure it for next time."

"There is no next time if Eugene's dead," said Cassidy.

* * *

Meanwhile, Eugene stood on the desktop as Eve opened the software.

She fumed. "Half the money's gone. It was supposed to last a month."

"Well, can't you just add more to the account?"

"That's not the point," she seethed. "You were supposed to be checking my work."

"Well, I—just figured—I mean, you're such a natural—"

"I'm not." She slammed a fist onto the opposite corner of the desk.

The shock of the blow shot through his body. Somehow he didn't soil himself.

"That was your job."

Neither of them wanted to acknowledge he'd been gawking at her. They scrolled through the lines in silence.

He cleared his throat. "Right there." He pointed. "That's—"

"I see it," she muttered, correcting the script.

They took a pass through, spot-checking.

Her phone vibrated. Quinn. Eve tensed, glaring at Eugene, and held up a threatening finger.

Her whisper hit like a concentrated hurricane. "Do not say a word."

He nodded, saturated in condensation.

"Hey, Quinn."

"Hey, I'm outside your place."

Eve's mind raced. "My-My place?"

"Yeah, I got your address from Barb a little while ago. I wanted to send you a thank-you."

"Well, uh—I'm on my way home, if you can wait like...?"

Eve grimaced at Eugene. He shrugged, and held up two fingers, forming an O with his other hand.

"Twenty minutes?" Eve suggested.

"Okay, sure. I mean, this isn't a great neighborhood, but I saw a coffee shop up the street. I can wait there."

"Awesome. All right—be there as fast as I can." She hung up, scowling at Eugene. "I'm still mad at you."

"I'm sorry," he said. "We were having fun, and I got—"

"Yeah, well, when we're working, I expect you to be more professional."

"Absolutely. It won't happen again."

* * *

Kevin, Zach, Shadi and Troy crept against the east wall. The tremble of her steps had warned them. Shadi stuck her improvised grappling hook under the barbecue grill's lid. Kevin and Troy coiled up the extension cords. They raced in through the sliding glass door, shoving the cords under the couch before Eugene entered.

Janelle, Darien and Cassidy rushed toward him, consuming his attention as much as possible.

"What happened?" asked Cassidy.

"Yeah." Zach stormed forward. "How're you still alive?"

"False alarm." Eugene put his hands up. "Just a mis-key, on her part. Don't get me wrong—I almost shit myself."

"So she doesn't suspect anything?" he asked.

"She has no idea." Eugene lowered his hands.

They backed off. Eugene paced with agitation.

"What was the mis-key?" asked Shadi.

Eugene huffed. "It was—it broke the schedule, and she freaked out. Sorry, but, uh—I need a minute."

He hurried down the hall into his bedroom.

The housemates huddled.

"He's not telling us everything," said Shadi in a hush.

"Yeah, no shit." Zach rasped.

"How high are the walls?" Cassidy whispered.

"Troy thinks he can get over them," said Kevin.

"I can probably do it in five." Troy shrugged.

"So we just need to get everything out of Eugene," said Janelle.

* * *

Lighter traffic made Eve's trip to the garage smooth, but her brain was a tangle of tangerine-and-chartreuse squiggles sprouting bands of mauve. The Russians might still be monitoring Kira's place. Not to mention the fact Eve hadn't been there in ages and had no idea the conditions inside.

She called Quinn to let her know she was nearby. Eve scoured the parking lot from the driver's seat. No dark blue sedan. No one loitered outside.

She stepped out as Quinn's car rolled into a space.

Her friend walked up with a wine bottle in hand.

"Quinn, I'm sorry, I—"

"No, I overreacted."

"No, it was important to you and I—I was so excited about doing this other thing, I forgot it was important to you, and I'm sorry."

Quinn restrained a smile. "You feel guilty when you listened to it?"

"Oh my god—I was trying to drive and I couldn't see because I was crying so much."

"Good." She smirked, holding up the bottle. "Want to get drunk?"

Eve sighed. "This one time, okay?"

Quinn chuckled.

Tension gripped her as she thumbed the key ring. Rather than fumble through them, she stuck the least familiar one into the lock. It worked. The door opened and they entered Kira's apartment. Though comfy—and not as dusty as she feared—it was unfamiliar. She remembered picking out the burnt-orange couches and distressed-wood living room set. But the random items she'd grabbed from thrift stores to fill in Kira's persona were alien to her.

"So, make yourself at home." Her head swiveled, unsure where to put her keys.

She headed for the bedroom while Quinn explored. Eve flipped the lights on. The bed was untouched. She dashed over and rumpled the comforter with her hand, pulling at the sheets. She darted to the bathroom to dishevel toiletries, flicking water around the sink and mirror. Anything to make it seem lived in.

The real problem was the *modifikator*. What if someone broke in and stole it? Or if Quinn found it? Eve left it in her jacket, unwilling to part with it.

She strolled into the living room as Quinn examined trinkets and figurines on a bookshelf.

"No pictures of family or anything?"

Eve exhaled as she headed for the kitchen.

Lie.

"No, I—" She shook her head, speaking louder. "Kind of got tired answering questions about my younger, smarter, taller, prettier, better-at-everything sister."

Dumbass.

"Damn." Quinn smiled. "Serious sibling rivalry."

"Rivalry implies I stood a chance." Eve hunted for a corkscrew.

Quinn sauntered over and staked the wine bottle onto the counter. "Bet she made your life miserable in high school."

"Worse." Eve looked up from the drawer. "She was super nice to me, like, all the time."

"That bitch."

"I know." She pulled open another drawer.

"Well, I think you're awesome."

"Thanks. Kind of want you to meet my family so you could tell them that, but then they would tell you really embarrassing stories, so—no."

Quinn laughed.

Eve returned to a previous drawer, finding a rosy-pink winged corkscrew with yellow levers. Her brow pinched—odd she hadn't spotted the peculiar item before. Had she bought it at the thrift store? She grabbed it and shut the drawer.

Quinn handed her the bottle.

"Don't get me wrong," said Eve. "I don't want to trash-talk her."

Quinn leaned against the counter. "Well, I thought that's what we were doing."

"And I appreciate you being totally on board for that." She tore off the bottle's wrapper. "But I don't hate her. I actually miss her a lot."

"You don't talk to her?"

Eve winced with regret. "I may have taken things too far."

She jammed in the corkscrew.

"You can always apologize." Quinn smiled. "And you're really good at it."

"Oh, thanks." Eve snickered, twisting the corkscrew. "But I haven't because...I didn't think I was wrong."

"Oh."

"Yeah. So what about you? Or are you the perfect one?"

Quinn grinned, recoiling. "No—I am not. That would be Tristan."

"Tristan? Well, he lost out in the names department."

"Yeah, but..." Quinn counted off on her fingers. "First to graduate college, first to go to grad school, first to get married, first to buy a house, first to have kids. I mean, it's not like I want all that, but—"

"You want the things you want."

"Yeah. And it's hard enough getting those."

"Yeah." Eve popped out the cork.

"Where are your wine-glasses?"

"No idea." Eve shrugged. "I usually drink straight from the bottle."

Quinn laughed. They found a couple in the back of the cupboard and poured their drinks.

Quinn lifted her glass. "Okay, so, before I met you, I was about to quit. Everybody was saying music's not a real career and I should get a job with Carmen's company, that maybe it was something I could do on the weekends—"

"I thought your friends were all musicians?"

The corner of her lip tugged to one side. "Some of them. But even they were like, *You need a better day job*. I think they play so they can tell people they're musicians, but they're more interested in living in the hottest neighborhood, going to the newest restaurants, buying organic butt plugs or something—I don't know."

Eve chuckled.

"That's why I didn't invite any of them. It's why I went along with Diego. I was desperate, and I...just wanted *something*. And then you showed up, and—"

Eve clinked the edge of her glass her friend's.

Quinn responded in kind. They sipped.

The conversation shifted to the wine itself and the possibility of more wine. Kira had another bottle in the fridge but not much else aside from condiments and nonperishables. Eve admitted she hadn't gone grocery shopping so they ordered pizza.

She thought about checking on the bots. Or peeking out the window for the dour man. But Quinn consumed her attention. The troubles drifted. She didn't have much time left with her. Might as well have fun.

While waiting for the delivery, they polished off the first bottle. They uncorked the second minutes before the pizza arrived, celebrating their timing with another toast. They moved to the living room and turned on the television, talking between bites and refilling their glasses.

"And we get into this argument," said Eve. "Whether or not the *Fast and Furious* series are car movies or heist movies."

"Oh, they're definitely heis—"

"They are car movies," Eve said with finality.

"I see you feel strongly about this." Quinn smirked.

"I do. The heists were an afterthought. They didn't add that in till, like, ten years later. Anyway—I ended up living with him for another three months."

"At least tell me the sex was good."

"It wasn't terrible."

Quinn chuckled. "That should've been your first clue."

"Well, whatever—point is I realized I was better off alone, and I guess I default to that now?" She shrugged.

"I read something somewhere that was like, it doesn't matter if all these relationships work out or not, because the one you end up with is The One."

"What if I already found The One?"

"Well, if he was, you'd still be with him, so, your One is still out there."

"Well, what if your One dies?"

Idiot.

Quinn tried, but Eve wouldn't meet her eyes. "Well, I guess they wouldn't be The One. Is that what happened?"

Eve's molars dug into her tongue. The sad story she'd repeated to herself countless times, the centerpiece of her life, which had driven away most of her friends, that she so much wanted to share with this new friend—she couldn't. The details, the timing, all of it. Anyone searching for Eve Kincaid who spoke to anyone she'd known for the past decade would know the same story.

She shook her head. "It was a long time ago. It doesn't matter."

"Well, I mean, I was really drunk, but I'm pretty sure I unloaded my latest tragic attempt at a relationship on you."

"Yeah." Eve smirked. "And you probably need to tell me again because I was a little wasted."

"Well, this sounds much worse. And fair is fair, so—"

"No, sorry—not doing this right now. We're having a good time, and I don't want to be a downer."

"Oh, so I'm the downer?" Quinn smiled. "Thanks!"

Eve chuckled. "To be honest, I couldn't hear most of what you were saying at the end of the night."

"I know, dude! Why do they do that?"

"To make you drink more."

"Seriously?"

"Yeah. The French studied it. Turning up the volume makes people drink faster. Plus you can't hear what people are saying, so there's no point in talking."

"All the more reason to drink at home."

They clinked glasses.

"Not to get back into it, but—how did you know he was The One?"

A lake of blue-gray fog flooded Eve's mind. Cozy brown quilt. Curly black locks. His laugh. His warmth. All of it wound on a single thread. "He wanted the real me. And I mean—I have a hard time with the real me."

Quinn's forehead scrunched.

Eve watched the blue-gray fog spread but sensed Quinn's attention. "Sorry."

"No, it's—"

"See?" She smiled. "Not fun."

"Yeah. I need water."

They nestled into the couch. Quinn's eyes closed during the late show's opening monologue. Talk of President Ramos's threats of war with Venezuela, a hackneyed pretense for obtaining oil in the Western Hemisphere. She turned off the television and draped a blanket over Quinn.

Eve lay wide awake in the strange bed. Troubled by the neighborhood's noises. Every set of passing headlights. She longed for the serenity of the penthouse. Her head swam in boozy paranoia. The Russians. The FBI. The detectives. Whatever passing fear she latched onto.

The *modifikator* remained in her purse, which had been hung from its strap on the bedpost above her head. She reached up, pulling out the case, checking inside to make sure it was still there. She clutched the case, contemplating how to sleep with it in hand. But she put it back. Someone could take it from her.

Restless, she hunted for the echo of every odd tap and slight rustle.

No more passing headlights. She feared the dark here and remembered something her mother had said about letting babies cry it out, that they'd done that to her. They'd run out of options.

A vague impression floated from the depths of her brain as she hovered between wake and sleep, exhausted by the day and drunkenness. She latched onto the feeling—thick, wet splotches of crimson, yellow, and bright blue melding into green, distasteful orange, and muddy brown—and reached back, uncertain if it was a dream or memory.

She was three, on the floor, learning to write numbers and letters with her mother. She'd drawn them on lined paper at angles, sideways, upside down, in different color crayons.

"What are you doing?" Her mother had smiled. "You're supposed to draw them right-side up. Like that."

She pointed to a number six (royal blue). "They dance."

Her mom beamed at her. "How do they dance?"

Instead of a funny little jig, Eve flipped and flapped and twisted her hands around in front of her face. Her mother laughed. Eve had gotten the sense she wasn't taking her seriously.

"And then they mix together and-and-and they fly away."

"Like a rainbow?"

"No...like, like in the air."

Mom had introduced her to fingerpainting. The feel of the paint had left much to be desired, but the ability to move colors around as she saw them had been a revelation. She could put these untouchable things into the real world. She had tried to tell mom, but hadn't had the words.

"It's very pretty." Her mom had smiled.

Her mom had needed to tend to Charlotte, so they'd washed up and put the paints away. After a nap, Eve had awoken energized to play with the colors again. She'd wanted another chance to show her mom, to make her understand. But her mom had started making dinner and Charlotte had needed to be fed, so she'd turned on the television for Eve.

But the allure of the paint had been unbearable.

Eve had wrapped a blanket around a large plush chipmunk toy to serve as her decoy. She'd pushed over a chair in the dining room, dragging it several feet and climbing its legs to reach the door knob of the hall closet. She'd pried it open, stretching to reach the paints on the shelf above. Construction paper had been too flimsy a canvas for the depth of color she wanted to express. The walls were much better. She'd painted what she'd seen. And gotten carried away. She'd smeared every square inch within range of her chubby little arms—the entire living room, hallway, dining room, and by the time her mother had turned around, the kitchen door.

"Eve?! What in god's name are you doing!?"

She'd turned, wide-eyed, clutching a duvet caked with paint, as she'd been wiping her hands on it to prevent improper mixing.

"Make." Her lip had quivered. "Making the colors dance."

"No! Bad! Very bad! Oh my god—oh my god, what is wrong with you?" Her mom had regained her composure. "You are in so much trouble. Don't ever do that again."

Tears had streamed down her cheeks. She'd just wanted to show her. "But Mom—"

"No. No more dancing colors, okay?"

"But—"

"*No more.*"

A special kind of fear had etched its mark deep within her. She'd never spoke of the dancing colors to anyone else until she met Gideon, though she'd learned the word for it many years before. Maybe that was why she'd shrouded herself in black. The absence of color. What her mother wanted to see.

25

(yellow, red)

The housemates gathered in the living room for another *Go-Kart WarZone X* tournament. At Cassidy's suggestion, it turned into a drinking game. Shadi didn't drink but continued to play. Troy sat alongside Eugene on the couch and tried to act natural. It was harder than guarding millions of dollars.

Cassidy returned with four bottles, reaching two out toward Troy and Eugene. She nodded. Troy took the cue, handing the most forward bottle to Eugene. She nodded again.

The game went on. Their voices grew louder. Except for Troy. He shifted on the couch cushion. He lost the race and handed off his controller. He leaned back, watching Eugene take sip after sip. Regret knotted in his chest.

It was one pill, he told himself. One night. He wouldn't remember.

But Troy himself would.

Eugene's head loosened on his neck. He laughed as he lost control of his go-kart, struggling to stay on the track. Zach handed him another beer. Eugene's head rocked about, tracing the game's fanfare with giddy fascination. He lost the round. Handed off his controller. Drank more beer.

Troy wanted to stop him.

Eugene sank into the couch and closed his eyes. Troy sat up. He tapped Janelle on the shoulder. She stood, waving her hand, and led everyone out except for Zach and Cassidy. They continued to duke it out in a head-to-head matchup.

Troy gently bumped his knee into Eugene's. Eugene awakened, sitting up. Relieved he wasn't totally knocked out, Troy scooted closer.

"Today had to be scary as hell, man." He slapped Eugene's knee. "But you held it together. Came through for us—again."

"Yeah." Eugene sat up, straighter. "Yeah, I guess I did."

"You really think she'll let us go?" Troy asked.

"Yeah, yeah. She-She's going to let us go. I mean, I'm going to stay, but..."

"What?" Troy asked.

Eugene's head rocked forward and back with a drunken grin. "I'm going to work for her."

Cassidy and Zach turned around, dumbfounded.

"You can't be serious," said Zach. He turned to Cassidy, muttering, "That's the drugs talking, right?"

She shrugged, her face drooping with doubt.

"Oh, I'm serious," Eugene slurred. "You're going to fire me anyway, so, like, screw you. And I've got nothing going on. It's, like, best thing that's ever happened to me. Meeting Selene."

"Her name's Selene?" Troy asked.

"Shhhhhhhhhh." Eugene hovered a finger over of his lips, lodging it against a nostril. "You're not supposed to know. Eugene and Selene. Like we're meant to be together, right?"

"Or," said Zach, "she just made it up because it rhymes and she knows you're an idiot."

Troy shot Zach an admonishing glare. "Dude."

Eugene's head bobbed. "She wouldn't...she wouldn't lie to me like that."

"He's clearly not going to remember this." Zach shrugged at Troy, then turned to Cassidy. "Is he?"

"No," she said. "But tomorrow he's going to wish he was dead."

Eugene's head snapped backward, his mouth open.

Troy leaned forward, whispering in concern. "Well, is it going to knock him out or is going to kill him?"

"He'll be fine—he'll just feel like shit," Cassidy answered. "Trust me. I had an ex-boyfriend who was a pharmacologist. No—pharmacist."

"You mean drug dealer," Troy corrected.

"Oh." Cassidy pondered. "I guess he was."

Troy patted Eugene's shoulder, reviving him. "So, you and Selene are pretty close, right?"

"Yeah." Eugene nodded, eyes closed.

"You see where she keeps that thing?" he asked.

"What thing?"

"The shrink ray," Zach said with annoyance.

"Oh, yeah, no—she never lets it out. It's always—she's got a case for it, started using. Always in a...pocket, *orrrr*...or some place."

"Which pocket?"

"Uhh—some? Depends. What she's wearing. Usually her pants, but if she's the jacket, it—it's inside there, in-in...side, inside the pocket."

"The inner jacket pocket?"

"Yeah."

"What side does she favor when it's in the pants pocket?"

"Favor." Eugene chuckled. "Favor. Can you do you a favor? Me a favor. It's a funny word. *Favor. Fay. Vur.* Like you're saying *favorite*—favoring, favoring something."

"What side does she keep it on?" Zach asked, impatient.

"Right. Left side. Always the left." He sighed. "I-I'm feeling really tired. You guys—are you guys—are you guys...tired?"

"You probably just need some water," said Troy. "Zach—get him some water."

Zach scowled. "Why don't you ge—"

"Don't harsh the kid's vibe," Cassidy scolded through gritted teeth. "Get him water."

Zach stood. "Ask him about the security flaw."

He headed to the kitchen while Troy and Cassidy followed the reflexive bob and jerk of Eugene's head as he fought slumber.

"You know where she keeps it at night?" asked Troy.

"Mmph, no," he murmured. "There's, uh—black box. Next to her bed."

"What kind of box? Does it have a lock on it?"

"I don't know—can't see that far."

"Eugene," said Cassidy. "When, specifically, is she letting us go?"

"Like," he whispered through a smile, eyes still closed. "Like... never."

Troy's brow crumpled. "But you just said—"

"I...I told her not to."

"What?" Cassidy's lips twisted into a snarl.

Eugene hunched over, confiding in them. "She wanted to know...if she could *truss* anyone. Not to call police. And-and I told her—I told her I didn't think so. She-she can only *truss* me."

Troy turned to Cassidy with dismay as Eugene lost consciousness. He slumped forward. His head thunked onto the coffee table.

Zach stood not far from the couch with a glass of water in hand.

"You know," Zach muttered, sarcastic, "we could just smother his head with a pillow, and no one would ever find out."

* * *

One of the perks of working at No Nukes were the flexible part-time schedules for hourly employees. Until Kira officially took over for Barb, she only had to come in Mondays, Wednesdays, and Fridays. Quinn was usually off on Thursdays as well, but had picked up a shift to make up hours. The alarm on her phone chimed at 7:00 a.m.

Kira had cereal but no milk, so Eve and Quinn visited the coffee shop up the street. They bought several pastries and sat at a table outside, immersing themselves in their phones. While Quinn checked her social media, Eve tended to her bots on the Diane phone.

"I haven't been using FriendBook lately," said Quinn. "So I really didn't think about it, but we haven't bookmarked each other."

Eve sipped her coffee. "Yeah, I'm not on there."

"Well, what about Tell-A-Photo?"

"Not on there either. Really don't do the social media thing anymore."

"Then what're you doing on your phone all the time?"

Eve shrugged. "Checking email, reading, games, shopping. Lots of shopping."

"I was wondering why I couldn't tag you."

She sat up. "You posted pictures of me?"

Quinn lifted her eyes, innocent. "Yeah. From the bar."

Eve softened, smiling. "Please take those down."

"You look fine, see?" Quinn held out her phone, showing a candid shot of an intoxicated Kira holding a highball glass.

"No." Her eyes flared. "I look wasted. Please take them down."

"I'm sorry I—"

"I know, and I should've said something, but—I haven't been out in so long I didn't think about it."

"Well, I mean, nobody really uses FriendBook anymore. Or Chitter for that matter. It's mostly Clip-Clop—"

"I don't want all the toxicity, you know? Had some bad experiences and decided to quit."

"Well, you can always block people."

"Tried that. Didn't stop."

"Stalkers?"

"Nothing like that."

"Trolls?"

"Assholes."

"Well, I mean, that's pretty much the whole internet."

Eve bobbed her head in agreement. "And don't we get enough of them in real life?"

Quinn leaned forward, concerned. "What happened?"

"Nothing." Stymied by her genuine tone, Eve couldn't lie. "I don't—maybe I'm just an asshole magnet."

"Is it because we're in public?" Quinn asked in a soft voice.

"No, it's—a philosophical position I've taken to best live among other people."

Quinn smirked. "So it's super embarrassing, huh?"

"No, it's my life philosophy, and I'm asking you to respect it."

"All right." Quinn leaned back, dubious. "I'll take them down."

She thumbed through her photo album, deleting any pictures of Kira.

Agonizing over her own carelessness, Eve abandoned her bots in favor of hunting down services to scrub traces of Kira Sloane's data from the web. For a hundred bucks, in a few days Kira Sloane would be unsearchable.

* * *

Simon led a herculean young man in a jumpsuit through the basement. He slapped a hand on the restoration technician's shoulder and grinned. "And for five grand a head, you and your crew don't mention this."

The technician pulled away, flummoxed. "This is serious damage, Dr. Pierce. I mean, an explosion. I have to report this."

"I'm already in contact with the manufacturer," said Simon. "Believe me."

"Look, I know you want to get it done—"

"Ten thousand a head. If no one ever mentioned this to anyone, I would consider it a personal favor."

"Yeah, but I've got to document it."

"But nothing happened." Simon spread his hands apart, gesturing to the disaster. The dangling light fixture crashed to the floor behind him. "It was confined to the basement. The fire-suppression system worked. And I'm miles from the nearest residence."

"But you've got a national forest right outside your door."

"And it's pristine." Simon's toothy smile persisted. "Untouched."

The technician shook his head. "Rules are rules."

Simon's smile sank. He'd have to dip into his emergency cash reserves. But this qualified as an urgent matter.

The technician sighed. "You wouldn't want me or my crew bending the rules when we're work—"

"Okay, so fifty for you? And ten for each of your crew?"

The technician's mouth hung open, his eyes processing the words.

The edges of Simon's lips curled up and out. "Make it a hundred. Ten for everyone else. That work?"

The technician blinked, his jaw struggling to form words.

Simon stuck out his palm, thumb in the air. "Let's just..."

He grabbed the technician's hand and shook it. The technician eased into the motion, firming up his grip.

"You like snakes?" asked Simon.

* * *

Velez sat in the bullpen with her back to the whiteboard. Tony Lam led the competition. Forty-three solves to her thirty-six.

"They've had deliveries there." Velez draped her arm over the back of her chair. "One of them was for a generator, another for a shed and enough freeze-dried meatloaf to feed an army. But the place was empty —"

"The guy's a nut." Russo leaned against the desk and folded his arms. "The whole business is basically this germophobe's bulletproof-bubble to wait out the Apocalypse."

"That's the other thing—the shell companies. We don't know what other properties they own."

"Not enough for a warrant."

"There's something going on. Maybe they crossed the wrong people."

"For what?"

"Buying weapons. That's doomsday stuff, right? Arming yourself for the end of the world?"

"Okay. So, Devereux's getting contraband from the Badlands?"

"Maybe." Velez shrugged. "Something unregistered. Or maybe he's hiding an arsenal at one of his residential properties."

"No good." He shook his head. "We got anything connecting the fires?"

"They haven't figured out what caused the first one."

"But we know this one was C-4. Cernik clearly wanted the place, and insurance ain't paying shit, so somebody wanted to send them a message."

"All right, maybe Devereux's laundering for them."

"Judge is going to ask for a money trail, which we don't got."

Velez chopped the air with her hand. "They didn't incorporate until this year."

"I don't know what to tell you. It looks shady, but we got nothing."

Her head tilted, annoyed and defeated. "So, hand it over to Gang Unit?"

"Based on the explosives" —Russo leaned off the desk— "I'm thinking Counterterrorism. And if Devereux's up to something, they'll turn him upside down and shake it out."

"Works for me."

The desk phone rang. Velez reached for the receiver. "I'll catch up."

Russo hurried out of the bullpen.

She brought the phone to her ear, the company's web page with Diane's picture still up on her laptop. Something about the angle bothered Velez, something about her face.

"This is Detective Velez," she said, reaching for her smartphone.

"Morning, Detective. This is Special Agent Manuel Guzman with the Federal Bureau of Investigation."

"What can I do for you, Agent Guzman?" She swiped through pictures on her phone.

"More about what we can do for you. I spoke with Detective Santiago, and we understand there's a couple overlapping missing persons cases. We'd like to offer our assistance."

Velez gazed at the picture of the tall redhead from days earlier. Same angle. Same face. Same bamboo wood-grain phone case.

"We just had a break in that, so we're going to follow up on a lead."

"Oh. All right. Mind if I ask who your suspect is?"

If the Bureau stepped in, she wouldn't get credit for the solve.

She smiled. "You know how it is—don't want to jinx anything."

"Sure, I got you. Well, either way, we'd like a follow-up."

"Will do. Thanks." She hung up.

No harm in checking it out. Counterterrorism was heavy on procedure and always backlogged. They wouldn't dig into the case for a week.

Diane's background was clean. Years of employment and rental history, credit checks, a few pictures in subpar industry websites. The address on her license was for a penthouse, owned by a holding company. No other associated properties. But in the absence of wrongdoing, their investigation was limited.

Velez saved Diane's image and accessed the facial-recognition database. After emailing herself the redhead's photo, she ran a comparison with Diane through the program.

Ninety-three-point-eight percent match.

Her brows clenched together as she studied the images. Velez added the still frame of the mystery woman from outside Milner's building. Ninety-three-point-eight percent match. She leaned back, snorting with aggravation. They'd been warned the software wasn't perfect. Results were only as good as the images loaded into the database.

She skimmed the analysis. Their first search using the still frame of Burglamazon had yielded results for a missing woman from the federal database named Eve Kincaid—fifteen inches shorter than their suspect. Her name had popped up again when Velez ran the redhead's picture.

Ninety-three-point-eight percent match.

Velez sighed as she closed the program. "Great technology, guys."

* * *

Quinn left for work. Eve headed to the waypoint garage, where she switched vehicles and personas. Half hour later, Diane bypassed the elevators at the high-rise. She headed to the lobby to pick up a delivery.

"What do you do with all this food?" asked the receptionist.

Eve signed the register. "Oh, well, since Mr. Devereux does everything over videoconference, rather than go out, we entertain. Hire a couple of caterers, and they put it all together."

"Wow," said the young woman. "Sounds like a lot of extra work for something that's kind of odd."

"And now you know Avery Devereux." Eve smiled as she handed over the clipboard.

She glimpsed at a photo posted behind the receptionist. A grainy image from the security camera in the lobby. The dour man.

"Excuse me." Eve pointed. "Who is that?"

The receptionist glanced over her shoulder. "Oh, some creep. Don't worry—security's all over it. You need any help with that?"

"No, thanks, I'm fine. I'll bring the cart back."

Eve wheeled the cart to the elevator and rode up to the penthouse.

Must've let her guard down. Or the waypoint garage had been compromised. He didn't seem to know the name of her other alter ego. Yet. And while she was unsettled at how close he'd gotten, she had another shot at capturing a spy. She smirked as the doors opened.

More work to do.

Eve changed clothes and made her deliveries.

Kevin met her outside the miniature house.

"Sorry," she said. "Still don't have your blood pressure medication. The Canadian supplier I was using has it on back order. Might be another week."

"It's okay, I've got some stockpiled," he answered. "I was wondering about the renovation stuff?"

She'd studied his list. Paint and dry wall, two-by-fours (mustard, plum, orchid), screws and nails. A spool of electrical wiring and some outlets. It looked like a renovation project. Which only made her more suspicious.

"Oh—yeah." Her head lilted to the side. "What are all the bungee cords for?"

"Tying up lumber, keeping extension cords together." He shrugged. "You know, organization. Just a good all-purpose thing to have. Like duct tape."

"Huh." Her eyes lingered on him, waiting for a tell.

He gazed back at her, expectant. "So...that a yes? I'd like to get started on something, 'cause these people are getting on my nerves."

She sucked her teeth. "Sure. I'll put in the order today."

"Thanks."

* * *

Armando's hobbies consisted of eating ice cream and watching DVD box sets. He'd missed decades of television running the streets in his youth. This was a chance to catch up. Besides, he couldn't fight her. Curtains drawn and lights out, he'd melded with the sofa, oblivious to the rumble of the sliding glass door.

"You're a dumbass, Ross! Rachel's too good for you."

The footsteps were harder to ignore. He sat up, wiping a hand on his shirt before meeting the woman outside. He shielded his eyes from the sun as she set down his groceries.

"You know, there is a washing machine in there."

"Yeah." Armando snickered. "I, uh, haven't gotten around to that."

She sat back on her haunches. "I'll give you some quarters, since I just came from the laundromat."

He hoisted the bags with a scowl.

"They torched my warehouse," she said. "Now the cops are investigating my business."

He shook his head. "I told you Lionel wouldn't quit."

"Then I need to shut him down." She stretched across the pond.

Armando stumbled backward, groceries scattering. Her weight jostled the island. She balanced on it with her palms, looming over him and blocking the sun.

"Where do they move the most money?"

He flattened against the sand. "The art gallery! They move everything out of there—cash, crypto—"

"You said they had twelve guys guarding the place."

"Well, I don't know—I don't know what you been doing. But based on what I seen, you can't do what you do. It's the middle of downtown."

"Anything you want to tell me? Anything you might've left out?"

"You need the banker, Shangkar. Kid's got all the passwords. Can't miss him. He's a toothpick with a goatee."

The woman sat back on her heels. Sunlight returned to the island. She stood. Armando picked himself up. She headed back inside while he gathered his groceries.

* * *

Eve's day descended into projects. She assembled the housing for the energy prototype, then rehearsed her presentation. She considered every question, every critique, every answer. Anxious she might fail, she retraced her steps on the diorama downstairs.

The chat bots needed little or no guidance. They'd found suitable targets, engaged them in conversation. Within days, they'd indoctrinated followers with environmental fervor. The earlier releases made executive decisions and influenced the bots in other groups. She hadn't told them her plans, yet they'd become an extension of her own mind. She only needed to give them words.

She broadened the target. Nuclear power plants. All power plants. Fossil fuels weren't the enemy, the way humankind got its energy was the enemy. The old way was obsolete. It must be overthrown, or else total annihilation—condemnation to a New Dark Age.

New Power, New World.

She sprinkled the tag across her botnets, along with another: *Free Energy, Free World*.

Let the people choose which one they liked more. The bots would recognize their patterns and push the favored tag en masse. A low, steady hum resonated in the backdrop. Part of her everyday existence. Like waiting for the sun to set.

* * *

Eugene awoke in late afternoon with a splitting headache, pain pulsating his eyes. Nauseated and disturbed by every sound, he found sanctuary in the kitchen, away from the banging and metallic screeches from the garage. He slumped at the table with a glass of water.

Zach opened the fridge. "Want any food?"

"*Mrrm*, no."

He scouted the shelves. "Over did it last night, huh?"

"I guess." Eugene forced his head up, eyes squeezed shut. "Didn't think I had that much."

"Well, you did. Passed out on the couch, talking in your sleep."

His belly filled with a different sort of queasiness. "I did?"

"Yeah." Zach smirked. "Who's Selene?"

Eugene's eyes popped open, blinding him. "Nobody." He covered his eyes, reeling from the pain in his temples. "This girl I went out with, like, a long time ago."

"Sure."

Zach grabbed a package of sliced ham and shut the fridge.

Eugene sipped his water.

Had he slipped up? If he'd confessed she'd never put in the security flaw, they would've been furious. So that wasn't it. But he'd said her name. A secret only the two of them shared. If one of the housemates called her Selene, she'd realize he'd broken her trust—she'd kill him!

He searched his disjointed memories from the night before.

What else had he said?

* * *

Eve left the penthouse at 11:00 p.m. She changed into the suit at the waypoint garage. The Badlands had to be dealt with. And since he'd tracked down her other alias, so did the dour man.

The police and F.B.I. wouldn't be far behind.

She mapped out their moves. Suspicious of Devereux's business, and with limited options, the detectives would hand the case off to federal law enforcement. Probably through the Counterterrorism division. Thanks to the fires, they'd scrutinize the explosions at the florist and laundromat for traces linking them together. Eventually, the investigation would land in front of McCrae.

Everyone will see how horrible you are.

"*No,*" she whispered. "I just need a few more days."

Violet, blue, scarlet. Invisible.

She had to control the message, same as she did with the bots. She was cleaning up the city, cleaning up the country, cleaning up the world.

Nobody will believe that. Nobody likes you.

"Quinn likes me." The helmet muffled her words.

She likes Kira.

"Shut up."

A homeless man huddled outside the parking garage lifted his head.

He searched for the voice. "Hello?"

But Eve was already crossing the street.

She marched several blocks to a polished storefront. Marble facade reflected the street lights. Thick white curtains in the windows. Cars rolled on by. A couple vans were parked along the curb. Gray, purple, gold. People passed through her. A guy with a bodybuilder's physique paced outside.

Across the street, bars were still open. Another meathead. He leaned against the wall, arms folded, facing the gallery.

Eve passed through the marble, entering a maze of paintings. Portraits and figures led into abstract art. Splotches and streaks of color.

Some with no particular form, others had the suggestion of order. Black lines, yellow streaks, red-and-blue dots—she and Charlotte were kids, bouncing on the couch cushions and singing until Charlotte slipped off. Eve had dashed forward to catch her. Their mother had rushed in, scolding Eve for allowing her younger sister to play so recklessly.

Another painting. Orbs of greens and blues layered on top of each other, denser and denser—her and Gideon cuddled in bed. The sun had warmed the window of a rented cabin in Lake Tahoe, the squeaky whistling pops of a Steller's jay outside.

Purple on turquoise, swaths of gold—she'd sat alone at picnic table eating lunch in an empty park, a cold breeze had swept over her. Last Christmas Day.

Faint movement on her wrist brought her back to the present. The arm cuff's settings had shifted.

In the corner of her eye, a dark figure. A tall, athletic man stalked through the aisle.

Eve passed through him, into the back.

Professional offices. Two men stood guard. The narrow corridor led to the rear exit. Another stood at a closed door. She passed through him into the fluorescent light of the office.

The banker, as big as the bodybuilder outside, sat at a laptop. Duffel bags of cash rested alongside the desk. No bodyguard for him.

Hadn't Armando said the banker was skinny?

Orange, scarlet, brown. Eve stepped forward, hitting a razor-thin trip wire. Two heavy cables snapped around her. She gasped. Yellow, white, and fuchsia. Her arms were pinned to her sides, her legs bound together. Her balance gave out. Gravity took over. She hit the floor.

Stupid, careless idiot!

"We got it!" The bodybuilder sprang from his chair, pulling his gun. "We got it!"

He kept the barrel trained on her as she writhed.

If she made herself intangible, the cables would be caught in the field, same with the floor.

The stampede of men neared the door.

Blue, yellow, silver. She reduced a few inches, the cable lengths outside the field breaking. Green, purple, blue. She enlarged. The cables fell away.

He fired two shots at her leg. The bullets glanced off, striking the wall.

Green, purple, blue. She got to her feet, rising higher. The bodybuilder backed away as the snares slid off her.

He'd call her an "it." But he should see. He should know.

Pink, white, orange. Visible.

His eyes widened. The men burst through the door, spellbound by the eight-foot figure. It wasn't just fear in their faces. It was awe. They had no clue what they were dealing with. And they responded the only way they knew how.

Bullets ricocheted off her. The slugs tore holes in the walls and ceiling.

The men retreated.

She backhanded the bodybuilder with her fist. The blow flung him into the desk. Earsplitting clatter and a concentrated shower of lead forced her backward. The pellets scattered. Machine gun fire. She stumbled into the wall, dropping onto her knees.

They paused to reload.

Her ears still rang.

"Holy shit!"

"What is that thing!?"

Violet, blue, scarlet. Eve vanished and jumped to her feet. Gray, purple, gold. She ran through the wall, back into the gallery. She caught her breath and listened.

Car doors. Voices. More men outside.

"It went through the wall!"

Eve peered out the windows. More vans had pulled up. Men in tactical gear leaped out of them. The private security force encircled the building.

A trio scanned the windows.

"Right there." One of them pointed. "See that?"

Eve checked herself. Lead soot stained her torso. They could see her. And she was surrounded. Orange, scarlet, brown.

But how did they–

The florist. Lionel had realized Armando was still alive. That she was getting information from him. She knew right where to go. And eventually, she'd come here. This was Lionel's play. Hit her from every angle. If the cops didn't get her, he would. He knew about her front, and he had to maintain his. So he needed it to look like she was robbing a legitimate business.

The private security outside. He wasn't just drawing her out, he wanted to expose her.

You got yourself caught! Everyone will see you're a thief!

"Oh, shit, shit!"

McCrae won't trust you now! No one will!

Tears leaked from her eyes.

Everyone's going to know what you did...

No energy source. No saving the planet. No fragments. No fame. No secrets of the universe.

You ruin everything.

Why did it always have to be this way?

Because you're defective.

Why couldn't she have anything good? Why did it always have to fall apart?

You're fucking worthless.

The hum buzzed. Crimson, black, magenta.

Levitate out of here. Run and hide. That's all you're good at, anyway. Run and hide before they take every—

"No." She pointed the arm cuff at the window. "They're going to hide from me."

Yellow, green, pink. White-hot energy sent shards of glass and men flying.

Innocent bystanders ran from the explosion, taking cover inside the bars across the street.

Eve strode out of the smokey haze. A squad assailed her with more machine-gun fire and high-powered assault rifles. She blasted the ground at their feet. Hunks of molten asphalt erupted and seared through their gear. They screamed and fell back.

A Badlander ran up behind her and bashed a sledgehammer into her backside. She flopped forward, landing on her hands and knees.

Green, purple, blue. Eve enlarged to twelve feet and kicked her heel into his head. Blue, yellow, silver. She reduced to seven feet and charged, punching another man in the face. Right hook to the next. Left jab.

The growling hum filled her ears. Crimson, black, magenta. She couldn't hear the bullets bouncing off her as she beat back dozens of them. Pink, emerald, violet.

The men struggled to retaliate. Nothing slowed her. Nothing hurt her.

Yellow, green, pink. She blasted the asphalt at random, and they scattered.

"Cowards!" One man stood his ground and reloaded.

Eve backhanded him in the chest. He choked, collapsing to his knees, and crawled away.

A van tore down the street on a suicide mission. The growl of its engine was no match for the one inside her. Nothing was going to stop her. Not ever again.

Gray, purple, gold. A black aura radiated around her. The van sped through her. The black waves rippled through the vehicle. The driver slammed on the brakes. Yellow-and-red lights flickered on the dashboard.

The brakes failed. The van careened, and the driver leaped out before it crashed into the gallery doors.

Embers fluttered around her. Smoke wafted past.

Eve surveyed the block as the men fled. Bet Lionel hadn't expected that.

Across the street. The dark blue sedan. Was he working with them? Had he tipped them off?

Orange, scarlet, brown. She marched toward the car.

The dour man was busy on his phone.

Crimson, black, magenta. Her fist smashed through the driver's side window. Pink, emerald, violet. He fumbled for the phone. She snatched his collar, pulling him up. Crimson, magenta, indigo, viridian, maroon. The black aura emanated from her fingers. His screams gurgled and screeched as the black waves warped his face, head, and throat.

Horrified, Eve let go, yanking her hand away. The waves and hum halted.

The dour man sat motionless—his head elongated and twisted, one eye bulging, the other popped from the socket, blood streaming from his orifices.

She backed away, glancing over her shoulder at the destruction, unsure where the waves had come from or what they meant.

Bystanders poked heads out from their hiding spots, probing the smoke for answers. Sirens echoed.

Violet, blue, scarlet. She sprinted off, already out of breath.

* * *

Eve raced into her bedroom. She enlarged the suit, inspecting it for damage and checking the connections. No wear aside from lead stains. She slipped it back on. What was that ripple? A drawback to layering fields? Or too rapid a succession, jumbling distorted realities? Or were the fields pulling reality apart?

She switched through settings, faster and faster, but couldn't reproduce the effect.

What was different?

The feeling. Before the waves, it had been...rage. Then pleasure.

When her fist had shattered the window and she'd grabbed him—crimson, magenta, indigo, viridian, maroon. She closed her eyes, switching settings, retracing the sequence.

Her eyes opened. Her left hand radiated black waves. She held the aura away from her body. The waves bent the air around them, drifting off and dissipating. She raised her arm to examine the phenomenon. Squinting, she caught her reflection in the closet mirror through the waves.

Her reflection through the aura didn't have an arm cuff.

And the suit was different. Jet black, running from her neck to her fingertips. The face was hers but not her—and as surprised to be seeing herself through the aura. No EEG net in her hair either. Eve turned her head. Her right hand ventured in search of a sensor. With the brush of her finger into her hair, the waves and the strange reflection vanished.

She flipped through settings again, trying to summon the aura, but couldn't reproduce it. Her frustration mounted. Burnt orange, then laurel green. Guilty visions of her fists cracking into men's skulls. Their screams. How thrilled she'd been to feel the bullets ricocheting off her like crumpled pellets. Smashing glass. Rippling black ether. The dour man's head twisting.

Eve paced, sucking in deep chunks of air, fingers pressed into her temples. "Think, think, think."

The hum. She'd first heard it the night she'd laid eyes on the fragment. It had been getting louder. Maybe, with Shadi's prototype, she had a direct link to it?

"No, that's crazy." She stared at her reflection, hands on her hips. "And everything else that's happened is totally plausible?"

Her eyes darted about as she reviewed the improbable events. She settled on the corkscrew she'd found at Kira's. Why hadn't she seen such a peculiar object earlier? Had she been in a hurry, or had it appeared because she'd needed it? Had she pulled it from another dimension? Or created it out of thin air?

"So, what? It's because...of what I think and feel?"

Her thoughts. Her feelings. The ultimate distortion of reality.

Her reflection stared back, mouth agape.

"No." She shook her head. "No, no, that—that can't be right." She pulled the zipper down. "I've got to get this thing off."

26

(yellow, royal blue)

Velez's cellphone rang at 4:30 a.m. It was Captain Harrell, an all-hands call. A robbery at an art gallery had led to a shoot-out and escalated. He said it looked liked a war zone. The building had structural damage and they feared the facade would come down.

She slipped on a pair of jeans and a top she didn't mind getting dirty before grabbing her leather jacket. She followed detours until she reached a block strung with yellow tape. Officers on the perimeter were setting up barricades. The haze had the sooty stink of gunfire. Craters blistered the asphalt leading up to the charred rupture.

Firefighters and paramedics in hazard suits searched the alien terrain, their every step with the crunch and roll of broken glass and bullet casings.

Velez spotted Russo talking with Porter.

"The hell happened?"

Russo turned, eyes a mix of confusion and awe. His lips parted. "Ally, you're not going to believe this."

Porter leaned in. "Badlanders got into a shoot-out with some woman. Said she was like seven feet tall."

"Burglamazon," Velez said in a vindicated hush.

"That ain't it."

"They said bullets bounced right off her," said Porter. "And she had this laser gun or something."

Her brow wrinkled. "A what?"

"Yeah." Porter shrugged. "I don't know."

"Nobody saw her face?"

"She was wearing a helmet. Footage on Tell-A-Photo's hard to make out. Found one that was pretty good."

Porter hit Play on his phone. A jumble of noise, gunfire, and explosions, the street already in shambles. Thick plumes of dust and smoke filled the frame. Flashes of white light erupted and red-orange cinders sprayed.

Men ran out of the murkiness, hobbled, desperate to escape. The injured fell to the ground, only to have fleeing men rush back to drag them away from the spreading cloud. A billow drifted off and revealed a towering dark figure in the haze.

She lifted her arm. Another blast. Heavy smoke consumed her.

More men rushed out. The clip ended.

"Holy shit." Velez turned to Russo with the same mix of confusion and awe.

"Yeah." He nodded.

"It's got to be her."

"Why? Because she's tall?"

"She took out all those cameras—"

"Not with that shit," said Russo. "We still got nothing linking whoever that was to Milner or any way to ID her."

"Yeah." Porter tilted his head. "I don't think they're looking for hunches."

* * *

Across the street, an intense man in a trench coat stepped away from Captain Harrell to take a call.

"This is McAndrews."

"This is Special Agent Kelly Callahan—"

"Callahan." He smirked. "Thought you were investigating a haunted house this morning?"

"It's an abandoned theme park—look, I think we may share the same suspect."

His eyebrows rose. "What makes you say that?"

"Protocol prevents me from—"

"This is a national-security situation," said McAndrews. "You have evidence linking someone, I want to hear it."

"Well—nothing concrete yet. But we're working on it."

"Uh-huh." He sighed. "Well, I appreciate your desire to—"

"I know that tone. Don't patronize me. I can't disclose anything, but at least eight people are missing. And we're finding more every day, along with cars and buildings and—"

"I see," he muttered.

"This is big," said Callahan. "And if you want access to my case file, you have to go to the top—Garza."

"All right, I will, uh...pose the question." He hung up, shaking his head.

* * *

Eve arrived at No Nukes in a daze. She didn't know what else to do but keep up appearances. Her night had been sleepless, ruminating over the events. Larry's words passed through her. Barb had gone into labor. Smile and nod.

She sat at Barb's desk, head balanced on her fingers and stared at the monitor.

Quinn rapped her knuckles on door jamb and darted in.

"Have you seen this shit?" Quinn stuck out her phone, playing an eyewitness clip of Eve's confrontation.

"No?" Eve lifted her head. "What?"

"They're calling it domestic terror."

She swallowed. "They are?"

"Yeah. They don't know who it is or what they want." Quinn lowered her phone.

"Yeah, that—that's crazy." She couldn't make eye contact, wringing her hands below the desk.

"Everything all right?"

She sat up straighter. "I'm—little freaked out with Barb gone. Thought I had more time to figure things out. And—maybe I'm not supposed to do this."

Quinn smiled. "You can handle this."

Eve cleared her throat. "Yeah, but maybe I'm not the best person... in the world? I have a tendency to screw things up."

"Think you're putting a lot of unnecessary pressure on yourself."

"Well, I mean, was it a mistake to give Lorenzo your demo?" Eve tossed her hands in the air. "I don't know. I thought I was doing something good, but what if I'm a jinx who destroys shit?"

"No—oh my god, no." Quinn sat on the edge of the desk.

"Is that my problem? Like, no matter what I do? I mean, for a while it felt like I knew what I was doing—I thought I knew what I wanted."

Quinn's face locked in concerned confusion.

Eve collected herself and placed her hands on the desktop. "Maybe I should go back to Sacramento."

"You're not going back to Sac-Town."

"Please don't call it that." Eve shook her head. "And that's the thing

—I just up and left. Who does that? Not a stable, successful adult. And I don't want to screw up your life by doing something I think is good but —"

"You've made my life incredibly better. I go to the gym now."

Her lip curled, puzzled. "I didn't tell you to go to the gym."

"It's because I'm not hungover anymore—most of the time."

"Oh. Well, that is good."

"Yeah," her friend said. "You're not a bad person. You do good things."

"Yeah, but what if—"

"No. No."

"But—"

"Shh." Quinn waved a finger to silence her. "You are not cursed. Thanks to your awesomeness, I have enough songs for my first solo album and a meeting with one of the most influential producers in the country. Barb can have her baby without worrying about this place. All great things made possible by you."

Eve mustered a small smile, unwilling to argue.

"So, no more of this"—Quinn fluttered a dismissive hand—"*leaving town* shit, okay?"

Laurel green. Eve fought back guilt as her smile widened. She nodded.

"Good, because I might've lost an earring at your place."

"I'll take a look."

* * *

Eighteen hours of bed rest was all Eugene needed. He walked into the kitchen, waving to Janelle.

"Morning." He smiled.

She hurried out.

That wasn't like her.

He dropped a couple frozen organic Belgian pastry waffles into the toaster. The faint whir of power tools from the garage. The kitchen door peeked open. Darien took a half step in but pulled back as Eugene turned his head.

"Hey," said Eugene.

The kitchen door swung. Darien never entered.

They were avoiding him. He'd said something awful. Despite wracking his brain, the memories had only gotten fuzzier.

Buzzes and whirs and hammering continued as he ate. They were up to something. Shadi had been pulling baseboards. She'd said it was remodeling, but that couldn't be it, could it?

Troy walked in, sweaty from a run, and headed straight to the cupboard.

"Hey."

"How're you feeling?" Troy asked.

"Great. Just a little hungover yesterday, that's all."

"Got to know your limits." Troy poured a glass of water from the fridge's dispenser.

"Yeah," said Eugene. "Was—was I talking to myself, or anything?"

"Uh, who told you that?"

"Zach. What was I saying?"

"Mostly gibberish." Troy shrugged. "You were drunk."

"Yeah, but—did I say something to piss everybody off?"

Troy guzzled some water. He wiped his mouth on his wrist. "No, but maybe they're still pissed about the shed? I mean, you took her side."

"But you told me the same thing. She's not a killer, right?"

"Well, yeah, but—"

"And I told everybody she's going to let us go."

"Maybe they don't believe it."

"Why would I lie?"

"Not you lying, her."

"She's not—"

"You trust her way too much."

"You guys don't know her like I do—"

"Look, having it come from you, she can turn around and be like, 'I didn't say that.' Or like, 'No, I said if this and this happened.' Or she can change her mind however she wants."

"But—"

"You're going to say she wouldn't do that. Yeah."

Troy walked out.

Eugene washed his plate and silverware. Was she using him? Had the VR set been a bribe? No—it was a token of appreciation. They'd toiled together over long nights, brainstorming solutions. And as mad as she'd been, her fist had pounded the opposite corner of the desk.

They thought he'd taken her side? What had he said?

Eugene tried the door to the garage. Locked. He knocked.

The noises stopped.

"Hey, what's up?" Kevin shouted from behind the door.

"Just curious what you're working on," said Eugene.

"Renovations, wiring," he answered. "It's not safe in here. Hard-hat zone, you know?"

"Oh. Okay."

Eugene wandered off.

He rolled open the sliding glass door and stepped outside. The lamp overhead warmed his skin. Was he being played? Or was everyone else dumping their frustrations onto him? He passed the water tower. The grass thinned, leading to a rugged stretch of dirt. His fingers ran across the plexiglass as he traced the perimeter of the box. He found a stray piece of the drone Shadi had built. He reached for the broken length of plastic.

A shoe print.

And another. Dozens of them. All focused around the same portion of the wall. He scanned the ground and jumped back, startled by a snake. But it couldn't be.

A brown extension cord. He picked it up. Someone had tried tying a lasso. He squinted, gazing up at the water tower and the lid overhead. Shadi had asked about the height of the walls when she'd first arrived. Now she and Kevin were building something in the garage.

He concentrated on the previous night, from the beginning.

Shadi never drank, but everyone else had. Or had they? Had they been trying to get him drunk?

Troy had taken beers from Cassidy and handed him one. They'd been playing games, and then everyone had gone somewhere. The kitchen, maybe? Had they been listening to him? He'd told someone something.

He tossed the extension cord onto the ground. The game controller. Troy had taken it from his hand. He and Zach had been asking Cassidy something. They'd been talking about him. They'd been talking about what he'd been saying, but he couldn't remember his own words.

He'd told Selene none of them were trustworthy enough to set free. If he'd mentioned that, the others would be furious. They'd redouble their efforts to escape or contact the authorities. They'd jeopardize everything he and Selene had built.

He had to warn her.

* * *

After a long morning of crowd control, Velez dropped into her desk chair in the afternoon. Russo couldn't sit, pacing around the bullpen.

"Hey, Paulie." She clicked on the facial recognition database. "Let me get your opinion."

The images from her last search popped up. He lumbered over, massaging his lower back.

He strained to lean forward. "We handed that case off."

"But you see what I'm saying? It's weird, right?"

"Might be a glitch." He shrugged. "What's the connection?"

"I don't know. Just a feeling."

"Then you've got to check it out." He smirked. "Me? My feeling is, I got to see the chiropractor."

She shook her head. "Told you not to move those barricades."

"We were there to help—I was helping," he said with a pained smile. "You find something, call me."

He shuffled out of the bullpen.

Velez studied the pictures. Kincaid was too short—and missing. If there was a glitch, it was her. Velez closed Eve's result. She stared at the grainy still frame of Burglamazon. Russo was right—they had no link between her and the art gallery. Captain Harrell expected them to work a case, not guess at it. And she was still four solves behind Tony Lam.

She'd blown off Guzman and with him, her shot at an assist from the Bureau. Now all their resources would be concentrated on the art gallery attack. They'd probably commandeer most of Counterterrorism. Which would give her more time. If she could prove Burglamazon's connection, she'd get credit for the solve. Big solves. Multiple solves.

Velez studied the pictures. If Diane Cernik was a fake identity, she would've needed a portfolio of falsified documents and someone to hack into various sites to plant them. Impractical, but not impossible. The redhead on the street bore the closest resemblance in both height and appearance. Her friend's back was turned in the picture, but she was holding a to-go bag from the Delirium Café at the Morpheus Theatre.

Maybe the staff could identify her. Velez shot out of her chair.

Twenty minutes later, she stepped across the thick red carpet of the historic Morpheus Theatre's lobby to a young man in a purple vest with too much gel in his hair. She held up her badge, startling the usher.

"Excuse me, were you working here last Thursday?"

"No, but Dana might've been." He looked over Velez's shoulder to a young woman sweeping the floor. "Hey, Dana—were you on last Thursday?"

Her ponytail swung and flopped against her back as she turned. "Yeah."

Velez pulled out her phone, striding toward her. "You remember seeing this woman?"

She held up the redhead's photo.

"Yeah."

"Were they here for a show?"

"No, just lunch. But they did sign the guestbook." She tilted the broom handle toward the ornate wooden podium on the opposite side of the hall. A huge leather guestbook rested with a black feather quill pen.

Velez flipped pages to the date in question, skimming the names. Some were intentionally offensive, others scribbled in illegible handwriting. She lifted her phone, taking shots of each page.

Back at the station, she uploaded the guestbook pictures into the forensic handwriting analysis software. She dropped in a document with Diane Cernik's signature. At worst, it would eliminate her as a possible suspect. The optical character recognition plucked out several matches. The *i*, *k*, and *ane* of Diane's full name along with a signature from the guestbook.

Kira Sloane.

Another identity?

Intrigued, Velez returned to the database and searched for the name. She scrolled through the entries, cross-referencing address information with driver's licenses. None of them looked like the woman in the photo. None of their signatures matched.

"Velez," said Captain Harrell. "Got a robbery on Pico."

"I'm on it."

She closed the program and locked her computer, pondering Diane Cernik and her possible alter ego.

* * *

Simon had moved his research to the study upstairs. Though his earlier gamble had been destructive, it'd paid off. He'd determined the shard was the same material and established plausible deniability. After all, if he'd already known it was the same, why would he risk firing electrons at it?

"The object produced a sound, like hum or a buzz. Since they didn't hear it until they reached the object, I suspect the material reacted to the noise in the tunnel."

He opened a polished wood box and took out a tuning fork. Simon started with a middle frequency. He worked his way up and down, using different methods to strike the forks and bringing the tines near the fragment.

But the shard didn't respond. Even at 512 hertz. So he struck two at a time. He started at the lowest frequencies and drew them closer. He altered the pairings, high and low frequencies together. He placed the shard in a granite box and ran through the whole experiment again. No response.

"Well, that doesn't make any sense." The tuning fork clanked onto the desk. "Jareima. Continuing dictation. New paragraph."

"Ready."

He smiled. "The reaction in the lab was more intense than I anticipated, considering its size."

Simon paced, his smile intensifying. "However, it doesn't respond to sound waves. Which doesn't make any sense because, clearly, it's the same material. So, why doesn't it respond?"

He focused on the little chunk of black crystal, his fingers intertwined. "Why?"

He neared the desk.

"You have visitors, my lord." The flat-screen monitor on the wall turned on, displaying the feed from the front door's surveillance camera. A van and a truck pulled up.

Simon spun around. "Ah, yes."

He checked his watch—10:14 a.m. "They're late."

Simon greeted the workmen and led them to the basement. It had been cleared of debris two days ago but not yet rebuilt.

The head contractor's belly hung over his belt, and it jiggled with the slightest movement. He surveyed the space and pulled off his baseball cap, running a hand over a fuzzy patch of hair.

"So after we drop the steel, it'll take about two weeks for the concrete to cure."

Simon grinned. "Really doesn't fit my time table."

The contractor smirked. "Well, we can't make it dry any faster. It is what it is."

The workmen snickered.

They thought they knew better. But they just weren't properly motivated.

"Allow me to propose an alternative solution, gentlemen." Simon waved his fingers and headed up the basement stairs.

The workmen followed. Simon led them outside to a prefabricated shed. He unveiled a smaller, robotic version of a Pierce Technologies-brand laser cannon. He picked up the control unit, activating the machine. It rolled forward on six chunky wheels.

"Thought you wanted us to—"

"In good time." Simon grabbed a pair of dark goggles. "Come."

He guided them and the robot through the trees to an enormous stone jutting from the earth. He punched commands into the unit. The machine's arm came to life. The laser head spun.

"Isn't this protected land?" asked one of the workmen.

"Might be—I don't know." Simon pulled the goggles over his eyes.

The men shielded their faces. A brilliant beam shot into the stone, eight feet up.

It carved an long incision across with a fearsome hiss. Then it shifted at a right angle and sliced downward. The mechanical arm swung over and around. The beam returned to its first cut and sizzled down. Another mechanical arm—smaller and thinner—reached out and pried into the rock.

The clean-cut slab fell forward, shaking the ground.

"Well?" Simon lifted the goggles. "It's not going to walk into my basement on its own."

"Thing's got to weigh a ton," said the head contractor.

Simon smiled. "Well, this is your job, and I already did half the work."

"You don't got a robot for that?" asked one of the men.

"Not one that goes down stairs."

The workmen glanced at each other in disbelief.

"Tell you what," said Simon. "I'll start at a hundred thousand dollars. Each."

Another gamble, considering his dwindling cash reserves. But time was on his side.

"For every hour it takes for you to move these and secure them into place, I subtract ten grand. You could all feasibly walk away with fifty thousand apiece. Up to you."

Simon pulled the goggles over his eyes, then punched commands into the unit.

* * *

Eve closed the door and immersed herself in work. While the numbers and colors were comforting, the patterns suffocated inside grids and bureaucratic forms. Like the purchase orders. Routine was safe yet confining. She'd longed for the endless possibilities of a probabilistic quantum universe. But now she had more uncertainty than she could handle.

She minimized the spreadsheet and turned away. The colors dissolved, leaving her with the inescapable sense her very nature was wrong. For reasons she couldn't place, her mother haunted her. Then the Other Eve's reflection, the details she'd been avoiding. No sensors. No arm cuff. Different suit.

Was it the future?

Or one possible outcome?

Had she perfected the technology?

Whatever it was, it hinted the fragment might interact with spacetime.

She turned back to the monitor. A browser window with news headlines running by default had been hidden behind the spreadsheets. Anti-nuke protests in India and Pakistan. She clicked the story, and a video auto-played.

A woman with a British accent reported: "Organized entirely online and between groups in both countries, protests have jammed the streets in recent days. Leading to crackdowns in Pakistan—"

Protesters ran from members of the Pakistani military.

"And India."

Indian soldiers pushed against dense crowds.

"Though separated by hundreds of miles, demonstrators are united."

A man drenched in sweat spoke to the camera. "We don't want war, India doesn't want war. It is what the people in power use to threaten them, to threaten us. But who suffers if there is nuclear war? Not people in power. People here would suffer, and people in the streets of India."

A woman in a lavender-and-white sari spoke next, her words translated by an interpreter. "This isn't simply about power in terms of politics or military might or energy. This is about the power that drives humanity and how we choose to live in the world."

Eve paused the video. Those were her words.

They believed in her cause. Enough to turn against their own leaders. Enough to risk their lives. Indigo, scarlet, black.

She couldn't stop now, not when she was so close. Not when she could do so much good. Maybe there was still a way to have everything she wanted.

She shut down the computer and gathered up her shoulder bag. She told Larry she wasn't feeling well.

"Oh, don't tell me you're pregnant, too," he said. "*Kidding*. Kidding—please don't sue me. I hope you feel better."

Eve glided through the cubicles, giving Quinn a wave. "I'll see if I can find your earring."

Quinn chased her down. "Hey—does this mean you're not coming to my show later?"

She couldn't get the Bad Friend Award twice. Eve nodded, keeping her voice down. "I'll be there."

* * *

The afternoon was an onslaught of calls, more than Quinn had ever remembered. She pulled off the headset, her ear sore and tailbone stiff. She clocked out after five and walked into the parking lot. A man in a navy suit and tie was trying to get a signal on his phone.

He was young, kind of cute, but ridiculous as he held the phone overhead and swung his whole body all around, focused on the screen. He stopped, his head snapped in her direction.

"Excuse me, sorry to bother you." He hurried over. "My GPS isn't working. Do you know where Three-Forty-Two West Oak is?"

"Oh, yeah, it's this block on the left." She pointed. "You actually have to go downstairs to see it."

"Thanks." He smiled. "Appreciate it."

"Sure." She nodded, turning to walk away.

"Oh, and, uh, if you don't mind me asking—"

Flarg. Quinn's eyes slid up and back. Here it comes. The inevitable pickup line. She turned around—and got an FBI badge in her face.

"What can you tell me about Kira Sloane?"

Air emptied from Quinn's lungs. What had Kira done? Had she robbed a bank?

Agent Dempsey closed up his badge. "You are Quinn Maxfield, right? And you know Diego Santana?"

Oh, yeah. That.

"All right." She help up a finger. "I don't know what he told you, but —"

"Not much. He didn't have a great recollection. Details came over time. Like the new client he met with."

She struggled for an answer.

"Eventually, he remembered enough for a sketch artist to draw another woman. Which, after we searched your name, found her pictures posted in your social media. But it looks like you took them down a couple days ago."

She didn't want to incriminate Kira, but she also didn't want to lie to the FBI.

"All right, I—"

"Let's sit down and talk, okay?"

Was he serious? Her brow collapsed forward, and she gave him a side-eye. "You're not going to arrest me?"

"I need to know about Kira."

Three-Forty-Two West Oak was an old-fashioned cocktail bar with the decor of a speakeasy, wood-paneling with stained glass and vintage lamps. Quinn clutched a Long Island iced tea. She sat across from Agent Dempsey in a back booth out of earshot of the happy hour crowd.

"You know where she lives?" he asked. "Where she works?"

"It's never come up." Quinn shrugged.

"You know lying to a federal agent is a felony, right?"

"And how do I know you're really with the FBI?" After a few sips of her drink, and a moment to think, she'd gotten the impression he was hiding something.

"Aside from my badge and all the information I just gave you? You can go into any local office—there's, like, seven of them—and they'll verify that I am in fact an FBI agent."

"I can just walk into an FBI office?" she challenged.

"As long as you're not waving a gun with a bomb strapped to your chest? Yeah. You should be fine. Want to change your answer?"

"I don't understand. Why not talk to her yourself?"

"It's complicated. For reasons I'm not permitted to speak on." He leaned forward. "But if she's the person we think she is, she came into contact with something dangerous, panicked, and ran. We're afraid if we get too close, she—she'll disappear again. And we need to find out what she knows so we can get a handle on the dangerous thing."

Quinn resisted his words. He was leaving out details. But maybe he had to?

Not Kira. Without her, Quinn would revert to awkward conversations with her roommates and superficial friendships. People who loved to listen to vinyl and criticize the music of others, but whose own songwriting amounted to jam sessions in someone's backyard on the weekends.

"This—it's got to be a mistake. It's not her."

"Well, let's see. Where's she from?"

"Sacramento."

"She have any siblings?"

"A sister."

"What's her name?"

"Uh…" Quinn searched the air. Had Kira mentioned her sister's name?

Agent Dempsey's expression didn't change.

"Well, I don't know." Her frustration rose. "They haven't spoken in a long time."

"Brothers?"

"No."

"What about a dead boyfriend?"

Quinn's heart dropped. "She mentioned that, but she didn't want to talk about it."

He nodded. "All right. She say or do anything unusual?"

"All the time. She's funny." She shrugged. "Is that unusual?"

"No. Why isn't she on social media?"

"Sounded like she got trolled pretty bad."

Agent Dempsey leaned back. A pensive sigh shot from his nose.

Quinn sucked down a third of her Long Island iced tea. She ran through everything she thought she knew, doubting it. Then she shook her head. "I—I don't know."

Dempsey sat forward. "All right, look, I want you to get the dead boyfriend story."

"And what if she lies to me?"

"I don't think she will. And if it turns out she's in trouble for other reasons—like maybe her boyfriend's alive and a douche bag—you let me know, and I'll hook her up with the resources she needs."

Quinn tilted away from her glass, touched by the gesture. She felt like he meant it. "You promise?"

"Yeah. Our investigation has a different focus. I'm not here to arrest everybody along the way."

The agent reached into his jacket and pulled out a burner phone. "Don't mention me, don't mention any of this. As far as we know, I'm wrong."

He slid the phone across the table. "This has my number and the field office's already in it. Get her to tell the story. Then when you're alone, you call me. Tell me what it is. That's it."

Quinn stared at the burner. A chance to rescue Kira. Or lose her forever and be condemned to the hollow companionship of vapid assholes until another rare soul crossed into her life.

She dragged the phone close.

27

(yellow, gold)

Motivated by an unexpected payday, the workmen employed every tool at their disposal. They devised rigs using winches, pulleys, straps, and tracks. They modified several steel dollies, and using one of their trucks, hauled the slabs to Simon's door step. One at a time, they slid the stone panels onto a dolly, rolling them into the foyer and down steel tracks over the stair into the basement.

Five men at a time guided the monstrous slabs, sliding them into heavy-duty steel brackets mounted into the floor. Once secured in place, the men sealed them together with concrete. They mounted a steel door onto the new chamber. Simon cut a square hole in the upper portion of one slab, and they used an industrial adhesive to secure a thick portion of impact glass.

The last ninety minutes, the workmen rehung the basement door and dismantled their rigs. Simon didn't count that as project time. Exhausted, they found little relief in the forty thousand dollars cash he handed them.

"Should be more," the head contractor grumbled.

"Let that be a lesson to you." Simon smiled. "You wasted time complaining."

The workmen drove off as the sky dimmed.

He delved into rewiring the basement's electrical systems. It was so routine that time passed without recognition. But as he configured the wireless, the process took on new meaning.

Signal bars lit up.

“A beacon.”

Radio waves, and energy, could be transmitted using wireless technology.

“Jareima?”

“Yes, my lord.”

“Open the log for dictation.”

“Ready.”

“What if it isn’t behaving like a mineral but a machine?” He smirked. “An incredibly complex machine, greater than the sum of its parts. On its own, it’s a component. I wonder if it would behave differently if it were connected to another piece...”

He turned to his rebuilt lab. The mortar wasn’t dry yet. That would take another forty-eight hours. Still wouldn’t be safe until it cured. But this new hypothesis demanded examination.

“Jareima, end dictation.”

He tore open a utility closet, and sifted through the shelves. With the parts on hand, he assembled a resonant transformer circuit—a Tesla coil. The design was rather open. The primary was an oscillator. And the secondary, included the fragment.

Simon positioned the coil on the counter inside the chamber and wired it to the external mainframe. He shut the door behind him, locking the hefty latch. At the mainframe, Simon flipped a switch. Lightning crackled from the ring atop the coil into the shard. It produced a bassy hum.

“That’s it!” He swung around, ready to fly out of his skin. “That’s it! That’s the sound! Jareima! Are you recording this!?”

“You did not request that I—”

“Shut up and record it! Record! Record!”

He stared at the electrical discharge with a toothy grin. “What is it? What does it mean?”

He switched off the coil. The hum stopped.

“Jareima, open the log.”

“Ready.”

“I’ve succeeded in recreating the same sound from the undisclosed project. The material doesn’t appear to react negatively. So far. I wonder if energy can be used more safely in this state. Of course, I should probably wait for the concrete to dry.” He shrugged. “It will, however, afford me the opportunity to design my next experiment.”

* * *

Later in the afternoon, Velez returned to the station to file her report. The eyewitnesses had been too flustered. She’d have to wait on a warrant for the camera footage. Fine by her. She was eager to puzzle over the mysterious redhead.

She revisited the profiles, sure she'd missed something. What was link between the redhead and Burglamazon? She rested her lips against knitted fingers, brows and forehead clenched. Their databases had limitations. Facial recognition was only as good as the information fed into it. She'd searched social media with no luck.

Her brow softened. She lifted her head.

If this was someone who'd never been arrested and they were using fake identification, they might not show up. Or maybe they were from another country.

Velez pulled out her phone and searched Kira Sloane's name. Results returned people-finder websites—some credible, some sketchy. She selected one which vacuumed up data from the internet without verification. Most of their results matched the law enforcement databases. Except one. A Kira Sloane between the ages of thirty-five and forty in a neighborhood outside downtown.

With a swipe and payment details, she purchased the identity report.

* * *

Eve tended to her projects. She assembled the energy-capture rig. After testing the wiring, she secured the power source within the nest of photovoltaic cells inside. Current flowed. She rehearsed her presentation, tweaking the bots between breaks, and followed the steady flow of reports of protests around the world.

Then there were the housemates. She couldn't face them, their judgmental little eyes.

They hate you. They're going to tell everyone about you...

Eugene would defend her. But even if the power source was a success, all her contingencies, the hush money—did it seem too guilty?

She needed more leverage. More proof she was good. A Russian spy would clench it.

The dour man's twisted head flashed in her memory.

Time had gotten away from her.

She'd forgotten to stop off at Kira's to look for Quinn's earring. Not an easy thing to lie about if she'd been home all day.

At six, she left the penthouse as Kira and drove straight to the apartment, no longer worried about her Russian shadow.

Eve dug through couch cushions and spotted the little golden dangle with yellow crescent moons on the carpet. The long whine of car brakes outside unnerved her. She leaned over, careful as she peered out of the blinds.

She caught the toss of the driver's ombré hair. The lady detective from the warehouse fire. Velez. The pearl gray sedan accelerated, rounding the corner and out of sight.

Eve backed away from the window and shut off all the lights. Where was the other one? The older guy with salt-and-pepper hair?

Figures. So close.

Two nosy cops weren't going to stop a revolution. Crimson, magenta, indigo.

She hit the lights off, then unlocked the door and pulled it open a crack.

* * *

Velez parked in the side street between two apartment complexes. She climbed onto the roof of her car and scaled the wall of the alley. Old-school PI stuff Russo had taught her. Never let them see you coming. And if you ain't got grounds to be there, don't look like you were there. For that same reason, she didn't call him and left her phone in the glove box.

She hustled to Sloane's apartment.

Velez rapped a knuckle on the door. It budged. Unlocked. She slid her gun from the holster and kept it at the ready. With a gentle push, the door creaked inward.

"Hello?" She stepped inside, running her hand against the wall for a light switch.

With a flick of her knuckle, the room lit up.

"Hello? Anybody here?"

She pulled the door shut behind her. Velez ventured into the hall, to the darkened bedroom. A ball of tension tightened in her gut. She raised her gun.

"Are you all right?"

A cautious step into the bedroom. No light switch nearby. She moved toward the bathroom, spying a switch there.

"Just want to make sure you're okay..."

Light filled her eyes. An intense flash reflected off the bathroom mirror. The room spun as she turned around, losing her balance. She steadied on her feet but felt like she was falling. The spots in her eyes faded. A large figure moved closer, growing larger.

"What the—what the fuck!?" Velez tripped and toppled to the carpet.

She raised her gun, aiming higher and higher. A giant ankle boot landed in front of her.

"Oh my god!"

She scurried up, screaming. Enormous fingers gently closed around her. She tumbled into the giant's cupped hand. Gravity thrust around her as she was lifted.

She'd found Kira Sloane.

"Stop it. No one can hear you."

Velez gasped. "What—"

"Who else is here?"

"No one."

"Sure about that?"

"Nobody knows I'm here, I swear!"

"Where's your car?"

* * *

Eve unzipped the inner pocket in her purse and gently scooped out Velez. She tilted her onto the high table.

"What is this?" Velez's head swiveled. "Where are we?"

"What were you doing in my apartment?"

She gazed up. "I was running a background on Diane Cernik, and you—your picture came up."

She's lying.

"I'm not listed. How'd you find it?"

"Some crappy people-search site."

Dumbass! Should've purged all that sooner.

"So you just let yourself in?" Eve shrugged. " 'Cause you couldn't get a warrant?"

"They're going to come looking for me."

"Yeah, how? Your car's gone. And you said no one knew you were there."

She backed away. "You can't just make people disappear."

Eve squatted, balancing with her fingers on the table's edge.

Velez stood her ground.

Eve lifted her hands, indicating surrender, then placed them on her knees. "I'm not going to kill you."

Velez glared with a cagey scowl.

"I'm trying to do something important. To make the world better—"

"If it means lying and kidnapping people—"

"You don't understand. Things got...messy. But once I'm done, everything will be better. Okay?"

"Look, Kira...or Diane—"

"You know who I am. Which is why"—Eve's lips wavered—"I have to put you in a jar."

"What?"

"Normally, I am much more hospitable—"

"What if I have to pee?"

Eve cringed. "Well, there will be a Port-A-Potty in there—"

"You're going to leave me in a jar with a Port-A-Potty? No food or water?"

"Well, that's not really sanitary, so—"

"There's got to be some other way..."

Eve huffed. If an LAPD detective had resorted to snooping, it meant the case was hot, and possibly taken out of their hands.

"How much do they know?"

"Who?"

Eve shook her head with annoyed glance toward the ceiling. "The FBI."

"I don't know, I haven't talked to them."

She scowled, unconvinced.

"I haven't talked—"

"How much do they know?"

"I don't know." Velez shook her head. "But we handed the warehouse fire over to Counterterrorism and the feds put a task force on the gallery."

Threads spun in Eve's mind. They were closing in. They'd focus on motive. They'd want to interview Diane and Devereux, sort through the network of shell companies to determine illicit activity. Dumping large sums would be too suspicious. She needed to stall them.

But maybe she already had.

They'd shift all their resources to the art gallery attack. Of course, whoever was working the initial search for Talbot and the fragment at the FBI would suspect her. They just couldn't prove it. So she'd have to purge Diane's online information. Unless a couple Badlanders broke their code of silence and started blabbing about an invisible monster raiding their laundering operations. In which case, she had cover as a vigilante, not a terrorist. But based on her conversation with Armando, Lionel didn't tolerate snitches.

The key was still the power source. Once she had investors—legitimacy—she'd have her lead in to McCrae. She could offer the Defense Department a solution to the existential threat of global climate change. Not as Diane, but herself. Within reach of the Mobius.

Or maybe they'd offer her a job, like Frank Abagnale Jr. in *Catch Me If You Can*. An elusive con artist turned expert for the government.

Won't work. Nobody likes you. And Abaganle was slick. You've bungled your way through everything.

But she still had the suit. And with it, she was untouchable. Stick to the plan.

Velez stared up at her and waved. "Yo. Hello?"

Eve blinked. "On second thought, doesn't matter."

"What?" The detective leaned back. "What doesn't matter?"

"Nothing." She smiled, standing.

"No—what are you talking about?"

"As much as I don't want to do this"—Eve reached for her—"I'm already running late."

Velez whipped out her gun, firing shots.

"Ah!" She jerked her hand away from the tiny stings.

Her opposite palm bumped against Velez, her fingers folded over her. "Drop it."

The tiny weapon tapped against the tabletop. She turned around, carrying Velez into the guest room. Eve propped up the lid and lowered her to the front porch.

"The hell is this?"

"Your new home. Just for a while. Write a list of whatever you want, I'll pick it up in the morning."

Velez's brow scrunched as the lid closed.

* * *

Velez turned around as Eve walked out, skeptical of the shelter. A hefty man poked out the front door, then stepped onto the porch. More people peered out from inside as she neared.

"You all right?" he asked.

"Ask me again in an hour."

"I'm Kevin," he said. "This is Shadi—"

Velez recognized a face behind him. "Janelle Sinclair?" She rushed inside. "And Eugene Hughes. What about Milner? Is he alive?"

"Unfortunately," said Shadi.

"Shut up," said Zach. "Who're you?"

"Detective Allegra Velez. Don't worry—they're going to find us."

"Yeah," said Zach. "Because you did such a great job."

"Okay." Velez gave Shadi a nod. "I see what you mean."

"Whatever," he said. "Once again, you're all missing the point—she's adding more people, not letting us go."

"She said she'd let you go?" asked Velez.

Zach tossed a hand in another young man's direction. "According to Eugene."

"I'm sure there's a good explanation," said Eugene. "If I could talk to her—"

"Wait." Velez stepped toward him. "She tells you what's going on?"

"Well, not exactly," he answered. "I've been helping her. With some software stuff."

"Building a botnet," said Janelle. "To stop nuclear weapons."

Velez's brow crumpled. "The One Is Too Much campaign?"

Eugene shrugged. "Well, I don't know if we settled on a name—"

"People are protesting in the streets," she said. "Like, all over the world."

"Wow." He seemed jubilant. "Maybe that's what she's waiting for."

"Or," said Janelle, "so she can use Shadi's invention to shrink everybody."

Velez turned to Shadi. "What did you help her with?"

"A suit," she answered.

Velez's jaw hung with disgust. "You helped her build that?"

The young woman drew back. "I—I don't know what she's doing—"

"She tore up downtown," said Velez. "Looks like it was bombed."

"I didn't know," Shadi defended. "She stole my prototype, kidnapped me, and tricked me. She threatened to hurt my friends—I didn't know she was keeping people alive at the time."

"Well, whatever she's doing," Kevin grumbled, "it's working."

"Not for long," said Velez. "The FBI, the ATF—the whole city's looking for her."

Eugene folded his arms, focusing on the floor.

"So you know who she really is?" asked Janelle.

Velez nodded. "Eve Kincaid."

* * *

The name was a gut punch. A queasy lump collected in Eugene's throat. The pang in his stomach grew heavier, dulled by the fact she'd lied to him. But she'd had to. To protect herself, and them, from the forces preventing global denuclearization. His information would be vital. Proof of his undying loyalty. In exchange, she'd give him new accommodations, since he'd no longer be safe in the house. He had to get her attention.

He realized the conversation had stopped. All eyes were on him. "What?"

Zach smirked. "Something wrong?"

"No." Eugene shrugged. "I'm fine."

* * *

The bar was nestled between a warehouse and a motorcycle repair shop in a dodgy part of town. Eve walked in, surprised by the artsy interior, and headed over to Quinn as she set up.

"Told you I'd make it." Eve smiled. "And—"

She held out the earring.

"Oh, you're the best." Quinn plucked it from her hand. "And I really mean that."

"Yeah, I'm sorry about earlier. I was stressed out—"

"It's cool. Happens to everybody. And you can talk to me about whatever's bothering you—you know that, right? I'm here for you."

She smiled. "I know."

"Good."

"All right, so, what are you drinking?"

"Uh, you know." Quinn shrugged. "Think I'm just going to stick with beer. Something light."

"Okay."

Eve headed to the bar. She blew out a heavy sigh as she leaned against the counter.

The woman alongside her studied Quinn tuning her guitar. "She's your friend, no?"

The accent struck Eve like a slap. She turned to the tall, athletic woman with long dark hair and eyes like ice picks. Dressed in all black. Knee-high boots.

A slow smirk rose on her lips. "It would be shame if something happened to her."

"She doesn't have anything to do with this," Eve said in a hush.

"Then hand it over."

"I don't have it on me."

"Get it and bring it here. If not, I slit her throat and leave her in the aqueduct."

"I can't leave—she's about to go on."

The woman shrugged. "Then she dies. You have one hour."

Eve sighed and dug into her bag. "All right, look—you already know where I live. Take my keys. Go in through the parking garage. No one will stop you."

The woman glanced at the keys. "No."

"What? Why not?"

"It's clearly a trap. The material amplifies energy. You will not use it in front of all these people. Not after last night."

Eve's face tightened. "Maybe...we should discuss this outside."

"Oh?" The woman sized up Eve with a lazy roll of her head, then smirked. "You think so?"

"Yeah." Eve shrugged, nodding.

"You have forty minutes." The woman sipped her drink. "She will not return to the stage after her first break."

Crimson. Bitch wasn't taking the bait. She needed her alone, outside. Get her to chase her. Eve leaned in.

"I just want to see if you're as weak as the others." She cocked a challenging eyebrow.

The woman regarded her glass with more concern than she did Eve.

She was tougher than Armando.

Of course.

"I mean," said Eve, "unless, they sent you to negotiate...Oh my god—that's it, isn't it? You start with an over-the-top ultimatum, but eventually we get into our feelings, girl-talk, cry it out, right?"

The woman sucked her teeth. Fire lit in her eyes. "Show me which car is yours."

* * *

Quinn spied the tense conversation between Kira and the leggy woman at the bar. The two women stood. Though the other woman was taller, Kira seemed much more substantial.

The bartender set down drinks. Kira asked him to hold them and her purse. She and the woman disappeared into the darkened back hall. Was this what Agent Dempsey had meant? Had things caught up with her friend?

Should she follow them outside?

No. Kira wasn't—was she? Was she in trouble?

And if Quinn saw it firsthand, what kind of trouble would she be in?

* * *

The Russian operative and Eve stepped into the cramped parking lot. Their eyes locked on each other as the door croaked on its hinges, closing...

Shut.

Eve darted toward the alley but the operative dashed in front of her.

"No, no, no." The woman smiled, whipping a dagger from her hip.

The operative advanced, wielding the knife like a small sword.

Eve stumbled backward onto the hood of a car as the Russian sliced at her.

She launched both heels into the operative, forcing her backward. Eve pushed herself from the hood and swung a kick into her hand, sending the dagger flying. She swung a fist at the woman's head. The operative ducked and swept Eve's legs, felling her to the ground. Pain radiated through her lower back. She had to get the woman to chase her.

From the asphalt, Eve jammed her heel into the operative's

abdomen, and the woman staggered back from the blow.

Eve sprang from the ground and stuck a jab into the woman's face.

The woman swiped a right hook into Eve's head, then thrust a side kick into her torso.

She blocked, grabbing her foot.

The operative twisted on her heel, sending her free leg flying at Eve's jaw.

Eve caught the woman's ankle. Bracing it against her forearm, she swung the operative into the side of the nearest car with all her might. The operative dropped to the ground.

Eve bolted. She heard the dagger's blade scrape against the asphalt behind her. Then the clomp of boots. She raced into the alleys behind rows of automotive repair shops.

Backed up against a wall, she took the *modifikator* from its case. Eve held her breath, listening for footfalls. She pocketed the case and palmed the *modifikator*. Traffic on the main road broke the stillness. She tilted forward, checking to see if her path to the next alley was clear. She had to get the drop on her.

Eve turned her head—a blade hovered against her throat. White and yellow.

Great plan, dumb shit. Now you're dead.

"You will take me to it." The operative pulled out handcuffs. "Try anything, and I will cut you just deep enough for you to bleed out in thirty minutes. That is all time you have. Move."

Eve crept away from the wall, the *modifikator* concealed under her left arm. "Wait—do you still have my keys?"

The woman's brow wrinkled. The flash of light forced her eyes shut.

The operative swiped the blade. Eve hopped back. The woman's reach shortened.

Eve recognized her confusion and backed off, but not too much.

The operative turned to run.

Eve raced after her. She lunged, reaching out with a cupped hand, and cornered the shrinking woman against the wall. With her edge of her opposite hand, she coaxed the two-inch woman into her palm.

She stood. Crimson, magenta, indigo, viridian, maroon. Brighter.

Eve grinned at her tiny prize. "Worth it."

She stuck the operative into her jacket pocket and returned to the bar's parking lot. Eve checked her face in a truck's side-view mirror. No blood or bruising. Though flushed, she was otherwise unscathed. She brushed off grit from her clothes. Back inside, the bartender returned her shoulder bag and drinks from behind the counter.

Quinn hurried over as she reached into her purse. "Hey. What happened? With that lady?"

Eve zipped up the inner pocket in her bag, pretending not to remember right away. "Oh—she needed directions."

"Really? Seemed kind of intense."

"She had a heavy accent." Eve shrugged. "So it was hard to understand her."

"Oh."

"Yeah."

* * *

Quinn took her beer to the stage. Her friend looked flushed. Maybe she'd rushed back in so not to miss anything? She turned over Kira's answers. She was sure Kira and the woman had been having an argument.

The crowd welcomed Quinn with applause. Unlike the tavern, these folks were here for music. Their attention focused on her as bits of conversation floated between them. Wes and his friends showed up. Their rambunctious appreciation irritated the regulars.

Encouraged, Quinn launched into her own songs after a handful of covers. She kicked off her second set with distortion, swapping the acoustic for an electric, playing a familiar track from her demo before a seamless segue into what seemed like an impromptu instrumental. Her next song flowed from it, rehearsed but seamless.

The crowd ate it up.

Next, a frustrated cover of Billy Idol's "Dancing with Myself," swapping out "girls" for "guys" in the lyrics. Quinn pulled out her phone, using a beat from a sound library, and strummed along, creating a hypnotic lo-fi tune. From the last chord, she started into her own rendition of "Owner of a Lonely Heart" and into a surprising close with Throwing Muse's "Shimmer," which half the crowd must've thought was hers.

She hopped off the low platform, barraged by eager music lovers.

"How're you not in band?"

"Hey, do you know Jesse?"

"Do you need a drummer?"

"Dude—give me a call."

Overwhelmed, Quinn chatted, noncommittal, edging toward Kira. But Kira had her own problems. Wes had dedicated a mission to befriend her.

They ended up sharing a booth with Wes and the guys. His friend with a crooked nose didn't seem to understand that Wes was interested in Quinn and vied for her attention while their skinny buddy tried his luck with Kira.

Kira sat with her shoulder bag in her lap, arms folded over it. "You do realize I'm old enough to be your mom, right?"

"Is Mommy going to give me a spanking?" the twerp asked.

"Quinn," said Kira, "could you come with me to the bathroom?"

"Sure."

They were steps from the ladies' room when Kira turned to her. "Flarg?"

Quinn nodded. "Flarg."

They paid their tab and snuck out the back.

"So, I was thinking we'd hit up—"

"Well, I was just going to go home." Kira shrugged.

"Oh. Well..."

"Figured you have work tomorrow, and being a little more sober is really good for your music." She smiled. "You were a star tonight."

Quinn tried to play it off, but couldn't resist grinning.

"Besides," said Kira, "after Wes and his buddies, I'm kind of done."

"Well, we can't let them ruin our night."

"It's not ruined. And you'll be happier when you get up and write that song."

She wrinkled her nose. "What song?"

"The one you're going to write tomorrow."

Quinn chuckled. No way Kira was wrapped up in some horrible shit. Agent Dempsey could wait another day. Or two. He'd never really given her a deadline. And she did have little bubbles of a new song floating about...

* * *

Back at the penthouse, Eve scooped out her tiny captive. She slid the woman into a decorative bowl on the dining table and left to change clothes. When she returned, she found the operative perched on the bowl's rim, assessing the living space.

Eve smirked. "*Dobro pozhalovat,* comrade."

The woman scowled, lowering herself into the bowl.

"I don't think we were properly introduced."

"Zilya Morozova." Her voice echoed in the bowl. "And you will die at my hands, Eve Kincaid."

"Well, you clearly don't know everything about me. Let's say we compare notes?"

"Fuck you."

It always surprised her when people weren't terrified. But more so how bold they were. It was like the only thing they understood was brutality. They had to push her, test her. The same way normal-size people did.

Eve cocked her head. "You know how cold it can get at your size?"

"I'm Russian. I am the cold."

"All right. I'll make it really hot, then."

"You cannot break me without killing me. And if you kill me, you get nothing."

"We'll see about that."

Zilya folded her arms. "No, foolish girl. You will kill me before I say a word."

She considered Zilya's shrewdness. And since Eve had abducted Velez, the operative had more value alive.

Let her think she won.

"You know what?" Eve sighed. "It's late. I'm tired; you're probably tired—"

Zilya scowled.

* * *

Armando slumped on the couch asleep, the DVD player still running episodes of early nineties network television. The thunder of the sliding glass door stirred him.

Though muffled, the woman's words were clear. "Should be plenty of food, and, you can get acquainted with your new roommate."

The isle shook. Heavy vibrations receded. The sliding door had closed. The front door opened and in walked a dark-haired, angry woman.

He sprang from the couch, brushing crumbs off himself.

She surveyed the place, passing a glance at Armando. "Fat American pig."

"Hey! I'm Filipino."

"Were you born in this country?"

"Yeah, but—"

"Then you're American. Idiot."

He charged toward her. "The fuck you think—?"

She spun around, and he froze—a dagger at his neck. She was good. Really good.

The woman stepped back and flipped on a lamp. She sheathed the dagger, striding through the house, and grimaced in distaste.

"Look, I know it's not ideal—"

"It's awful." She put her hands on her hips. "What's in the water?"

"Fish. Really aggressive, hungry fish."

"Have you tried building a raft?"

"No." He scoffed. "Because of the fish. And the birds. You'll see."

An irritated sigh hissed through her teeth as she paced. "What about weapons?"

"No." He shook his head. "Everything at our size is weak."

She turned around. "No. Make weapons."

Holy shit. He hadn't thought of that.

"You have silverware?" she asked. "Stainless steel?"

"Well, yeah." He didn't want to admit he'd given up. But it was probably obvious.

"We melt them down. Forge stronger blades. Wood made our size should be lighter, float better. We are lighter."

She glanced at Armando's girth and ice cream stained shirt and reconsidered. "Well, mostly."

Embarrassed, he wiped away an offending smudge. "Look, I don't see what—"

"Of course not, because you are lazy." She strode toward him, declaring her orders with each step. "We are going to get off this island, into that apartment, get that device, and fucking kill her."

28

(yellow, purple)

Eve lay in bed, fretting over tomorrow's presentation. Orange squiggles and violet dots. It was finally coming together. After fifteen years. Orbs of greens and blues. Denser and denser. She could still hear his voice.

"So, it's like QCD, where colors represent charges?" asked Gideon.

"Well—they're colors." Eve had answered, glassy eyed. "But they don't have anything to do with charges."

She'd been working on her theory for over a year and still couldn't find the words.

"Okay." His head wiggled. "You lost me."

Together they'd polished off three-quarters of a bottle of vodka in his apartment studying for finals. Textbooks and notebooks had cluttered the chipped Formica coffee table along with an empty pizza box. The two of them had slumped shoulder to shoulder on a beaten-up futon.

Eve had sat up straighter. "All right, let me start over—"

"Well." He'd brushed crumbs off his black Nirvana T-shirt. "I get what you're saying...it's a language of colors. But all right—language implies cognition. Then you get into the whole issue of consciousness—"

"I know, I know, and I can hear Professor Beckett now." She sighed. "But I'm saying, the particles know. They know all these rules and laws we discover, and maybe *consciousness* isn't the right word."

"Well—does blue know it's blue?"

Her face had contorted, holding a smile. "I don't...know?" Her eyes searched the corner of the ceiling for answers.

She could feel him watching her. Not with ridicule but warmth.

She'd turned to him. "Blue understands what blue is."

"Sound pretty confident about that," he'd said with a slow smile.

"I am." She'd grinned.

"And you're comfortable speaking on behalf of blue?"

"Blue and I go way back."

He'd tittered. "Best buds."

"Got diaper rash together." She'd chuckled. "That's how we met red."

"And doo-doo brown."

She'd clapped her hands, the two of them collapsing into laughter. A textbook had slid off the table and Gideon had sat up to recover it.

"I mean, I get what you're saying," he'd said. "It's just—capturing that nuance."

"Well, I think whatever it is, it's necessary to information."

"Consciousness?"

"Yeah, we're not special. We forget we're part of this...massive quantum system and if we have something like that, they have something like that, too."

He'd placed the book on the table, his eyes wandering with drunken fascination. "Symmetry."

He'd actually listened, and thought about what she'd said. Like what she said mattered.

"Okay, let's come back to that." He'd circled a finger. "So, this language...doesn't have rules like conjugation limiting combinations. Combinations are only limited by...probability?"

"Right, but there's a certain set of combinations we know probably won't happen—like, there isn't a word made up of six *H*s."

"Sure there is. It's *hhhhhh...*" A heavy breath had rasped from his mouth.

She'd snickered, and shaken her head. "Okay, well, a blip made of all yellow is improbable but possible." She'd bitten her thumbnail, mumbling. "Or it represents a pure quantum state...?"

"All right—and don't take this the wrong way, but—what's wrong with good old-fashioned QED?"

"Nothing. Love QED. And QCD. This doesn't—okay." She'd lurched forward, grabbing a pen and a sketchbook. "So, information is the fundamental element of universe. It's both created by the universe and essential to its existence."

Gideon had grimaced. "Well, matter and energy are—"

"No." She'd known where he was going and held up a finger. "Charges, spins, quarks, strings—they don't exist without information." She flipped to a blank page. "And if you understand how information is transmitted, you understand reality itself."

The cuffs of her fuzzy black sweater had fallen around her wrists as she'd sketched out a diagram. "Let's say there's a photon transfer, and we know the most likely outcome, and yet it could still do something else before getting to where it's going."

"Okay." He'd nodded. "With you so far."

She clenched her eyes shut, fighting intoxication to choose her words. It was hard enough getting what was in her head out into the world when she was sober.

"Okay—and I'm saying in the past, we know there's all these possible outcomes and we're only concerned with what happened, what can be measured. Even though other outcomes have happened in similar instances, we wouldn't know why or care."

"Right."

She'd taken a deep breath and opened her eyes. "But—if we start using blips, cataloging exchanges, we build a dictionary of all possible outcomes—"

"You're talking about an insane level of processing power. And, QED is already pretty accurate."

"And this doesn't get rid of quantum electrodynamics or chromodynamics. This is expanding on them and melding them. If there's a common language, or dialects, linking the fundamental forces and we can translate it, we get closer to a grand unified theory."

Gideon had picked up his glass. "But mapping every possible outcome, every possible blip? It's incalculable."

"No—well—it seems that way, but look." She wrote out the colors. "So, a blip comprised of a color sequence of blue-green-red-purple would therefore have a return blip of purple-red-green-blue, communicating all of the information we can describe in QED between the particles themselves."

He'd set his glass down without taking a sip.

"Return blip?" He'd smirked. "Wouldn't it be a *pilb*? I mean, it sounds like you're describing chirality in action."

"Yeah." She'd smiled, nodding. "Through information transmission."

"And—Devil's advocate—how is that not a string?"

"Because a string is still the vibration of something at a higher level. Information isn't just spin or charges, it's qualitative, and there's... nuance relative to the context of the system it's describing."

"Well, that's—I-I just don't understand how you would do that—"

"Well, I don't have it all worked out—but I—I have this." She flipped pages ahead. "Color expression. You take a quality and define it by a sequence."

"But how do you know what the starting point is? Couldn't it be any combination of colors?"

"I've built sort of a matrix for that." She hadn't shown it to anyone else.

Eve had hesitated, then handed it to him. Her chest had gone cold. Chartreuse and electric blue.

He's going to see how stupid and crazy you are.

He'd grimaced, his brow pulling together over the lengthy series of formulas.

"See." She'd pointed. "Since color's in a continuum, you use it to define a range..."

He'd thumbed through the sketchbook with slow fascination to a three-dimensional grid, several points denoted with their corresponding colors—silver, red, yellow. On the opposite page, her attempt at grids in fourth and fifth dimensions. Gideon had flipped to earlier pages, then back to the grid.

"You think I'm nuts," she'd muttered.

"No." He'd shaken his head.

He's being polite.

"This is—this is daring. And it's still early stages, you should keep working on it."

"Really?"

"Yeah, I mean, there's other things to consider, like—well, okay—so, what about when a photon pops out of existence? Where does the blip go?"

She'd shaken her head. "I don't believe in virtual photons. Well, at least, I don't think things just pop in and out of existence. They're always there. Whatever blips are transmitted project a photon or electron from this deeper layer we can't perceive before sinking back into it."

"So." His forehead had furrowed. "It would be like...if we could see the words we were saying?" He'd smiled. "And they became the things we're talking about?"

"Sort of." She'd bitten the side of her lip. "Imagine these...endless ribbons of color sequences, not just overlapping, but intersecting, passing through each other—constantly transmitting information. And these...blip-*pilb* exchanges rise into strings, into the different elementary particles, and what we perceive as reality."

Gideon's eyes had wandered. He'd gone off in abstract realm, a place without mass and energy as it had been known to him yet the source of everything. He'd blinked, rediscovering Eve. Their eyes met.

Rays of rose, brass, and azure. She'd seen him gaze at her with the same wonder as when she'd studied a feather or moth.

"It might be where"—he'd muttered—"all these other imperceptible things exist. Dark matter. Dark energy. A whole new set of particles. But they couldn't be particles..."

"Colors." She'd nodded.

"Right." He'd mused, searching the air, his eyes again finding hers. "So it would be, what? Ground state? Zero-dimensional space?"

"Infinite black."

* * *

Thanks to the botnets, the world spun further out of control with each passing hour. Only Eve understood why. She turned on the television as she got ready, listening to the too-perky host of *Get Up, America.*

"The holidays are four months away, but we're going to show you the must-have gifts you need on your shopping list. And celebrity chef Chawker Miner will teach us how to cook with the hottest trending superfood—split peas! But first, let's go to Lamar with the headlines."

"Thanks Zara," said her dapper cohost. "Breaking overnight, havoc in North Korea as an improvised explosive detonated in the capital at nine a.m. Pyongyang time, killing five senior members of the ruling party. Early reports say the leader was not injured and has vowed retaliation—"

Eve switched to another channel with a more venerable, solemn anchor.

"Protests have ground the Chinese economy to a halt as millions of workers fill the streets of Beijing, Shanghai, and other major cities. Hong Kong has closed entrance from the mainland as the government struggles to quell the chaos—"

Another station. An anchor spoke over images of lawmakers in discussion.

"Congress is feeling the pressure to eliminate nuclear stockpiles as protests have intensified around the capitol. While India and Pakistan have entered into negotiations aimed at reducing their—"

Another channel. A more sensational anchor's words highlighted a montage of footage.

"A world rocked by protests. Iran's government overthrown as a violent coup in Tehran has ousted the leadership. In neighboring Saudi Arabia, the capital Riyadh surrounded by thousands of protesters while the nation's oil fields go dormant, threatening the global economy. This just days after online activists expanded their focus from nuclear weapons and nuclear power to fossil fuels. Here, too, in the United States citizens have taken to the streets. Hundreds of cars have been abandoned across American highways, blocking traffic in major cities.

Outside the White House, thousands have gathered to protest President Ramos's incursion into Venezuela, largely believed to be a grab at the nation's oil supply."

The anchor pivoted to two commentators, a staid middle-aged woman and an older man so languid he might have been asleep.

* * *

Watching the program in the Oval Office, President Ramos muted the television. He tossed the remote onto the desk.

"We're preserving democracy in the Western Hemisphere," he groused. "We were up twenty points in the polls."

He ran fingers through his thinning black hair, then settled them onto his neck to rub out the tension with a sigh.

"That was a week ago, sir," said a young woman, his chief of staff. "Things have changed."

"It's democracy and oil." Ramos paced. "What else does this country want?"

She hesitated to answer. Ramos waved a finger over his head. "I know—I heard right after I said it."

She nodded.

"It appears to be to a series of botnets, sir," said the national security adviser. "Originating in India or Pakistan."

"Then shut them down," said Ramos.

"We've tried," the older man answered. "They've infected devices around the globe and operate without direction or supervision."

"We've got the world's greatest surveillance network," said Ramos. "You're telling me we can't stop this thing?"

"Well..." The older man cleared his throat. "Given your law enforcement campaign, we believe hackers may have taken it as a challenge. To be honest, if the Chinese couldn't identify the source and eliminate it, there's no way in hell we can."

"Okay." Ramos stepped back. "How about we shut down the internet?"

The chief of staff and national security adviser exchanged wary glances, unwilling to question the President's intelligence.

"Sir, that's not possible," said the chief of staff.

"Why not?" asked Ramos. "The North Koreans did it. So did Iran."

"Mr. President," said the security adviser, "those are not democracies—"

"And I'm talking about a direct threat to our democracy," said Ramos. "Our allies, global stability. We order all internet providers to shut down service—"

"Sir—"

"For twenty-four hours. For reasons of national security. We call on UN members to do the same. Every country, every company, no exceptions—Russia and China would be all in. Easiest sell ever. India and Pakistan are looking for an out. We could finally get a handle on this thing."

"I understand what you're saying, sir," said the chief of staff. "But we can't just hit Pause on the world econ—"

"That's exactly what needs to happen. We need to break the spell." He pointed to the television running images of protesters. "This is barreling out of control, and the opportunity to catch it already slipped through our fingers. If it sounds crazy and drastic, that's because that's where we're at."

Ramos lowered his arm. Both of his counsel were disquieted.

"Get me the joint chiefs," said Ramos. "If they've got better ideas, I want to hear it."

* * *

Eve arrived at the posh downtown office early. She wheeled a cart with a black cloth draped over it into the conference room. She requested a lamp, a standing fan, and a spare computer monitor. Eager staff brought in the equipment. Eve closed the door behind them and reviewed her presentation on note cards, ignoring dots of yellow and chartreuse.

Diane's phone buzzed.

The colors floated. She didn't recognize the number. The buzz repeated.

"This is Diane Cernik."

"Ms. Cernik, it's Detective Russo. I was wondering if you could come down to the station so we can talk."

Yellow, then black.

"Unfortunately I'm in meetings most of the day. I do have availability around one, if you'd like to come to the workspace building off Main. I can meet you in the lobby."

"See you then." He hung up.

A complication she'd anticipated—though sooner than expected. She bit the edge of her lip, dragging the flesh through her teeth.

The attorney knocked. They exchanged pleasantries. They were soon joined by an older woman with flaxen hair, Christina Yarrow. A longtime idol of hers, Eve had never dreamed she'd meet her, let alone present her with a radical invention. Marty Glick entered with Adrian Borg, a towering man with a coarse beard. The attorney doled out nondisclosure agreements.

Borg turned up his nose. “This is highly irregular. And unnecessary.”

“Necessary if you want to see it,” said Eve.

Marty shrugged. “Price of admission.”

He signed, as did Yarrow. Borg grumbled as he dashed off his name. The attorney thanked them, gathered up the documents and left.

Eve stepped to the front of the room.

You’re going to blow it.

“The three of you represent the leading edge of technology in the United States,” she said. “Mr. Devereux—”

“Where is Mr. Devereux?” asked Borg.

They can see right through you.

“Due to extenuating circumstances, he couldn’t attend—”

“Why not?” he asked. “He can’t videoconference?”

Yeah—why can’t he?

“Ah, Avery—Mister—Mr. Devereux...” *Diane. Be Diane.* “Suffers from a severe form of mysophobia. It’s worsened with age, and he’s currently in treatment. In his absence, I’ve been tasked with certain executive responsibilities.”

Marty smiled. “So talking to you is like talking to him?”

“Minus the slight Cajun accent, yes, for the most part.” Eve nodded.

Yarrow and Glick smiled at the joke. Borg glowered.

Eve spread her hands. “As you may have noticed, the world’s in chaos. We’re at a crossroads. The energy sources humanity has tied itself to are either unsustainable or not worth the long-term risk. The public knows this, nations know this. Alternative energy—solar and wind, while scalable, are still lagging behind.”

She brought her hands together. “Which is why several months ago, when Mr. Devereux was approached with the promise of a revolutionary energy source, he made the unthinkable decision to venture out and meet with the inventor in person.”

She lifted the cloth, unveiling the black box underneath.

“Doesn’t look like much,” she said. “But this technology can provide limitless power—without waste, without radiation—for everyone on Earth and be integrated into existing power grids.”

“That is...” Borg scoffed. “Do you have any proof to back up these claims?”

“Allow me.” She plugged the cords into a row of outlets on the bottom edge of the box. The lamp glowed. The blades of the standing fan spun. The monitor lit up before displaying *Cable Not Connected.*

She popped in her phone charger and plugged in her phone.

“This is a classic con.” Borg snickered. “How do we know there isn’t a car battery in there?"

Yarrow nodded. "I'm skeptical as well. Can we see inside?"

Eve pulled the plugs. She unclasped the latches on the box and opened the housing, revealing the glowing cylinder. It radiated orange particles which burned white as they floated off, absorbed into the surrounding photovoltaic cells on the box's interior.

The CEOs reared back.

Borg jumped out of his chair, moving to the farthest end of the room. "What is that?"

Yarrow squirmed. "You're saying there's no radiation?"

"There is not," Eve said with placid calm. "It's completely safe. No radiation. Little or no residual heat."

She reached into her jacket and held up a dosimeter. "I was in this room, with this box, an hour before you all arrived. The reading has not changed."

Yarrow eased into her chair. Glick remained motionless, his posture still angled away, studying Diane.

Borg took two steps forward, hands on his hips, keeping his distance. "Not possible."

"It is," Eve said. "You want to wave your hand under the cart? There's no mirrors here."

"How does it work?"

"Right now," she said, "the panels lining the inside capture the particles and convert them into electricity. We believe, with your help, we can engineer more efficient ways to harness the power. But the key to all of it is that material. This is the answer to the future."

"Tell me," said Marty, "why did the inventor approach Mr. Devereux, as opposed to say, one of us?"

"The inventor was aware of Mr. Devereux's reputation for privacy." Eve nodded. "As you can imagine, they were reluctant to go public, as many powerful people would be threatened by it. We're seeing that play out today. They believed their life would be at risk."

"This is a con," said Borg.

"All right, so Mr. Borg is out." Eve gestured to the door. "You're free to go."

He lingered, unwilling to pass by the glowing cylinder.

"Just remember you signed a legally binding document," said Eve.

He huffed, taking a circuitous route around the table to exit.

"I'm optimistic." Yarrow nodded. "But I need more detail. I'd like an opportunity to test the material."

"That can be arranged." Eve smiled.

Yarrow stood. "We'll be in touch."

She left in a hurry.

"Mr. Glick?"

Marty stood. "I have a couple questions—well, maybe just one." He neared her. "It's you, isn't it?"

"I'm sorry?"

"You're the inventor."

She broke into a self-conscious smile. "While I do possess a wide range of skills, none of them allow me to create something like this."

He smirked. "You know how you can tell when people are lying?"

Her smiled dropped. "Excuse me?"

"These little micro-expressions—not microaggressions, microexpressions." He pointed to his own face. "Tiny little movements people make with their eyes, corners of their mouth, the muscles in their cheeks, jaw, which are usually imperceptible...except to those who are practiced in catching them."

The door was closed. They were alone. Her mind ran through the scenarios of a well-known billionaire and head of a multinational corporation vanishing.

"And you think in the few minutes we've spent, you have enough information to determine I'm a liar?"

"Well, just about that."

"I'm flattered you think so highly of me." She smiled. "But I'm brilliant in other ways."

"Your secret's safe with me. Let's build the future." He offered a hand.

They shook on it.

"I'll be in touch, Ms. Cernik."

He left the room.

Eve gasped for breath like she'd run a marathon. Electric blue, pink, and violet. She'd done it. Once Yarrow's tests came back, she'd jump on board. Borg would come crawling back. Everything was coming together. Her gasps eased into breathy laughter, then settled into a deep, calming cadence.

* * *

Velez and Troy slowed to a trot, cooling down from their jog as they neared the house.

"How long you been a cop?"

"Nine years."

"Think you make a difference?"

"I don't think you need to be a cop to make a difference—just how I do it. Why?"

He wiped his brow. "Thought about it. Wasn't sure if it was for me."

"So you protect money for banks instead?"

He shrugged. "Figured it's like being a cop without the politics. Like a test run. See if I like it."

"Not the same." She shook her head. "You'll never know what it's like to give somebody closure. To take someone off the street you know is going to hurt people. And that little...hit." She pointed to her temple. "When you solve a case. There's nothing like it."

Troy grew pensive as they neared the door. He rapped his knuckles against it twice. A hefty latch unbolted inside. Kevin pulled the door open. They slipped in, joining Kevin, Shadi and Zach around a large crossbow on a cart filling the length of the garage.

Shadi's neck swerved. "I know you think making explosives is second nature to me—"

"Oh, I didn't say anything like that," said Zach.

"But it's not. I'm not a chemist."

"Wow," he said. "You're admitting you can't do something? *That's* amazing to me."

Kevin stepped between them. "Will you keep it down?"

"Look, look," said Troy. "There's gasoline in the truck. We can siphon some out tonight."

"It's flammable, not explosive," said Shadi. "It would just be a giant Molotov cocktail."

"Napalm," Zach said. "Styrofoam, gasoline. Light it on fire. It'll stick to whatever it lands on."

"Yeah," said Kevin. "Including us and the house."

Zach threw up his hands. "Well, then I don't know."

"Oh, you don't know something?" asked Shadi.

"Oh my god—stop," said Velez. "This is a bad idea. She'll go ballistic."

"Which is why we want to blind her," said Shadi.

"Okay." Velez balked. "And then what?"

"I scale the wall," said Troy. "Find out where she keeps that thing."

"But he only has enough food and water for a couple days," said Shadi. "We can't consume anything unless it's been shrunk."

"So it's a suicide mission," said Velez.

"No." He shook his head. "See, we've got the layout. This room's across from her office. The main bedroom's right next to that one. Eugene says there's a box on her nightstand—"

"And what if he lied?" asked Velez. "What if it's in a safe?"

"He says it never leaves her side," said Troy. "She wouldn't put it somewhere she couldn't get it to it right away."

Velez sighed. "If you can wait a little longer, the FBI—"

"We've got to take a shot at this," he said.

"I know you're desperate, but there's no telling what she'll do if she's blinded."

"We've been waiting too long," said Kevin. "And if things go sideways for her, there's no telling what she's going to do with us."

* * *

The hum was as enigmatic as the shard.

What was it? If the shard and Mobius produced the same noise for different reasons, what did it mean? And why did the shard react to energy the same way as the Mobius without the sound present?

Simon downloaded several audio-mixing programs. Playback in digital form altered its tone and pitch, creating a sound like water in a suction tube at a dental hygienist's office. He tried different approaches. Altering its speed. Playing it backwards. Examining it through a digital oscilloscope. The signal registered as white noise, a cacophony of irreducible frequencies.

He dug an analog oscilloscope from the storage closet in the basement and connected a microphone. Simon activated the coil. The sound fried the machine.

Why did that happen?

He sat at the console, absorbed by the droning noise. Another day before the concrete dried and the chamber would be sturdy enough.

Perhaps a vacuum tube to house the coil while firing electrons at the shard?

He considered the inelegant arrangement he'd already devised. It would be better—maybe safer—for an electric arc to pass through the fragment, using the air to diffuse the power. Then the fragment's reaction might not be as intense.

Running low on cash, he couldn't afford another catastrophe.

Simon shut off the coil and set up a negative cathode and a positive anode disc. He wired them to separate power sources and placed the fragment between them.

He locked the chamber and turned on the coil. The signal hummed. Then, he switched on the cathode-anode pair. A flash. But nothing more.

Simon stared into the chamber. Any amount of energy should have been enough.

"Why?" He smiled. "Jareima, open log."

"Ready."

"Attempts at passing a current into the fragment while the signal is generated produce no effect. Whatever this material is, I believe it exhibits properties of negative mass. Improbable but could explain its bizarre relationship with energy."

He stepped from behind the console. "I believe in this state, energy might have a different function, and I may be able to attenuate to the signal's frequency."

Simon floated toward the chamber's window, fixated on the shard. "Maybe its producing a new, novel field. One which requires different methodology. An entirely new science."

* * *

Eve packed up her equipment and left the meeting space. She returned an hour later, loitering in the chic lobby until Russo arrived.

"Thank you for making the time, Ms. Cernik."

"Of course." Eve smiled. "Hoping it's good news."

"You've spoken with Detective Velez?"

Chartreuse. She shook her head. "No. Why?"

"Sure about that?" His New York accent rose.

"Yeah? Does she know who set the fire?"

"No. And unfortunately, Detective Velez is MIA."

"Oh—okay?"

"Based on what I found at her desk, she thinks you got an alias. Kira Sloane."

"I don't understand...what does that have to do with our warehouse?"

"Well, nothing. But she seems to think you're a suspect in other crimes."

"And..." Eve shook her head, disbelieving. "What crimes?"

"Robbery, kidnapping, possibly the art gallery attack."

She squinted. "What the fuck do you people do all day?"

"Look, if you could just come down to the station, we can clear all this up."

"I'm not going anywhere with you—there's nothing to clear up. Do I need protection from your partner?"

"I don't think she would do anything crazy—"

"Oh, like concoct some wild conspiracy and then disappear from her job?"

"Well, I mean, the thing is"—he shrugged—"she pegs you as a suspect, and then she disappears."

"So, you're buying into this lunacy?"

"Don't make me do this the hard way, Ms. Cernik. Just come down to the station."

"I want your badge number and the name of your superior."

"Oh, really?" The New Yorker in him lit up.

“Yeah. Really. Your job is to protect and serve. Now, I want protection from your partner and for you to serve me your badge number.”

His eyes tightened on her. He reached into his jacket.

Hot yellow. Eve backed off, bracing herself.

He took out his badge and read off the number. He held it up for her. “I report to Captain Harrell.”

She loosened and smirked. “Captain Marcus Harrell?”

“You heard of him?”

“When you donate over ten grand to the police association, your local captain contacts you to say thanks.”

Russo zeroed in on her phone.

She’d changed the case. Still a wood-grain but now Zebrano. Close enough to bamboo at a distance, but up close, distinctive.

She held it to her ear. “Captain Harrell, please. That’s unacceptable—I need to speak with him immediately regarding a serious issue with a couple of his detectives.”

She watched Russo lose focus. He was second-guessing himself.

Eve smiled. “Hi, Captain Harrell, it’s Diane Cernik. We spoke—yes, that’s right. Well, I wish it was under better circumstances. Detectives Russo and Velez were assigned to investigate arson at one of our properties. Now I’ve come to find out Velez has gone rogue and is accusing me of unrelated crimes, and Detective Russo is here to arrest me.”

She gazed into Russo’s eyes.

“Yes. Thank you. I appreciate it. You have a lovely day as well.” She hung up.

A buzz vibrated in Russo’s pants pocket.

“Might want to get that,” she whispered.

He answered the call. “Detect—Y-yes—I understand, sir.” He sighed, scowling at Diane. “Thank you for your time, ma’am.”

He turned and walked out of the lobby, the phone still to his ear.

She restrained a smile. Too soon to celebrate. Time to lay low. Violet, blue, scarlet; gray, purple, gold.

29

(yellow, brown)

Voicemail messages from Agent Dempsey gnawed at Quinn. Kira had passed on hanging out two nights in a row. Was Kira avoiding her?

She at least had to tell the FBI she'd tried to get the story. If she couldn't get Kira drunk, she had to find another way.

Quinn glided into the IT department, her sunflower-print skirt flowing behind. "Heeeey Powell."

His eyes slid in her direction.

She smiled. "Could you do me a big favor?"

"What did you download?" he asked in a dry, accusing tone.

"Nothing." She recoiled. "That was one time, I swear."

"Sure."

She planted her elbows on the partition and leaned over, lowering her voice. "I need you put down your joystick and ask Kira out already."

"Okay, first off—wow. Second, none of your business. And third, I don't think we're allowed to do that anymore."

"Oh—so, you're not interested?"

Powell struggled. "I—look, dating in the work place aside, I think there's something there, but..."

"Well, you won't know until you ask."

"Are you telling me it's a sure thing?"

"Uh, no. I just want you both to stop acting like awkward teenagers."

He heaved a sigh, shaking his head.

"Do I need to make the clucking sound?"

"That would not persuade me."

"You haven't heard me do it yet. I have three older brothers—it's pretty irritating."

"I just need to find the right time."

Quinn clasped her hands together, pointing with two joined fingers. "Whatever time you do it is the right time. But today would be great."

She drifted out of the room, certain she'd set the stage to draw out Kira's past heartache. On her way to the cubicles, Quinn spied Larry with another man entering Kira's office. He was tall, young, dashing, with the sort of magnetic eyes and radiant smile that melted hearts.

She hurried over.

"Kira, I'd like you to meet Tyler Thomas," Larry's voice carried. "He's going to help expand our brand."

"Nice to meet you."

"Pleasure's all mine."

Tyler and Kira finished a handshake as Quinn reached the door.

She poked her head in. "Morning, everybody."

Larry beamed. "Quinn, this is Tyler. He's our new public relations insider."

"Ooh, insider." A smile crept across her face. "Sounds so... undercover."

She reached out for a handshake and was not disappointed.

"It's actually just a lot of lunches." Tyler smirked. "And drinking."

"Maybe I should get into public relations," Quinn quipped.

He nodded. "Don't get me wrong—it's fun, but also a lot of work."

"I like fun," she said, lost in his eyes.

"I'm...going to stop shaking your hand now."

"Oh—yeah. Guess you're going to need that back." She released him and straightened her jacket.

"Thanks."

"Well, speaking of work, I should get going," said Quinn. "Nice meeting you."

She floated to her cubicle daydreaming about her romance with Tyler. She'd build a music career while he wined and dined politicians and journalists. She'd take him to seedy bars and nightclubs. He'd be uncomfortable at first, only to befriend some biker dudes by the end of the night. He'd bring her to boring seminars at fancy hotels where they'd get caught having sex in the linen closets. Double dates with Kira and Powell. Lazy Sunday mornings at his place.

* * *

Tyler's eyes and warm smile fixed onto Eve.

"This whole One Is Too Much protest has put us on the map," said Larry. "I had a conversation a couple days ago with some congresspersons—who shall remain nameless—and we're in a position to lobby ahead of groups who been around decades longer. We can make a serious impact."

"Not everybody sees it as a good thing," said Tyler. "We need to strike a balance. There is a danger in being too hot." He glanced at Eve. "And I'd say we're pretty hot right now."

She returned a small smile. His eyes lingered on her.

"And that's what we wanted to talk to you about," said Larry. "Donations are up and we're going to have to increase our spend, so I need you to check the numbers, revise the budget, see how much leeway we actually have. Tyler and I have hashed out some ideas—"

"We can sit down one-on-one if you want and go over what I'm thinking," said Tyler.

"Oh, no—you can just send me the numbers." Eve nodded. "I'm better with numbers. I'll put some things together."

"That'd be great," said Larry. "Thanks, Kira."

He led Tyler out. "Come on, I'll finish showing you around."

Once they were down the hall, Eve rushed to the door and shut it.

"Maybe he has a thing for redheads," she muttered.

Seriously? Larry suddenly hires an Adonis who wants you alone and doesn't give Quinn a second look?

Her eyes flared. Breathless. "Undercover."

Either a fed or a Russian.

She darted to her desk and grabbed her Diane phone to research Tyler Thomas.

* * *

Dempsey meandered into the office, exhausted.

Callahan looked up from her laptop. "Any luck?"

"Chop shop operation."

"You sure?"

"Yep." Dempsey dropped into a chair. "We nailed the tow truck they were using."

"Damn."

Masuda strolled in, coffee in hand.

"What about you, Mel?"

"I'm thinking it was Kincaid. Al-Sana and her prototype went missing the same night—nothing on camera."

Callahan fumed. "How's that possible?"

"Well," said Masuda, "based on the art gallery, looks like she figured out how to get it to do other things."

"Yeah, but...become invisible?" asked Dempsey.

Masuda shrugged. "Maybe."

Callahan's phone vibrated. She grabbed it.

"It's Manny. You got a minute?"

"Yeah, putting you on speaker." Callahan set the phone down.

"All right, so the missing Winnebago was a dead-end," said Guzman. "But there were these two warehouse fires on the same block. One of the detectives assigned was Velez. So I went to follow up with her about the Milner case. Come to find out she's missing now, too, and the last couple searches she ran were for a Kira Sloane."

Callahan locked on Dempsey. "Reid—"

He sat up. "I've left three messages—"

"Let me finish," said Guzman. "Velez's partner got reprimanded for harassing a woman named Diane Cernik. She looks like Kincaid with a makeover."

"Got an address for her?" asked Callahan.

"Some penthouse, but it's not in her name."

"That's why we can't find her," said Masuda. "She's nesting shell companies."

"All right, send me the address," said Callahan. "I'll work on getting a warrant."

"No way she's living there." Masuda shook her head. "She probably has multiple dummy addresses—"

"I don't care if it's a front at this point," said Callahan. "We need a trail."

"Well, hang on," said Guzman. "Captain Harrell wants to know why I'm interested in these cases. I tell him we investigate strange occurrences. So he shows me this picture of a body they found in a car outside the art gallery. Something broke the window and twisted this guy's head like it was pottery clay."

"What?" asked Callahan. "What do you mean?"

"I'll send you a pic," said Guzman. "But don't expect to eat anything for a few days. The victim's ID was an expert forgery. They found him with a burner phone and a handgun with no registration, no serial numbers."

"You tracing the burner?" she asked.

"You know it."

"Let's see how long the Russian was tailing her and if we can build a map," said Callahan. "Maybe we can figure out where she's going. Nobody engages her alone, understand?"

* * *

Velez and Troy walked into the kitchen. Janelle, Shadi and Zach sat at the table eating breakfast while Kevin washed dishes.

"Morning, everybody." Troy filled a glass at the water dispenser.

"Morning."

Velez poured herself a cup of coffee and took a seat at the table.

The kitchen door swung open. Eugene walked in. "Morning."

"Morning." Troy sat alongside Velez.

Eugene sifted through a wall of frosty packages in the freezer. He turned around, finding Zach eating waffles.

"Hey," said Eugene. "Those were mine."

"Your name wasn't on them." He shrugged.

"Dude, I specifically asked for them. She got them for me."

"Eugene." Janelle sighed. "Just get something else."

"No," said Eugene. "He did it on purpose."

"Go cry about it to your girlfriend." Zach muttered.

"She's not—Shut up," said Eugene.

"Yeah, you want her to be."

"This happen every morning?" Velez mumbled to Troy.

He shook his head.

"All right," said Eugene. "You don't know anything about her."

"Oh, and you do?" Zach asked with a snide smirk.

"More than you."

"You're delusional," said Zach. "She's using you."

"Will you two stop?" Kevin shut off the faucet.

"Just let them get it out," Janelle muttered.

"How is she using me?" asked Eugene. "I haven't seen in her days."

"Yeah," said Zach. "Because she's done with you. She doesn't need you anymore."

Troy flagged a hand. "All right, that's enough—"

"And you're still waiting like a lovesick puppy dog," said Zach. "When are you going to realize she doesn't care about you?"

"What do you know?" asked Eugene. "You been wrong about everything. You were wrong about negotiating with her. You were wrong about the drone. You were wrong about the wireless—"

"I was right about the security flaw!" Zach sneered. "That should've worked. And that was on you. So why hasn't she gotten caught yet?"

"Because I didn't tell her to put it in, asshole!"

"I knew it!" Janelle shot from her chair, pointing an accusing finger. "I fucking knew it!"

"You son of a bitch!" Kevin clenched his fists. "I'm going to fucking kill you!"

Eugene lurched back and whipped a chef's knife from the butcher block in a desperate bid to defend himself. He pointed it at Zach and then swung the blade toward Kevin, unsure how to fend them both off.

Zach leaped from his chair to escape as Eugene sliced the air.

"Whoa!" Velez jumped to her feet. "Hang on!"

Janelle flung her plate at Eugene, toast and eggs sailing. He deflected the projectile with his other arm as Zach attempted to fence with him using a butter knife.

"Hey!" Troy stood. "Stop! Stop!"

Kevin sprayed Eugene with the sink attachment while Shadi and Janelle pelted him with the remaining dishes and silverware from the table. Eugene slashed, batting them away. Utensils zinged around, plates shattered on the floor.

"Stop!" Velez edged closer. "Everybody stop!"

Kevin tossed aside the sink attachment. He seized a cast-iron skillet, wielding it like a club.

"I'm going to kill him," he seethed. "I'm going to kill him."

Eugene held the knife overhead like a katana sword.

"No, you're not!" Velez held up a hand, stepping closer. "When you get out of here—"

"We're never getting out of here," said Kevin. "He trapped us!"

"You can't think like that," she said. "When we get out. If you kill him, when we get out, you'll go to prison for murder, all right?"

"She's right, Kev," said Troy. "Think about Jeanie and the kids. You want to get out of here only to be locked up somewhere else?"

Kevin flung the pan onto the counter, cracking the backsplash tile.

"Drop the knife," said Velez. "Both of you."

"Are you kidding?" asked Zach. "He just tried turning my face into fajita meat."

Velez charged forward, snatching Zach's wrist and twisting his arm. In one swift move, she pinned him to the table and forced the knife from his hand. It clanked onto the floor.

"Now put yours down," she said to Eugene.

The door opened. Cassidy and Darien hung back.

"Oh, wow," said Cassidy. "So I guess he found out you're planning on killing her, huh?"

"What?!" asked Eugene.

"Cassidy!" Janelle scolded.

"I think they settled on maiming her," said Darien.

Eugene's head swiveled between the housemates. "What about going to jail for murder once we get out of here?"

"It's different when it's your kidnapper and you're escaping," said Shadi.

"Is it, though?" asked Cassidy. "Look, we're not really involved, so can we get cereal?"

"No!" Eugene swept the knife tip across the room. "Nobody gets shit until you listen to me."

They awaited his words.

"I was scared, all right?" He sighed. "At the time, I thought I was protecting us—"

"You were saving your own ass." Zach muttered.

Velez leaned on him. "Shut up."

"I was," said Eugene. "But I saw she was going to figure it out. Which is what I told you. She's had a plan—and it's not bad. She's not bad—"

"She's holding us hostage." Janelle folded her arms.

"She stole from me." Zach's words muffled against the table.

"And me," said Shadi.

"And us," said Kevin.

"And whatever she's doing is affecting people all over the world," said Troy.

"All right, so she's not perfect," said Eugene. "But I'm pretty sure my roommates drugged me, lied to me, and are hiding something in the garage to kill her with. So you're not perfect either. Maybe except for Troy."

"No." Troy sighed. "I lied to you. And I'm the one who drugged you. Well, Cassidy's the one who got the drugs, but—"

"Whatever," said Eugene. "I know you want to escape, but Darien's right. All you're going to do is piss her off. Just wait until she lets us go."

Kevin grumbled, "You told her not to."

"Like she listens to me," said Eugene. "She's been ten steps ahead the entire time. We're just in her way."

"You can help stop her," said Velez.

Eugene snickered. "You're the ones who are delusional. I've accepted the fact she's going to do whatever she wants. And look—we're changing the world together!"

He stormed towards Cassidy and Darien, still clutching the knife. They backed way, allowing him to exit the kitchen.

"Probably a bad time," Zach mumbled, "but I actually didn't eat all the waffles. I hid them in the back of the freezer."

Velez leaned into the hold, pressing onto Zach's arm, back and face. He grunted in pain.

Eugene tried the door to the garage. Locked.

"What do you think you're doing?" Kevin asked from behind.

He spun around, taking an *en garde* stance with the blade. "I'm not letting you destroy everything we've built together."

Kevin and Shadi inched toward him. The others crept up behind them.

“It’s the only way, Eugene,” said Shadi.

“You’re going to get us all killed,” said Eugene. “Just let her finish it.”

He made a break for the front door and raced out of the house.

“Well, it’s not like he can go anywhere,” Janelle muttered.

Kevin shook his head. “He’s going to try to warn her.”

“He’s right about one thing,” said Velez. “You should reconsider this plan.”

“You want to sleep outside, too?” asked Kevin.

“Dude.” Troy stepped forward. “All right, that’s not you. And this isn’t it me. Drugging somebody, lying to them? You know me. I’ve never done any shit like that before.”

“Because you want to survive,” said Kevin.

“No,” said Troy. “We’re letting her turn us into terrible people. We need to back up and stop.”

“This has gone on long enough.” Kevin tilted his chin at Velez. “What’s it matter if she’s right and the cops show up?”

Shadi nodded. “We’d be preventing her from doing any more harm in the world.”

“Or to us,” said Janelle. “Are you backing out?”

Troy took a thoughtful breath. “Truth is we don’t know what she’s going to do—”

“Forget it—we don’t need you.” Zach joined ranks with Janelle, Shadi and Kevin. “I’ll go.”

Cassidy and Darien stepped up behind Velez and Troy.

* * *

At first, Armando was furious when Zilya smashed the television. But once the withdrawal waned and he embraced her rigorous exercise routine, he recovered a sense of focus and clarity. They brainstormed, taking notes, challenging the other’s ideas, and perfecting their escape strategies. She was impressed with his cunning, far more artful than the gluttonous sloth he appeared to be. He was both wary and in awe of her ruthlessness. She was direct and deliberate. There was no second-guessing, no hesitation.

She improvised a small forge using a large decorative ceramic pot, several bricks from the front porch, a blow dryer and beach sand. They set aside a fork, knife, and spoon each. Then they melted down the rest along with other metals in the house to create stronger alloy which they smithed into larger blades, small swords, and lance tips.

They examined the wood furniture and architecture, settling on an armoire as their primary hold. They mounted two hulls on either side, creating a sturdy catamaran. From the kitchen pantry, they stocked survival packs for days of trekking through the apartment.

In a few cycles, they learned Eve's schedule. Once she'd made her delivery, she didn't return to check on them for three days. She did, however, have a cup of coffee on the terrace every morning. Since she'd delivered this morning, their escape had to be tonight.

They shut off the power to the house and tore out the wiring. They fashioned climbing cables and secured homemade grappling hooks onto them.

"Got to watch out for the birds," said Armando.

"That's what the flamethrowers are for," Zilya said with a slow smile.

He smirked. "Think she'll notice a cooked pigeon on her backdoor step."

She shrugged. "Maybe." Her smile fell away. "So we are clear, there is no room for error."

He nodded. "I know."

"Best case, we both survive. But if something should happen, promise me you will kill her."

Armando stopped winding his cable and met her eyes. "You have my word, Zilya. I will slit her throat."

* * *

Simon flung open the aluminum trunks in the basement. He'd intended on perfecting the laser system for his fusion reactor. But now he only needed one. He assembled the parts of the scaled-down system, modifying it to extend the beam's duration and reduce heat. Satisfied with the initial tests, he focused a beam of low-range ultraviolet radiation into the activated fragment.

A pulse of light and his heart jumped.

The luminous holographic grid inside the shard projected outside, filling the chamber with a three-dimensional grid above. He gazed in wonder as liquid streamed from its center.

He shut off the beam and the coil, fearing a short circuit. Simon raced into the chamber where a murky brown puddle spread across the floor. Perplexed, he knelt down to examine it and within seconds recognized the odor—

Fresh, hot coffee.

* * *

Eve stared at the stream shooting into her cup from the dispenser, consumed by the troubling discovery that Tyler's previous employers no longer existed. She suspected he was a fabrication, designed to obtain access without people questioning his confidence and good looks. The real Tyler Thomas, from what she'd pieced together, had tired of the advertising game and relocated to Wyoming around the time this new Tyler had assumed his identity. Another Russian operative. She was sure of it.

"Larry can't stop singing your praises." His warm baritone resounded behind her.

Eve tensed, grabbing her coffee. Tyler leaned on the counter alongside her.

"If I didn't know better..." He smiled. "I'd say he had a little crush on you."

This could work—let him think she was enamored, then get him alone.

"Oh, no." Eve blushed. "He's just being nice."

"No, no, he says you get it. Which is why I'd like to pick your brain. Hear your thoughts on nuclear disarmament. Maybe over dinner tomorrow night?"

Quinn had another show. She shook her head. "Tomorrow night's no good." She lowered her voice. "But Larry's got me on a special project. Kind of a secret."

She leaned in a touch.

The heavy lids of her bedroom eyes were more like an uncertain squint to him and then a scowl as she calibrated.

"Might have to stay late tonight," she said, breathier. "It uses a lot of...pivot tables."

"Well." Tyler leaned in. "If there's anything I can help with..."

"Could use an extra pair of hands," she whispered. "It's...really hard." She leaned back a touch. "I mean, you know I'm not talking about real tables, right?"

"Yeah, got that," he said. "I'm sure the two of us can—"

Powell cleared his throat.

Lemon and laurel green. She had no idea how long Powell had been there. If there was anything between them, she'd just squelched it.

Wow, you managed to kill him without killing him. Impressive.

Tyler backed off.

"Hey, Powell," said Eve.

"Hey," he said. "Don't mind me."

"No worries," said Tyler. "We were talking strategy."

"Right." Powell refused eye contact and headed for the snack machine.

"Remember," Eve whispered to Tyler. "It's a secret."

She sipped her coffee and walked away with a little sway in her hips and then stumbled off her heel, coffee scalding her hand. She ignored the pain, straightening and casting another seductive bedroom scowl at Tyler on her way out.

* * *

McCrae's conversation with a pair of officers in the base's administration center was cut short as a formidable woman cruised past the desks toward them.

"Ah—goddammit," he growled. "Why're you here?"

She smirked. "Nice to see you, too, Rusty."

"It's Russell, Maria—I mean, General," he grumbled, collecting himself, and turned to the officers. "We'll resume this later. Dismissed."

The officers departed.

"And it's Deputy Director Garza," she said.

"And I'm usually notified before someone arrives on my base."

"Well, that's why I'm here. You don't seem informed about your own command."

"That's an unfair—"

"The president is deeply concerned. Given the escalation in global events, he's tasked me with closing this egregious lapse in security."

McCrae scoffed. "Global events? What in god's—"

"The terrorist attack in Los Angeles? The perpetrator used some sort of energy weapon. I suspect a very dedicated agent contacted McAndrews who in turn, reached out to me."

A soldier escorted Callahan through the door.

Garza smiled. "Don't you love it when things work out like that?"

They sat in McCrae's office to review the situation. Satisfied with Callahan's progress and the prospect of closing in on their prime suspect, Garza turned to McCrae.

"So where are the rest of them?" she asked.

"The fragments have been locked in storage since the breach," he answered.

"And you've tested them?"

"No."

"Why not?"

"They'd never been taken out for experimentation. It was determined removing them posed a greater security risk until Agent Callahan completed her investigation."

"So, you don't know if the other fragments have been replaced with decoys?"

He sighed, then answered slowly. "They were never removed from storage for experimentation."

"But we've established that foreign operatives had access to the material. Correct, Agent Callahan?"

"Yes, Director." Callahan nodded.

Garza gazed at McCrae. "Test them."

McCrae gave the order. The trio waited in his office, making awkward small talk. Garza received a call and excused herself.

"So, you two used to date?" asked Callahan.

"God, no," McCrae grunted. "First had a run-in with her a decade ago, working on a guidance system. Another bureaucrat out to make a name for themselves. Guess she did a pretty good job."

"Seems like there's more to it."

"She has what we like to call an olfactory impairment of reality."

Callahan squinted.

"She thinks her shit doesn't stink," he said. "And I don't tolerate that well."

McCrae's desk phone rang. An officer notified him their findings were available on a secure drive. He opened the file as Garza returned.

He huffed. "Impossible."

"What is?" asked Garza.

"Epsilon"—hot air shot through his nostrils—"is obsidian."

Garza folded her arms, rather smug.

Much less delighted, Callahan faced McCrae, the same conclusion forming.

"Son of a bitch," he said.

"Excuse me?" asked Garza.

"We think we know who has it," said Callahan. "Someone with early access to the project, a collection of mineral samples, and incentive to hang onto it in case the government didn't give them rights to the technology."

Garza nodded, clear on the culprit. "I want it recovered in the next twelve hours."

* * *

Since Kira hadn't mentioned him at lunch, Quinn popped into IT as Powell packed up for the day.

"So." She grinned. "How did it go?"

"Uh, it didn't."

Her smile weakened.

"She's more interested in the new guy."

"The new guy?"

"Yeah. They were having some...private conversation."

Quinn blinked in surprise. No, Kira was into Powell, not– "What did they say?"

He shrugged. "Like I said, private. They were really close."

"Oh."

"Yeah." He picked up his laptop bag. "Whatever. Guess it's better to find out before I tried and looked stupid. Or maybe I waited too long–I don't know. Doesn't matter. I'll see you later. Have a good night."

"Yeah. You, too. Good night."

Quinn's jaw jutted. Her fantastical romance with Tyler shattered. She stewed in her cubicle as her coworkers left. The lights dimmed around her. How could he? How could she? What was her deal anyway? Quinn snatched her purse and stormed toward Kira's office.

* * *

Quinn leaned in the doorway. "Hey, want to grab a drink?"

"Uh, no, thanks." Eve shook her head. "Need to finish up here."

She meandered in. "Anything I can help with?"

"No, just some stuff for Larry."

"I can keep you company." Quinn shrugged.

"It's all right. You don't have to–"

"I want to."

Eve smiled. "I know you want to get out of here."

"It's no big deal." Quinn dropped into a chair.

"Quinn, you can't be here," Eve bluffed. "It's...payroll stuff."

She nodded, seeming irritated. "Payroll stuff?"

"Yeah."

She stood. "Okay."

"Look, I–"

"I thought we were friends. But lately, it's like something's going on and you don't want to tell me. Is that what you do? Pretend to like somebody until something better comes along?"

"What are you talking about?"

"Powell. He walked in on you and Tyler. You know, he really liked you, and you led him on."

Eve's mouth hung open, wondering how much Powell had heard. She'd jeopardized her alibi. There was no secret Larry-project. Damage control.

"All right, Tyler's a little flirty, and I mean–you saw him–"

"Oh, I saw him."

A lump formed in Eve's throat. Coral and tangerine. She needed an out.

"Okay." Eve nodded. "That's what this is about. You're calling dibs. Oh my god—you think I'm too old for him."

"I did not say th—"

"That's what you're thinking. Or I'm not—someone like me couldn't possibly be with someone like him? Is that it?"

"Are you being serious right now?"

"He's yours, all right?" Eve put up her hands. "I'm not even in a place right now for it anyway. I have work to do."

"Will you—"

"I don't have time for this shit, okay? I'm done. I have nothing else to say to you."

Laurel green. Silver, coral, Persian orange. She felt awful. But she had to meet Tyler alone. No one could know. And this way, saying goodbye to Quinn wouldn't be as hard.

Quinn's brow wrinkled, her mouth sagging.

Eve stared on the monitor as Quinn backed out of the office. She counted the seconds, hoping they didn't cross paths.

* * *

Quinn charged into the parking lot. She dug into her purse, fumbling for her keys. Her fingers brushed the burner phone. She wanted to throw it against the wall. Her stomach churned. She'd done it. She'd dredged up painful memories in her friend and let some guy they barely knew come between them—

"Fuck that."

Kira wouldn't do that. Then why did—

She was just trying to get rid of her. Because she was expecting Tyler. But why?

Quinn swung around, steaming toward the building.

* * *

Meanwhile, Tyler rapped his knuckles on the door jamb. Eve lifted her eyes with a pleasant startle.

"Still need a hand?" He glided in.

Eve rose from her chair. "Remember what I said?"

He raised an eyebrow. "It's a secret."

A smile curled the edge of her lip. "Close the door."

He turned around. Eve slid the *modifikator* from her jacket. This one last time, and she'd have enough leverage.

Tyler glanced over his shoulder. She hit the dial button.

His eyes squeezed shut with the flash. "What—what was that?"

Eve dashed from around her desk as he spun on his heel, rubbing his eyes. He was level with her knee and then below it. She bent down and scooped him up. Admiring her quarry, she lifted him to her face.

"Kira?"

Eve's eyes widened at Quinn's voice. Like a reflex, she hit the dial button.

30

(blue green, black)

Armando and Zilya pushed the boat into the pond as dusk fell over the terrace. They climbed in and paddled with oars fashioned from the coffee table. Cichlids churned below, bumping the bottom of the catamaran. The fish grew more inquisitive. A hefty thump lifted the portside. They steadied the vessel, then lifted their oars. They rocked with the waves, waiting for the fish to lose interest. The ripples leveled off. They dipped their paddles back in and a fish nipped off the end off Armando's oar.

"Take mine." Zilya handed over hers.

She pulled up a spear and made her way to the bow.

"What're you doing?" he asked.

"Giving them what they want."

She braced a foot on the bow, reared back the lance, and plunged it into the surface again and again. The water frothed as the spear whipped back and forth. She'd lodged it in the creature's eye. The catamaran faltered, and Zilya dropped to her knees. Armando flattened against the stern. The splashes lessened.

The fish swarmed deeper to eviscerate the injured one.

Zilya picked up a spare paddle from the deck, and Armando righted himself. They resumed paddling with slower, more deliberate strokes. Twilight dimmed the world, turning the cerulean waves black. The eerie slosh licking the sides of the boat toyed with their senses. An icy breeze. Another thump. This time from the edge of the pond. No place to anchor, only smooth stone tile.

Zilya leaped onto the terrace. Armando tossed her a cable secured to a crossbeam. She pulled the other end while Armando tossed over their packs of supplies and weapons.

The boat fumbled, knocking Armando down.

A vicious splash broke the water—they'd been found.

Zilya released the cable and snatched another spear. She thrust the tip into the ripples, striking the creature's head with a crunch. It thrashed about, then relented.

She helped Armando onto shore. They heaved the craft from the water and dragged it for a half hour. Then they concealed it in the undergrowth. They hoisted their packs and weapons, starting out into the vast, dark expanse. A boxy wicker patio table towered in the distance, back lit by the apartment. There they would camp for the night.

* * *

Rapid rumbles alerted the housemates their captor had returned.

"This is it! This is it!" Kevin flung open the garage's roll-up door.

Troy and Velez rushed in front of Shadi and Kevin as they wheeled out the car-sized crossbow.

"You can't do this," said Velez.

"Get out of the way." Janelle marched toward her with a lit tiki torch.

Velez stood aside. Shadi and Kevin tilted the contraption's firing end upward and locked it into position.

"Look, we are not unified here," said Troy. "And this affects all of us. You can't do this."

"You want to go home or what?" Kevin turned a crank, winding up the winch against ratchets and pawls.

"Yeah," said Troy. "And I want to be alive to enjoy it."

"Then it's us or her." Shadi pinned the taut cable with a claw, setting the trigger.

Kevin and Zach hoisted a sealed, plastic tub into the rail.

Velez slapped a hand onto the tub. "Shooting a fireball into her face is not a good idea!"

Eve rushed into the guest room and set something onto the table's edge.

She yanked off the lid. "All right, guys, I know this is kind of crazy and I don't have time to explain but this guy's a Russian spy and you shouldn't—Wait a second—"

The jostle tripped the lever. The ballista's payload shot from the rail, sailing toward Eve.

"Selene!" Eugene waved his arms from atop the water tower. "Watch out!"

The plastic tub struck Eve's chest and burst, the pungent liquid splattering across her top.

"What are you doing!?" She checked her stained clothing. "Oh my god—you're like the worst pets ever!"

She snatched the crossbow, crushing it to pieces, and flung it into the wall.

The housemates ran into the garage, desperate to escape her wrath.

"I don't have time for this." Eve slammed the lid onto the box and stormed out.

The impact sent the housemates to their knees and Eugene off the tower. He screamed as he fell. He struck the ground and bounced. The others ran to his motionless body.

"Eugene?" asked Troy.

He sat up in disbelief. "I'm alive."

"We're lighter." Shadi nodded. "Gravity doesn't have the same effect."

"Wait," said Janelle. "She say something about a spy?"

* * *

Under the cover of the wicker table, Zilya had started a campfire. A long, rolling rumble shook them. They hurried to the edge of the table leg as Eve sprinted to the island.

"The hell is she doing?" asked Armando.

Eve leaned across the pond and then dashed away. The quaking ended with a final thunderous clunk as the door shut. They stared out into the dark, wondering who she'd condemned to the island.

"Whoever that is," said Armando, "they ratted us out without even knowing it."

Zilya shook her head. "We must be ready to run for the door before she wakes."

* * *

Tyler's shoes turned up the sand as he got his bearings. The darkened bungalow seemed uninviting. The sand appeared swept, like someone had covered their tracks. He searched the night. Across the water, a small orange ember under a boxy wicker table. Other captives had escaped.

"Hey!" He waved his arms. "Hey!"

Too far to hear him.

He trotted to the shore, gauging the distance. He pulled off his shoes, tied the laces together, and swung them under his armpit. Tyler jumped into the cold water and swam, motivated by the promise of warming himself by a fire. A hefty current passed in front him. Another below. His foot hit a large, smooth surface. Visceral fear gripped his ribs.

He turned back to the shore. The suction of furious mouths dragged him down, drowning his screams.

* * *

Flurries of color cluttered up Eve's vision as she dragged fingers through her hair. "Okay—it-it's not—so bad. I mean—I don't have to say goodbye to her now..."

Silver linings are not your thing.

"Oh god." Eve bolted into her bedroom and changed into a T-shirt and jeans. She couldn't give Quinn a terrible impression.

"Comfy, homey, relaxed," she whispered. "It's not so bad. It's a great place to be."

She slipped on a pair of canvas shoes, wringing her hands. "Everything's fine. You're fine. It's okay."

A long breath trembled out, her eyes filling with the reality she was about to face Quinn.

Can you trust her?

Angst, doubt, and fear seeped through her like an oil slick—charcoal and dingy rust, chartreuse splotches and mauve stripes.

She couldn't let Quinn think she was a monster. But her plans weren't finished. She couldn't risk letting her go. She unzipped the pocket in her purse and scooped out Quinn.

She looked distraught as Eve set her down.

Eve mustered an airy smile. "Heeeey..."

"Kira?" Quinn shook. "What—what is this? Where's Tyler?"

"He's fine. He's—in a tiny house. With...some other people."

Quinn hugged herself. "What? What other people? You mean—you do this all the time?"

"Well, not all the time." Eve cringed. "But probably a lot more than I should?"

"Wh-Where are we?"

"Well, this is where I actually live, and—" Eve cleared her throat. "All right, try not to freak out."

"I'm already freaking out!"

Eve muttered. "Okay, well—"

She slid off the glasses and put them aside. Eve bowed her head and dug her fingers into her hair to unfasten the clasps, then pried off the wig. She slipped off a hair tie, freeing her chaotic black mop.

* * *

Quinn stared up, breathless. Everything Agent Dempsey said about Kira being in trouble took on a horrifying, new meaning.

"I thought it was a dye job!"

"I know. It's a really great wig."

"Oh my god, oh my god."

"My real name's Eve. But I'm still your friend—that's not different."

Was it? Who was this person? Why had she brought her here?

"Are you?" asked Quinn. "You were pretty mad when I left—"

"I know, I'm sorry. I was just trying to get rid of you."

"Please change me back. Please."

"Yeah, I—I can't do that."

Can't? Or won't?

"But—"

"Yeah, see—nobody knows about this place, or this." Eve held up the device.

Quinn frowned. "I—I thought we were friends..." She needed to yank serious heartstrings.

"Please don't cry—you're my best friend, and I love you, but I kind of have this other thing going on—"

"With..." Quinn pointed at the device. "With that?"

"Yeah." Eve struggled. "I—I didn't know what to do, because—it's really complicated and I'm not supposed to have it, but—I saw myself as this gigantic savior of the planet, and now I think I can do so much more. Well, okay—not sure I want to be gigantic or not yet..."

What in god's name was she talking about?

"What?"

"I know, there's pros and cons to it." Eve shrugged, and then gasped a relieved smile. "Oh my god—you have no idea how good it feels to finally tell somebody all this."

Quinn didn't know what to believe. She pieced it together as best she could. "So, you're a super-villain?"

"No." Eve recoiled. "I'm saving the planet. And I don't have an archenemy—well, not since that Russian guy."

"But, you're keeping a bunch of tiny people—"

"Yeah, that situation got way out of hand." She nodded. "It's actually kind of a funny story..."

"I won't tell anybody, I promise. You can do whatever you want—just please put me back."

"I will. I promise. But not yet."

"But I'm your best friend."

"You are, and—now we'll be more like roommates."

She couldn't be serious.

Quinn trembled. "But I don't want to live in a tiny house. I want to go home!"

"No, no—you'll go home. Eventually. And you're not living with those assholes. You'll have your own place. Maybe I can clear off a shelf, or—"

"A shelf?" Quinn whimpered.

"No, uh—you know what? I have the perfect spot." She laid her palm up on the table.

Quinn gazed at it and then Eve, alarmed she expected her to hop into her hand.

"It's okay." Eve nodded. "Go ahead."

"You promise? You're not feeding me to your cat, right?"

A pained expression flashed across Eve's face. "No. I don't have a cat. And I'd never do that. Or feed you to any other animal."

Quinn poked the tip of her shoe into Eve's hand, testing the squishy flesh. She bent forward and clambered into the middle of her palm. It was uncomfortably warm and damp.

"I'm going to lift you, okay? Real slow, all right?"

The world shifted around Quinn. She planted her hands onto Eve's skin, desperate for stability.

"It's all right, see? I'm going to start walking, okay?"

Each step sent a tremor through Quinn until Eve knelt. She opened the door to the crawl space with two fingers, the device cradled in her other palm. Eve lowered her hand to the floor.

Quinn climbed off.

Eve crouched. "I totally forgot this was here. I never use it."

"This is where you want me to live?" Quinn wandered in, a little recessed light like a dull yellow sun overhead.

"Well, yeah. I'll get a house and put it in here. And whatever you want. Furniture, decorations, anything. Oh—and I'll build a little walkway so you can go into the living area. But this will be like your own room. I'm going to take such good care of you. And this isn't forever, I promise."

It was Kira's voice. The same sincerity. Quinn twisted slow, right to left, examining the space. She got the sinking feeling she'd never leave.

"Don't take this the wrong way." She faced Eve. "But I want to go home."

"I know, but...look how much space you have." Eve balanced an elbow on the floor as she leaned through the doorway.

Quinn backed away, apprehensive.

Eve set the device down and edged further inside.

Adrenaline shot into Quinn's brain. While Eve was fidgeting, she sprinted and leaped onto the dial button.

The blast struck Eve, enlarging her, to Quinn's dismay.

Eve filled the doorway. She angled around, smiling as she reached for the device. "All right, I'm going to let that slide."

Quinn hopped up and down on the dial button at a frenetic pace. "You want to be gigantic!?"

"No—Quinn!"

"Dance Party Apocalypse, bitch!"

* * *

Jolt after jolt struck her, the staccato effect of the fields rippling through her. "That's not how it's supposed to work!"

Eve's mind raced as she tried to predict the compounding effect of the fields. A flash of terror as she considered her molecules stretching and snapping apart. Already too large for the crawlspace, she wrenched her shoulders free and tore apart the door jamb. She landed on her backside as her body convulsed with the overlapping fields.

She needed a stylus in order to reduce herself with the *modifikator*. Eve spotted a decorative arrangement of reeds in a vase and stood. Her head shot through the ceiling and burst apart the roof. Her body stretched up and out. She backpedaled, losing her footing. Her butt crashed down and took out the west end of the building.

* * *

Zilya and Armando crouched by the hearth, cooking a pot of canned stew. Troubled by the shouts and thundering from inside, they readied their weapons.

She stalked to the edge, peering into the apartment. Shadows danced on the wall. Was someone attacking Eve?

Then, an eruption. More shadows. Something dark filled the room.

"Run!" Zilya turned around.

Armando turned on his heel. A broken beam crashed against the tile. They both stopped cold, then backed away from the edges. Chunks of roofing rained onto the terrace.

From their hiding spot, they watched another beam smash the patio chairs. The wicker table overhead crunched. Before they could react, the table collapsed under the weight of the beams, crushing the two of them into goo.

Debris splashed into the pond, leaving the bungalow untouched.

* * *

The tremors sent the housemates huddling in the interior doorways. The quakes grew more volatile. Then they heard the crash. And another. And another.

"Everybody in here!" Zach held open the garage door.

"No!" said Shadi. "The basement!"

"There isn't enough room!" He ducked into the garage.

The others ran from the doorways toward Shadi. The penthouse roof crashed into the enclosure's lid, cracking it into uneven sections. One part smashed through the garage. The other portion plowed through the kitchen and hall. Shadi lost her balance and stumbled down the stairs. The last thing she heard was Janelle's scream as the roof fell in.

* * *

The night sky filled Eve's vision. She floated up and then backward.

She was falling, while hunks of concrete and glass rained around her.

Time slowed as she reflected.

This was it.

She was dead.

You deserve it, you stupid bitch! You worthless, careless asshole.

Her expanding back slammed into something. That was right—she was outside. And across the street was...a department store. It crumbled under her like a gritty sandcastle. She braced herself as the walls collapsed over her.

The worst possible scenarios she'd contemplated had involved someone taking the *modifikator* and shrinking her. She hadn't considered being hundreds of feet tall, with no way to use to the *modifikator*—that is, if Quinn hadn't broken it. Or it hadn't been crushed to pieces, along with Quinn.

She ran through probabilities. Quinn should be too light to damage it. Whether or not she and the *modifikator* had survived was another matter.

Eve needed another stylus, something big and long enough and tapered to a fine point so she could reduce herself before the city's police department deployed its paramilitary arsenal. But to do that, she'd still have to dig through the wreckage and not destroy the *modifikator*.

How is that a good plan? It's like King Kong trying to thread a needle.

Why this? Why now? Everything had been coming together.

It's you. Everything you touch turns into shit.

She grunted and shoved off the debris like beach sand. She sat up, rubble flooding the street.

The street below was murky. Filled with dust and smoke and the spray of busted hydrants. She could make out tiny people running away on the edges of the blocks.

Eve twisted her arm, planting a hand onto the asphalt with a booming thump.

She swept her foot under her, and set it down. Thunder echoed with screeching and crinkles as a row of parked cars were flattened. Hunched over, she caught a glimpse of her faint reflection in an office building. The din of the city was replaced by the hum. She cracked a smile. Indigo, viridian, maroon. If this was a mere five or six hundred feet—

She had to get to the suit. Eve pivoted to the penthouse, her hip smashing an adjacent building, showering the street with broken glass.

* * *

Quinn sat up, gasping, surrounded by crumbled drywall. She'd wanted to escape, not kill her. Another violent tremor. The whole building might come down.

She needed to get back to normal, fast. She ran to a chunk of drywall the size of a basketball and picked it up. Too light. She dropped it and ran to a larger one, as big as she was—too heavy. Then she found a length of splintered wood. She raised one end and dragged it.

Once close enough, she positioned the stick alongside the device. With all her might, she hoisted the end and propped it onto the dial button. She dashed to the other end, lining up in front of the antenna. Quinn squatted and jumped, lifting the stick. The button pressed, blasting her shin. She enlarged, falling onto her butt. Several inches taller now, she poked the button for another zap.

She picked up the device and climbed out of the crawlspace into the wreckage. The only sign of Eve was the city's skyline where the walls and ceiling had been. Dots of lights spread for miles in the night.

Quinn examined the device. A setting between the pluses and minuses read *00*. She dialed the knob and restored herself to normal.

She stepped toward the ragged opening. "Shit."

The building shook with an intense quake. The tremors rattled on and on. Quinn struggled to stand, grabbing the couch's armrest, awestruck as the top of Eve's head continued to rise before her. "Oh, fuck."

Dusted with concrete, Eve's tense expression softened as they made eye contact.

Not wanting to find out why Eve had pondered being gigantic, Quinn turned the dial and hit the button, again and again.

Eve goggled as the fields yanked her downward. She reached up, her contracting hands managed to grip a hanging slab of concrete. The bent girders sagged.

Quinn fled to more stable flooring as the steel whined and warped. The ledge sloughed off like ice from a glacier.

Eve clawed for whatever she could—"Quinn!"—then disappeared over the side.

Quinn edged toward the chasm, peering over. "Kira!? I mean—Eve?"

No answer. Then the distant crunch of concrete hitting the pavement below.

"Shit." Quinn searched the cloudy darkness. "Oh god, what did I do?"

Giant fingers clamped around Quinn's wrist from behind. Her stomach clenched. Eve had faked her out and scaled the side of the building. The ten-foot woman raised her into the air.

"I'll take that." Eve plucked the device from her fingers.

"No!"

"You have no idea what you've done." She lowered Quinn. "I was so close!"

Close to what?

Quinn turned to run and the world widened. She slowed as she shrank, unwilling to hide in the ruins. Now Eve was pissed—no telling what she'd do. Quinn felt her resolve slip. She wanted to cry. She caught her breath, more determined than ever to escape.

* * *

Eve tuned the dial and set the *modifikator* on the counter. She pressed the button and returned to six feet. With a swift lunge, she scooped up the five-inch-tall woman.

"Put me down!" Quinn pummeled her fists against Eve's fingers. "Put me down!"

Eve reached into a busted kitchen cupboard and pulled out an extra large mixing bowl, slipping Quinn inside. "For god's sake, don't move."

There was no hiding now that her face had been the size of a billboard. The Russian spies were her best shot at a plea deal. If they were alive. She grabbed the *modifikator* and dragged open the cracked sliding glass door. The wreckage of beams and roofing was piled onto the terrace. With a couple blasts, her path was cleared. Eve tread around the remaining chunks to the pond. No lights. No curious little people.

"Tyler?" She leaned across the pond. "Zilya?"

She peered into a window, the faint glow of the penthouse's remaining light behind her.

Ransacked. Furniture missing. They'd torn up the walls.

"No..."

Eve stooped to her haunches, sweeping her head for any sign of them. They would've needed a boat.

Under a thick patch of salvia, she found a thin wooden hull. She pushed aside the leaves, revealing a little catamaran.

Eve spun around. The deck furniture was gone, piled under the broken beams and sheeting, and shrunk. Any chance of bargaining with the government wiped away with it.

* * *

The rapid bounds of Eve's rush into the guest room startled Quinn. She climbed the bowl and slid back. The sides were too smooth and steep. She ran back, building momentum, attempting to overcome the curvature.

Even if she could get out, what then? What could she do? Where could she go?

She couldn't stay hopeless.

Quinn had to get her hands on the device again. And to do that, she'd need Eve to trust her.

* * *

Eve reduced the collapsed roof blocking her path. The table was broken, the front of the enclosure smashed apart. Before she could move, the rest of the ceiling caved in, burying the box.

"No!"

She dropped to her knees, digging into the debris. "Guys!? I'm going to get you out of here!"

Something wet her fingertips.

Blood.

She pawed through the scraps, slowing as she reached shards of plexiglass mixed with the splintered wood.

"Fuck!" Tears streamed down her face as she pulled her fingers through her hair. "Fuck!"

No time to search for tiny body parts. No time to identify remains.

No time for proper burials. She reared back, sobered by the untold casualties across the street.

They're all coming after you. The FBI, the cops, the military. And they're going to take away the fragment—they're going to take everything away. No one will listen to you now. No one will help you. No one cares about you because you're defective, and you just showed the world what a monstrous fuck-up you really are.

The hum returned in a faint pulse.

Plan F wasn't a last-ditch option anymore. It was the only option. But the tunnels, if she uprooted them, were they stable enough to—

"Levitate the base," she whispered.

Dialed to the right level, the soldiers, their guns—everything—would float in mid-air. A castle in the sky. Once she nabbed the fragments and the Mobius, she could gently lower the base back in the ground and disappear.

She ran to the office.

* * *

Eugene had taken cover under the dining room table, which had been buried under the ceiling. When he'd heard Eve's voice, he'd hesitated. Whatever had happened, whatever she'd done, he hadn't wanted to know. His life had flashed before his eyes twice in ten minutes. And she'd been the reason, both times. He'd heard her sob and felt vindicated. She should feel awful.

He pushed his way through the wreckage and crawled out. He could hear Janelle shouting and used a two-by-four to pry debris aside. She'd hidden in the hall closet. They could hear muffled voices, unsure where they were coming from. Pounding from under the floor. Shadi, in the basement.

With the two-by-four, Eugene thrust apart the splintered wood and shattered drywall. Janelle used a smaller pole to the same but slowed, then stopped. Eugene glanced up. Blood and guts were splattered against the remaining edge of the wall to the garage.

Zach. No part of him was recognizable.

"Oh...fuck." Eugene swallowed, then forced aside the last chunk.

Shadi flung open the door. Eugene reached out a hand.

"Hey!" Velez crawled from under a heap. "Hey!"

"Over here!" Janelle turned around.

The detective hobbled toward Janelle. She and Eugene helped her up, all of them bruised and scraped.

"Help! I need help!"

They searched the vicinity, spotting Kevin struggling to his feet.

"Troy?!"

Kevin rushed to a pile of broken lumber and chunks of plexiglass. Using a split beam, he pushed aside pieces until he found Troy laying on his back.

"My leg." Troy wheezed. "I think it's broken."

Kevin choked. "It's not broken."

The others rushed to his aid, dumbstruck by the deep slice.

"We need to tie that off," said Velez.

Shadi nodded. "I'll see if there's any cable from the crossbow."

Eugene and Shadi ran off.

Kevin knelt alongside Troy. "I'm sorry—"

"You didn't do this."

"I should've listened to you. I'm sorry."

"You just wanted to see your kids again."

"We're going to get you out of here, all right?"

"Yeah." Troy winced in pain. "Where's everybody else?"

Kevin shook his head. "Don't know if they made it."

* * *

Quinn was perched on the rim of the bowl, judging the drop, when Eve's wail startled her. She tensed as Eve reappeared and wiped her eyes before darting into another room. Quinn had considered the other people Eve mentioned as prisoners. But they were something else to her. Other friends?

* * *

Eve grabbed the laptop and opened a safe hidden in the desk. Inside packs of thousands of dollars, another fake ID, and several flash drives. All of it was shoved into a bug-out bag along with her notes and the suit, miniaturized in its case. She slung the pack over her shoulder and shrank the server tower. The cables snapped away. The tower toppled. She stomped it.

Eve shot into the kitchen wearing a black jacket, Diane's wig, and holding an acrylic tumbler.

"Sorry, but this is the safest way for you to get around."

Quinn scowled. "Wouldn't normal-sized be the safest way?"

Eve grumbled. "Don't make this any harder than it has to be."

"Yeah." She dropped into the bowl. "Because it turned out so great for everybody else."

Blue gray and mauve, then crimson. Eve fumed, reaching for her.

"No!" Quinn swatted at her fingers. "Stop!"

With a flick of her wrist, Eve tripped Quinn into her palm. She tilted the tumbler and slid her in, then secured the top. She left the mouthpiece tab open.

Quinn pressed her hands against the sides as Eve slipped the tumbler into the bug-out bag.

Eve spied her shoulder bag under the breakfast bar and zapped it, sticking the tiny purse into her pocket. She sighed, taking a last look at her once-wonderful penthouse. Then she crept through the torn walls and made a careful free climb into the floor below, descending into the exposed stairwell.

The murmur of other residents echoed below. By the time she reached street level, they'd crowded outside. Eve pulled the collar of her T-shirt over her nose as they did and pushed through the horde.

She trekked past onlookers gathering on the corners.

A man flagged her down. "What happened?"

"Don't know." She shook her head. "But I'm getting the hell out of here."

The dust thinned out blocks later. With sirens ringing across the city, Eve ran through side streets. She popped out her escape car once she'd reached an empty spot in an alley and restored it to normal.

The black Camaro revved, bounding onto the street and sped onto the freeway, headed north.

31

(blue green, silver)

Simon had discovered an unexpected property of the fragment. It appeared to project energy into different states, even matter. Fascinated, he tested the substance.

The litmus paper turned pink, confirming his suspicion it was coffee. After a quick mopping, he placed a bucket in the chamber and mounted a camera to record his next test. He switched on the coil, and dialed up the beam's intensity. The holographic projection formed. No liquid, but a cascade of colors. Red, blue green, purple, green, silver, orange, gold, red, blue, purple. No pattern emerged as they swirled and blurred.

What was happening inside the shard? And how could he observe it?

He turned up the beam's intensity. The holographic grid faded, but the aura came into greater focus. The colors returned and melded, coalescing into distinct shapes.

Another room appeared in the portal, the clarity sharpening. He could see several computer mainframes in protective casings with cooling systems.

His eyebrow rose as two soldiers entered. Where was this room? Was it real? Or had he created it?

Two people approached them wearing security badges. Scientists. The soldiers escorted them through the heavy door.

A military project? What was the connection?

Simon smiled. He switched off the beam, then the coil. "Jareima..."

"Yes, my lord."

"Dictation."

"Ready."

Simon stared into the chamber. "Ionizing radiation coupled with the discharge from the coil projects a field from the fragment...unlike anything we're aware of. As the level of ionization increases, the projection stabilizes."

His eyebrows lowered into place. "I suspect the projection may be the vantage point of other fragments. Possibly through quantum entanglement. If so, by determining the frequency, one might be able to communicate with or even control—Jareima, delete that last sentence."

"Deleted."

"Play back the last three seconds."

His voice answered: "Vantage point of other fragments. Possibly through quantum entanglement."

Communicate with and control the fragments. Maybe control their reaction to energy. What other effects could they produce? This one seemed like a wormhole. And if stable enough, it meant instantaneous travel, anywhere.

"Resume dictation."

"Ready."

"Maybe I should have exposed the fragment to ionizing radiation first, in the form of beta waves, then introduced an electric charge. Using lower voltage. That will have to be my next battery of tests. For now, I'll finish with this configuration and increase the beam to the X-ray level. End dictation."

He switched on the coil. The hum returned. He grinned.

Love that sound.

***

"We've got him on infrared," the technician said to Callahan. "Looks like he's in the basement."

Simon's story had checked out. He'd taken up residence at his winter home. With the assistance of local FBI, Callahan had organized a raid in a few hours' time. McCrae had insisted upon military support, and a National Guard brigade secured the perimeter around Simon's property.

"What's up with these guys and basement labs?" asked Masuda.

Callahan shrugged. "You can ask him yourself in twenty seconds."

***

Meanwhile, the beam intensified. Black waves radiated around the projection of the empty lab and shifted into a different, yet similar room. A familiar figure appeared.

Simon's smile sank, mouth hanging, as he watched himself—though not himself—working on a machine. This Simon wore a lab coat, goggles, his hair in need of styling.

He strained to decipher what his alternate self assembled. Some handheld device. Like a medallion.

"You have visitors, my lord."

"Tell them I'm busy."

* * *

A battering ram bashed through the front doors. Agents flooded in.

"Anything and everything is evidence," said Callahan. "Computers, laptops, documents—all of it needs to come back with us."

She flung open the basement door, bringing a walkie-talkie her lips. "Cut the power."

* * *

The blare of the alarm broke Simon's concentration.

Was it the projection or his own reality?

A heavy pop answered his question. Power in the lab remained, running on separate units. But the unfortunate chain of events about to unfold flashed through his brain. The coil and beam were wired to different power sources. If they cut the coil's power first, the beam would strike the shard at X-ray-level intensity without a buffer.

He ran to the door. "Jareima! Terminate! Terminate!"

The lab went dark. Simon yanked open the door—Callahan. Her face was illuminated by the brilliant beam behind him. The boom squeezed his ear drums. Stinging pressure needled through every inch of skin. He flew forward, thrust into her. The two of them were hurled into the stairs.

* * *

Callahan had rushed to the basement without backup. Masuda hurried after when a shock wave swept through the house. She lost her balance and tumbled down several steps. She braced herself and stopped her fall, clenching her teeth. The bone jutted out of her shin. Heat radiated from the wall. At the bottom of the stairs, Callahan and Pierce were crumpled on top of each other, motionless.

"Kelly!?"

She could hear the building shift and creak. The basement crumbled. Concrete dust billowed. Agents above her screamed, the voices moving away, falling into the hot sinkhole. The building shook. She could hear snaps and loud cracks. The house was losing structural integrity. Masuda covered her head, tightening into a ball. The second story buckled. The crash above seemed unending as the building imploded and she was buried inside.

* * *

Dempsey and a small team of agents made a precarious offload by helicopter into the penthouse ruins. They split up, searching for signs of their suspect.

Agent Tabares shone a flashlight into the guest room, examining the destruction. She stepped in, and swept the light across the floor. Broken plexiglass. And what looked like the shattered remains of a model house. Blood streaks glistened.

She crouched for a closer look.

Faint voices. Whispers.

"Someone's here."

"What if it's her?"

"Who cares?"

"Hey!"

"No—stop!"

"Careful! We're down here!"

Tabares brushed aside debris, expecting to find a radio or cellphone. She stumbled backward, stunned to discover tiny people huddled in a clearing.

"Oh my god!" Janelle cried. "Oh my god, we're saved!"

Tabares regained her senses. "Agent Dempsey!?"

Dempsey strode in. Tabares kept the light on the housemates.

He didn't seem as shocked. Dempsey kneeled.

"You have to change us back," said Velez. "We have people in need of medical attention."

"Yeah," said Dempsey. "We...don't have that capability."

"What happened to the shrink ray?" asked Kevin.

He shook his head. "It's probably still with her."

"What?!" Shadi stormed forward.

"Everything's going to be okay," said Dempsey.

"No!" said Shadi. "We can't eat regular food! We don't have enough water! We're going to die like this!"

Velez lay a hand on her shoulder. "It's all right. They're going to find her—"

"The water tower's gone!" Shadi smacked her hand away. "Whatever's not contaminated in the basement is all we have!"

"We're going to find her," said Dempsey. "We know her aliases. She can't get far."

"Agent Dempsey?" Hamilton leaned through the doorway.

* * *

The wind whipped as Agent Hamilton led Dempsey toward a fissure allowing passage into the floor below. They climbed down the crinkled ramp. The interior was wall obliterated, opening into the apartment under the penthouse. A strange diorama-map filled the living space.

Dempsey squatted nearby it. "You got pictures?"

"A few."

"Take more."

"See the footprints?"

His followed the path in the sand. "Yeah. Let's get a cast."

"Where is that?"

Dempsey's eyes floated to a cluster of white plastic buildings. He stood. "Let's figure out how to get this thing out of here."

He climbed through the hole, lingering in the hallway and checked his phone. No word from Callahan. But someone else had called. He hit redial.

"Agent?"

"General?"

"Glad you called, son." McCrae sighed. "FBI raided Pierce's property. There was an explosion, and several agents are in critical condition."

"What about Callahan and Mel—Masuda?"

"We're still looking."

His words shook at first. "Yeah, uh—I don't know if you've heard the news, but Kincaid went Godzilla on us. Tore up the middle of downtown, disappeared. There's no way to keep a lid on this, sir. Every news outlet in the world has her picture."

"Ah, Jesus..."

"And it looks like she may target the base."

"The base?"

"That or some other unmarked buildings in the desert. They've got roadblocks set up for miles, but you need to be on high alert."

* * *

In the twenty minutes it took authorities to set up roadblocks, Eve had reached Descanso Gardens and banked onto the Crest Highway. She plodded the winding curves and crept up the peaks. Her turn onto the Forest Highway felt more treacherous. The headlights only revealed rock walls on one side of the thin road and a drop into darkness on the other.

Thirty miles later, her grip on the wheel relaxed. They'd reached the desert. She pulled onto the shoulder, reaching for the tumbler.

"Um, cover your ears," she said. "Or wait—don't cover your ears."

"Why?" Quinn asked.

"Because the change in air pressure might blow your ear drums."

"What?!"

"Or not. I—I don't know."

"How do you not know!? I mean, how am I even like this!?"

"Well, the *pilbs* are responding to the blips, and the blips are producing the effect they told the *pilbs* to make."

Quinn stared back, dismayed. "Oh my god—you're insane!"

"No, I'm not. Just because you don't understand it doesn't mean I'm crazy." Her fingers dug into the lid's seam. "If I'm right, information is the fundamental element of the universe. Except unlike mass and energy, it's being created and stored all the time as everything increases in complexity. Which means the universe is a massive...computational system. And why it exists, for what reason, I want to know."

"No! Stop—"

The lid slipped off. Quinn paused. She seemed surprised she was fine.

Eve shifted into gear and rolled onto the road.

Quinn propped herself on the tumbler's lip. "So where are we going? Your secret lair?"

"We aren't going anywhere," said Eve. "I need to figure out where to drop you off."

"So you can go to your secret lair!?"

"It's not a secret lair. It's just an underground bunker I was going to use as my base of operations while I—" She considered her next words. "All right, it's my secret lair."

"I knew it!"

She sees you for who you really are.

"No." Eve shook her head. "Okay. I didn't want to brag about it, but I busted up the art gallery."

"You're proud of being a terrorist?"

"It was a money-laundering operation, and—"

"And you know what? I don't think I ever heard Kira say anything about the environment."

"I drove a hybrid," said Eve. "And I didn't want to blow my cover."

"Nobody knew who you were. How would you blow your cover?"

See? Everything you do is wrong.

"I—I don't know. Leave me alone. I need to think."

"Everyone knows what you look like now," said Quinn. "You should just turn yourself in."

Eve clenched the wheel. "Shut up, or you're going back in the bag."

She jammed on the accelerator. The abrupt boost knocked Quinn into the tumbler.

Quinn stood but didn't attempt another climb. She folded her arms, keeping a watchful eye on Eve.

"Goddammit," Eve muttered.

You're the dumb ass who shrank her. You're the idiot who put the modifikator down.

"Leave me alone," she mumbled. "I need a plan."

What's the point? All your plans turn to shit.

Self-conscious, she glanced at the tumbler. Quinn had heard the whispers. Stupid. Dumb. Idiot.

Eve withdrew deeper into herself, into silence.

She hates you. Everyone does. No one will ever forgive you.

Eugene, Kevin, Shadi—all of them. She'd been trying to keep them safe. Yes, they'd pissed her off, but she couldn't blame them. Then there was the department store. How many employees had still been closing up shop? Security guards? Janitorial staff? An accident? No one would believe that had been an accident. Orange and chartreuse. Nausea bubbled into her throat. What had she done?

They were going to find the diorama. The cops wouldn't understand it, but the FBI would recognize the base's location. They might not know what her plans were, but it wouldn't matter.

Turn herself in and try to cut a deal? At best, it would be a hundred life sentences. Prosecutors would be out for blood. Opposite ends of the political spectrum would unite in their hatred of her. If they didn't give her the death penalty, people would revolt. That was if someone didn't try to kill her first. The distraught kin of one of her victims. Or the CIA would make it look that way. Erase her knowledge and any link to the project. Create whatever cover story they wanted. She'd go down in history as an unspeakable monster. A deranged lunatic who'd ravaged the city and sowed anarchy across the planet.

Vacancy flickered in the silver marquee up ahead.

Eve shook off the last of her self-degradation and returned to the waking world, exhausted. She slowed, pulling into the lot.

Quinn climbed up as Eve reached for her pack. "Where are we?"

Eve dug into the bug-out bag, discovering the Steller's jay feather she'd grabbed when she'd abandoned her apartment. Another time. Another place. She stared at the crumpled quill, the barbules frayed and faded, wondering what had become of her. She shoved it into her pocket and resumed her search.

A new wig. Longer, dark with infrequent strands of silver. She tied it into a loose ponytail and slid on a pair of blue-framed glasses.

"All right, if something goes wrong, it might get a little cramped in there."

"Oh my god—you have to stop shrinking people!"

"I don't know if I can." Eve shrugged. "I mean, it's gotten me this far."

"Yeah." Quinn gestured to herself. "Exactly."

Blue gray, laurel green. Eve winced, on the verge of tears. She snatched the tumbler lid, more stern. "Don't move."

Quinn dropped into the cup. Eve rested the lid overhead.

* * *

Copper bells jangled. The night clerk turned his attention away from the soft core porn playing on an old television mounted to the wall.

Eve glanced at the screen as the clerk sat up.

"Just the night?" he asked.

"Yeah. All I have is cash."

"That's fine. Got ID?"

She handed over her license. He checked the picture, studying her face. With a nod, he jotted down her information and handed it back.

"Car trouble?"

"Hm?"

He pointed to her clothes, smudged with dust.

"Oh. Yeah." She nodded. "Had to change a tire."

"Mechanic down the street opens at eight."

"Any place to get some food?"

"Sorry." He shrugged. "Everything around here's closed."

* * *

Quinn stepped out of the tumbler onto a long dresser. An out-of-date television rested on the other end. The motel room was sparse. Cleaner than expected. A bed with green comforter and a nightstand alongside it. A wooden table and two chairs by the window. She folded her arms, chilled.

Eve switched off the air conditioner.

"Here." She flipped on a nearby lamp.

Quinn moved toward bulb's warmth while Eve took out a laptop and sat on the edge of the bed.

"What're you doing?"

Eve didn't answer.

"Shit." She slapped the laptop closed, shoving it aside.

"Can we talk about this now?"

She stood, tossing the wig onto the nightstand. "There's nothing to talk about, Quinn."

"Are you kidding? You were supposed to be my best friend. Was anything you said real?"

Eve huffed. "All right. I'm not from Sacramento, and I didn't sell a condo." She slid off the glasses. "But I do have a sister, who's better than me in every way possible—which, really isn't that hard. And my parents did make me a moth costume."

So she had told her the truth? Or at least parts of it.

Eve sat on the end of the bed. "And I flunked my sophomore year. That's how I met Gideon."

"The One?" Quinn stepped closer.

She nodded. "He was a transfer. We ended up in the same classes, became lab partners, hit it off, and—things just happened. We moved in together. Became like this...physics department power couple. Started grad school. Everyone else said my theories were ill-conceived and childish, but he pushed me to refine them."

"Thanks, Gideon."

"That's a whole different story. Anyway, one of his friends, Dennis..." She shook her head, "Such a pig. He organized this guys-only weekend for his own birthday, which was really just an excuse to get wasted and act stupid."

Quinn smirked. "Right."

"I didn't want him to go. He knew I hated Dennis, but I didn't want to say anything because..." She sighed. "I might've been a little bit of a control freak."

"Yeah, I can't imagine." Quinn scowled.

"I was trying not to be, and everything was going so well—"

"You didn't want the fight."

"Yeah." Eve bit the side of her lip. "So, I get a call Sunday morning. His car had skidded off one of the passes in the snow, and he had to be airlifted. I pretty much lived at the hospital after that. Slept in the lobby, ate at the vending machines. Nurses told me to go home—there was no telling when he'd wake up."

It was sad, but Eve seemed distant. Like she was watching it all over again.

"And then, one night, all these doctors were running in, and they wouldn't... I don't know how long I stood there. But at three forty-three a.m., they pronounce him dead. He'd left early to get home for me. If I would've just said *I don't want you to go*, he wouldn't have gone."

Odd twist. She'd blamed herself, and carried it around for years. Sounded like she needed an understanding friend. And maybe she'd be so grateful, she'd return that friend to normal.

Quinn shook her head. "That's—no—okay, look, that wasn't your fault."

"If it were Kyle, you would've told him flat out, *Dennis is an asshole*."

"Well, okay, that sounds like me, but—"

"All Gideon ever wanted me to do was tell him what I thought. How many women would kill for a guy like that? And when it counted, I couldn't. I was so afraid of screwing everything up, and—screwed it up anyway. Because I *suck*."

Harsh emphasis on "suck." It was Kira's voice, but not her.

Quinn's brow scrunched, remembering the moth costume. Some deep-rooted issues there. Maybe Kira was who Eve wanted to be but didn't think she could be?

"Everything fell apart after that," Eve said quietly. "Everybody told me it would take time, it would get easier, but it didn't. Tried working on our thesis, but..." She sighed, her eyes watering. "I couldn't get it together. Went to therapy, got on meds. Couldn't afford the apartment by myself, and I ran out of bereavement. So I had no work to show, and the dean told me, I'd have to re-apply. But it'd been over a year, and I didn't have the money."

"Your parents wouldn't help?"

"Well, they'd already bailed me out before, and..."

"You didn't tell them."

"No. So when I got this"—she held up the device—"I thought I had a second chance. And I ran. As fast and as hard as I could because I knew I was going to fuck it up somehow."

"All right, to be fair, and without you getting mad at me"—Quinn ventured a smile—"I am the one who jumped on it."

"You were scared, and I didn't do a very good job making you feel comfortable."

Eve only seemed to find fault with herself. And although puzzling, Quinn was relieved. It meant she felt remorse and guilt. Maybe she still thought of Quinn as her friend.

Quinn, however, wasn't sure how to feel.

"I'm sorry," Eve muttered. "I didn't mean for any of this to happen, it's just what I do."

"That's not true—"

"Look where you are." She spread her hands.

"You can still change me back. And I mean, right now I think you could really use a hug."

Eve shook her head and stood. "I need sleep. And to get the blood out of my hair. I promise to let you go tomorrow. Safe and sound, back to normal."

Probably for the best. No telling how Eve would react if she felt betrayed.

Eve dug into the pack and enlarged something. She returned to the dresser and set down a small one-bedroom house under the lamp.

Quinn gazed at the house. Doubt twinged in her stomach. Was it a trap? Was she going to lock her inside? Shrink it even smaller and hold her hostage forever?

"It's a micro-house." Eve shrugged. "Well, it's a mini micro-house now. There's clean sheets, granola bars, and limited running water—just don't flush the toilet a lot."

The peace offering felt more like an apology.

"Thank you."

"Told you I'd take good care of you."

32

(blue-green, yellow)

Simon's left eye cracked open. He presumed it was five forty-five, his usual wake-up time. Pain pulsed in spots all over his body. The room was white, save for a dull gray cabinet. A hiss and a beep. He grunted, groping for the control box. The head of the bed rose with a laborious whir.

He touched his face. Fresh bandages. It stung. His vision sharpened. No windows.

The blanket rolled off his chest. Standard issue, hospital grade. Warm, but not comfortable. He'd always regarded hospital blankets somewhere between fabric and a foam material. He would have preferred something more substantial, like a woven quilt, and remembered the one he had in the linen closet.

The change began from his fingers, spreading out. The hospital blanket transformed into the same material, weave, texture, pattern and colors as the Southwestern-style quilt until he jerked his hand away.

He touched the blanket again. No change.

Again, he recalled the quilt, it's fibers and color, warmth and pattern. The blanket resumed its metamorphosis, becoming the quilt in his mind's eye down to his toes. He clutched the cover in wonder, and tossed it off. He yanked out the IV, and then planted his feet on the cold linoleum.

Simon turned to the wall mirror, startled by the bandages on the right side of his head. He pried them off, ignoring the searing pain. He had to see.

His skin had been melted. His fingers hovered above the area, but wouldn't touch it. He lamented the loss of his gorgeous, handsome face. The skin shifted, lifting on its own, and spread—same as the blanket—until it became his gorgeous, handsome face again. An awed, grateful smile broke out. Fingers ran across his right cheek, same as it ever was. The pain was gone. He checked his forearm, scarred as well, though not as severe. It, too, returned to its former health.

How was it possible?

He recalled his last conscious moments. The X-rays striking the shard. Possibly within the residual current of the coil.

He snatched a plastic fork from the meal tray resting on the nightstand and concentrated. The fork folded inward, changing in color and consistency. Its shape smoothed and luster improved until it formed the shard. But the black crystal lacked the strange luminous lattice interior.

"Of course," he muttered. "That'd be too easy."

He set down the crystal and grabbed the plastic tray, dumping the food and utensils. He considered its atoms, protons, electrons, and mass, altering it to copper, then silver, then sand. The grains poured from one hand into the other, becoming mercury, the liquid running down his arm and changing to titanium. With concentration on the desired structure, its configuration and mechanics, the metal formed into plates with pins.

A gauntlet.

He made a fist, examining his craftsmanship. A replica of the mystical armor worn by Batir the Mighty in *The Hollow Earth Chronicles*, forged from opal ore in the Talistaeryn Caves, and the only material durable enough to resist the edge of the FireLance. The metal illuminated, taking on the multicolored flecks of the mystical substance.

It couldn't be as strong as opal ore. There was no such thing. But Simon knew other metals. Maybe he could combine them now without heat or time. Nickel, aluminum, chromium, platinum and lead. Tungsten, taltanium, and molybdenum. Corundum and diamond. The gauntlet's exterior didn't change, but he felt its alteration. A super-lightweight alloy with extreme durability and heat resistance.

With his comprehension of materials and their structure, his imagination freed him from classical physics. And his knowledge wasn't limited to geology and lasers. He understood electronics and computer hardware, mechanical engineering, chemistry, biology, biochemistry, genetics, the emergent field of epigenetics—

Further experimentation was obligatory.

But he'd stolen top-secret military property. The door would be guarded. If he were to stay and hide his ability, he'd have less chance to explore its potential. His calendar would fill with court dates and jail time, under constant surveillance. Then he'd never learn the full scope of the Mobius.

Simon studied his face in the mirror and remembered the contractor sent to clean out his basement. His features shifted, forming into the young man's. The hospital gown lengthened and divided into standard-issue scrubs. An ordinary orderly.

The gauntlet thinned and dissipated, wrapping the length of his arm and melding into his skin as a tattoo of the mythical serpent Jǫrmungandr. He clutched the pillow, concentrating on his form and likeness. It shifted into a leathery vinyl, and an unflattering version of his face. Bits of splintered plastic trickled out, having once been down feathers.

Perhaps he couldn't create living things from inanimate objects. He took another pillow, joining the two, and formed a mannequin. He restored the quilt to hospital issue and pulled it over the decoy.

A nurse with a stubble beard and a hulking soldier entered before he could get to the door.

"How'd you get in here?" asked the soldier.

The orderly smiled. "Just making rounds."

"Did you disconnect his heart monitor?" asked the nurse.

"Is that what that was?" the orderly answered.

"Stay right here." The soldier clutched the orderly's shoulder while the nurse approached the bed.

"Why is there a sheet pulled over him?"

So much for talking his way out.

The soldier reached for a radio on his hip, and Simon grabbed the man's face.

"What—" The alteration seeped through the soldier's head, down his neck, transforming his body and clothes into solid iron.

The nurse pulled back the blanket, discovering the mannequin. Startled, he spun around, losing his footing, and braced against the bed. His eyes widened in horror at the soldier statue.

"Relax. Just an experiment." Simon faced him, returning to his true form. The scrubs shifted into a ruby-red tailored suit and tie.

Disoriented, the nurse struggled. "Get—Get away from me."

"Nothing to worry about." Simon's toothy grin neared. "I'm an innovator. I make people's lives better. Now let's see how I can improve upon you."

"Hel—" Simon's hand smothered the nurse's holler. The change coursed through the man's face and skull.

Simon released him.

The copy blinked. Something had happened. He didn't know what.
"Who are you?"
"I—I'm Simon Pierce." The copy stared back, puzzled. "But—can you see what I'm seeing?"
"No?" Simon leaned forward. "What's the last thing you remember?"
"Changing that—" The copy examined his own clothes. "Nurse."
"You remember the explosion?"
"Yes, but, then I woke up here."
"See if you have the same ability."
The copy gripped the bed rail, squeezing tight. It remained metal and plastic.
"So, not an exact copy."
"But still a perfect one." His doppelganger smiled.
"Can't argue with that."
Simon placed a hand on the iron statue's head. The metal receded, returning the soldier to flesh and blood. But no breath came from him. His head, neck and shoulders slackened, falling forward. The body crumpled to the floor, lifeless.
"Couldn't make a copy out of a pillow." Simon picked up the soldier's handheld radio. "But I can out of a person. Can't make a person inanimate without...de-animating them."
He concentrated on the radio. The plastic shifted into new shapes, color, and textures while the inner workings reconfigured and reorganized, becoming a Qiopa virtual assistant.
The copy smiled. "You can only alter something within the context of what it already is."
"A system." Simon grinned, tossing his copy the Qiopa unit.
He knelt alongside the dead soldier, transforming him into another copy of himself wearing a hospital gown. He changed the mannequin back into pillows. The two Simons hoisted the body into bed.
A double knock. The copy darted away, backing against the wall alongside the door. Simon transformed back into the orderly.
Another solider entered. "You okay in here?"
Simon grinned. "Fantastic."
The copy seized the soldier from behind, muffling his mouth and restraining his arms. The soldier slammed an elbow into the copy's chest, knocking the wind of him.
Simon grabbed the soldier's wrist.
Moments later, the nurse exited the room accompanied by two soldiers. They passed the nurse's station.
"Hey," said the head nurse. "Monitor's still not back up."
"Better call maintenance." The nurse shrugged. "It's reconnected."

They proceeded down the hall.

"The hell you think you're going?" asked the head nurse. "Get back here!"

The nurse and soldiers boarded an elevator. The nurse pointed to his own ear as the doors closed, shaking his head.

He pressed the button for the lobby and returned to his own form.

"All right," said Simon. "So, just gaming this out—they're going to find my dead body, realize there's a nurse and two soldiers missing, and check the security footage. They won't know what's going on, but they'll know it's something. So, what is that, like an hour?"

"Maybe half," said the first soldier.

"Let's call it forty-five minutes." Simon shrugged. "They go into investigation mode, inform McCrae, McCrae calls his higher-ups, they'll set up blockades in every direction—"

"Infiltrate the ranks," said the second soldier. "Sneak across the border, transform the whole battalion."

"Well, once they figure it out," said the first soldier. "The other units will surround us. And what about air support?"

"Ah." Simon grinned and pointed two fingers into the air. "You're both forgetting we have unlimited resources."

His hospital scrubs shifted and spread with the luster of opal ore, solidifying into a full suit of glorious armor.

"You're not seriously walking around like that, are you?" the second soldier asked.

"Jealous?" Simon grinned.

"A little, yeah." The second solider nodded.

The elevator opened.

"That's just great!" A bright young woman in a peach pant-suit boarded, marveling at his costume.

"The kids are going to love that." She beamed. "But the children's ward is on the second floor."

"Oh." Simon smiled. "Could you give me directions?"

"Of course. Second floor. As soon as you get off, make a left, and it's at the end of the hall on the right."

"Thank you very much."

"My pleasure, Mister...?"

He reached out a hand as the doors closed. "Oh, it's Doctor, actually."

She shook his hand. "Really?"

"Yes, Doctor—"

"Simon Pierce." The new copy grinned.

The elevator doors opened on a pair of physicians conversing on the second floor. Baffled, they glanced about at the four Simons, the one in the iridescent armor in particular.

"It's okay," said Simon. "They're with me."

The clones lunged, snagging the doctors as Simon outstretched his hands.

"And now, so are you."

The doors closed.

"All right, given the last three floors," said Simon. "We may have to change our approach."

"Well, if you would lose the armor," said the second copy.

"This is what's going to keep me alive," said Simon.

"What about the rest of us?" asked the third.

"This is what's going to keep me alive," said Simon. "Your job is to acquire two military-grade vehicles while I create a diversion."

"Or," said the second, "you could not wear the armor."

Simon fluttered a dismissive wave. "You know that thing that's always getting in the way of what we want?"

"You mean other people?" asked the first.

"Yeah, that." Simon snapped his fingers, pointing. "It's no longer an issue."

"Don't you think we're losing the element of surprise?" asked the third.

"Oh." He smirked. "There will be surprises."

The five copies clad in military fatigues hurried down the maintenance corridor. Simon strode through the main thoroughfare, doctors and nurses gawping at the fantastic knight.

He threw open the lobby doors in all his spectacular glory. But no one paid much attention, his grand debut muted by screaming babies. Sallow patients slouched in the waiting area while overworked nurses muddled through their registration.

Simon flipped up the helmet's visor, disappointed. A well-dressed pharmaceutical sales rep pushed past him, visibly frustrated.

"Move it, freak."

He snatched her arm.

"Hey!"

Now he had their attention.

Or, rather the monstrosity alongside him did. The bloated, hairless body had the complexion of scrambled eggs, dotted with blue and green, its sunken eyes wide with horror. The creature did its best to run from Simon with its stubby legs and webbed feet. Its tongue had been shriveled to a useless appendage in its wide mouth, shrieking a hideous wail.

The lobby exploded with fright, people scattering as soldiers ran in. They raised their M16s, striking the creature square in the head. It keeled with a thump, revealing Simon in the entryway.

Predictable. Shoot first. He'd have to attempt resurrection some other time.

He snapped the helmet's visor down and marched toward them.

"Stay where you are!"

"On your knees, now!"

Their bullets whizzed off his armor.

Simon pointed the Qiopa unit, transforming it into a ray gun. He pulled the trigger and a ring of energy struck a soldier's chest.

The man flopped onto his back, convulsing.

"It's okay!" Simon's voice rang from the helmet. "He's just unconscious. I need your bodies!"

Ring after ring whirled into the fleeing troops, felling them all.

Simon strode out with a squad of Simon soldiers. Outside, patients and medical staff had taken cover behind parked cars.

The onlookers cheered. The soldiers slowed and waved, soaking up the applause.

Two Humvees peeled out of the lot, braking only to let the Simon soldiers jump in before tearing over curbs and speeding onto the main road.

"Ha!" said Simon. "And you thought it wouldn't work!"

The fourth copy pointed the second. "You mean him, not me."

"Whatever," said the second. "We all look the same. I still think we lost our advantage."

"They have no clue what's going on," said Simon.

"Somebody want to tell me where we're going?" the first asked from the driver's seat.

"The base, obviously," said the fourth.

"We have a couple stops first," said Simon. "Cut off this bus—make sure they can't pull around. After this, you're going to the machinery depot off the interstate."

"There's already sixteen of us," said the third.

"And we need more," said Simon. "You're all too preoccupied thinking about how you're going to overthrow me."

"Get out of my head!" The third, fourth, and sixth clones grinned.

Simon leaned over to the driver. "Radio the others—tell them to block the lane. Stop here."

He sprang from the Humvee and hopped aboard the waiting city bus.

The bus driver glared at him. The riders tittered and jeered. Simon placed a hand on the driver's shoulder, then leaned over and gave the Humvee blocking the lane a thumb's-up. The Humvee shifted into gear and drove off.

"The machinery depot," Simon said to the bus driver.

The copy hit the gas, thrusting passengers into their seats.

"The hell's going on up there?" asked a passenger in the back.

Simon gripped the handrails. "Taking a little detour."

"I don't think so, pal. I need to get to work!"

"You all work for me now." Simon stamped forward as the bus careened, placing his hands on riders' shoulders as he passed.

Riders in the back weren't sure what was happening as people upfront seized other passengers, dragging them toward Simon. Frightened by the commotion, riders pulled the cords as the bus raced past its stops. One passenger wrestled free, pulling a switchblade, and stabbed Simon between the helm and gorget. Simon's skin blunted the knife tip to a nub.

"Organic graphene." Simon smiled. "My own special blend."

He grabbed the attacker's neck and allowed the others to witness their fate.

Ten minutes later, the bus barreled through the chain link gates of the Holcomb Machinery Depot and slowed to a stop. The engineers peered out of the warehouses as the iridescent knight dismounted from the bus. A rosy-cheeked man wandered over, looking dubious.

"Morning!" Simon reached out a welcoming hand. "Just here to inspect some of our products."

"Uh, sure." The manager shook his hand. "Who are you with?"

"Pierce Technologies. We're planning a major global expansion."

The engineers blinked as their boss transformed into a Simon.

The two Humvees rolled in, blocking the entrance. The engineers ducked into the workhouses as copies streamed from the vehicles.

Prepared to make a stand, the engineers armed themselves with tools, only to be subdued at the sight of the M16s. They dropped their hardware and raised their hands.

Simon and the second copy strolled into the bay doors of a warehouse where several bright yellow Pierce Technologies laser cannons sat in storage.

"Couldn't you just make your own lasers?" asked the copy.

"Well, of course." Simon shrugged. "But first we needed to make a daring escape—"

"From Cidara's citadel!"

"Exactly." A wild flare filled his eyes. "Now I have an army, and we can storm the walls of the Eternal Temple and take what's rightfully ours."

"You mean the Mobius, right?"

"Yeah, of course. Just having a little fun with it, you know?"

"Oh, no, no—I'm right there with you."

* * *

After hours of excavation and rescue operations, McCrae and his team returned to the base. Major Bellamy caught up alongside him.

"Director Garza is asking to see you, sir."

"Tell her I am neck-deep and cannot be extricated, Major."

"She's asking about the fragment, sir."

"Recovered and secured. That's all she needs to know."

Never mind the fact that he didn't have answers. The situation had nosedived beyond their comprehension.

McCrae hustled into a unmarked building and rode the elevator to the laboratories below ground. He strode through the dim corridor. With a swipe of his key card and a retinal scan, he accessed the depository, two sentries were already inside. McCrae deposited the fragment, locking it in a safe with a barrel key.

Two levels below, a woman in a drab green hazmat suit approached him.

"She's been awake for about twenty minutes," she said, her husky voice stifled by a gas mask.

"How bad is it?" he asked.

"Her condition's deteriorated." The scientist shook her head. "Or advanced. I'm not sure."

McCrae donned a hazmat suit. At the end of the hall, the woman punched in a code. The bolts retracted, unsealing a heavy steel threshold. Inside the vault, a large chamber of concrete and lead.

A flickering figure peered through a narrow window of thick, polarized glass.

"General!" The chamber muted Callahan's voice. "What happened!?"

"We don't know," he said. "Recovery team pulled you and Pierce out of the rubble. Soon as they hooked you up to a heart monitor in the ambulance, you started doing that."

Callahan shifted between transparent and opaque and translucent, over and over. It reminded McCrae of a strobe light, but the cadence was broken and erratic. Although he didn't rely on intuition alone, that particular detail made his overall gut feeling negative.

"Our best guess at the moment is that you're switching between different frequencies of the electromagnetic spectrum."

"What does that mean?!"

"Well, for us, it means you're potentially producing dangerously high levels of radiation."

Her eyes and mouth sagged.

"We're going to figure this out, okay?"

"I thought you didn't know how it worked!" said Callahan.

"Well, we have several competing theories." McCrae nodded. "It's a matter of picking the right one."

Callahan's eyes tightened in grim dismay.

"What about Pierce?!" she asked. "He was right next to me!"

"He's in a coma, in a hospital back in Flagstaff," said McCrae. "We're airlifting him out here at oh-nine-hundred."

* * *

Eve rose before the sun. Her secret back-up identity's account was untouched.

Doubts percolated. If the Bureau had found the other accounts, they could've left it as a trap. She shut down the laptop. If they knew about Devereux, they knew about the bunker. Federal law enforcement and National Guard troops might be waiting in southeast Oregon. She could run for Mexico—it would be easy with the suit. But if she had the suit, why run?

Her eyes drew to the mini micro-house.

Quinn poked out. "Morning."

"Morning."

"Um—I used all your water."

Eve smiled a little. "I'll refill it."

"And I ate all your granola bars."

They ordered takeout breakfast from a diner up the road. Quinn got a huevos-rancheros burrito, and Eve a vegetable omelet. She reduced the room's table and a chair along with a coffee mug for Quinn. Eve pulled up the second chair alongside the dresser. She kept her eyes down, guilty about the dining arrangements. They ate in silence until Eve refilled her mug and sat down.

"You always want to be a scientist?" asked Quinn.

"I'm not a scientist," she mumbled, sipping her coffee.

"Well, you're really good at math."

Eve shook her head. "I remember patterns, and..." She sighed. "I have synesthesia."

"Oh yeah—a girl I knew in college had that. She could see sounds."

Eve nodded. "Mine's linked to numbers and symbols and how I feel in certain situations. It's why I got into physics."

Quinn smirked. "*That* got you into physics?"

"Colors are waves of light. Well, then I found out most everything is actually empty space. Not just the universe but inside atoms, between the nucleus and electrons—lots of nothing. I didn't think that was true...

or didn't want to believe it. Then I got into quantum physics, and that says there's almost always something, you just can't see it. So, I wanted to prove there's something to all this nothing, something we can't perceive."

"So." Quinn ventured. "What's...seven?"

"Gold."

She smiled. "What's red?"

"Five. The letter *A*. September."

"What's black?"

"Technically not a color. It's neutral, but it makes other colors possible." She set down the mug. "Guess that's why I used to wear it a lot. It was...easier."

"Well, yeah." Quinn nodded. "It could be whatever you wanted. Like a blank canvas."

Eve blinked. This wasn't how she wanted to say goodbye. She didn't want to say goodbye, but—

You ruin everything. Everything about you is wrong.

"What's *M*?"

"Quinn." She sighed. "They raided my accounts—"

"You could turn yourself in."

She knows. She's not your friend. Nobody likes you.

Eve's gaze hardened. "Once we get far enough out, I'll give you a car, half of what I have in cash—"

"I don't want it if it's stolen."

"You're taking it. And you're meeting with Lorenzo and getting the life you're supposed to have."

Quinn's brow scrunched. "And how does that fit into your plan? What's it matter to you?"

"I don't know." Autumn gold and sky blue. "I guess, because...my sister never needed me? Everything always came so easy for her, and you actually wanted my help. Felt like it mattered."

"Probably mattered to her a lot more than you think."

"Guess we'll never know." She stood, grabbed the empty container, and tossed it into the trash.

Quinn stood. "And how was I going to meet Lorenzo while living in your crawlspace?"

"All right." Eve turned around, cracking a smile. "I didn't have all that worked out."

"Yeah." She smirked.

"I want you to be happy, Quinn. I wanted you to have your dreams."

"I appreciate it, but I didn't need that. I was happy because I thought I had a good friend."

The words stung.

"Shit, he might've already called you."
"Well, I lost my purse—"
"Oh. No—I have it."
She stiffened. "What?"
Eve dug into her pocket.
Quinn wandered toward the edge of the dresser, folding her arms. "Well, I mean, won't they track the signal or something?"
Eve took out the *modifikator*. "Reception out here sucks. Besides, I'm not dialing out, just checking to see if he called."
"But it'll still...ping the tower, right?"
"We'll be long gone." She enlarged the purse and set the *modifikator* on the nightstand.
She dug around in Quinn's bag—her heart skipped. Ice blue, gray, and mustard.
"Quinn." Eve held up two phones. "Why do you have a burner?"
"All right." Quinn smiled. "You caught me. I really wanted to pay Kira back, and I may have considered dealing drugs."
"You were going to deal drugs." Eve listened to her own words. "To pay me back?"
"I know. Stupid idea. Didn't even do it."
She angled the phone against the lamp light, divining the smudges. Yellow, pink, purple, gold. She tried a few combinations and unlocked it.
"It—it's nothing."
Eve thumbed through the burner, pulling up the contacts. "Then why are there two numbers in here?"
"Well, somebody gave me their dealer, and—"
Eve swiped open a browser on the burner.
"What are you doing?"
"Checking to see who they belong to."
An FBI field office. Charcoal and rust. Eve sickened. "You were giving them information about me?"
"No." Quinn waved hands in front of her. "I didn't tell them anything, I swear."
"Oh my god. You knew. They told you who I was."
"No—no, they didn't. I didn't—They didn't tell me anything. They weren't even sure you were the Kira they were looking for."
She's lying.
"No," Eve whispered.
Why else would she want anything to do with you? She's not your friend.
"That's why you wanted me turn myself in." The hum droned in her ears.

She was never your friend. Nobody cares about you.

"No," said Quinn. "They said Kira was in trouble, and—"

Eve picked up the *modifikator*. She shoved the phones back into the purse and shrank it.

"I thought I was helping you!" Quinn pleaded. "They said they would help you!"

It was only to get information.

She pocketed the *modifikator* and stormed toward the dresser.

"Please!" Quinn ran for the sanctuary of the mini micro-house. "Just listen to me!"

The micro-house darkened with Eve's shadow. The dresser trembled.

Quinn lunged for the door knob and missed.

Eve lifted the micro-house. With her other hand, she lowered the green plastic tumbler around Quinn.

"Eve?!" her voice echoed inside.

She turned away, and knelt, digging into her pack.

Faint scraping against the dresser, followed by a light tapping. Quinn was trying to knock over the tumbler. Probably ramming her shoulder against it. The clatter of the plastic.

Eve snatched it.

Quinn turned on her heel, only to be stopped by Eve planting a silver SUV in front of her.

"Get in."

She spun around. "Will you just let me—"

"Now."

Their glares locked.

"You don't understand—"

"Quinn—"

"They wanted to help Kira."

"There is no Kira." Her lips curled with a harsh whisper. "Get in."

33

(teal)

In an hour's time, Simon had outfitted his troops with laser guns, shock helmets, and lightweight ultra impact-resistant body armor. The machinery depot's ample raw materials were loaded into trucks altered into more durable all-terrain designs with armor plating and puncture-proof tires. The convoy roared across the highway at breakneck pace with no regard for other drivers, taking up lanes and forcing cars off the road.

Simon commanded his militia from a captain's chair aboard the bus, converted into a hulking battle rover embossed with the features of the fearsome dragon god, Oroleg.

"So, we all have a field around us?" asked the third copy. "But you're generating it without the fragment—"

The tenth copy snapped his fingers and pointed at the third. "I had the same thought."

"Right," said Simon. "What's the energy source? Based on what we —"

"It's the energy absorption," said the second.

Simon nodded. "And it's projected into a field using resonance coupled with low-level ionizing radiation. It appears the X-ray burst flipped, or folded, this projecting effect onto me."

"So another fragment could—"

"Doubtful they know." Simon shrugged. "They were reluctant to use high energy—"

"After the cave-in," said the second and fifth.

"Exactly."

"But," said the fourth, "excessive ionizing radiation—"

"Should be absorbed," said Simon. "Possibly amplified. Higher levels might collapse a field, you know, something catastrophic. But there's no way they'd use that much firepower."

They all grinned in a wave of understanding. Though apart from him, they were of the same mind. A new sense of power arose within him. He'd never felt such deep connection to other people before.

"We're fifty miles from the California border," the driver announced.

Simon stood. "Tell everyone to stop."

He hopped out of the battle rover. The copies were already offloading power tools and computer hardware.

"We've detected four UAVs," the second copy advised.

"Bring them down." He flicked a dismissive hand. "Somewhere close by."

While the copies aimed the laser cannons, Simon crafted his next masterpieces.

* * *

Unfazed by the loss of their UAVs, Major General Rogers ordered another squadron launched. The National Guard's fortification on the western side of the Colorado River concentrated on the interstate, ready to assail Simon's forces once they crossed the bridge. Lieutenant Colonel Pike's garrisons stationed to the north and south on California's eastern border would close in behind.

The radio crackled with Colonel Pike's voice. "Keeping an eye on us, Rogers?"

Puzzled by the comment, Rogers picked up his radio. "Always got your back—"

Explosions rolled in the east. A dark, smoky cloud mushroomed in the distance. Faint trails of missile fire sprayed behind Pike's garrisons.

"What in God's name are you doing!?"

"Colonel?" Rogers awaited an answer. "Colonel?!"

The long rasp of aircraft echoed, followed by the searing tear of missiles.

Rogers' troops on the western side of the river scrambled as explosions erupted ahead their ranks.

"Holy shit—friendly fire, friendly fire! Get those fucking UAV pilots new glasses!"

The bushwhacked troops rushed to the river. Sleek metal boomerangs hissed overhead.

* * *

Simon's unmanned aircraft broke off into pairs, sweeping wide to take another pass at the beleaguered troops to the north and south before reconvening on the interstate's western path. The first brigade of his foot soldiers marched across the bridge, drawing fire from the regrouping guardsmen. Heavy rounds obliterated his infantry. Their parts moved stiffly.

Robotic decoys.

"Fall back! Fall back!"

Laser cannons blasted at the troops from across the river, blowing chunks of desert into the sky. A monstrous mechanical reptile the length of a city bus rose from the riverbank. The serpentine body was comprised of thick scales of tungsten carbide. Streams of fiery vapor shot from its nostrils and jaws. Its segmented tail whipped behind, demolishing the Guard's armaments. While Oroleg sent the troops running, levitating hovercraft soared over the river and up the banks. Copies sprang out, unleashing barrages of laser rings upon the frantic troops.

The infantry returned fire. Their munitions bounced off the copies. The troops retreated, rallying into smaller units to hold their position. They scattered when laser fire rained from overhead, unwilling to run to the higher ground in the west.

Simon hovered into the battlefield atop a levitating chariot.

"Remember!" Simon held up a finger as copies charged past him. "We need them alive!"

He pressed the touchscreen on his gauntlet and his UAVs overhead relented, holding a circling pattern.

"Not that I'm ungrateful to be us," said the fourth copy, "but you could've just make a super-android army."

"And how does that help humanity?" asked Simon.

The chariot lowered. He hopped off and approached the mechanical dragon, placing a hand on its side. "Good boy."

The creature tamed, its scales unfurling and resettling into new shapes as it straightened, returning to its previous form as the battle rover. Machine gunfire ricocheted off Simon's armor.

A brazen band of troops rushed him.

He turned, jamming his right sabaton into the sand. The patch of earth before the troops churned, thickening into tar. The soldiers plunged, sloshing desperately to escape.

"Round them up!" Simon checked the display on his wrist. "We're making excellent time!"

* * *

Miles north of the motel, Eve pulled off the highway and swapped the Camaro for a Jeep behind an overgrowth of mesquite trees. She turned onto the 395 (blue green, brown, red), and detoured through the desert.

Get the fragments, get the Mobius, then you'll finally be something great.

The wheels on the highway droned.

All the secrets of the universe...you'll be a god. Show them all.

What had they already seen?

They'll all be meaningless little specks.

But they were all specks now.

Blood on her fingertips flashed through her mind. The house in splinters. Their little bodies somewhere inside. She'd wanted to let them go. She just hadn't known how.

What do you expect? You're a horrible person.

She glanced at the tiny SUV resting below the gauges on the dashboard's instrument panel. Colors floated, obscuring it.

She doesn't care about you. Nobody does.

Every nasty word Eve had ever sputtered repeated in her mind. She'd been too angry to apologize. And then too scared. And then it had been too long. The invisible wall which had blocked her had spread into a chasm she couldn't cross. Now she was about to maroon Quinn in the desert, condemning her to a four-and-a-half-hour journey back to the city further delayed by whatever cataclysm Plan F created.

For what?

A never-ending equation with no answer? To prove herself to the world?

Wasn't that all Quinn was after? To prove she could achieve her dreams?

Wasn't that what she wanted for her?

"Was it?"

* * *

Quinn trembled from the heavy rumble of the car's engine. She studied the movement of Eve's lips, her big gray eyes focused in Quinn's direction.

She'd seen that look before. Regret. Guilt. She remembered Eve's distraught wail in the penthouse. Grief. She wasn't an emotionless psychopath.

She was, however, reactive. Conflicted.

Eve's attention drifted to the road, her gaze stretching long, sinking deep.

She'd taken care of her. And the other people. Enough to care about them. But at the same time, something bothered Eve inside.

Her eyes darted in Quinn's direction. Guilt again. Then anger.

"Okay...?" Quinn muttered.

She watched Eve's expression twist through emotions. Another glance her way.

The bitch wanted to talk to her but she didn't know how. Quinn was less than an inch tall, and Eve was terrified of her.

She folded her arms and settled into her seat, prepared to wait her out. "Okay, okay."

* * *

Nobody. That's why you need the fragments.

"Shut up."

You know it's true.

"I hate you."

The first road signs in ages appeared. Eve glanced at the SUV. Autumn gold, sky blue. Laurel green. Desert sand. She couldn't let it end like that. Not again.

With a gentle pinch, she plucked the SUV from the dash. Eve set it into a crevice in the passenger seat's cushion. She dug into her jacket, steadying the wheel, and took out the *modifikator*. A glance at the settings, then the road. She hit the dial button.

Eve stuck the *modifikator* in her jacket and bit the side of her lip, glimpsing at the car that filled three-quarters of the passenger seat.

"Hey." She cleared her throat. "How're you doing in there?"

Quinn rolled down the window. "I'm okay. I guess."

"You hungry? I need to get gas, and—did you want snacks or anything?"

"Yeah. I could go for some Hot Fries and Funyuns."

"Ugh." Eve grimaced disgust. "Really?"

"Yeah. And you can hold the judgment, thanks." She smiled.

The Jeep rolled into a lone gas station. A guy in a denim shirt slept outside the convenience store in a chair, a baseball cap pulled over his eyes. Behind the counter, a little old man with a thick white mustache watched a soccer match on an ancient television.

Eve dumped a pile of snacks in front of him along with a calling card and handed him cash.

"Need forty on the first pump."

"How much you want on the card?"

"Twenty."

"Won't get you much time."

"It's enough."

She dropped the bag of snacks alongside Quinn's SUV and filled the Jeep's tank. She pulled around, parking several feet from a payphone mounted to a pole.

She rolled down the passenger side window. "Be right back."

Eve flipped over the calling card and dialed, the colors guiding her through numbers she'd used a lifetime ago. She hoped they still worked. The line rang and rang, the connection spotty. She didn't expect an answer.

A familiar voice asked her to leave a message. Ice-cold blue. Her throat clenched. The air in her lungs thinned.

A beep.

She forced out the words. "Hey, Charlotte. It's Eve. I don't know if I'm ever going to see you again, so I wanted to say I'm sorry. For what I said. You didn't do anything wrong. It was me. I was jealous. And angry, and—I shouldn't have taken it out on you, any of you. And I hope one day you can forgive me. But I-I just wanted to say—"

Quinn screamed.

The guy in the denim shirt had broken into the Jeep, and was gawping at the five-inch woman inside.

"Hey!" Eve slammed the receiver onto the hook. "Get away from there!" She stormed toward the Jeep, pulling out the *modifikator*.

The startled man spun around, tripping as he fled. The step of her car-sized shoe shook the ground. She bent over and reached for him. He hollered as her fingers wrapped around him. Eve lifted him and reared back, about to hurl him into the horizon.

He whimpered, pleading, and Eve hesitated. He was an unlucky thief, like her. Tired of spreading misery, she hung him off the tarnished knob atop the flagpole by his belt, letting him dangle.

Eve knelt, peering into the Jeep. "You all right?"

Quinn clamped her hands over her ears. "Oh my god!"

She cringed, whispering. "Oh, yeah—sorry."

She reduced to six feet and rushed to the driver's side. They tore out of the station and raced down the road.

The Jeep jounced across the scraggy terrain and Eve placed a hand onto the SUV.

"Hang on."

Quinn fumbled to buckle up, clinging to the seat for stability. Several miles later, among the foothills, they slowed to a stop. Eve jumped out with the SUV in hand.

* * *

Quinn felt herself expand, the world outside shrinking as she and the car returned to normal.

She tore off the seat belt and charged out.

Eve blubbered, tears running down her face. "I'm so sorry, Quinn! The keys are in the glove box. Just go!"

"No." Quinn slammed the door. "First off—this thing isn't road safe."

She pointed to the SUV's warped side panels stained with oils in the patterns of Eve's fingerprints.

"Get away from me! For your own good! You have no idea—just being around me is a vortex of flaming shit and misery!"

"Stop. Stop it." Quinn neared her. "Get it together."

Eve sniffled, wiping the back on her hand across her cheeks.

"When I first met you," she said, "you were a good person who did the right thing."

Eve shook her head. "No..."

"Yes—and I think you still are."

"I'm horrible." Eve crumpled into herself as she choked out the words. "Everything about me is wrong." She sobbed, shriveling inward. If it was an act, it was a hell of a performance.

"I don't think so," said Quinn. "I don't think you mean...some of the things you do. You still care about me. You cared about those people, even though you called them assholes."

Eve lifted her head and nodded, her lips twisted in angst.

"The FBI said you were in danger. I was trying to help you—they wanted to help you."

"Yeah, well." She sniffled. "That was before I fell onto a building."

"I'll tell them what happened. Maybe they'll reduce your sentence."

"Sentence?" She grimaced. "They're going to give me the death penalty! You have no idea what I've done." Her fingers tore through her chaotic hair. "I'm just going to run, find somewhere to hide—which is probably what I should have done in the first place. Hopefully, at some point, I can build a time machine and make sure none of this ever happens."

"So you and I would never meet?"

"You'd be better off."

"Oh—with Diego conning me out of all my money?"

"I don't know." Eve shrugged. "Maybe he was a legit producer?"

Quinn folded her arms. "The FBI agent seemed like a good guy. He wanted to help Kira."

"I'm not her, okay?"

"I think it's you when you give yourself a chance."

"You don't understand—"

"If you just explain to them—"

"No, because—"

"Nobody would believe you?"

"Yeah, because—"

"Because they're all against you?"

"Well—"

"Because they don't like you? Because everyone thinks the worst of you? Because nothing good could ever possibly happen to you?"

Eve's eyes widened, panicked. "Oh my god. Oh my god." She clasped a hand over her mouth.

"It's okay." Quinn edged closer. "I don't think you're a bad person. I think you have some problems—which is okay; we all have problems—but you're really hard on yourself."

"I am." Eve lowered her hand. "I really am. But—you don't know what I did. Oh my god, Quinn—"

"You can still make things right," she said. "Like how you put me back."

Eve folded her arms, her eyes distant as she shook her head. Her breath trembled.

She needed more convincing. Maybe if Quinn recreated the day they'd met, she could rekindle Eve's better nature.

"Don't know about you." Quinn smirked. "But I could use a drink."

She shot her a confounded glare. "We're in the middle of the desert."

"There's a town with a bar somewhere." Quinn shrugged.

Eve scowled, pointing a warning finger. "No tricks."

"No way." Quinn put her hands up. "I just got back to normal."

She held a suspicious squint on Quinn as she reduced the SUV, picked it up, and dug into the bug-out bag for another vehicle. Eve tossed the bag of snacks to Quinn. With the bug-out bag in hand, she shrank the Jeep and enlarged a pickup truck.

"How many cars did you steal?"

"I bought some of them, " Eve defended. "Just...not...these."

The truck rattled across the dunes until they reached the main road, following signs toward the nearest town.

"Okay," said Quinn. "Now talk to me."

* * *

Eve recounted the events of the night she'd gotten the *modifikator*.

"I can't believe you did all that."

"I know. I suck."

"Okay, you've got to stop talking about yourself like you're garbage. It's like distortion. Everybody uses a little bit here and there, but it can't be a whole song."

"Is that what it's doing?" Eve muttered.

"Yeah, totally. And you're blasting your brain with it."

"No—the fragment projects distortions of reality. And I can hear this noise sometimes. Like a buzzing or—" She dropped into a lower register making a harsh, nasal growl.

"So..." Quinn eyed her with concern. "You're hearing noises?"

"Well, not all the time. When I feel a certain way."

Was she linked with the fragment—the Mobius—because she already lived in a distorted reality? A kind of symmetry? Was the hum a manifestation of the same frequency as the Mobius? And what if now, because she'd become aware of it, the link was broken?

Oh my god, it's like the only thing you know how to do is fuck shit up.

"Eve?" Quinn leaned over. "What are you thinking? Don't shut me out, okay?"

"What if I got entangled with it? Or it thinks I'm the Mobius?"

"How does a rock think?"

"Maybe it's not a rock. Maybe it's an organic computational system, operating on its own. I mean, sometimes—a couple times—I heard it, and I wasn't sure what was happening. I don't think I was controlling it."

"All right, you need to get rid of this thing."

She's playing up to you. It's a trick. Think about it—she got your whole story, and now she wants you to give up the fragment.

"No, it's the greatest discovery in human history. And it proves all of my theories. That's why I thought I had a second chance. And if I'm entangled—still entangled, then—"

"Then you need to stop being so negative."

She shrugged. "It's just the way I am."

"That's not true. What about the person who cared about my dreams?"

"Okay, that's different. I wanted good things for you."

Quinn leaned over. "I want good things for you. But I can't make them happen. Only you can."

Oh, please. There's no hope for you.

"Too late for that," Eve mumbled.

* * *

A bartender with a Burnside mustache dried glasses behind the bar of the empty saloon. Eve wondered what he made of them. Some Amazon with hair down her shoulders wearing glasses and a leather jacket, and a disheveled younger woman in a flowing sunflower skirt.

He gave them a nod and a smile. "Afternoon, ladies. How're you doing today?"

They sat on the silver-rimmed robin's-egg stools.

Quinn nodded. "Better now."

"Been better." Eve scrutinized his sturdy build.

Careful. TVs in here have local stations on. And it's another bar in the desert. What if Quinn knows this guy?

Eve sighed.

He raised an eyebrow. "Get you all something to drink?"

"Whiskey," they answered.

"Got you covered."

He poured them two doubles. "Will you be wanting any food?"

"Definitely," said Quinn.

He handed them menus, and stepped away to watch the baseball game.

Quinn picked up her drink, and hesitated a toast. Eve clinked the edge of her glass against hers. They sipped.

Quinn snapped up the menu. "I'm famished. Being in a constant state of panic burns a lot of calories."

"Sorry."

"It wasn't— It was a joke."

Eve shook her head.

The bartender grumbled. "Ah, come on."

Yellow flashed in her periphery. She turned to the screen.

The midday anchor appeared unprepared. "We interrupt this regularly scheduled broadcast for a special report. Less than an hour ago, a blockade of National Guard at the Arizona border was attacked, allegedly, by Simon Pierce. Pierce had been brought to the hospital late last night after an explosion in his home and reportedly escaped, avoiding being taken into custody."

Images of large, burnt craters around the highway replaced the game.

"Jesus Christ." The bartender folded his arms.

"The number of casualties has not yet been released. However, early reports indicate Pierce has an army. We are attempting to verify that information. Governor Owens has issued a state of emergency. Local and state officials are shutting down access to the southeast corner of the state. Residents are being advised to stay in their homes and seek shelter until more information is available."

"Flarg." The women gasped.

Quinn leaned closer, whispering. "This is your chance. You can be a hero. A superhero."

"Not if he's got one of them," Eve whispered. "He's smarter than I am."

"But you figured it out—"

"Not all of it," she rasped.

"You know it better than he does, and—you're entangled."

Eve bit her lip, shaking her head as dismal blue-gray puffs bubbled up inside.

"That just means my particles and its particles share a link over a large distance," Eve muttered. "It doesn't give me any special—anything."

"You're the only one who can stop him—"

"There's no way—"

"There is if you stop listening to all the terrible shit you tell yourself."

"I can't—I can't beat him."

"You saw what he did. What do you think he's going to do if he wins?"

The prospect of planetary rule by a narcissistic lunatic filled Eve's mind. If there was no wreckage, no bodies, and he had an army, then he'd either obliterated everything or he'd figured out how to alter matter. What if he could change whatever he wanted? The only truth would be his truth, the world his personal playground. A vast real-life *Hollow Earth Chronicles* theme park populated with genetic abominations replicating the mythical beasts and races. All natural flora and fauna eradicated. All music played by minstrels on lutes and ocarinas. All alcohol either ale or mead. No more tacos. No more sushi. No Thai food. Just giant turkey legs and chickens sewn into roasted pigs. No more people, not as they were. Whatever he wanted them to be. She thought of her family. Quinn's family. Everyone's family.

"Uh, hello?" Quinn waved a hand in her face. "Still there?"

Eve glanced at the bartender. He was scrutinizing her.

Shit. You've been made, dumbass.

He strolled over, reaching under the counter. "You ladies ready to order?"

"Maybe next time." Eve knocked back her drink and stood.

She dug into her pocket, spotting the tension in his arm. Didn't seem like the kind of place where they kept a baseball bat behind the bar. Probably a revolver or shotgun.

Their eyes locked as she stuck several bills onto the counter.

Quinn set down her empty glass. He glanced her way.

"We have to go," she said softly.

He focused back on Eve, loosening his grip, and placed both hands on the counter.

"Thanks." Quinn stood.

He gave her a nod, and they rushed out.

* * *

They drove to an outcrop not far from the highway where Eve changed into the suit. She stepped out from behind the rock, securing the EEG net onto her head.

"How did you not know you were a supervillain?" Quinn asked.

"I was fighting crime." Eve put her hands on her hips. "Sort of."

"Well, I mean, don't get me wrong—it makes your butt look awesome."

"Really?" She checked her posterior. "You're just saying th—"

"For god's sake, take the compliment. You're hot as an evil bitch."

Eve blushed. "Thanks."

"Head gear's a little weird." Quinn pointed.

"That's how you control it."

Eve aimed at a rock formation several yards away. Yellow, green, pink. A white orb blasted the rock into glowing nuggets.

Quinn leaped back, an anxious grin peeking behind her clasped hands. "Flarg."

"Wait—I thought that's what we said when a guy was being an asshole?"

She shrugged. "I've been using it as a general exclamation."

"Oh. Cool."

"What else can you do?"

Eve turned around. Violet, blue, scarlet. She vanished.

Quinn's jaw dropped.

Pink, white, orange. She appeared alongside Quinn, who laughed in startled delight.

Eve counted off on her fingers. "I can walk through walls, make myself bulletproof, grow, shrink, levitate."

"You can fly?"

"Mmm." Eve shrugged. "More like floating."

Quinn beamed. "You're incredible."

"No, I—"

"Yes. You are. Now say it."

Eve sighed, shaking her head. "Quinn—"

"Say it."

She mumbled, self-conscious.

"Louder. Like you mean it."

"I'm incredible."

Quinn glared, unconvinced. "Again. And more. You're brilliant. Come on."

"I'm...incredible. I'm brilliant. I'm amazing. I'm...I'm a genius. I am brilliant!"

"Yes!"

"I can do anything!" Eve clenched her fists. "Nothing can stop me! And I'm going to take over the world! I mean—save the world, save the world."

Quinn eyed her, skeptical. "Sure about that?"

"Yeah, I got carried away. I'm saving the world."

"Like, I want to believe you..."

"I am. And I don't need money, or superpowers or to be some gigantic tree hugger. I just have to know that I can, that what I do matters. That I'm capable."

Quinn smiled. "Good for you."

"But I mean, the technology's really important." Eve shrugged. "Because the planet's dying and we're not going to be able to fix it without major innovations."

"Kind of went a little negative there."

"Sorry, sorry."

"It's okay. You're a work in progress."

"Yeah." Eve headed for the Jeep. "Come on—we don't have a lot of time."

Quinn raced up behind her, swatting her rear with playful slap.

Eve yelped—yellow, green, pink—blowing a charred hole in the sand.

Quinn leaped back in fright.

She spun around. "Don't do that."

"Sorry."

34

(blue green, pink)

McCrae blew into the administration building along with a tall, lean officer.

Garza stormed toward them. "We have to evacuate."

"That ain't happening." McCrae shook his head.

"He's headed right for us."

"Yeah, well, we can't get the Mobius topside and haul it in a couple hours, and he knows it. Then there's Agent Callahan's condition."

"We can't stay here."

"Director, you're free to do whatever you like. Just know them lasers took down six UAVs not in visual range. If you get on that helicopter, there's no guarantee you're going to make it to safety."

She huffed, redoubling her composure. "What are our options?"

"You need to convince the president to authorize a nuclear strike."

"Russell—"

"It's nothing I take lightly—"

"We've dumped hundreds of millions of dollars into this project. You're telling me that's the best you can come up with?"

"Colonel Das." McCrae pivoted.

"Director." The officer stepped forward. "Based on what we know, the material amplifies energy—"

"He doesn't have the fragment," she said.

"And neither does Agent Callahan," said Das. "We believe it generated a field and higher energies could destabilize and collapse it."

"Collapse meaning, what?" she asked.

"Well." Das glanced at McCrae. "Presumably, eliminate the field. However, there is a chance it could annihilate everything in a fifty-mile radius."

"Okay." She folded her hands in front of her. "And why can't we devise a less drastic solution using all of the very expensive equipment on hand?"

Das nodded. "The issue is, again, getting everything above ground. In speaking with our chief engineer, we would need to modify and reconfigure several elements. We'd be cutting it extremely close."

"So you're opting for brute force."

"We would all be underground," said McCrae.

Garza cast out a hand. "And what about everyone else?"

"Maria," said McCrae. "If Pierce gets the Mobius, it's over for human civilization. We can't let someone like that have that much power."

She inhaled with a gentle fury, hands on her hips. "All right. I'll call Ramos."

* * *

Eve gripped the wheel as the pickup truck sped southbound.

"Once we're twenty miles out, I'll give you the Jeep. Go south for nine miles, watch the odometer. You're looking for a dirt road on the left, under a set of power lines. Turn onto it and don't speed—forty miles an hour. You're technically on a military base after five miles."

"Should I be writing this down?" asked Quinn.

"Couple Humvees will probably stop you before you get too far."

"How do you know all this?"

"Because." Eve sighed. "That was my plan. Get onto the base. Get the fragments. Pierce must've had one of his own, so that's where he's going."

"So, wait a minute—"

"When you see the trucks, stop the car. Open the door and put your hands up."

"You don't have a gun or anything?"

"If they see a gun, they'll shoot you. Tell them you're unarmed and you need to talk to General Russell McCrae, and...that I sent you."

"Can't you just call him?"

"Well, I don't know him personally, but—I'm pretty sure he knows who I am."

"Sure." Quinn's head bobbled. "Okay."

"He built a guidance system, like, ten years ago, and now they use it for repurposed nukes. You tell him, if it comes to it, the suit I'm wearing can withstand a small, low-yield nuclear warhead as long as I'm over a couple hundred feet."

"*What?*"

"Problem is I don't even know if I can hurt Pierce. In my experiments, the distortion fields got along. But that's why I need you to tell McCrae I'm on their side."

"Are you?"

"Well, for the most part." She shrugged. "I mean, I fundamentally disagree with nuclear weapons, but under the circum—"

"Eve!"

"All right—yeah! Yes. Okay? And if they need to, they can use a bigger one."

"I don't think they're going to go for any of this."

"With a larger payload, the energy should still be absorbed by the fields, but Pierce and I—our atoms will be ripped to shreds."

"There has to be another way."

"We can't let him win. Otherwise, the planet turns into a never-ending Hollow Earth LARP."

Quinn squinted, bewildered.

Eve glanced at her. "Live-action role-playing?"

"What are you talking about?"

She checked the odometer. "Never mind. This is it."

Eve pulled the truck over. She dug the Jeep out of her pack and enlarged it on the roadside.

"Be careful. Remember, nine more miles, on the left. Drive slow, put your hands up when you get out. Ask for General Russell McCrae."

"I will." Quinn nodded. "He can use a small nuclear warhead."

"Low-yield. Small, low-yield nuclear warhead."

"Right."

Dismal blue-gray puffs sagged into soggy purple and abysmal pea-soup green. Impending doom.

"Look, if I don't see you again—"

"Don't say that." Quinn raised a warning finger. "Don't think like that. You're going to do great."

Eve nodded, looking askance with regret.

"What's wrong?"

"I just remembered there's no way to pee out of this thing."

She cracked a smile, chuckling. Eve smirked.

Quinn opened her arms. "Good luck."

They hugged. "You, too."

They got in their respective vehicles, driving in tandem for a stretch of road, until Eve waved and veered off into the desert.

* * *

Quinn swallowed hard, repeating Eve's instructions. She'd forgotten to check the odometer when she'd started the Jeep. Frantic, she scanned the highway ahead for any sign of a dirt road among the chaparral.

"Shit."

She glanced in the rearview mirror, pondering a vain attempt at gauging the distance she'd traveled. Behind her, more desert and a couple of power lines. The brakes squealed as the Jeep swung a U-turn, racing back to the landmark.

* * *

The pickup rumbled across the sand until Eve reached a long hillside. The truck ascended the ridge. From the top, she could see Simon's militia on the horizon. She slid out of the cab, grabbing her helmet, and shrank the pickup. She pocketed it and made her way down the slope. Her pace slowed. She braced the helmet against her hip, watching the legion advance.

"All right," she muttered. "Time to put your big girl pants on."

She clutched the helmet, ready to slide it on. Blue ice and drab gray lilac. Her resolve crumbled. She collapsed into herself. "Oh my god. I don't want to die."

She strained to breathe, managing to straighten upright.

You can still run.

"What about everybody else?" she whispered.

They all hate you anyway.

"Fuck—I can't do this."

She mulled over her words.

"Stop, stop it." Her jaw clenched. "Yes, you can. You did this. You made all of this. Not Diane. Not Kira. Not the fragment. You. You built the arm band. You designed the suit. You set all of it into motion. And I mean, look how far you got?"

And still couldn't finish it. Fucked all that up, too.

Desert wind passed over her. She stared at the legion's encroaching dust cloud. "This is finishing it. If you don't stop him, no one else will."

He's an actual genius. You're just some weirdo loser nobody likes.

"No, no." Eve shook her head. "That's not true. Stop telling yourself—All right, that's it—we're having this out right now." She pointed authoritatively at the ground.

"Oh yeah?" She folded her arms. "What do you got?"

"Quinn likes you—I mean me. She likes me. Larry and Barb liked me. And so did Powell before I screwed that up." She grimaced. "And for some reason, Eugene still liked me."

"But they didn't really know you, did they?"

"Yeah, they did. I mean, I—I may have been disguised, but I shared things about me. And they liked them."

"But you lied to them. Because you're a liar, and a thief—"

"Because you make me hide."

"I know you're too stupid to realize it, but I'm protecting you."

"I understand that, and—" She bit edge of her lip, twisting the flesh in her teeth and releasing it. "You know, I probably don't say this enough, or at all, but...thank you. I love you, Eve."

She paused, searching for a reply. "All right, so, just going to let that hang out there?"

"Well, I was kind of taking it in."

"Well, don't feel obligated to say it back or anything."

"Oh." She scowled. "But I'm supposed to?"

"It would be nice..."

She let out a long, harsh sigh, then softened. "I love you, Eve. And I don't say it enough. Or at all. I'm sorry I'm so hard on you."

Tiny beads of color floated and faded. She wasn't sure what the feeling was. But it left her calm.

"You wanted to save the world, right?"

"Yeah." She shrugged. "Might get to kill Simon, so that's kind of cool."

"Yeah."

"All right."

She tilted her head and slipped on the helmet.

"Hope you know what you're doing, bitch." She flipped down the visor.

Violet, blue, scarlet.

* * *

Simon sat in the captain's chair, twirling a bullet casing in his fingers, altering it into gold, then agate, then silver, then granite, then tourmaline, then platinum. A sensation rippled through the cabin, quieting the copies. He perked up, the casing caught between turquoise and rosy quartz, and clutched it in his fist. A stream of fine sand ran out.

"Tell everyone to stop."

The war machines halted. Simon and his legion dismounted. Copies from other units scanned the area.

"Is that what I think it is?" one asked. "Out here?"

"Another Mobius." Simon grinned.

A copy stepped forward. "Our unit can stay behind and start

digging."

"Nice try," he said.

"Well," said the third copy. "We should at least mark the spot."

Simon scoffed. "I'm not sure any of you can—"

An explosion flipped a laser tank on top of another, spurting twisted metal and scattering bolts.

"All right," said Simon, shrapnel bouncing off his armor. "Someone's not doing their job."

Another explosion on the opposite side of the formation. Another tank upended and slammed to the ground. The discombobulated copies ran for cover. A burst, and another tank flipped. Simon raced to the battle rover, catching a glimpse of the giant, invisible figure in the smoke and dust.

"There!" He pointed.

* * *

A white-hot streak from a laser cannon struck Eve with a frizzling pop. Knocked off her heels, she dropped onto her backside, demolishing a transport underneath. The earth trembled.

Blue, yellow, silver; pink, white, orange. She contracted to six feet.

"What manner of sorcery is this?" Simon stalked through the haze.

Eve stood.

He reared back as the copies closed in behind him. The face mask lifted on the helmet.

His brow crumpled. "You look familiar..."

"Oh, don't even play with me."

"Kincaid?!" An incredulous grin swept across his face. "Never in a million years did I think it would be you."

"Yeah, well, this may not be my worst nightmare, but it's definitely in the top ten." She eyed the smiling Simons. "Top five."

His grin grew. "Doesn't have to be like this. Surrender now, and I'll let you live."

"And be a member of the worldwide Simon Pierce circle-jerk?" She aimed the arm cuff. "I'd rather die."

Did you seriously think that sounded cool?

"Shut up," she whispered. "That was cool."

Simon and the copies snickered.

"Afraid I've lost my fragment," he said with heavy sarcasm.

"Sucks to be you."

"I'll manage." With a quick draw, Simon fired the laser pistol.

Yellow, green, pink. Eve let loose a white-hot orb.

But the orb rode an unseen boundary around Simon's head. His laser blast crackled against her own fields and zoomed off into the distance. Eve's orb detonated behind him, flinging copies in all directions.

Puzzled, Eve and Simon lowered their weapons, taking stock.

Their fields were in polarity. Should've known when the tanks had flipped instead of exploded. More troubling, Simon didn't have a fragment and could generate his own distortion fields.

All right, this was a huge mistake.

"You're supposed to be on my side," Eve muttered.

Kind of having a hard time coming up with anything positive...

Simon broke into a fiendish smirk.

Eve snapped her head down, dropping the helmet's face shield.

Violet, blue, scarlet; orange, scarlet, brown. Green, purple, blue.

Simon searched the ground, trained on her enlarging footprints. He dashed away, scaling a dune. His fingers dragged through the sand, transforming it to steel.

Her fist slammed into the dune with a deep gong and furious sizzle from the repelling fields.

Simon reached the apex.

Eve threw another fist. The steel transformed to talc. Chalky powder filled the air.

A barrage of heavy gunfire ricocheted off her. The copies marched in with unaltered M16s.

Eve raised the arm cuff to return fire, but sensed a shift in the earth. Mighty steel needles sprang forth and she leaped back. A spiked pillar caught her heel with a fizzle. Blue, yellow, silver. She stumbled, reducing, and wafted away the thick haze.

An iridescent glint scampered through the talc and gun smoke. Eve reared back a heel—green, purple, blue—and expanded as she punted Simon into a rocky outcrop.

Pink, white, orange. Eve abandoned invisibility. If she could amplify her fields enough, it might overpower his. Green, purple, blue. She enlarged to over a hundred feet.

An intense bolt flashed alongside her head. A crunching fireball erupted in the sky behind her, miles away. The other jet fighters dispersed, veering off to reassess their strategy.

Eve turned around to find three grinning Simons standing on the bed of a laser tank.

* * *

Quinn held steady at thirty-five miles an hour, scouting for Humvees. Two of them flanked her out of nowhere.

She slammed on the brakes and threw the Jeep into Park. With a deep breath, she popped open the door and stuck out her hands.

"Don't shoot!" She pushed the door with her knee. "Don't shoot! I'm unarmed."

A loudspeaker blared. "Ma'am, you are on restricted property. If you need assistance, we will guide you back to the main road."

Quinn stepped out. "I need to talk to General McCrae."

"Ma'am, get back into your vehicle!"

Three brawny soldiers jumped out with large, scary-looking rifles trained on her.

She waffled between the dirt and the car door. "Uhh—okay, look. " She edged closer. "It's really important—"

"Ma'am!" The squad leader leaned out. "Get on the ground immediately, or we'll be forced to open fire!"

"Oh my god!" Quinn dropped to her knees. "I need to talk to General McCrae! Please!"

"On the ground, now!"

"Oh my god!" She planted a cheek against the sand. "Please don't shoot me!"

The jet fighter's explosion captured the soldiers' attention.

"The hell was that?"

Quinn raised her hand. "I have information! I need to talk to General McCrae!"

"Don't move!" The squad leader ordered. "Put your hand down!"

She lowered her arm.

* * *

The ground shuddered as Eve bounded from torrents of laser fire. Yellow, green, pink. She returned a blast. The orb ruptured under a laser tank. It soared and crashed inside the dark, noxious haze.

Her helmet rang with the clanking impact of a boulder. She stumbled, fanning a hand to clear the smoke and find its source. Another boulder thwacked against the visor, and she faltered, landing on her butt with a thunder.

Through the smog, she spied two robotic workers on a ridge, loading another hulking rock into the pouch of huge slingshot. She took aim—yellow, green, pink. The orb bowled over the battlefield before winging the robots apart and smashing the slingshot against the hillside. The top of the ridge blew into red-hot pebbles.

The earth tottered under her. Eve sprang to her feet as a carpet of jagged crystalline spikes sprouted, matching her height. The fields crackled as she swung the back of her fist across a row of them. The splinters rained into a line of copies and their advancing war machines. The copies scattered from the spiny cascade while the vehicles took the brunt of the heavier chunks. She caught a glimpse of Simon dashing through the fray. She charged a remaining crystal with her shoulder, the crackling field flung her backward.

Simon leaped away as the huge pike plowed into the soil.

She took aim at him. The earth under her deteriorated into a steaming lake of acid. The fields jittered, buzzing and buffering her fall. She hovered above the frothing waves—red, yellow, white.

Eve levitated from the surface as a smattering of laser fire lit up her field and bounced off her. Green, purple, blue. She swung her foot, batting the laser cannon across the shore while the acid hardened into a salt bed.

Blue, yellow, silver. She reduced to a mere hundred feet. Blue brown black. She returned to earth. Orange, scarlet, brown. She'd lost Simon again.

He arose on a pillar of sandstone.

She swung at him. A spire of titanium shot up in front of her. She dodged it, stumbling back.

Another spire shot up behind her. Then another before her and another behind. Another and another, meeting overhead, forming a cage. The opposing fields buzzed, intensifying around her. The cage narrowed. Gray, purple, gold—her intangibility stalled.

The enclosing fields crackled. Blue, yellow, silver. Normal size. She watched through the fields' blur as Simon's pillar lowered.

He stepped off, revealing bare soles under the sabatons. "Well, that was fun."

Eve flipped up the visor, out of breath. She gauged her options. Best she could figure, he needed only to narrow the bars and let the force of the fields obliterate her.

Fuck this plastic prick.

"Look," she said. "I know all this better than anyone."

"Based on your current condition?" He winked. "I'd have to disagree."

"I-I can help you."

"You will." He nodded, drawing closer. "As a test subject."

The bars tightened around her. Eve pressed against the ground.

"Just between you and me"—Simon leaned in, the fields amplifying —"and me and me and me...your ideas were always brilliant."

What? Was he serious?

Wait for it...

"Which is why I made sure to take credit for them after I rejected your applications."

She snarled—crimson, magenta, indigo, viridian, maroon—black waves burst forth, shattering the bars and sending Simon soaring. The copies gawked at the swaths of color blending within the dark aura. The air vibrated with a hellacious growl.

Orange, scarlet, brown; green, purple, blue. Eve took a menacing step forward, rising larger and larger.

* * *

A handful of Simons perched on a surviving laser tank witnessed the unexpected turn.

"Wait," said a copy. "If she's still using a fragment to project fields, and it's the inverse configuration, we can—"

"Already on it." A copy stationed at the cannon's console punched in commands.

* * *

Eve loomed as Simon sat up, digging his fingers into the soil—but the effect of his field dissipated as the aura neared.

Powerless, he scuttled back like a hermit crab, smiling wide. "Let's talk about this! You—you're not a killer! Don't let this change you into something you're not!"

"Shows what you know." She took aim. "I'm a fucking supervillain."

But as she gazed down the length of her arm through the aura, she didn't see the Simon she knew. His hair wasn't so perfectly coiffed. And instead of a suit of illustrious armor, he wore slacks and an Oxford shirt.

From his vantage point, Simon squinted at a haggard Eve—forehead furrows and dark circles under her eyes, hair as chaotic as ever.

A blast of reverse polarity from the reconfigured laser tank struck Eve's chest with a furious crack, launching her backward. The waves surged, then neutralized.

She slid across the sand, shaking off the blow as she lifted her head. Normal sized again. And not superdense.

Simon scrambled to his feet, his armor returning. He checked over his shoulder. The laser cannon was a melted husk. The tank had devolved into a pickup truck and various machine parts. The copies, too, had reverted. The confused, terrified people ran to the road Simon had forged from sand back to the main highway.

Violet, blue, scarlet. The dial didn't move.

35

(blue green, red)

The soldiers finished patting Quinn down and searched the Jeep.

"This is serious," she said. "You have to listen to me."

"Ma'am," said the squad leader. "You're in a restricted area with no license in a vehicle with no registration. Why should we believe you?"

"Well, all right, because—wow, this really is hard to explain—okay, so—I was sent by Eve Kincaid and she knows General McCrae, but not like personally. But he knows who she is because she's the person who stole that thing you guys are looking for—well, she didn't steal it, but she has it."

"So, you're saying you know someone in possession of stolen government property?"

"Okay." Quinn reconsidered her words. "I know how it sounds—"

"We're going to have to detain you for questioning."

"No—okay, look—can't you just call McCrae and tell him what I'm saying?"

"No, ma'am."

A soldier sidled up beside the squad leader. "Vehicle's stolen."

"Goddammit, Eve!" Quinn huffed. "All right, I can explain—"

"Plenty of time once you're in custody, ma'am." The soldier took out a pair of handcuffs.

The radio crinkled. "Snipe Hunter, this is Litterbox. What's your position?"

The squad leader held the radio to his lips. "Litterbox, this Snipe Hunter. We're on the outer perimeter, thirteen mikes from the main road, over."

"Snipe Hunter, you need to fallback immediately, over."

"We got a Space Camper in irons—"

"That is a no-go, Snipe Hunter. Catch and release. Return immediately. Do you copy?"

A boom resounded in the east.

"Litterbox," said the squad leader. "The hell is going on out there?"

The delay in response disquieted the men. They gathered round the squad leader.

"Snipe Hunter, that's not for discussion over coms." The radio fizzed. "Return to base, A-SAP."

"What? What is this?"

"I'm trying to tell you," said Quinn. "I know what it is."

The squad leader's eyes swept back and forth, reading her face. He spoke into the radio. "Our Space Camper—"

"Stop calling me that." Quinn scowled.

"May have information regarding the high-alert situation. We need a direct line with McCrae."

"Negative, Snipe Hunter," dispatch answered. "Top brass is preoccupied."

Quinn folded her arms. "How's it feel when nobody listens to you?"

* * *

"All right," Ramos said through the speaker phone. "And what about this woman on aerial surveillance? She seems to be stalling him pretty well."

"No telling how long she'll last," said McCrae. "And we don't have enough intel—"

"She's a criminal, sir," said Garza. "FBI believes she has the other fragment."

"Well, that poses a serious complication, doesn't it, General?" asked Ramos. "What happens if there's a nuclear reaction near the material?"

"It could amplify the reaction, sir, however—"

"What does that mean? Amplify how?"

McCrae pursed his lips. "It could expand the area of devastation...beyond our estimate."

Ramos hissed.

"But," said McCrae, "Colonel Das and his team believe a nuclear detonation will cause the fields to breakdown. And a targeted strike should limit the radius."

"Okay," said Ramos. "Let's say we allow him to take the base—"

"Mr. President—"

“Hang on,” he said. “You’re asking me to order a nuclear strike on American soil. I need to know other options have been exhausted. We can’t devise a trap?”

“That might have been feasible five hours ago, but we can’t risk him getting anywhere near Callahan.”

“She was affected as well, sir,” said Garza. “They don’t know what’s wrong with her.”

“Oh, fantastic,” said Ramos. “Okay, so what if he gets his hands on this thing?”

McCrae folded his arms. “You see what he can do right now? The piece he had was smaller than a person’s thumb. Use your imagination.”

Silence from the White House.

Garza and McCrae glanced at each other, then the phone.

“Sir?” asked Garza.

“No matter what happens,” said Ramos, “I’m shutting this project down.”

“Until the situation with Agent Callahan is resolved,” said Garza, “that might not be possible, sir.”

“Director, General.” Ramos sighed. “Thank you for your counsel. I’ll speak to you once all personnel have taken cover underground.”

36

(blue green, royal blue)

Eve hit the button—superdense. Relieved, she counted the settings, jumping up as Simon neared.

"Wait!" She held up a hand. "What did you see?"

He hesitated, suspicious. "What did you see?"

"I saw you, but...not you."

"I saw you." Simon smirked. "But she needed a makeover."

"Ouch." Eve nodded. "Okay, well, the Simon I saw knew the right amount of gel to put in his hair."

"It's pomade."

"Look, maybe we can work together."

"And why would I—"

Eve raised the arm cuff and cocked an eyebrow.

He chuckled, then held up a fist. The encroaching militia stopped.

"How many more fragments are there?"

"You'll find out after we take the base." Simon lowered his hand and turned around, addressing the copies. "She's with us now."

The nearest copy smiled. "Of course."

Other copies dragged wreckage toward Simon. With a pass of his hands, the parts melded into sleek designs, rising from the sand as another levitating battle rover. He climbed aboard with a new crew.

"Her arm band is damaged." He muttered to a copy. "We'll get everything we need out of her soon enough."

A copy outstretched a hand, offering Eve a ride in an unaltered

Humvee. She turned away with a surreptitious press of the dial button.
She enlarged several hundred feet, allowing the convoy to roll past her.
Fuck. Fuck. Fuck. We're fucked. We're so fucked.
She turned the dial discreetly, counting clicks.
Simon's UAVs shuttled ahead and split off. Overhead, the two pairs of UAVS circled the caravan.
Screw this. Make a break for it.
Eve grumbled.
Ghost-mode to the base while they're distract—
"Stop," Eve whispered. "Stop it."
The faint rushing scream of fighter jets. A finger-four formation appeared on the western horizon.

* * *

The flight leader opened a channel. "Commander, Kincaid's joined ranks with Pierce, over."
Ramos and his team in the war room deliberated over the displays of the aircraft's viewpoints.
"Garza said we couldn't trust her." Ramos nodded. "Terminate them both."

* * *

The jets bent a wide curve to the northeast.
Eve vanished, invisible.
"Oh." Simon sighed. "We get to kill her sooner than I thought."
The UAVs sizzled and floundered overhead, exploding into metallic hail. Simon's caravan halted, laser-cannons converging on Eve's giant form in the smoke—she vanished.
A copy tore away from a monitor. "She's gone!"
"She's just invisible." Simon stepped to the console.
"No, she's gone," said the copy. "There's nothing on infrared."
"Well, that—" His smile wavered. "That's improbable."
"Maybe she can teleport?"
"Teleport?" He snickered. "She probably shrank or something. Everybody check the ground for footprints!"
Copies patrolled the area, ill at ease. Jets screamed in the distance.
Simon's head swept around, uncertain and unwilling to believe—he convulsed, overwhelmed by Eve's field as her intangible fingers pushed him off the battle rover's platform. He hollered as her palm pressed him into the sand. His armor wilted back into a hospital gown.

The charged field interaction revealed her.

His copies raced to reposition the laser-cannons as she fought to aim the arm cuff with every ounce of her being.

The arm cuff charged as laser blasts struck her, the reaction coursing through her, into Simon's field, and back.

She spilled backward, the disruption shredding the battle rover. Restored machine parts smashed into the rest of Simon's artillery. Her orb whizzed into a mountain ridge, blowing it to gravel.

* * *

Eve sat up, no longer intangible. No longer invisible. Still huge.

You know, you could still—

"Stop." Eve scowled.

She dialed and hit the button—no effect. Terror flooded her belly. Pearls of mauve, charcoal dots, chartreuse flashes. She glanced at Simon.

He pulled himself up. His iridescent armor returned. The bridge of his nose wrinkled under an icy glare.

No smile.

He snatched a broken laser rifle. The parts flipped and folded, reorganizing.

But Eve was too busy with the arm cuff. The other settings didn't respond. A fiery ignition called her attention from Simon's direction. He held a plasma sword, an intense beam of energy and light streaming from the hilt.

"Oh, you've got to be kidding me," she muttered.

"We both know you can't win." He pointed the sword at her, stepping closer. "The arm band's broken, and you can't fix it. But I can help you, Eve. I can end your lifetime of misery."

Eve pressed the button, surprised as she reduced to six feet. She turned the dial up and pressed it again, enlarging to a giant size. She jammed her boot heel into Simon.

He flew into his armaments and lost control of the sword. The copies fled as the torch seared through a laser-tank, detonating the machine in a hideous fireball.

Eve stood in a frantic search of the sky. She flipped up the helmet's face shield and waved to the jets.

"We're good, right!?" She gave a thumbs-up.

* * *

The wing-woman tilted her head in Eve's direction. "Uh, Flight Leader, you catch that?"

"Yeah, I did Wing." The flight leader switched channels. "Commander, this is Flight Leader. Looks like Kincaid's trying to signal us?"

"We can't afford to let them get any closer," Ramos answered. "Proceed as planned."

"Affirmative, Commander."

* * *

Eve followed the jets' flight path as they veered southwest.

This was a stupid plan.

"Well, I didn't hear you coming up with anything."

Quinn probably ran away. I mean, why would they listen to her? Or trust you for that matter?

"Stop thinking the worst."

This is the worst possible situation! It's exactly what you were afraid of. No one trusts you, no one's coming to save you—

"Then I'll do it myself." She snapped the face shield down and turned up the dial.

Eve enlarged, towering above the battlefield, and stomped through Simon's remaining forces. The copies abandoned their war machines and fled.

Simon recovered his plasma sword from the blackened earth only to be overtaken by temblors.

The air hissed as Eve's fingers flicked away the smoldering rubble. Her fingers closed around him. Their opposing fields crackled, the intense boundaries trapping him inside. He rattled about at the mercy of the inverse fields, armorless.

Ferocity ran up her arm and into her shoulder, shaking to the bones and joints, strengthening in its effort to drive them apart. Eve gritted her teeth as the jets made their final approach. She fought to lift her arm and straighten her elbow. A wisp of fire and smoke. The searing roar coursed towards her. Her whole body shook. Her muscles burned as she traced the path of the missile, straining to grip the fields imprisoning Simon.

The lithe warhead sailed between her fingertips—a brilliant flash and magnificent jolt. The burgeoning fireball's fission chain reaction surged. The fields blazed, resisting then absorbing the exponential flux. Simon screamed. Energy streamed into his molecules and atoms. His vision filled with endless ribbons of color stretching into infinity until he realized the ribbons were him. His very essence tore apart and dissipated.

The tremendous rupture hurled Eve onto her back with an earthquake. She sat up, shaking her hand to alleviate the scorching sting. She flipped up the face shield, checking the glove's damage. Charred, but still intact. Something seemed off. A concussion?

Dazed, she twisted her hand back and forth, unable to place it. She was overcome by a strange motion, as though the world was moving.

No...

She was moving. Expanding. She hadn't reverted to normal. The field was absorbing the fallout.

"N-N-N-No."

* * *

A rolling rumble shook the earth. Quinn and the soldiers gawked as Eve filled the eastern sky.

Quinn's jaw hung open. "Holy fuck."

* * *

Eve slid off the helmet and gaped at her surroundings. The mountains were mere bumps. She scanned the golden horizon. The sprawling metropolis was a patchwork of grays and browns, the azure-green Pacific stretched beyond. Exhilarated, an uncontrollable smile broke across her face followed by a breathy chuckle.

* * *

The deep, resounding booms shook Quinn to her core.

"Ohhh no," she muttered. "No, no, no, no..."

"What?" the squad leader asked. "What's she going to do?"

"I don't know."

* * *

Eve cupped a hand over her lips, realizing the power of her voice. She whispered through her fingers. "Sorry, sorry."

The land trembled as she shifted her magnitude. Quinn and the soldiers clung to the Humvees for stability. The vehicles bounced along with them. Eve planted her foot down. The planet quaked, bringing Quinn and the men to the ground.

Upper level winds whipped across Eve's face as she rose. The gusts stripped off skin mites. Dozens of the harmless bugs sailed several thousand yards, crashing into the main street of a small desert town where they crushed cars and store fronts. The residents fled, screaming, convinced of an alien invasion. The confused mites writhed and plodded in the unfamiliar environment until heroic gun owners fought back.

Eve took a deep breath, estimating she'd have little atmosphere. She straightened her legs, towering. Immense. Twice the height she'd planned for taking the base.

You can still do it. You can take it right now. Nothing can stop you.

But she'd decimate hundreds of thousands of acres of civilization. And that was what she could see. Quinn was down there somewhere, terrified.

You don't know that. She might be in jail. Or dead.

Eve shook her head. She spotted the cloudy ulcer she'd created in the middle of downtown. And right below her, the scarred land she and Simon had torn apart. Some environmentalist she'd turned out to be.

You see that? You are in deep shit, okay? You still have a chance. Take it.

But without the ability to change her density, she couldn't get the fragments or evade the military. Without invisibility, they'd track her down in a matter of days. She could shrink the base, but then she'd have hundreds of uncooperative soldiers to feed. Their lives in her hands. She thought of their families. The department store. Blue gray and soggy purple. Tears welled in her eyes. The government would mobilize every resource to hunt her down.

A new noise filled her ears. The din of an unceasing gong. The motion of the planet itself. She lifted her head as though breaking the surface of a pond and gazed into the endless expanse of stars, feeling small again. No more than a tiny speck. All the same questions about the universe still unanswered. Her chest and throat tightened with the desire for air. Another reminder of inescapable reality.

The land quaked as she lowered to one knee, surveying the mosaic of reddish browns, tans, and greens, streaked and splotched with the slate and gray of roads and towns.

Come on, you're so close.

Eve sighed.

Okay—not this size. But smaller. You could find Quinn.

She bit the side of her lip.

And...just take the lowest level of the base?

A couple days might be enough to repair the arm cuff.

She slid on the helmet, then turned the dial down. A third of her size should work. She pressed the button. A shattering pop. The field jolted her—she was overtaken by the rush of contraction.

* * *

Tremors jostled Quinn and the soldiers as Eve reduced on the horizon. She'd looked startled. Something was wrong.

Once sure of her footing, Quinn made a break for the Jeep.

"Hey!" The squad leader took off after her.

"If you're going to shoot me, just do it!" She glanced over her shoulder but didn't stop.

"You can't go out there!" The squad leader slowed. "There's radioactive fallout!"

Quinn yanked open the Jeep. "She said the field would absorb all of it!"

She slammed the door. Quinn couldn't abandon her now. She had to make sure Eve was okay, that she knew someone cared about her. And that she still needed to do the right thing.

The Jeep revved, tearing a tight curve and raced to the main road.

* * *

The military took a more methodical approach. Garza had a drone deployed from Edwards Air Force Base to scan for radioactivity. But after an hour of sweeping the area, none registered. Das and his researchers didn't have a ready answer. Concerned the drone's sensors had malfunctioned, Garza ordered another one from a different location armed with more-sensitive diagnostics.

The delay gave Quinn ample time. She sped toward the thinning smoke of Simon's fallen army, abandoning the roads until a mountainous crest of earth appeared where Eve's boots had been.

Quinn followed the massive outline for miles. She expected to see a giant Eve step out at any moment. But she didn't appear. She remembered her talking about her atoms ripping apart. Had that been the look on her face?

Quinn's anxiety turned to the gas tank, wondering how much longer she could hunt. A landslide of soil and rock had been flattened by the sole of a footprint. Then a smaller one. She drove along the edge of the impression until she spied a little figure sitting in the dirt, fiddling with something.

She threw the Jeep into Park and ran out. "You did it!"

Eve lifted her head, subdued.

She slowed. "You all right?"

Eve nodded. "I-I think I might've inhaled a flock of birds."

"Oh...okay." She helped her up. "You know, for a second there I—"

Quinn was stunned to find herself looking down on Eve.

Refusing to meet her eyes, Eve held out the device, the cover removed. “In case you wanted to see what all the fuss was about.”

Quinn reached for it, reluctant to touch it.

“It’s okay—it’s fried. I can’t get it to work.”

Quinn gazed at the fragment. The slightest tilt of her hand was enough to illuminate a grid inside. Captivated, she tilted it again. The hologram vanished.

Eve shrugged. “Maybe they’ll still cut me a deal.”

The patter of helicopters drew their attention. Chinooks floated into view from the West. Eve’s eyes widened at the full breadth of what awaited her.

“I changed my mind. I want it back!” She lunged for the device.

“No, Eve!” Quinn dodged, yanking it away. “It’s okay. I’m going to help you. We’re going to talk to them—”

“No!” She thrashed for the device. “I can fix it! We can still run!”

“No—Eve! Stop it!” Quinn threw up a hand, pushing her back.

Eve faltered on the overturned soil and tumbled to the ground.

“All right.” She heaved a sigh. “I deserved that.”

* * *

They were brought to the base and separated. The military provided Eve with a change of clothes and a medical evaluation before federal agents snapped handcuffs on her wrists. After they led her out, McCrae took the medic aside.

“How is she?” he asked.

“Aside from some nasty scrapes and bruises,” said the medic, “amazingly well, considering she got hit with a nuclear bomb.”

“What’s the prognosis long-term?”

She shook her head. “Biohazard team didn’t find anything, and so far she has no symptoms of radiation poisoning. That being said, she is in shock. Probably should wait before interrogating her.”

“Yeah,” he grumbled. “Garza ain’t waiting.”

* * *

The soldiers sat Eve in a small room with a table and three chairs. They posted at either side of the door in silence. Garza and McCrae walked in and the soldiers exited, shutting the door.

“Well.” Garza sat across from her. “You’ve done some serious damage.”

McCrae pulled up a chair and folded his hands.

“We don’t have a full count yet,” Garza said with a stony glare. “But

I can tell you, we lost good people. Others are in the hospital, some in comas. Some still missing."

"I'm sorry," said Eve. "I didn't—"

"You'll get your chance." She produced a digital voice recorder from her jacket, setting it between them.

Garza hit Record. "It is five twenty-three p.m. This is Deputy Director Maria Garza. I am here with General Russell T. McCrae at an undisclosed military location. Please state your full name for the record."

"Eve Elizabeth Kincaid."

"Ms. Kincaid, would you please detail the events which brought you here?"

Eve blew a puff of air, then the words flowed without much effort. They didn't interrupt or ask questions as she divulged the altercation that had led to her acquisition of the *modifikator*. She confessed her panic, her ruminations and aspirations, the unfortunate people she'd crossed paths with before and after her discovery of its unique properties to distort reality, her experimentation and its applications, and her well-intended yet ill-fated plans. By the time she finished, Eve felt as though she'd lived it all again.

"And you were confident enough in your theory to take on Dr. Pierce?" asked Garza.

"Well, yeah, for the most part."

"And your theory, the suit, its components..." she said. "You'd be willing to share how they work?"

Eve's eyes darted between their faces. "Yes, but, on the cond—"

"This isn't a negotiation."

She leaned forward. "Can I just ask—"

"You may not," said Garza. She turned to McCrae. "General?"

He answered with a short nod.

"Thank you for your time, Ms. Kincaid." Garza turned off the recorder and scooped it up.

They walked out, the soldiers resumed their posts. They didn't answer questions either. Pale mauve.

Eve could only hope Quinn would absolve her.

If they believe her.

"Stop," she whispered.

The soldiers glanced at her. She looked away. It was cold. Quiet. The hum was gone. She slumped forward, elbows on the table, lulling close to sleep.

Garza returned some time later, her entrance rousing Eve. The deputy director sat, opened a portfolio and read the FBI's cursory briefing aloud. She cited evidence collected from the penthouse, Diane's penthouse, and Kira's apartment before enumerating a series of offenses which included grand theft, grand theft auto, grand larceny, theft of classified government property, counterfeiting, wire fraud, credit fraud, cryptocurrency fraud, cyber crimes, money laundering, concealment of assets, failure to report offshore funds, destruction of public and private property, identity theft, possession and use of false identification, spread of false information, manslaughter, murder, kidnapping, creation and use of weapons of mass destruction, conspiracy to attack government facilities, seditious conspiracy, and conspiracy to commit treason.

"Do you understand the charges being brought against you?"

Laurel. Mauve. Sand. Mustard. Periwinkle. White.

Eve blinked. It had all happened. It had all been her. She swallowed. "Yes."

"Given your heroic effort to stop Dr. Pierce and your intimate knowledge of the material, we are willing to forgo the death penalty in exchange for your continued assistance as a resource and helping those affected by these events. Would you be amenable to that arrangement?"

"So." She brightened. "That would mean I—"

"Would be housed in a maximum security federal penitentiary for the rest of your life."

"Don't—don't I get an attorney?"

"You take your chances with an attorney"—Garza's fingers slid under the papers—"and you never see this deal again."

* * *

Quinn's examination was enjoyable. She felt that was Garza serious but pleasant and diplomatic. Maybe because she had been a victim of Eve's plans, or she'd agreed to assist Agent Dempsey. Quinn emphasized Eve's good deeds and explained that her fall from the high-rise had been an accident.

Garza smiled and nodded but made no promises.

Afterwards, another pair of soldiers guarded Quinn. They made conversation and shared stories. Garza returned an hour later. She'd determined Quinn had been dragged into perilous circumstances against her will. The government didn't believe prosecuting her as an accessory was warranted. Her possession of stolen property and false information presented to Agent Dempsey had been due to Eve's deceit. Garza was willing to overlook trespassing, and Quinn would be released, on the condition she sign a nondisclosure agreement.

Quinn picked up the pen. She hesitated with a smirk. "You—you're not going to shoot me in the head, like, as soon as I walk out of here, are you?"

"Of course not," said Garza. "The movies get it wrong."

"Oh, yeah—I figured." Quinn signed her name.

"We only do that if you violate the agreement."

She expected the woman to smile or a laugh, but Garza didn't move.

By the time the soldiers led Quinn outside, layers of deep purple, pink, and blazing orange lit the sky. A cool breeze wafted as federal agents escorted Eve toward them. Whatever questions Quinn had were wiped away by the handcuffs and shackles.

"I know I already said it," Eve muttered. "But I'm sorry. About everything."

"It's okay. You don't have to keep—"

"I do. I feel awful. You didn't deserve any of that, and I didn't want —"

"I know. But you have to stop beating yourself up."

"I haven't had a friend like you in a long time."

Quinn stifled a laugh. "I don't think I've ever had a friend like you."

"You really were my best friend."

"Still am."

"Well, if you ever want to hang out again..." Eve raised her wrists. "You know where I'll be."

The agents led her away. The breeze sank into a chill.

* * *

Within twelve hours, the remnants of any former life were stripped away. Documents filed. Photos taken. Jumpsuits issued. None of it seemed real until Eve stepped into the cell. A bed. A sink. A toilet. The heavy door slammed shut behind her. She clung to its echo. But that faded as well.

Eve shuddered, placing the stack of prison uniforms on the bed and taking another pass of the cell. Gripped by cold, she wrapped her arms tight and gazed at the vent overhead. The louvers were attached to a lever. Maybe if she could close them, even part way, she wouldn't freeze.

She stepped onto the bed. No springs. With a huff, she reached up and jumped. Well below any hope of touching the vent. She bent her knees, adding more effort to her leap. Still coming up short. Eve glanced at the wall, gauging if she could vault off it to increase her range without falling and bashing her head into the sink. She leaped once more, straight up, her fingers touching the louver blades. And stayed there.

Over eight feet tall. She smiled. A breathy little laugh. Green, purple, blue.

Black.

ACKNOWLEDGMENTS

Thank you to my family for your love and support, confidence, and putting up with me.

Thank you to Scott Barrow for artwork, cover design, encouragement, brainstorming, and patience with draft after draft.

Thank you to Aaron Valle for motivation, conversation, guidance, and, of course, random absurdity.

Thank you to M. Ehrenshaft. You saw me as a writer even when I didn't, and with perseverance and enthusiasm, waited until I believed it myself.

Thank you to Amelia Beamer for your empathy and perceptivity, thoughtful guidance and wit.

Thank you to Mandi Andrejka for your keen eye, instructive inky pen, and helpful suggestions.

Thank you to the Drop Everything gang for your support and advice, humor and philosophical discussions, and just a touch of nihilism.

Thank you to Daniel B. for your knowledge and patience in fielding my numerous requests and questions.

Thank you to Cathy Barrow, Stephanie Francis, and Amanda Ryan for your invaluable insights and perspectives.

ABOUT THE AUTHOR

Joe Palazzo is a writer living in Central Florida. *Incalculable* is his first novel.

www.jpalazzowriter.com

www.ingramcontent.com/pod-product-compliance
Lightning Source LLC
LaVergne TN
LVHW090546110826
845146LV00001B/36

* 9 7 9 8 9 9 1 9 5 4 1 0 5 *